PRETTY THINGS

PRETTY THINGS

JANELLE BROWN

THORNDIKE PRESS
A part of Gale, a Cengage Company

Copyright © 2020 by Janelle Brown.
Thorndike Press, a part of Gale, a Cengage Company.

Thorndike Press® Large Print Core.
The text of this Large Print edition is unabridged.
Other aspects of the book may vary from the original edition.
Set in 16 pt. Plantin.

LIBRARY OF CONGRESS CIP DATA ON FILE.
CATALOGUING IN PUBLICATION FOR THIS BOOK
IS AVAILABLE FROM THE LIBRARY OF CONGRESS

ISBN-13: 978-1-4328-8053-8 (hardcover alk. paper)

Published in 2020 by arrangement with Random House, an imprint and division of Penguin Random House LLC

Printed in Mexico
Print Number: 01   Print Year: 2020

To Greg

Even if when I met you I had not happened to like you, I should still have been bound to change my attitude, because when you meet anyone in the flesh you realize immediately that he is a human being and not a sort of caricature embodying certain ideas. It is partly for this reason that I don't mix much in literary circles, because I know from experience that once I have met & spoken to anyone I shall never again be able to show any intellectual brutality towards him, even when I feel that I ought to.

— LETTER FROM GEORGE ORWELL
TO STEPHEN SPENDER, APRIL 15, 1938

PROLOGUE

When a body goes down in Lake Tahoe, they say, it does not rise again. The frigid temperature of the lake, its vast depths, conspire to keep bacteria at bay. What once was human fails to decompose. Instead, the body is doomed to drift along the lake bed, in perpetual limbo; just more organic matter joining the mysterious menagerie that lives in Tahoe's uncharted depths.

In death, there is no disparity.

Lake Tahoe is over a quarter mile deep and two million years old. Locals have laid claim to a fistful of superlatives: Their lake is one of the deepest in America, the purest, the bluest, the coldest, the oldest. No one really knows what's at the bottom of that water, but everyone is sure it's something dark and enigmatic. There are myths about a Loch Ness monster–like creature called Tahoe Tessie, which no one really takes seriously even though Tessie sells a lot of T-shirts. But deep-sea cameras have also captured mysterious fish on the lake bed, 1,600 feet down: creatures pale white and shark-like, evolved to withstand the near-freezing temperatures, their blood slowing to a crawl in their veins. Creatures perhaps as old as the lake itself.

And then there are other stories: Stories about how the lake was used by the Mafia as a dumping ground for its victims, back when they controlled the Nevada casinos. Stories about the Gold Rush railroad barons who considered the lake a convenient mass grave for the Chinese migrant workers they worked to death building the tracks over the Sierras. Stories about vengeful wives, cops gone bad, killing trails that led to the lake's edge and then went cold. Kids tell each other bedtime stories about corpses bumping along the bottom of the lake, eyes open, hair floating, in permanent limbo.

Above the surface of the lake, the snow is softly falling. Below, the body drifts slowly down, lifeless eyes lifted toward the vanishing light, until it sinks into darkness and is gone.

NINA

1.

The nightclub is a temple, devoted to the sacred worship of indulgence. Inside these walls there is no judgment: You'll find no populists, no protestors, no spoilsports who might ruin the fun. (The velvet ropes out front stand sentry against all *that*.) Instead, there are girls in fur and designer silk, swanning and preening like exotic birds, and men with diamonds in their teeth. There are fireworks erupting from bottles of thousand-dollar vodka. There is marble and leather and brass that is polished until it gleams like gold.

The DJ drops a bass beat. The dancers cheer. They lift their phones toward the sky and vamp and click, because if this is a church then social media is their scripture; and that tiny screen is how they deify themselves.

Here they are: the one percent. The young and ultra-rich. Billionaire babies, millionaire millennials, fabu-grammers. "Influencers." They have it all and they want the whole

13

world to know. *Pretty things, so many pretty things in the world; and we get them all,* says their every Instagram photo. *Covet this life, for it is the best life, and we are #blessed.*

Out there, in the middle of it all, is a woman. She's dancing with abandon in a spot where the light hits her just *so* and glimmers on her skin. A faint sheen of sweat dampens her face; her glossy dark hair whips around her face as she swivels her body to the grinding beat. The waitresses headed to the bottle-service tables have to maneuver around her, the fizzing sparklers on their trays in danger of setting the woman's hair alight. Just another L.A. party girl, looking for a good time.

Look close, though, and you can see that her half-closed eyes are sharp and alert, dark with watching. She is watching one person in particular, a man at a table a few feet away.

The man is drunk. He lounges in a booth with a group of male friends — gelled hair, leather jackets, Gucci sunglasses at night; twentysomethings who shout over the music in broken English and baldly leer at the women who career past. Occasionally, this man will plunge his face to the table to do a line of cocaine, narrowly missing the flotilla of empty glasses that litter its surface. When a Jay-Z song comes on, the man climbs up on the seat of his banquette and shakes up a giant bottle of champagne — a rare large-format bottle of Cristal — and then sprays it over the heads of the crowd. Girls shriek as $50,000 worth of bubbly ruins their dresses and drips to the floor, making them slip in their heels. The man laughs so hard he nearly falls down.

A waitress lugs over a replacement bottle of champagne, and as she sets it on the table the man slips his hand right up under her skirt as if he's purchased her along with the bottle. The waitress blanches, afraid to push him off lest she lose what promises to be a sizable tip: her rent for the month, at the very least. Her eyes rise helplessly to meet those of the dark-haired woman who is still dancing a few feet away. And this is when the woman makes her move.

She dances toward the man and then — oops! — she trips and falls right into him, dislodging his hand from the waitress's crotch. The waitress, grateful, flees. The man swears in Russian, until his eyes focus enough to register the windfall that has just landed in his lap. Because the woman is pretty — as all the women here must be in order to get past the bouncers — dark-featured and slight, maybe a hint of Spanish or Latina? Not the sexiest girl in the club, not the most ostentatious, but she's well dressed, her skirt suggestively short. Most important: She doesn't blink as the man swiftly shifts his attention to her; doesn't react at all to the possessive hand on her thigh, the sour breath in her ear.

Instead, she sits with him and his friends, letting him pour her champagne, sipping it slowly even as the man puts back another half-dozen drinks. Women come and go from the table; she stays. Smiling and flirting, waiting for the moment when the men are all distracted by the arrival of a tabloid-friendly basketball star a few tables over; and then she swiftly and silently tips the contents of a clear vial of liquid into the man's drink.

A few minutes pass as he finishes his drink. He pushes back from the table, working to upright himself. This is when she leans in and kisses him, closing her eyes to push away her revulsion as his tongue — a thick, chalky slug — probes hers. His friends goggle and jeer obscenities in Russian. When she can't take it anymore, she pulls back and whispers something in his ear, then stands, tugging at his hand. Within a few minutes they are on their way out of the club, where a valet jumps to attention and conjures up a banana-yellow Bugatti.

But the man is feeling odd now, on the verge of collapse; it's the champagne or the cocaine, he's not sure which, but he finds he can't object when the woman tugs the keys from his hand and slips behind the wheel herself. Before he passes out in the passenger seat, he manages to give her an address in the Hollywood Hills.

The woman carefully maneuvers the Bugatti up through the streets of West Hollywood, past the illuminated billboards selling sunglasses and calfskin purses, the buildings with fifty-foot-tall ads hawking Emmy-nominated TV series. She turns up the quieter winding roads that lead to Mulholland, white-knuckling it the whole time. The man snores beside her and rubs irritably at his crotch. When they finally get to the gate of his house, she reaches over and gives his cheek a hard pinch, startling him awake so that he can give her the code for entry.

The gate draws back to reveal a modernist behemoth, with walls entirely of glass, an enormous translucent birdcage hovering over the city.

It takes some effort to coax the man out of the passenger seat, and the woman has to prop him upright as they walk to the door. She notes the security camera and steps out of its range, then notes the numbers that the man punches into the door's keyless entry. When it opens, the pair is greeted by the shrieking of a burglar alarm. The man fumbles with the alarm keypad and the woman studies this, too.

Inside, the house is cold as a museum, and just as inviting. The man's interior decorator has clearly been given the mandate of "more is more" and emptied the contents of a

Sotheby's catalog into these rooms. Everything is rendered in leather and gold and glass, with furniture the size of small cars positioned under crystal chandeliers and art clogging every wall. The woman's heels clack on marble floors polished to a mirror gleam. Through the windows, the lights of Los Angeles shimmer and pulse: the lives of the common people below on display as this man floats here in the sky, safely above it all.

The man is slipping back into oblivion as the woman half drags him through the cavernous home in search of his bedroom. She finds it up a set of stairs, a frigid white mausoleum with zebra skin on the floors and chinchilla on the pillows, overlooking an illuminated pool that glows like an alien beacon in the night. She maneuvers him to the bed, dropping him onto its rumpled sheets just moments before he rolls over and vomits. She leaps back so that the mess doesn't splash her sandals, and regards the man coolly.

Once he's passed out again, she slips into the bathroom and frantically scrubs her tongue with toothpaste. She can't get his taste out of her mouth. She shudders, studies herself in the mirror, breathes deeply.

Back in the bedroom, she tiptoes around the vomit puddle on the floor, pokes the man with a tentative finger. He doesn't respond. He's pissed the bed.

18

That's when her real work begins. First, to the man's walk-in closet, with its floor-to-ceiling displays of Japanese jeans and limited-edition sneakers; a rainbow of silk button-downs in ice cream colors; fine-weave suits still in their garment bags. The woman zeroes in on a glass-topped display table in the center of the room, under which an array of diamond-encrusted watches gleam. She pulls a phone out of her purse and snaps a photo.

She leaves the closet and goes back into the living room, making a careful inventory as she goes: furniture, paintings, objets d'art. There's a side table with a clutch of silver-framed photos, and she picks one up to examine it, curious. It's a shot of the man standing with his arm flung over the shoulders of a much older man whose pink baby lips are twisted up in a moist grin, his wobbly folds of flesh tucked defensively back into his chin. The older man looks like a smug titan of industry, which is exactly what he is: Mikael Petrov, the Russian potash oligarch and occasional sidekick to the current dictator. The inebriated man in the other room: his son, Alexi, aka "Alex" to his friends, the fellow Russian rich kids with whom he pals around the planet. The mansion full of art and antiques: a time-honored means of laundering less-than-clean money.

The woman circles the house, noting items that she recognizes from Alexi's social media feed. There's a pair of Gio Ponti armchairs from the 1960s, probably worth $35,000, and a rosewood Ruhlmann dining set that would go for well into the six figures. A vintage Italian end table worth $62,000 — she knows this for sure because she looked it up after spotting it on Alex's Instagram (where it was stacked with Roberto Cavalli shopping bags and captioned with the hashtag *#ballershopping*). Because Alexi — like his friends, like the other people in the club, like every child of privilege between the ages of thirteen and thirty-three — documents his every move online, and she has been paying close attention.

She spins, takes stock, listens to the room. She has learned, over the years, how houses have character of their own; their own emotional palette that can be discerned in quiet moments. The way they stir and settle, tick and groan, the echoes that give away the secrets they contain. In its shimmery silence this house speaks to her of the coldness of life inside it. It is a house that is indifferent to suffering, that cares only about gleam and polish and the surface of things. It is a house that is empty even when it is full.

The woman takes a moment she shouldn't, absorbing all the beautiful works that Alexi owns; noting paintings by Christopher Wool, Brice Marden, Elizabeth Peyton. She lingers in front of a Richard Prince painting of a nurse in a bloodstained surgical mask, being gripped from behind by a shadowy figure. The nurse's dark eyes gaze watchfully out of the frame, biding their time.

The woman is out of time, herself: It's nearly three A.M. She does a last pass of the rooms, peering up into the corners, looking for the telling gleam of interior video cameras, but sees nothing: too dangerous for a party boy like Alexi to keep footage of his own misdeeds. Finally, she slips out of the house and walks barefoot down to Mulholland Drive, heels in hand, and calls a taxi. The adrenaline is wearing off, fatigue setting in.

The taxi drives east, to a part of town where the houses aren't hidden behind gates and the meridians are filled with weeds rather than manicured grass. By the time her taxi deposits her at a bougainvillea-covered bungalow in Echo Park, she is nearly asleep.

Her house is dark and silent. She changes clothes and creeps into her bed, too tired to rinse off the film of sweat and smoke that clings to her skin.

There is a man already there, sheets wrapped around his bare torso. He wakes instantly when she climbs into bed, props himself up on an elbow, and studies her in the dark.

"I saw you kissing him. Should I be jealous?" His voice is lightly accented, thick with sleep.

21

She can still taste the other man on her mouth. "God, no."

He reaches across her and flicks on the lamp so that he can examine her more closely. He runs his eyes across her face, looking for invisible bruises. "You had me worried. Those Russians don't joke around."

She blinks in the light as her boyfriend runs his palm across her cheek. "I'm fine," she says, and all the bravado finally runs out of her so that she's shaking, her whole body quivering from stress (but also, it's true, with giddiness, with the high of it all). "I drove him home, in his Bugatti. Lachlan, I got inside. I got everything."

Lachlan's face lights up. "Fair play! My clever girl." He pulls the woman to him and kisses her hard, his stubble scraping her chin, his hands reaching under her pajama top.

The woman reaches back for him, sliding her hands up across the smooth skin of his back, feeling the clench of his muscles under her palm. And as she lets herself sink into that twilight state between arousal and exhaustion, a kind of waking dream in which the past and present and future come together into a timeless blur, she thinks of the glass house on Mulholland. She thinks of the Richard Prince painting, of the bloodied nurse watching over the frigid rooms below, silent guardian against the night. Trapped in her glass prison, waiting.

■ ■ ■ ■

As for Alexi? In the morning, he will wake up in a dried puddle of his own urine, wishing he could detach his head from his body. He will text his friends, who will tell him he left with a hot brunette, but he will remember nothing. He will wonder first whether he managed to fuck the woman before he passed out, and whether it counts if he doesn't remember it; and then, somewhat idly, he will wonder who the woman was. No one will be able to tell him.

I could tell him, though, because that woman — she is me.

2.

Every criminal has an M.O. and this is mine: I watch and I wait. I study what people have, and where they have it. It's easy because they show me. Their social media accounts are like windows into their worlds that they've flung open, begging me to peer inside and take inventory.

I found Alexi Petrov on Instagram, for example — just another day of scrolling through photos of strangers until my eye was caught by a banana-yellow Bugatti and the man sitting on its hood with a self-satisfied grin that told me exactly what he thought of himself. By the end of the week, I knew everything about him: who his friends and family were, where he liked to party, the boutiques where he shopped, the restaurants where he dined, the clubs where he drank, as well as his lack of respect for women, his casual racism, his raging ego. All of it conveniently geotagged, hashtagged, cataloged, documented.

I watch, I wait. And then, when the opportunity arises, I take.

It's easier than you'd think to get to these kinds of people. After all, they provide the world with minute-by-minute documentation of their itineraries: All I have to do is put myself in their path. People open the door to pretty, well-dressed girls without bothering to ask a lot of questions. And then, once you're inside, it's all about timing. Waiting for the purse to be abandoned at a table while its owner is in the bathroom; waiting for the vape pens to come out and the proper level of inebriation to be achieved; waiting for a party crowd to sweep you along in its wake and that perfect moment of carelessness to present itself to you.

I have learned that the rich — the young rich, in particular — are so very careless.

So this is what is going to happen to Alexi Petrov: A few weeks from now, when this night (and my presence in it) has faded into a vague, cocaine-addled memory, he will pack up his LV luggage for a week in Los Cabos with a dozen of his jet-setting friends. He'll post Instagram photos of himself climbing aboard a *#gulfstream* swaddled in *#versace,* drinking *#domperignon* from a *#solidgold* ice bucket, sunbathing on the deck of a yacht with the *#beautifulpeople* in *#mexico.*

And while he is gone, a van will pull up to his empty mansion. The van will bear a sign advertising a nonexistent furniture restoration and art storage business, just in case any neighbors are watching from inside their own gated fortresses. (They won't be.) My partner — Lachlan, the man from my bed — will enter the house, using the gate and alarm codes that I've collected. He'll select the pieces that I've pointed out for him — two of the slightly less valuable watches, a pair of diamond cuff links, the Gio Ponti armchairs, that Italian end table, and a few other items of note — and he'll load them into the truck.

We could steal so much more from Alexi, but we don't. Instead, we follow the rules I set when I first got in this game a few years back: Don't take too much; don't get greedy. Take only what won't be missed. And only steal from those who can afford it.

Theft, a Primer:

1. Never steal artwork. Tempting as it might be, that multimillion-dollar painting — anything by a recognizable artist — is going to be impossible to move. Even Latin American drug lords won't shell out for a stolen Basquiat that they'll never be able to resell on the open market.
2. Jewels are easy to steal, but the really valuable pieces are often one of a kind, and therefore too identifiable.

Take lesser pieces, dismantle the jewelry, sell the gems.

3. Brand items — expensive watches, designer clothes, purses — are *always* a good bet. Throw that Patek Philippe up on eBay, sell it to a tech bro in Hoboken who just got his first big paycheck and wants to impress his friends. (Patience, here, is the key: best to wait six months in case authorities are monitoring the Web for stolen goods.)

4. Cash. Always the thief's ideal. But also the most difficult to get your hands on. Rich kids carry Centurion Cards, they don't tote around bundles of cash. Although once I found $12,000 in the side pocket of a limousine owned by the son of a telecom magnate from Chengdu. That was a good night.

5. Furniture. Now, this takes a real eye. You have to know your antiques — which I do, that's what a degree in art history will get you (if not much else) — and you have to have a way to sell them. You can't just set up on the corner with a Nakashima Minguren coffee table and hope that someone walking by has $30,000 in their pocket.

I've stolen three Birkin bags and a mink Fendi coat out of the closet of the star of the reality TV show *Shopaholix*. I walked out of a party at the mansion of a hedge fund manager with a Ming vase tucked in my tote; and slipped a yellow diamond ring off the finger of a Chinese steel heiress who had passed out in a bathroom at the Beverly Hills Hotel. Once, I even drove a Maserati right out of the garage of a twentysomething YouTube star best known for his videos of reckless car stunts, although I had to ditch it in Culver City because it was too identifiable to resell.

So — Alexi's cuff links will go to a jeweler of ill repute downtown, to be dismantled and resold; the watches will be placed in an online luxury consignment store, at a price that will be impossible to resist; and the furniture will end up in a storage locker in Van Nuys, awaiting its final destination.

Eventually, an Israeli antiques dealer named Efram will come by the storage locker to peruse its contents. He will pack our acquisitions into crates and ship them to a free port in Switzerland, where no one will bother to check on provenance and customers tend to pay in ill-begotten cash. What we take from Alexi will end up in collections in São Paulo, Shanghai, Bahrain, Kiev. For this, Efram will take seventy percent of the profit, which is highway robbery, but without him, we are nothing.

And at the end of the process, Lachlan and I will end up splitting $145,000.

How long will it take Alexi to notice that he's been robbed? Judging by the activity on his Instagram account, it will take three days after his return from Mexico to finally sleep off the hangover, wander into his living room, and realize that something is slightly amiss. Wasn't there once a pair of gold velvet armchairs sitting in that corner? (That will be the day that he posts a photo of a bottle of Patron at eight A.M. with the caption *Shit think Im going crazy need tequila.*) Before long, he'll register the missing watches. (Another post: a shot of shiny new timepieces lined up along his hairy arm, geotagged at Feldmar Watch Company in Beverly Hills. *Can't pick just gonna buy them all.*) Still, he won't report the robbery to the police; his ilk rarely do. Because who wants to deal with paperwork and nosy authorities, and all that unpleasant rigmarole over a few trinkets that will likely never be recovered and can be so easily replaced?

The super-rich are not like you or me, you see. We know exactly where our money is each minute of every day, the value and location of our most treasured belongings. The fabulously wealthy, on the other hand, have their money in so many places that they often forget what they have and where it's supposed to be. The pride in the value of the things

29

they own — *$2.3 million for this McLaren convertible!* — is often a disguise for a laziness in the care of those things. The car is crashed; the painting gets ruined by cigarette smoke; the couture dress gets trashed on the first wearing. Bragging rights aside, beauty is ephemeral: There's always a newer, brighter bauble to replace it.

Easy come, easy go.

3.

November in Los Angeles feels like summer just about anywhere else. A heat wave has blown in with the Santa Anas, and the sun bakes the packed dirt of the canyons, bringing up the scents of skunk and jasmine. Inside my bungalow, the bougainvillea vines rattle against the windows, shedding their leaves in passionate heaps of despair.

On a Friday, a month after the Alexi job, I wake up late to an empty house. I drive down the hill for coffee and a yoga class, and when I return I take a novel onto the stoop of my porch and settle in for a quiet morning. Next door, my neighbor Lisa is ferrying supplies from her car to her backyard, bags of fertilizer that are most likely destined for the marijuana patch she's growing. She nods at me as she passes.

I've lived here for three years now: my little aerie, a woodsy, two-story bungalow that started its life a hundred years earlier as a hunting cabin. I share it with my mother. Our

31

home is tucked up in a forgotten corner of Echo Park, bedraggled and overgrown, too inaccessible for real estate developers and too uncool for the gentrifying hipsters raising real estate prices down the hill. If you stand outside on an overcast day you can hear the groan of the interstate at the bottom of the hill; but otherwise, up here, it feels like you are far from the rest of the city.

My neighbors grow pot in their gardens; they collect broken pottery; they write poetry and political manifestos and decorate their fences with bits of sea glass. No one worries about maintaining their lawns up here; no one even has lawns to trim. What people value instead: space and privacy and a lack of judgment. I'd lived here for a year before I learned Lisa's name, and then only because her copy of *The Herb Quarterly* ended up in my mailbox by mistake.

On Lisa's next trip through, I wave her over, and pick my way across my own neglected clutter of succulents to the collapsing fence that separates our properties. "Hey there, I have something for you."

She pushes a wild lock of graying hair out of her face with a gardening glove, and walks to meet me. When she's close enough, I reach over the fence and tuck a folded check into the pocket of her jeans. "For the kids," I say.

She wipes her gloves on the back of her jeans, leaving brown crescents of dirt across her rear. "Again?"

"Work has been going well."

She nods, and gives me a crooked smile. "Well. Good for you. Good for us, too." Perhaps she finds it suspicious that her neighbor, the "antiques dealer," regularly gives her four-figure checks, but she has never said a thing. Even if she knew, though, I think she might not judge me anyway. Lisa runs a nonprofit that advocates for children in court, children who are there because of abuse and neglect: I'm sure it would secretly delight her, as it does me, to know that some of the money that I take from the most spoiled children in the world goes to children who have the least.

(And yes, I'm aware that the check is an attempt to assuage my own conscience — like the robber barons who write checks to charities and call themselves "philanthropists" — but really, it's a win-win for everyone, right?)

Lisa peers over my shoulder at the bungalow. "I saw your mom head off in a taxi at the crack of dawn."

"She went in for a CT scan."

A pucker of concern. "Everything OK?"

"Yes — it's just a routine follow-up. Her doctor's optimistic — her last few scans were promising. So it's likely that . . ." I leave the thought dangling there, too superstitious to articulate the word that I most want to say: *remission.*

"That must be a relief." She rocks back and forth on the heels of her work boots. "So, what then? You going to stick around if she's clear?"

That word — *clear* — triggers a little spasm inside me. *Clear* connotes clarity, but also blue skies, freedom, an open path to the future. Lately, I've been letting myself imagine, just a little. I've found myself in bed at night, listening to Lachlan's shallow breath beside me, and turning over the possibilities in my head. *What might be next.* Despite the adrenaline kick that I get from what I do — the self-righteous thrill of it all, not to mention the financial upside — I never intended to do *this* forever.

"I'm not sure," I say. "I'm feeling a little restless here. I've been thinking about going back to New York." Which is true, although when I mentioned this to my mother a few months ago — *Maybe when you're really and truly healthy again I'll head back to the East Coast* — the look of horror on her face was enough to stop the rest of that sentence right in my throat.

"Might be good for you to start fresh," Lisa says mildly. She pushes her hair from her eyes and settles them on me. I blush.

A car turns in to the road and slowly bumps along the rutted asphalt. It's Lachlan's vintage BMW, its engine clicking and whirring from the effort of ascending the hill.

Lisa raises an eyebrow, tucks the check deeper into her pocket with a pinkie, and shoulders her bag of fertilizer. "Come by one of these days for some matcha," she says as Lachlan parks in the driveway behind me. She vanishes into her garden.

There's the slam of a car door, and then I feel Lachlan's arms slip around my waist, his pelvis pressing against my backside. I turn in his arms so that I'm facing him. His lips slide across my forehead, down the side of my cheek, and end at my neck.

"You're in a good mood," I say.

He steps back, unfastening the top button of his shirt collar and wiping a bead of sweat off his hairline. With one palm, he shades his face against the sun: My partner is a nocturnal animal, his translucent blue eyes and pale skin more suited to dark places than the incinerating L.A. sun. "Eh. I'm a fair bit annoyed, actually. Efram didn't show."

"What? Why?" Efram still owes me $47,000 from the Alexi job. *Perhaps I shouldn't have given Lisa that check after all,* I think with alarm.

Lachlan shrugs. "Who knows? He's done this before; he probably got himself bolloxed or something and couldn't ring. I left a message. Anyway, I'm going to run back to my place later today, check in on things for a while, so maybe I'll stop in at his shop while I'm on the west side."

"Ah." So, Lachlan plans to disappear again, until we have another job lined up. I know better than to ask when he'll be back.

Things I know about Lachlan: He grew up in Ireland, in abject poverty, in one of those enormous Catholic families with a kid in every cupboard. He saw theater as his ticket out of this hardscrabble life and came to the States when he was twenty to try to make it on Broadway. That was two decades ago and the events that conspired between then and the day that I met him, three years back, remain murky. You could drive a semi through the gaps in what he chooses to share.

But this much I know: He didn't make it as an actor. He puttered along in background roles and fringe theater, in New York and Chicago and finally L.A., and got fired on the first day of his one big break in an indie film because his accent was "too Irish." Eventually, however, he discovered that his acting talents could be put to more lucrative, if less legal, uses. He became a confidence man.

I didn't much like Lachlan when we first met; but over time I came to realize that he was a kindred spirit. Someone who knew what it meant to drift along the edges of life, looking in. Who knew what it meant to be a child eating canned beans for supper while wondering what it would take to be a person who ate steak. Someone who believed the

36

golden beacon of the arts — theater, in his case; fine arts, in mine — would light the path out of an ugly life, only to find walls thrown up along the way. Someone who understood innately why one would choose to conceal one's past.

Lachlan is a reliable partner, but not a very good boyfriend. We'll do a job together, joined at the hip for however long it takes, and then he'll disappear for weeks without answering any of his phone numbers. I know he does jobs without me; he won't tell me what they are. Eventually I'll wake up in the middle of the night to find that he's slipped into my bed and is sliding a hand up between my legs. And every time I roll over to him and open myself wide. I don't ask where he's been; I don't want to know. I'm just glad that he's back — and frankly, I need him too much to press the subject.

Do I love him? I couldn't clearly say that I do, but I also couldn't say that I don't. I know this one last thing about him: That his hand on my bare skin makes me go liquid. That when he walks into a room that I'm in, it feels like there's an electric current running between us. That he is the only person in the world who knows everything about what I am and where I've come from, and that this makes me vulnerable to him in a way that is both excruciating and thrilling.

There are so many varieties of love — the

menu does not have just one flavor — and I see no reason why this can't be one of them. Love can be anything you choose to wrap around the word, as long as the two people involved agree upon the terms.

He told me he loved me just weeks after we met. I chose to believe him.

Or maybe he's just a very good actor, after all.

"I have to go pick up my mom from the clinic," I say.

I drive west into the midday sun, back toward the side of town where my marks usually live. The imaging clinic is in West Hollywood, a low-lying building that clings like a barnacle to the Cedars-Sinai sprawl. As I pull up, I spy my mother sitting on the steps of the clinic, an unlit cigarette poised between her fingers, sundress strap slipping off her shoulder.

I slow my car, squinting through the windshield at her. My mind crawls through the strange elements of this tableau as I pull past the parking lot entrance: That my mother is here, outside, when I am supposed to be meeting her inside the clinic. That she has a cigarette in hand, although she quit smoking three years back. The empty, distant look of her as she blinks in the thin November light.

She raises her head when I pull up in front of her and roll the window down. She offers a wan smile. Her lipstick, too pink, is smudged across the bow of her upper lip.

"Am I late?"

"No," she says. "I'm done already."

I glance at the clock on the dashboard; I could have sworn she said to come at noon, and it's only 11:53. "Why are you out here? I thought I was going to meet you inside."

She sighs and struggles to right herself, the cords in her wrist straining painfully as she pushes herself to her feet. "I can't stand it in there. It's so cold. I had to get out into the sun. Anyway, we finished early."

She pulls open the door and settles herself gingerly into the cracked leather seat. By some sleight of hand, she has already vanished the cigarette into the purse on her hip. She fluffs her hair with her fingers and stares out the windshield. "Let's go."

My mother, my beautiful mother — my God, I worshipped her as a child. The way her hair smelled like coconut and glimmered gold in the sunshine; the moist stickiness of her glossed lips plump against my cheek, leaving behind the marks of her love; the way it felt to be pressed against her chest, as if I might climb into all that soft flesh and hide safely inside her. Her laugh was an ascending scale, airborne, and she laughed at everything: the sour expression on my face when she served me frozen corn dogs for dinner, the way the repo man scratched his enormous rear as he hitched up our car to the tow truck, how we hid in the bathroom when the landlady banged on our door demanding the delinquent rent.

"You just have to laugh," she'd say, shaking her head as if she was helpless in the face of such mirth.

My mother doesn't laugh much anymore. And that, more than anything else about what has happened to her, breaks my heart. She stopped laughing the day that the doctor gave us the prognosis: She wasn't just "tired," like she protested; she wasn't losing weight because she had lost her appetite. She had non-Hodgkin's lymphoma, a cancer that was likely treatable but only at great cost, and that also had a pernicious tendency to battle itself back from the brink and recur, ad nauseam.

You couldn't *just laugh* at that, though my mom tried. "Oh, honey, it's OK, I'll figure it out. It's all going to be fine in the end," she said to me after the doctor left the room that first day, gripping my hand as I cried. She was trying to keep her voice light, but I heard the lie in her words.

My mother had always lived her life as if she was on a train journey, anticipating the next stop: If you didn't like where you got off, you just got right back on and moved to the next station. In the doctor's office that day, she learned that not only had she been booted off the train at the worst station on the line, but that this was quite possibly her final destination.

That was almost three years ago.

So this is my mother now: Hair that's still short and choppy since it grew back from the last round of chemo, its curl now coarse, the blond color a little too close to desperate. Bosom gone concave, ribs visible beneath. Soft hands now veiny despite the cherry-red polish designed to distract. Gaunt, frail, not soft and glimmering at all. Forty-eight years old and you'd think she was ten years older.

She's made an effort today — the sundress, the lipstick — which is heartening. But I can't shake the feeling that something is off. I notice a stack of paper folded into quarters and shoved into the pocket of her skirt. "Wait — you got results already? What did the doctor say?"

"Nothing," she says. "He said nothing."

"Bullshit." I reach across the car and try to pluck the paper from her pocket. She smacks my hand away.

"What do you say we go get pedicures?" she says, her voice as false and sticky as a child with an aspartame lollipop.

"What do you say you tell me what those test results say?" I make another grab for them and this time my mother remains motionless as I snag the papers from her pocket, careful not to tear the pages, my heart

41

building up to a rapid staccato because I know, already, what they say. I know from the resigned expression on my mother's face, the faint black smudges under her eyes where mascara recently melted and was wiped away. I know because this is what life is like: Just when you think you've reached the end zone, you look up to realize that the goal posts were moved back while you were focused on the turf right in front of your eyes.

And so even as my eyes scuttle across the CT scan results on the pages — the inscrutable charts, the dense paragraphs of medical jargon — I already know what I am going to see. And sure enough, on the last page, there they are: the familiar gray tumors bleeding shadows across slices of my mother's body, wrapping their amorphous fingers around her spleen, her stomach, her spine.

"I relapsed," my mother says. "Again."

I feel it in my own stomach then, the familiar dark spread of helplessness. "Oh God. No. No no no."

She plucks the papers from my fingers and carefully folds them along the crease marks. "We knew this was probably going to happen," she says softly.

"No we *didn't*. The last treatment was supposed to be *it*, the doctor said, that's why we . . . Jesus. I don't understand. . . ." I trail off before I finish, because this is not the point I mean to make; but my first thought is that we were sold a false bill of goods. *But he said . . . It's not fair,* I think, like a child having a temper tantrum. I throw the transmission into park. "I'm going in to talk to the doctor. This can't be right."

"Don't," she says. "Please. I talked it through with Dr. Hawthorne, we already have a plan. He wants to try radioimmunotherapy this time. There's a brand-new drug — I think it's called Advextrix? — just approved by the FDA, with really promising results. Even better than the stem cell transplant. He thinks I'm a good candidate." A soft laugh. "The upside is I won't lose my hair this time. You won't have to see me looking like a cue ball."

"Oh, Mom." I manage a wan smile. "I don't care about what your hair looks like."

She stares resolutely out the windshield at the cars that whiz past on Beverly Boulevard. "The drug. It's expensive, is all. It's not covered by my insurance plan."

Of course it isn't. "I'll figure it out."

She looks at me sideways, blinking her clotted lashes. "Each dose is about fifteen thousand dollars. I'll need sixteen of them."

"You don't worry about that. You worry about getting healthy again. Trust me to take care of the rest."

"I do. You're the *only person* I trust, you know that." She looks at me. "Oh, honey, don't look so upset. The only important thing

43

is that you and I still have each other. That's all we've ever had."

I nod and reach over to take her hand. I think of a bill still sitting on my desk at home, the final invoice for my mother's *last* round of treatments — the bill that Efram's payment was supposed to cover. This will make a third recurrence of her non-Hodgkin's lymphoma: Neither the first treatment (basic chemo, only partially covered by my mother's bare-bones insurance) nor the second (an aggressive stem cell transplant, not at all covered) kept the tumors at bay for more than a year. When I recently totaled up the cost of my mother's illness, we were approaching a high six-figure mark. This — her third round — will put us well into seven figures.

I want to scream. The stem cell transplant was supposed to have an eighty-two percent success rate; so I had taken remission as a certainty, because what were the odds that my mother would be that eighteen percent? Wasn't that why I had nodded, so unblinking, at the boggling price tag for the transplant? Wasn't that certainty the justification for everything I've let myself do over the past few years?

We were almost in the clear is what I think to myself now, as I turn over the engine and pull out into the traffic. It isn't until I feel my mother's cool hand on mine, tucking a tissue into my fist, that I realize that I'm crying. But I'm not quite sure what the tears are about: my mother, and the invisible tumors once again devouring her from within, or my own future, and how cloudy it once again seems.

My mother and I drive back home in near silence, her diagnosis sitting heavy as a boulder between us. In my mind, I am running through the *what next* of it all: The medication will be only the half of it, the cost of this round will certainly top a half million. Optimistically, I had no new marks lined up; how naïve I was, to think I might be able to move on to something else entirely. Now I mentally run through the faces I still have bookmarked on social media, the princelings and celebutantes currently cavorting their way across Beverly Hills. I try to recall the ostentatious inventory of their Instagrams. Thinking about this gives me a nasty little sparkle, a lift of anger that helps me rise above my underlying weariness. *Here we are, at this, again.*

When we arrive home, I am surprised to see that Lachlan's car is still parked in my driveway. There's a movement at the curtain as we park; his pale face flashing behind the glass, and then he's gone again.

When we get inside, I find that the lights are off and the blinds are down, casting my home into gloom. I flip on the light switch and see Lachlan standing behind the door, blinking in the sudden wash of light. He turns the light back off and pulls me out of the doorway.

My mother hesitates in the doorway behind me, and he stops to look over my shoulder at her. "Lily-belle, you all right? How'd those tests go?"

"Not so good," my mother answers. "But I don't feel like talking about it right now. Why are the lights off in here?"

Lachlan peers down at me, his face shadowed with concern. "You and I have to talk," he says softly. He grabs my elbow and guides me toward the corner of the living room. "Lily-belle, you mind? I need a moment with Nina."

She nods but moves toward the kitchen with glacial slowness, eyes glittering with curiosity. "I'll make us some lunch."

Once she's out of earshot, he pulls me in close and whispers in my ear, "The police were here."

I lurch back. "What? When?"

"Just an hour or two ago. Not long after you left to pick up your mom."

"What did they want? Did you talk to them?"

"Christ, *no,* I'm not a bloody idiot. I hid in the bathroom, didn't answer their knock, yeah? But they were looking for you. I could

46

never admit it out loud to her. I couldn't bear to witness my mother's disappointment in me.

But now I wonder if I was an idiot to think that I had *ever* fooled her. Because judging by the expression on her face, she knows exactly why the police were at our door.

"I did nothing," I say quickly. "Don't worry about it. I'm sure it's a mistake."

But I can tell by the way my mom's eyes dart back and forth across mine that she *is* worrying. She looks over my shoulder at Lachlan and her face changes as she reads something there.

"You should leave," she says flatly. "Right now. Get out of town. Before they come back."

I laugh. *Leave.* Of course.

If there's one thing my mother was a real expert at when I was growing up, it was leaving. The first time we left was the night that my mother chased my father out of our apartment with a shotgun, when I was seven, but by my count we left again nearly two dozen times before I graduated from high school. We left when we couldn't cover the rent; we left when a jealous wife showed up on our doorstep; we left when the police did a sweep of the casino and brought my mother in for interrogation. We left because my mother thought she might get arrested if we stayed; we left when opportunity dried up; and we

49

left because she plain old didn't like where we were anymore. We left Miami, Atlantic City, San Francisco, Las Vegas, Dallas, New Orleans, Lake Tahoe. We left even when my mother promised me that we wouldn't leave anymore.

"I am not going to leave you, Mom. Don't be ridiculous. You've got *cancer.* You're going to need me to take care of you."

I expect her to weep, and soften; but instead her face hardens into something immobile and cool. "For God's sake, Nina," she says softly. "You are no help to me at all if you're in jail."

In my mother's expression, I read disillusionment, even anger, like I have failed her and we are both going to pay the price. And for the first time since I came to Los Angeles I am truly frightened by what I have become.

4.

So I'm a grifter. You might say that the apple doesn't fall far from the tree — I come from a long line of bagmen and petty thieves, opportunists and outright criminals — but the truth is that I was not raised for this. I had a Future. That, at least, is what my mother used to say to me late at night when she found me reading *Pride and Prejudice* under the covers by flashlight: "You have a Future, baby, the first one in this family." When I performed on command for her male visitors, doing long division in my head while they sipped dirty martinis on our sagging settee: "Isn't my girl smart? She has a Future." When I told her I wanted to go to college but I knew we couldn't afford it: "Don't worry about the money, sweetie. This is about your Future."

And for a while there, I even believed her. Got caught up in the great American myth, the Puritan ethic of nose-to-the-grindstone-and-thou-shalt-prevail. That was back when I thought the playing field was even, before I learned that it was not flat at all; and that, in fact, for most people not born into privilege, the playing field is a steep incline and you are at the bottom with boulders tied to your ankles.

My mother had the ability to make you believe, though. This was her great gift, her sweet con. The way she could fix a man with those innocent eyes of hers, as wide and blue as a spring lake, and convince him of anything she wanted: that the check was on the way, that the necklace in her purse had ended up there by mistake, that she loved him like no one had ever been loved before.

The only person she *truly* loved was me; I knew that much. It was just the two of us against the world; it had been that way since she kicked my father out. And so I always believed that my mother couldn't possibly lie to me, not about this person I was going to become.

And probably she *wasn't* lying to me, at least not intentionally. Instead, the person she was really lying to was herself.

My mother may have been a con artist, but she wasn't a cynic. She believed, she truly did, in the great opportunity of life. We were always on the verge of hitting the big time, even as my shoes were being held together with duct tape or we were eating baked potatoes for dinner for the third week running. And when those opportunities did come

— when she won big at the card tables or managed to hook herself a big fish — we lived like queens. Dinners out at hotel restaurants, a red convertible in the driveway, a Barbie DreamHouse with a bow on it. And if she wasn't looking far enough down the road, saving up in anticipation of that convertible being hauled away by the repo man, who could fault her? She trusted that life would take care of us, and it always did, right up until the moment when it didn't.

My mother was pretty but not a beauty; though what she was, was more dangerous than that. She had a kind of sex-kitten innocence, with the summer-peach complexion of a child, those big blue eyes, blond hair only slightly enhanced with a bottle. Her body boasted an abundance of flesh that she had trained to swing in just the right way. (Once, I overheard a junior high kid in Vegas call her "Tits McGee," but after I slugged him he never did it again.)

Lilla Russo was her real name, though she went by Lily Ross most of the time. She was Italian, her family had been Mafia-adjacent, or so she said. I wouldn't know — I never met my grandparents, who had cut her off entirely after she had a baby (me) out of wedlock with a Colombian poker player. (I'm not sure which sin was the unforgivable one: the baby, the lack of a ring, or the lover's country of origin.) She once told me that my grandfather had been a mob soldier in Baltimore, with half a dozen bodies under his belt. She didn't seem to want to be around her family any more than they wanted to be around us.

The first years of my life were dictated by my father, whose gambling career kept us moving like migratory birds, our resting spot changing with the seasons or whenever his luck ran out. When I think of him now I mostly remember the lemony scent of his aftershave and the way he used to pick me up and fling me so high in the air that my hair would graze the ceiling, laughing at my screams of terror and my mother's shrieks of protest. He was less of a grifter than a bully.

Back then, my mother worked odd jobs — waitressing, mostly — but her main job was defending me from him: barricading me in my room when he came home drunk, putting herself in the way of his fists so that they wouldn't land on me. One night, when I was seven, she didn't quite manage to get me out of the way, and he threw me against the wall so hard that I temporarily blacked out. When I regained consciousness, there was my mother, blood dripping down her face, pointing my father's shotgun at his crotch. Her feathery, soft voice hardened to something sharp and lethal: "If you touch her again I swear I will shoot you right in the balls. Now, get the fuck out of here and don't come back."

And he did, skulking away like a dog with its tail between its legs. Before the sun rose the next morning, my mother had packed up the car. As we drove out of New Orleans — headed to Florida, where she had "a friend who had a friend" — she turned to look at me in the passenger seat and grabbed my hand. "You and I are all each other has," she whispered hoarsely. "And I will never, ever let anyone hurt you again. I promise."

She didn't, either. When a boy at our next apartment building stole my bike, she marched straight down to the courtyard and pushed the kid up against the wall until he cried and told her where it was hidden. When the girls in my class teased me about my weight, she went straight to their homes, rang the doorbells, and screamed at their parents. No teacher could give me a failing grade without facing my mother's ire in the school parking lot.

And when confrontation wouldn't solve the problem, she would just whip out her ultimate solution. "OK," she'd say to me. "Let's move and just try it again."

Chasing off my father had unintended conse-quences. My mother couldn't pay the bills with part-time waitressing anymore. Instead, she moved into the only other profession she knew: crime.

My mother's hustle was soft coercion. She used seduction as a means of access: to a credit card, a bank account, a chump who might cover the rent for a while. She targeted married men, misbehaving cads who were too afraid of getting caught by their wives to file a police report when $5,000 suddenly went missing from their checking accounts. Powerful men too wrapped up in their own egos to admit they'd been conned by a woman. I think it was her revenge on every man who had ever underestimated her: the English teacher who molested her in high school, the father who disavowed her, the husband who blackened her eye.

When she didn't have a mark on the line, she would hang out at casinos, working the card tables and waiting for opportunity to present itself. Sometimes my mother would dress me up in my fanciest outfit — blue velvet, pink taffeta, itchy yellow lace, bought on sale at Ross Dress for Less — and take me to the glitzy palaces where she plied her trade. She'd deposit me in the casino's nicest restaurant with a fat book and a ten-dollar bill; the waitresses would coddle me with bar nuts and fizzy orange drinks while my mother cruised the floor. If it was a quiet night, my mother would take me around with her and show me how to slip a billfold out of a jacket pocket, hook a wallet from a purse on the back of a chair. Imparting little lessons along the way: *A bulging back pocket is a better bet than an open purse. Men link their egos to the size of their billfold, while women find cash too bulky.* Or: *Don't be impulsive. Always look for opportunity, but don't act on it until you've thought three steps ahead.*

"It's not big money," she'd whisper as she rifled through a money clip in a casino bathroom, "but enough to cover a car payment. So, not bad, right?"

It all seemed so normal to me when I was young. This was just my mother's job. Other people's parents cleaned houses or scraped plaque off teeth or sat in offices typing at computers; my mother went to casinos and took money from strangers. And really what she did was no different from what the casino owners did; or, at least, that's what she told me. "The world can be divided into two kinds of people: those who wait to have things given to them and those who take what they want." She would hug me close, her false eyelashes brushing my forehead, the scent of her skin like honey. "I know better than to wait."

My world was my mother, her body the only home I'd ever known. It was the one place where I always belonged, in a world in which everything else was permanently in flux; where "friends" were girls you left behind, a name on a spindled pen pal postcard. I don't blame her, even now, for my misfit childhood. We moved so often not because she wasn't trying to be a good mom but because she was trying *too hard.* She always believed that the next stop would be better, for her and for me. That's why we didn't speak to her parents, that's why we left my father behind: because she was protecting *me.*

As an adolescent, I skated through school by making myself invisible — always sitting in the back of the classroom, reading a novel that I'd sandwich between the pages of my textbooks. I was overweight, rainbow-haired, and dressed in aggressively emo ensembles that deterred potential friends and staved off the disappointment of their ultimate rejection. I made perfectly mediocre grades that were neither bad enough for anyone in charge to flag my existence, nor good enough to be singled out for special attention. But by my freshman year at a goliath, cracked-concrete high school in Las Vegas, an English teacher finally noted my "missed potential" and called my mother in for a conference. And suddenly I was being sent in for mysterious tests, the results of which my mother wouldn't show me, but they made her walk around our apartment with her lips pressed into a thin line of determination. Pamphlets began piling up on the counters; my mother pressing stamps onto fat envelopes with triumphant gusto. A new Future was being planned for me.

One spring night toward the end of freshman year, my mother slipped into my bedroom just before lights-out. She perched on the edge of my bed in her cocktail dress, gently pried the book I was reading out of my hands, and began a speech in her soft, whispery voice: "Nina, baby, it's time we started really focusing on your future."

I laughed. "You mean, like, do I want to be an astronaut or a ballerina when I grow up?" I grabbed for my book.

My mother held the book out of reach. "I'm dead serious, Nina Ross. You are *not* going to end up like me, OK? And that's what *will* happen if we don't start taking advantage of the opportunities available to you."

"What's wrong with being like you?" And yet, even as I asked, I knew what she meant. I knew that mothers weren't supposed to stay out all night and sleep all day; they weren't supposed to monitor the neighbors' mailboxes for credit cards and new checkbooks; they weren't supposed to pack up the car overnight and move because the local law enforcement was breathing down their necks. I loved my mom, I forgave everything she did, but as I sat there on the lumpy bed in our latest cockroach-infested rental apartment, I recognized that I *didn't* want to be like her. Not anymore. I knew that what I felt when I

59

walked through the halls of my school with her — the teachers staring at her skintight bandage dresses and stiletto heels, her peroxided nimbus of hair and her berry-stained lips — was a desire to be anything *but* her.

But what did I want to be?

She looked down at the book in her hands, puzzling over the title. I was reading *Great Expectations,* which the English teacher had given me not long after she sent me for testing. "*Very superior intelligence.* That's what the IQ tests said. You can be anything you want to be. Anything that's more than a two-bit hustler."

"So I *can* be a ballerina?"

She gave me a withering look. "I never got a fair shot at life and you're getting one, so dammit, you're going to take it. So we're moving. *Again,* I know. But there's a prep school up in the Sierra Nevada, Lake Tahoe, that's offering us financial aid. We're going to move there and you're going to focus on your studies and I'm going to get a job."

"A *job* job?"

She nodded. "A *job* job. I got work as a hostess, at one of the casinos up there."

And even though I felt something jump and quiver inside me at these words — maybe we were about to become a normal family after all — the jaded fifteen-year-old cynic in me couldn't quite believe it. "And so, what, I took a test and now you think that I'll go to

Harvard someday? Become the first female president of the United States? Come on."

She sat back and regarded me with frank, blue eyes, wide as silver dollars and as calm as a moonlit night. "Oh, sweetheart. Why the fuck *not*?"

Needless to say, I didn't become the first female president. Or an astronaut, or even a goddamn ballerina.

No, instead I went to a college (not Harvard in the end, not even close) and got a liberal arts degree. I walked away with a six-figure student-loan debt and a piece of paper that qualified me to do absolutely nothing of value whatsoever. I figured that just being smart and working hard would clear my path toward a different life.

So is it any surprise that I ended up a grifter, after all?

5.

"Your mother is right. We should leave. Today." It is later that day and Lachlan and I have decamped to the darkest corner of an anonymous Hollywood sports bar, whispering as if someone might be listening in, although the only people in this bar are a group of frat types in football jerseys who are too drunk to pay us any attention. Sports games blare from televisions on every surface. "Let's just get out of town for a little while, until we know what's going on."

"But maybe it's nothing," I protest. "Maybe it has nothing to do with us. Maybe the police just came by my place because . . . I don't know. Community outreach. Maybe there's been a crime spree in my neighborhood and they want to warn us."

Lachlan laughs. "Darling, we *are* the crime spree." He kneads the knuckles of one hand in the other. "Listen, I made some calls after the cops came by. Efram has vanished. No one's seen him since last week and he's still

62

not answering his phone. Word on the street is that he was picked up by the police. So —"

"He owes me forty-seven thousand dollars!" I protest. "And there's still a few pieces in the storage unit that he was going to move for us. The Gio Ponti armchairs — he said he'd get at least fifteen grand each for them."

He prods at his dry lips with the tip of his tongue. "Yeah, well, that's the least of our problems. The police were *at your house.* Maybe Efram gave us up in a plea deal, or maybe your name was just in his contact files and they're fishing for information. But, either way, we should get out of town for a while and let the dust settle. And if we hear through the grapevine that they've issued a warrant for our arrest, we'll know we have to run for real, but at least we'll have a head start."

"We have to *run?*" My head spins. "But that's not possible. I've got to take care of Lily."

"Yeah, well, your mom was right about that, too. You're not going to be able to take care of her if you're in jail." He starts cracking his knuckles, gently tugging at each finger until it yields with a sickening *pop.* "Look, let's just take a breather and do a job somewhere else. There's clearly too much heat in L.A., so we're not going to be able to work here for a while anyway. It can't hurt to go find new hunting grounds, for a few months at least." He snaps his pinkie, and I wince.

"A few *months*?" I think of the cancer once again spreading its creeping tentacles through my mother's body. I imagine her lying alone in a hospital bed, an IV snaking into her veins, the steady bleat of the machines. I want to say something like, *This is more than I signed up for,* but it's not true. It *is* what I signed up for, it's just that I believed that Lachlan knew what he was doing and we would never get caught. We were being careful. We never took too much, even when we could. The *rules* — they were supposed to be our safeguard against this.

He looks at me coolly. "Or we can go our separate ways. It's up to you. But I'm leaving town."

I'm dumbstruck by the icy calculation in his words. Am I just a business proposition, so easily discarded when I start to be inconvenient? I can't finish my drink. "I thought . . ." I don't know how to finish the sentence. What did I think? That we would be together forever? Go straight together, get a house in the suburbs and have a kid or two? No, that was never in the cards. So why does this sting so much? *Because I have no one else,* I realize.

"Oh, c'mon Nina, love. Don't look like that." He reaches across the table and laces his fingers between mine. "It will all be fine.

Look, come with me. I promise we'll figure this out. We'll go someplace close enough that you can still come back and check on your mom periodically. Someplace within driving distance, like Northern California, or Nevada. But it needs to be a little off the beaten path, so we can lay low. A resort destination, maybe. Like Monterey, or Napa." He squeezes my hand. "Or, hey — What about Lake Tahoe? That's where all the Silicon Valley billionaires spend their weekends, right? Have you been tracking anyone up there?"

But I'm thinking about what will have to happen if I leave town: the home care I'll have to bring in to take care of my mother when she's weak from the treatment, the help I'll have to hire to get her to and from her appointments, the staggering bills that will need to be opened and paid. Assuming I even *have* the money to pay them. My mother's life is on the line: As long as our bank account remains depleted, there *will* be no experimental radio-immunotherapy treatment. I don't really have a choice.

We need a job that is fast, with a big payoff; and my thoughts catch on something that Lachlan just said. *Tahoe.*

There's a ruckus at the bar and I look over in time to see one of the football fans vomiting all over the floor. His friends are laughing as if this is hilarious. The bartender, a blond girl with tattoo sleeves, catches my eye with a murderous expression on her face, and I know that she is going to have to clean up their mess. Women always do.

I turn back to Lachlan.

"I have, actually," I say. "Have you ever heard of Vanessa Liebling?"

Vanessa Liebling. A name and face that I've followed for twelve years, although she didn't materialize on social media until four years ago. An heiress from the West Coast Liebling clan, one of those old moneyed families with their fingers jammed in lots of pies, from real estate to casinos. Instead of going into the family business, however, Vanessa's made a career as an "Instagram fashion influencer." In English: She travels the world taking photos of herself in dresses that cost more than the annual income of the women who sewed them. For this dubious skill set — wearing Balmain in Bahrain, Prada in Prague, Celine in Copenhagen — she has a half-million followers. She's dubbed her Instagram feed *V-Life.*

Study her Instagram feed — as I have, in detail — and you'll see that the earliest posts on her account are your standard rich-girl fare: loving (if blurry) snapshots of her new Valentino bag; close-up selfies of herself hugging her Maltipoo, Mr. Buggles; an occasional shot of the New York skyline from the window of her Tribeca loft. And then, fifty posts in, having likely realized the career-changing potential of being Instagram-famous, the quality of her photos improves dramatically. Suddenly, they are no longer selfies. Instead, another person is taking the pictures, probably a photo assistant paid to document her every wardrobe change and sip of macchiato. There is Vanessa, strolling through SoHo with Mr. Buggles, holding a fistful of helium balloons. There is Vanessa, in the front row of a Chanel fashion show, wearing sunglasses in the dark. There is Vanessa in a red silk dress, posing next to a snaggle-toothed sticky-rice vendor in Hanoi: *Vietnamese people are so colorful and authentic! (Dress by #gucci, sandals by #valentino.)*

Often, she travels to these exotic locales with other expensively clad women, a network of fellow influencers she's dubbed her *#stylesquad.* There are hundreds — thousands! — of other women on Instagram doing the exact same thing she does; she is by no means among the highest profile, nor the most ostentatious, but she's clearly found her audience. And an income stream, too, as she starts shilling jewelry lines and bottled green juices in sponsored posts.

A handsome boyfriend appears, usually in exuberant clinches, as if to prove to her followers how much he really adores her. The dog gets his own hashtag. Meanwhile, she grows skinnier and skinnier, her tan darker and darker, her hair more and more blond. Eventually, a diamond appears on her ring finger as she peers coyly through her fingers at the camera. *Guys,* she writes, *I have news.* There are photos of the interior of an exclusive bridal salon; her eyes peeking over the top of a flower arrangement. *I'm thinking peonies.*

But then, starting last February, the tone of her account suddenly shifts. There's a close-up snapshot of a man's hand, liver-spotted with age and resting on the edge of a hospital bed. The caption reads: *My poor daddy, RIP.* Then, for a few weeks, nothing, just a note: *Sorry guys, taking some family time, back soon.* When she returns, the photos of her outfits — black now, lots of black — are interspersed with generic inspirational quotes. *Nothing is impossible — the word itself says "I'm possible!" The only person you should strive to be better than is the person you were yesterday. Happiness is not something ready-made; it comes from your own actions.*

The ring has disappeared from her left hand.

And then, finally, there's a shot of her Manhattan loft, stripped of furniture, floors piled high with boxes. *Guys: It's time for a new adventure. I'm moving back to my family's historic vacation home in Lake Tahoe. I'm going to fix it up while spending some "me time" in great Mother Nature! Stay tuned for my new adventures!*

For the last few years, I've watched all this from afar, judging her with distaste. She was a spoiled trust fund kid, I told myself. Not terribly bright, skilled at nothing but self-aggrandizement, lever-aging her own insider access to get more of everything that she had done nothing to deserve. Canny at self-image; shallow at heart. Careless with her privilege and hopelessly out of touch with the real world, she was someone who liked to use those with less as props for her own fabulous-ness: a deluded elitist who believed she was actually a populist. She was clearly at a low point in her life and making some stab at self-actualization, judging by all those motivational quotes.

But it wasn't until she announced that she was moving to Lake Tahoe that I started to pay close attention to her. For the last six months since she moved, I've been tracking Vanessa's life closely: Watching as the glossy, professional quality of her photos disappeared, replaced once again by selfies. Watching as the fashion shots vanished, replaced by image after image of a crystalline mountain lake surrounded by stately pines. Looking for a familiar glimpse of a house I know so well, a house that has haunted my dreams since I was a teenager.

Looking for Stonehaven.

A few months back, I finally found it. She'd posted a photo of herself hiking with a young couple, everyone tanned and glowing with health. They stood on the summit of a mountain, the lake spreading out below them as they laughed with their arms flung around each other. The caption: *Showing my new BFFs my favorite Tahoe spots! #hiking #athleisure #beautifulview.* The friends were tagged. I clicked on one and found myself on the Instagram feed of a young Frenchwoman documenting her travels across the United States. Three photos in, there it was: a shot of the couple sitting on a familiar cottage stoop, surrounded by ferns. The open door behind them allowed a shadowy glimpse of a cozy living room, a couch upholstered in old-fashioned brocade that made my heart beat faster. The caption: *Cet JetSet était merveilleux. Nous avons adoré notre hôtesse, Vanessa.*

My high school French was rusty, but I knew what this meant.

Vanessa had started renting out the cottage.

It takes just an hour to pack a bag. When I tell my mother that I am leaving town — that I'll call often, visit as soon as I can — she starts blinking rapidly and I wonder if she is

70

going to cry. But she doesn't. "Good girl," she says instead. "*Smart* girl."

"I'm calling that home aide we used last year. I'll have her come and check on you daily once the radiation starts. She'll clean and do the shopping. OK?"

"For goodness' sake, Nina. I'm capable of setting up my own home care. I'm not an invalid."

Yet, I think to myself. "And the bills — you'll have to pay them instead of me. You're already on my bank account; I'll top it up as soon as some money comes in." I don't want to think about what will happen to my mother if it doesn't.

"Don't worry about me. I'm an old hand at this now."

I kiss her forehead, and wait until I am out of sight before I let myself cry.

Lachlan and I check in to a budget hotel in Santa Barbara. Nothing near the beach where we might hear the waves; just a concrete slab and a pool with gray crust soiling the tiles and leaves growing slimy on the bottom. The shower is prefab and it leaks, and instead of miniature bottles of soap and shampoo they offer one bottle of catch-all "washing liquid."

We lie side by side on the bed, sipping wine from disposable cups, my browser open to JetSet.com. I type *Lake Tahoe* into the search field and then start scrolling through the listings until one jumps out at me. I turn the

71

laptop around and display the page for Lachlan. "This is it," I say.

"That?" He gives me a quizzical look and I can see why: The photograph is of a modest shingled cottage, timbered and painted pale green, nestled in a stand of pines. Compared to some of the other lakefront listings, this one is humble, easily overlooked. The cottage has a worn, Hansel and Gretel quality to it: slatted wooden shutters, window boxes laden with ferns, moss growing up the stones of the foundation. *Cozy Caretaker's Cottage,* the listing reads. *Lakefront 2 Bedroom, Short- or Long-Term Rental.*

"Click on it," I command him. He raises an eyebrow at me but he obeys, and takes the laptop.

The listing has six pictures. The first is of a tiny living room anchored by a stone fireplace and a faded brocade couch, artwork tiled along the walls and antiques crowding the corners. The furniture is all slightly too large for the cottage, almost hodgepodge, as if someone had emptied the contents of a different house here and then thrown up their hands and walked away. The second photo shows a vintage kitchen dominated by a classic enamel O'Keefe & Merritt stove, the wood cabinetry hand-painted with stencils. There's a photo of a pristine lake view and another of a modest bathroom and yet another of a bedroom with twin sleigh beds nestled up against each other under the eaves.

Lachlan squints at the photos. "This is your area of expertise, not mine, but that dresser . . . isn't it Louis XIV?"

I ignore this, reaching over him to click forward to the last photo in the series. It shows a bedroom with a four-poster bed, positioned alongside a picture window framed in gauzy curtains. There's a white lace coverlet draped across the bed, and a painting of a farmhouse perched over a cascading river. The glass in the picture window is thick and warped with age, but through it you can glimpse the blue of the lake beyond.

I know that bed. I know that painting. I know that view.

"That's the bed I lost my virginity in," I hear myself say.

Lachlan jerks around to stare at me, and at the serious expression on my face he starts to laugh. "Seriously? This very same bed."

"It's a different bedspread," I say. "But everything else is the same. And the dresser is rococo, not Louis XIV."

He's rocking back and forth with laughter. "My God, no wonder you have a thing for antiques. You got deflowered on bloody rococo."

"That's the dresser. Don't know what the bed is, but it's not rococo," I murmur. "Don't think the bed's that valuable, actually."

"What the fuck *is* this place? Who puts

eighteenth-century French furniture in a crumbling old cottage like that?" He scrolls down the listing and reads the summary. I peer over his shoulder.

Enjoy a magical stay at the Caretaker's Cottage, part of a classic estate on the West Shore of Lake Tahoe! So much charm packed into two cozy bedrooms: Vintage kitchen, beautiful antiques, a working stone fireplace! Lake views, nearby hiking, and just steps away from a private beach. A perfect sojourn for a couple or an artist seeking inspiration!

He turns to look at me, quizzical. "Classic estate?"

"Stonehaven." That name in my mouth conjures up a strange stew of emotions: remorse and nostalgia and loss and a hot blast of rage. I enlarge the photo of the bedroom and examine it closely. I feel disembodied, my present and past selves split between these two beds, neither of them mine. "It's a huge lakeside mansion that's belonged to the Lieblings for over a hundred years."

"These Lieblings. Am I supposed to know who they are?"

"Founders of the Liebling Group, a real estate investment firm based in San Francisco. They used to be Fortune 500, though I think they fell off a while back. Old money, though. West Coast royalty."

74

"And you know them." He is studying me with an expression on his face that suggests I've betrayed him in some way by keeping this valuable connection to myself until now.

Fragments of memories are surfacing from someplace deep within me: The darkness of that cottage, even with the setting sun cutting sideways through the glass windows. The way the coverlet — blue wool back then, I recall it was woven with some sort of crest — scraped against the backs of my bare thighs. The frothy cascade of the river in the painting, water descending to the edge of the painting as if ready to spill over and anoint me. The tender red curls of a boy who smelled like marijuana and spearmint chewing gum. Vulnerability, loss, the sensation that something precious inside me had been dragged out and exposed to air for the first time.

So much that felt so vital then that I have since managed to forget.

I am disoriented, feeling as if I've tumbled back a dozen years and landed in the body of the chubby, lost teenager I once was. "I *knew* them. Just a little. A long time ago. I lived in Lake Tahoe for a year, back when I was a sophomore in high school. I was friendly with their son." I shrug. "It's all a bit of a blur, frankly. I was a kid."

"Sounds like you knew them more than a *little.*" He clicks back through the photos in the listing, studying them. "So wait. Will this woman —"

"Vanessa."

"Vanessa. Will she remember you?"

I shake my head. "She'd already gone off to college when I was living there. I mostly knew her brother. I met her only once, briefly, twelve years ago. So she'd never recognize me now — I look nothing like I did then. I was overweight and had pink hair. The one time we crossed paths she barely even looked at me." I remember it clearly, too — the way her eyes skidded across me, as if I was so insignificant that she couldn't be bothered to register my presence. The way my face burned hot underneath the thick makeup I'd so carefully applied to hide my adolescent acne, my rampant insecurity.

Benny, though: He'd recognize me now. But I know where he is these days, and it's not Stonehaven.

I'm not ready to think about him. I push him from my mind and pull up Vanessa's Instagram feed for Lachlan to peruse.

Lachlan clicks through the photos, pausing to examine a photo of Vanessa on a gondola in Venice, the hem of her Valentino dress trailing behind her in a soft breeze. I can see him registering her practiced prettiness, the way she casually ignores the gondolier, the complacent expression on her face suggesting that the picturesque canal and sweating old man

76

exist for her pleasure alone. "Still, I don't get it. If she's so rich, why is she renting out her caretaker's cottage?"

"My guess is she's lonely. Her father died, she just broke up with her fiancé and moved from New York. Stonehaven is pretty isolated. She probably wants company."

"And we will be that company." As he scrolls through Vanessa's photos, I can see his mind running through its calculations. He is already starting to map our way in: the gentle persuasion we will use to convince her to invite us into her world, the vulnerabilities we will discover and exploit. "So, what are we shooting for here? The antiques? Family jewels? All those handbags she's been collecting?"

"Not the antiques this time," I say. I realize that I'm trembling a little, maybe because I can't believe I'm finally opening this door after all these years. I feel a warm rush of vindictive anticipation, underlined by a whisper of disbelief that this is where the last decade has taken me: from that idyllic lakeside cottage to this cheap hotel, where I'm conspiring with a con man. I realize, with a twinge of self-awareness, that I am about to break two of my own rules: *Don't get greedy. Take only what won't be missed.*

"There's a safe hidden somewhere inside Stonehaven itself," I say. "Inside that safe should be a million dollars in cash. And get this — I already know the combination."

Next to me, Lachlan is suddenly alert and quivering. "Jaysus, Nina. You've been holding out on me." He leans in and breathes into my ear, the tip of his nose cold against my earlobe. "So," he whispers lasciviously, "did you lose your virginity to a Liebling, or to their caretaker?"

78

6.

Lachlan and I leave Southern California in the sunshine, the kind of morning when café windows are flung open and people eat breakfast *en plein air*. By the time we make it to the Sierra Nevada foothills the temperature has dropped thirty degrees and rain clouds are gathering overhead.

We stop in a small town halfway up the mountains and eat hamburgers at a Gold Rush–themed restaurant called Pioneer Burger with red-checkered tablecloths and wagon wheels hanging on the walls. Forest animals carved from tree stumps lurk near the ladies' restroom. I order a surprisingly good burger and surprisingly bad fries.

Lachlan carefully brushes crumbs from his lap, frowning at a ketchup stain on his button-down shirt. He's left his tailored suits behind in Los Angeles, and packed jeans and sneakers instead.

"Your name is . . ." he suddenly says.

"Ashley Smith." The name still feels sticky

in my mouth, unwilling to roll off my tongue despite the time I spent in front of the mirror, practicing. "Ash for short. And you're Michael O'Brien, my devoted boyfriend. You worship the ground I walk upon."

"As well you deserve." His expression is wry. "Your hometown is . . ."

"Bend, Oregon. And you are on sabbatical from teaching . . ."

"English 101, Marshall Junior College." He smiles at this, apparently amused by the notion of guiding the youth of tomorrow. "Am I a good professor?"

"The very best. Beloved by your students." I laugh along with him, but really, I think he *would* have made a very good teacher in another life. He has a good ear for articulation and the patience required for the long con. And isn't that what a college education is, after all? It's the longest con of all: a promise that leaves your pockets empty and rarely deposits you where it says you'll land. But maybe Lachlan's talents are more suited for one-on-one tutoring — intense and focused and intimate. The way he'd once tutored me.

Together, we have studied Vanessa's Instagram page, using the thousands of photos and captions she's posted there as a road map of her vulnerabilities. She often poses with classic novels, using *Anna Karenina* or *Wuthering Heights* as a prop while she's lying on the beach or sitting at a café. Clearly, she wants to be perceived as intelligent and creative. So Lachlan will become a writer and a poet, will appeal to her as an "artistic soul." As for her recent turn to inspirational quotes: She is attempting to be deep and grounded, perhaps as a counterbalance to the frivolousness of all that couture. So I will be a yoga teacher, the Zen ideal to which she aspires.

She's lonely; we will offer friendship. And then there's the matter of all those come-hither poses, the glittery little minidresses and the bikini shots. "She wants to be desired, obviously," Lachlan offers. "I'll flirt with her. Just a little. Keep her interested."

"Not in front of me, or she'll think you're a cad."

He smears a fry in ketchup, forks it into his mouth, winks. "Wouldn't dream of it."

And one critical, final touch: Lachlan will pretend to be from old money, a ginned-up family heritage back in Ireland that will be difficult for her to verify. The rich are always the most comfortable around their own kind: Familiarity breeds affection.

We seeded the Internet with our new identities before we left town: A Facebook page for "Ashley," jammed full of inspirational quotes from Oprah and the Dalai Lama, and photos of women in contortionist yoga poses that I skimmed off other websites. (Plus: A thousand "friends" bought for a mere $2.95.) A

81

professional website, advertising my services as a private yoga instructor. (Safe enough since I've sweated through enough Bikram classes in Los Angeles to be able to fake it.) "Michael" got a personal Web page with clips of his writing (lifted from the home page of an unpublished experimental novelist from Minnesota), plus a LinkedIn bio listing his teaching credentials.

The whole thing took less than a week. This is what the Internet has given my generation: the ability to play God. We can make man in our own image, birth an entire human being out of nothing at all. All it takes is a spark, flung out there somewhere alongside the billions of other websites, Facebook pages, Instagram accounts: just one profile, a photo and a bio, and suddenly an existence has flamed into life. (It is also much, much harder to snuff that existence out once it's been created, but that's another story altogether.)

The odds are slim that Vanessa will ever see how diligently we've worked on our social media profiles for her sole benefit. There are thousands of other Michael O'Briens and Ashley Smiths online; it will be difficult for her to locate our particular set in a sea of them. But if she looks hard enough, there we will be, with just enough of an Internet presence to assuage any fears. After all, if you aren't willing to display yourself for public dissection these days, people assume you must be devious and unworthy of trust.

A little poking around and Vanessa will be reassured that Ashley and Michael are just as normal as we said we were in our rental-site profile. A nice creative young couple from Portland, taking a year off from our lives to travel across America and work on creative projects. We've always wanted to spend time at Lake Tahoe, we wrote her; we're even thinking of staying through the snowfall to get some skiing in. *That sounds so lovely,* Vanessa had written back almost immediately. *It's a quiet time of year, you can stay as long as you like.*

How long *will* we stay? Exactly as long as it takes to infiltrate her life, uncover Stonehaven's secrets, and rob her blind. And at this thought, I feel a little stab of satisfaction, something vindictive and small that I know I need to suppress. *Don't make this personal. Don't make this about the past.*

Lachlan finishes his soda, crumples his napkin, tosses it in the direction of the snarling wooden bear that looms behind us. The napkin lands in the bear's open mouth and lodges there, snagged on splintered incisors. "Let's get this show on the road," he says.

Dusk comes early in the mountains. The rain begins not long after we leave the restaurant, a fine gray mist, making the road slick and perilous. Long-haul trucks belch their way up the mountain in the slow lane; four-wheel-drive SUVs jacked up on hydraulics whiz past us on the left; we, in Lachlan's vintage BMW, stay steady in the center lane. (One should always drive the speed limit when one has fake Oregon license plates on one's car.) At Donner Pass the mountains already have a crust of dirty snow on the highest peaks, and it gleams in the waning light.

Nothing about this part of the drive feels familiar to me. I've only been on this length of highway once, the day that my mother and I fled Tahoe, down the hill toward an uncertain future. And yet I carefully study the damp pines and mountain lakes we pass, nerves on edge, waiting for that nostalgic *ping* of recognition.

It comes once we descend toward Tahoe City, and the highway begins paralleling the Truckee River. Suddenly the curves of the road have a kinetic familiarity. Each passing landmark tugs at me with a flash of recognition: a German restaurant in a crumbling chalet that flies by in the mist; a log cabin with a tin roof huddling in a clearing down by the water; the raw granite of the river boulders, water descending down their faces. They come back to me as visual echoes: memories surfacing from the bottom of a mind that long ago paved over them with more pressing concerns.

It's dark by the time we come to the edge

of Tahoe City, with its low huddle of shops. We turn right just before town in order to follow the lakeshore south. As we drive farther from town, the vacation homes grow larger, newer, denser; classic A-frames make way for behemoth ski homes with two-story windows and wraparound decks. The pines grow closer to the edge of the road. A snow-less ski resort flies past, its dirt slopes carved up with paths from the mountain bikers of the previous summer.

Occasionally, we get glimpses of the lake from between the houses, a dark void, drawn up for the winter. The pleasure boats are already dry-docked, to remain covered until May. Even the pier lights have been turned off for the season. I remember this about November at Tahoe, how it felt like you were stuck in a kind of no-man's-land: the summer crowd departed and the skiers yet to arrive, the sun absent but the snow still holding off, everything quiet and still and dormant. A useless chill, devoid of winter pleasures, too damp and cold to even hike. The locals scurrying about their errands like squirrels, hoarding acorns for winter.

Lachlan and I drive the last few miles in silence. I stare out at the trees, mulling over my story, puzzling at the edges of the narrative we'd conceived — Ashley and Michael — until the pieces feel like they fit together smoothly enough. A strange mood has come over me, a churning mix of anticipation and nostalgia, a feeling that something is lurking in the shadow of the pines that I should be trying harder to see. I don't realize that my knee is jittering until Lachlan puts a hand on my leg to steady it.

"Having second thoughts, love?" He looks at me askance, squeezes my thigh with long warm fingers.

The weight of his hand on my leg anchors me. I weave my fingers between his. "Not at all. Are you?"

He gives me a bemused look. "Too late now, isn't it? She's expecting us before bedtime. If we don't show up she might call the cops and God knows that's the last thing we need."

And then the address is before us. From the road, you wouldn't even know the estate was there. The property is unmarked, just a high stone wall with an iron gate along Lake Shore Drive. Lachlan buzzes at the intercom and has barely taken his finger off when the gate creaks open, squeaking on its iron hinges. The driveway stretches into the pines, which are softly lit from underneath by solar lights. I roll down my window and sniff at the air. It smells like damp things: tree roots and decomposing needles and the moss growing down at the lake. It stirs something inside me, a familiar juvenile melancholia: Those lights, the way they dance like spirits

86

in the wind-tossed trees. The mist, the way it reflects diamonds in our headlights. Something magical is here in this grove; all the possibility of my past youth gathering here again, feelings I'd long ago forgotten.

We pass a grass tennis court, the net sagging with mildew, and a handful of small wooden outbuildings: maids' quarters, a butlers' cabin, all dark and shuttered. Down the tree-lined slope toward the lake, I glimpse the boathouse, a hulking stone structure that hugs the shore. Finally, the road makes a sharp turn and Stonehaven shoots up before us like a great gray ghost in the gloom. I make a strange sound in my throat despite myself. I'd spent so long looking at photos of the house online, but they hadn't steeled me for the familiar coldness of Stonehaven, monumental and admonishing.

The mansion is an anachronism, a stone monolith crouching under the dense pines of Tahoe's West Shore, timbered and guarded like some sort of medieval fortress. The house hinges at its center, the two wings connected by a three-story stone tower with narrow windows at its peak; it stands watch, like a castle keep, as if girded for an onslaught of intruders. Two chimneys bookend the home, stones mossy and streaked orange with age. The entire house is surrounded by a portico, with the trunks of enormous pine trees serving as pillars. Everything about the house that isn't stone is shingled and painted brown, presumably to blend in with its natural surroundings; but it also gives visitors the sense that the house itself is retreating into the darkness of an encroaching forest.

Stonehaven. Three stories, forty-two rooms, 18,000 square feet, plus seven outbuildings. I'd done some reading before we drove up, dug up a handful of photos in a back issue of *Heritage Home* magazine. The house was built in the early 1900s by the first American-born Liebling, a Gold Rush opportunist who had lifted his family out of their immigrant poverty and launched them into the new century as American aristocrats. At the turn of the last century Lake Tahoe had already become the chosen summer residence of the West Coast industrialist tribes. Liebling bought himself a mile of pristine lakefront forest, built his pile, and settled in to study his fellow millionaires across the lake.

Somehow the family has hung on to all that land, five generations on. The house itself has been largely untouched since the day it was built, other than the occasional interior decorating whims of the successive residents.

Lachlan stops the car in the drive and we stare at the house together. There must be something audibly wrong about the way I'm breathing — as in, I've practically stopped altogether — because he turns to me, his expression growing suspicious. His grip on my leg is suddenly too tight. "I thought you said you didn't remember much about this place?"

"I *don't* remember much," I lie, oddly reluctant to tell him the truth. He holds his cards close; I will hold mine. "Honestly, I don't. I only came here three or four times, and that was over a decade ago."

"You look disoriented. You need to pull it together." His voice is even and low, but I can hear the frustration building behind it. I am too emotional; this has always been his diagnosis of me, from the very beginning. *You can't be emotional when you're pulling a con; emotion makes you vulnerable.*

"Not disoriented. It's just odd, that's all, to be back here again after all this time."

"This was your idea. I just want you to remember that if this somehow gets cocked up."

I push his hand off my leg. "I am fully aware of that. And I'm not going to *cock it up.*" I look up at the house, smoke coming from one of the great chimneys, lights burning in every window. "I'm Ashley. You're Michael. We're on vacation. We're surprised and delighted at how lovely the house is. Never been to Tahoe before, always wanted to come, so excited to see the area."

Lachlan nods. "Good girl."

"No need to be patronizing."

There is movement from the house in front

89

of us. The front door swings open and a woman appears in a rectangle of light. Her blond hair glints in a halo around her, her face inscrutable in the shadows of the porch. She stands there watching us, arms folded tight against the cold, likely wondering why we're just sitting there idling in her driveway. I reach across Lachlan and turn off the ignition.

"Vanessa is watching us," I observe. "Smile."

"I'm smiling," Lachlan says. He flips on the radio, tunes it until he finds a classical station, and cranks it loud. Then he reaches out and hooks me around the neck and pulls me in for a long, lusty kiss, and I'm not sure whether it's intended as an apology or a show for her. *The lovebirds, taking a moment for themselves before they get out of the car.*

Then he pulls away, wipes his mouth, straightens his shirt. "OK. Let's go meet our hostess."

7.

My mother and I made the eight-hour drive from Las Vegas to Tahoe City on the day after I finished my freshman year of high school. The highway traced the border of Nevada and California, and as we drove north and west I could feel the temperature dropping, the oppressive desert heat making way for the mountain chill of the Sierra Nevada.

I didn't mind leaving Vegas behind. We'd been there two years — an eternity in our lives — and I'd hated every minute of it. There was something about the overwhelming heat of the place: the way the relentlessly beating sun made everyone laconic and mean, the way it drove you into the sterile embrace of air-conditioning. The halls of my high school smelled chronically like sweat, sharp and animal, as if the entire student body was living in a constant state of fear. Vegas didn't feel like a place that anyone should actually live. Even though our apart-

91

ment building was miles away from downtown, in a cookie-cutter stucco development that could have been torn from the sprawl of any western suburb, the shadows of the Strip still fell on our neighborhood. The whole city seemed to turn toward the money pit at its center: Why would anyone live there if they *weren't* hustling for a quick buck?

My mother and I had lived in the airport flight path and every few minutes you could look up and see the planes arriving, the transient hordes coming in for Mega Fortune and margaritas-by-the-foot. "Suckers." My mother dismissed them, as though these suckers weren't the whole reason my mom and I were there in the first place. Every night, she parked me in front of the TV and drove down to the casinos to try to rip those suckers off.

But now we were headed to genteel Lake Tahoe, land of vacation homes and summer people and vintage wooden ski boats. "I found a place in Tahoe City, on the California side of the lake," my mother explained as we drove. She had tied a scarf over her blond hair, movie-star style, as if she was sitting behind the wheel of a vintage convertible rather than a Honda hatchback with spotty air-conditioning. "It's classier than South Shore, where the casinos are."

God, I wanted to believe her. We were going to be classy. And as we drove over the summit and then descended into the lake basin, it did feel like we were shedding our old selves, trying on new, better identities. I was going to be a scholar — I closed my eyes and imagined myself walking across a stage with a valedictorian scroll in my fist, *Harvard* inked on my cap. And my mother — well, she was going to be working the legal side of the casinos, which was a major achievement in itself. I studied the pines and let myself believe that the long list of places where we had lived might finally finish here, in a quiet mountain town where we could fulfill some previously missed potential.

Call me naïve. You wouldn't be wrong.

Tahoe City, it turned out, wasn't a city at all, but a woodsy little town that fronted on the lake. The town's main drag was a lazy stretch of hamburger restaurants and ski rental shops, real estate agencies and art galleries selling mountain landscapes daubed in thick paint. The Truckee River spilled out of the lake at the south end of town, weaving its leisurely way down the mountain toward the distant valleys, its current dense with tourists in rubber boats and inner tubes.

Nor was our new home an apartment: It was a cabin, on a quiet street that backed up to forest. I fell in love with it the moment I saw it — with its cheerful yellow paint, riverstone chimney, and window shutters with hearts cut from their centers, a promise of the happiness to be found inside. The front yard was a carpet of pine needles, softly rotting underfoot. The cabin was better maintained on the outside than the inside — the living room was dark and the carpet smelled like dust, the kitchen Formica chipped and the bedroom closets missing their doors. But every interior surface was covered with knotty pine, which made me feel like we were chipmunks, nesting inside a tree.

We arrived at the beginning of June, just as the speedboats were coming out of winter storage and the boat ramps were backed up to the main road. Those first few weeks, I would walk down to the lake in the mornings to watch the boat boys throwing the rubber bumpers out over the ends of the piers, like fat squeaking hot dogs, and the restaurant owners pulling the sun umbrellas out of storage, killing the brown widows that had nested in the folds. At eight A.M. the surface of the lake was glass, so clear in the shallows that you could see the crawdads creeping along the silty floor below. By ten, the wakes from the speedboats and water-skiers would turn the surface into an icy chop. The lake was filled with snowmelt. It wasn't really warm enough to swim in, not without a wet suit. Still, you couldn't walk down the pier without some summer kid doing a cannonball off the end. They'd climb out a few minutes later, goose-pimpled and pale.

I didn't swim. I spent the summer on the shore, perched on a rusty lawn chair that I'd found abandoned in the sand one day, working my way through the reading list that my new school had provided me. *The Mayor of Casterbridge* and *Tortilla Flat* and *A Lesson Before Dying.* I was alone most of the time, but I didn't mind: Friends were an afterthought for me, they always had been. Every evening, my mother girded herself in a spangled cobalt cocktail dress with a slit so high you could almost see her panties, and a name tag — *Lily* — pinned into her cleavage. She'd drive the forty-five minutes across the border into Nevada, where she'd serve watered-down G&Ts to poker players at the Fond du Lac Casino.

I remember her elation the first night that she came home with a paycheck, like a child with a new toy she couldn't wait to show off. I woke up to the smell of cigarette smoke and rancid cologne and there she was, sitting on the edge of my mattress, an envelope in her hands. She waved at me. "A paycheck, honey. So *legit,* right?" She ripped it open with gusto and pulled out the frail piece of paper, but something in her face collapsed a little as she read the number on the check. "Oh. I didn't realize they'd take out *so much* for taxes." She stared at it for a while, then straightened up and smiled. "Well. I knew it was all about the tips. One guy tonight, he gave me a green chip for one drink. That's twenty-five dollars. I hear once you get assigned the high-stakes tables, the players sometimes tip in hundreds."

But I heard something in her voice that worried me: a soft flicker of doubt about the path she was taking for my sake. She tugged at the collar of her dress and I could see the pale skin of her cleavage, rubbed red and raw by the sequined trim. I wondered whether the reason that my mom hadn't been able to hold a real job until now was not because no one would hire her without a high school degree and a résumé, but because she didn't really want to be hired.

"I'll get a job, too," I reassured my mom. "You shouldn't work at the casino if you hate it."

She stared down at the check and shook her head. "No, I *should*. It's for you, baby, so it's worth it." She reached out and smoothed my hair against the pillow. "*Your* job here is to study. I'll figure out the rest of it."

I started at North Lake Academy the day after Labor Day, the same day that the summer crowds vanished back down the mountain. The roads were suddenly empty of luxury SUVs; no more lines for brunch at Rosie's. My mother drove me to school, still bleary-eyed and mascara-smeared from her late shift the night before, and as we pulled into the entrance she made a move to park and go in with me. I put a hand on her wrist before she could pull the keys from the ignition. "No, Mom. I can do this myself."

She stared out at the stream of kids pouring past our car, and then flashed a smile at me. "Of course, baby."

North Lake Academy was a small, progressive high school with the stated aim of "building well-rounded citizens of the world," endowed by a Silicon Valley mogul who had retired at forty-nine to become a philanthropist and amateur BASE jumper. The campus was a collection of glass buildings surrounded by pines, tucked into a mountain valley within eyeshot of a ski resort. The Academy's website was heavy on buzzwords — *challenges, self-reliance, actualization, teamwork* — and it also boasted that twenty percent of its graduates went to Ivy League schools.

The minute I walked through the front door of the school in my urban Vegas alternagirl garb — the black-on-black palette of my wardrobe and makeup broken only by the magenta streaks in my hair — I knew that I was doomed not to fit in at the Academy. The kids thronging the halls were swaddled in Patagonia and denim, athletic gear dangling from their backpacks. The girls were all fresh-faced, makeup-free, their bare calves muscled and tight. There were more mountain bikes parked in front of the entrance to the school than there were cars. But sports were foreign to me; all the years of fast-food meals and sedentary reading had left me thick-hipped and soft in the face. I was a baby Goth with baby fat.

In first period, as we watched the teacher writing her name — *Jo Dillard, call me Jo* — on the white board, the girl in front of me turned around and smiled at me. "I'm Hilary. You're new," she said.

"I am."

"There's a new guy in the junior class, too. Benjamin Liebling. Have you met him?"

"No. But I wouldn't know if I did. Everyone is new to me."

She wrapped a curl of her hair around a finger and pulled it across her face. Her nose was peeling and her hair was crispy from chlorine; I could see over her shoulder that her binder was covered with snowboarding stickers. "What's your jam?"

"I dunno," I said. "Strawberry? I like apricot, too."

She laughed. "I mean, what's your *thing*. Do you board?"

"I've never been on a ski slope in my life."

She raised an eyebrow. "Jesus, you really *are* new here. So, what then? Mountain biking? Lacrosse?"

I shrugged. "Books?"

"Ah." She nodded soberly, as if this answer required deep contemplation. "Well. You

98

really should meet the new guy."

I didn't meet the new guy for months, though I sometimes saw him in the halls — the only other person besides me who always seemed to be surrounded by a bubble of solitude. It wasn't that the other students weren't nice to me — they were always, like Hilary, pleasant in a wholesome, *responsible-citizen* sort of way. They invited me to study sessions and let me sit at their tables at lunch and asked me for help with their English papers. It was just that, beyond academics, we didn't have much in common. My mother had enrolled me in a school that believed in the concept of the "outdoor classroom," a school that planned kayaking adventures and overnight camping trips and mandated "stretch breaks" that consisted of wandering through the pines in the yard. We didn't take tests; we went on ropes courses.

Most of the other kids had ended up here because they *were* that kind of kid — locals whose parents had migrated to the mountains because they wanted their kids to be out-doorsy individualists. My mother had selected this school, I suspected, purely because of the financial aid packages, the proximity to the South Lake casinos, and the Academy's willingness to embrace a student who was more "promising" than distinguished. The Academy, in turn, probably looked at me —

at my half-Colombian ancestry and my low-income single mother — and saw "diversity."

Benjamin — Benny — Liebling was the only other kid at the school who didn't clearly fit into the Academy's outdoorsy vision of the world. He'd recently moved into town from San Francisco, I heard; his family was rich; they owned some fancy mansion on the West Shore. Kids whispered that he'd been kicked out of a much more exclusive prep school, and that's why he'd ended up here. He stood out, with his flaming orange hair and his long, articulated limbs; a pale giraffe ducking awkwardly through the doors. Like me, he arrived on campus with a foreign aura clinging to him, although in his case it was wealth, not the urban stench of Las Vegas. His T-shirts were always pressed and spotless; his sunglasses had an unmistakable Gucci logo on the earpiece that he'd failed to disguise with duct tape. Every morning he unfolded himself from the passenger seat of his mother's gold Land Rover and dashed to the front door of the school as if he thought his speed might make him invisible. Every-one noticed anyway, because how could you *not* notice a six-foot-two kid with hair the color of a jack-o'-lantern?

Curious, I looked up his family name on the computer in the school library, and the first thing that came up was a photo of his parents: a woman draped in white furs, neck heavy with diamonds, leaning on the arm of a bald, older man in a tuxedo, his fleshy face rubbery and sour. *Patrons Judith and William Liebling IV attend the opening night of the San Francisco Opera.*

I saw Benny during lunch sometimes, in the library, where I usually retreated to read after wolfing down my PB&J on white bread. He'd be hunched over a notebook, inking comic-book-style drawings in dense black ballpoint pen. A few times we'd catch each other's eyes across the room, in our tentative smiles a recognition of our shared "new kids" status. Once, he sat in front of me at assembly and I spent the hour gazing into the magnificent nest of his hair, wondering if he would ever turn around and say hi; and even though he didn't, his neck slowly flushed pink, as if he somehow intuited that I was staring. But he was a year ahead of me; we didn't have classes together. And neither of us belonged to any teams that might force us to interact.

And there was this: His family was loaded, while my mother was struggling to pay the gas bill every month. There was no reason for us to talk, other than our mutual failure to be the right sort of wholesome, responsible citizens.

I kept my head down and focused on my studies; the years of bouncing from school to school had left me miles behind my classmates in most subjects and I had to scramble to catch up. Summer turned to fall and then winter descended, and with it came a kind of cloistering, the world bracing itself against the ice and slush. School to home and back again; heat blasting, mittens on. I sat on the bus twice a day, wearing my secondhand parka and leaky snow boots, struck dumb by the magnificence of the snowcapped forests, the achingly blue lake. It was all so foreign to me. I still dreamed in concrete blocks and mirrored skyscrapers.

My mother had settled into her job. She'd finagled her way into the high-stakes poker rooms, and even if they weren't exactly the promised land she'd expected — hundred-dollar chips were still few and far between — she was happy to be there. In the evenings, I'd study at the chipped kitchen table while she clattered around the cabin in her heels, applying mascara, smelling like Shalimar and lemon verbena soap. The bills that I pulled from our mailbox didn't have past due emblazoned on the envelopes anymore, which probably had to do with the extra shifts she was starting to pull. Sometimes she wouldn't get home until I was waking up to go to school. She'd stand by the coffeepot, her sequins sagging and her hair tangled, watching me put books in my backpack with a dazed, complacent expression on her face that I interpreted as satisfaction, or maybe pride.

One day, I noticed that she'd taken her blond down a few notches, from Marilyn platinum to Gwyneth gold. When I asked her why, she just touched her hair and glanced in the mirror with a little smile. "More elegant, isn't it? We're not in Vegas anymore, baby. The men here, they're looking for different."

I worried that this also meant that she was looking for men. But as the winter went on, no one showed up in our living room at three A.M. and I took that to mean that things had changed for real. Maybe we really had gotten off at the right stop, for once. I imagined her working her way up the casino hierarchy, maybe to a floor manager, or even into a bona fide day job at the hotel's front desk. Maybe she'd take up with a *nice* guy, someone normal, like the genial café manager with the salt-and-pepper beard who gave us extra lox on our bagels when we came in together on Sundays.

The shield of vigilance that I'd erected for all those years was slipping. And even if I wasn't exactly Miss Popularity at North Lake Academy — even if Harvard was still an awful long shot — I felt some measure of content. Stability can do that to a person. My happiness was so tied to my mother's happiness that it was impossible to figure out where hers ended and mine began.

One snowy afternoon in late January, a day

when most of my classmates had decamped to the ski slopes after the last bell, I climbed on the bus back into town and found that I wasn't alone. Benjamin Liebling was sitting there in the back row, limbs splayed across the seats surrounding him. I saw him watching me climb aboard, but when I caught his eye, he quickly looked away.

I took a seat toward the front and opened up my algebra textbook. The doors clattered shut and the bus shuddered and heaved, snow tires scraping against the icy crust of the road. I sat there trying to wrap my mind around the concept of logarithmic expressions for a few minutes, acutely conscious of the only other student on the bus. Was he lonely? Did he think I was rude for never talking to him? Why did our non-relationship feel so awkward? Abruptly, I stood up and lurched my way along the rubbery mat to the back and flung myself in the seat in front of him. I swung my legs into the aisle and turned to face him.

"You're Benjamin," I said.

His eyes were a coppery brown, and up close I could see that his lashes were obscenely long. He blinked at me, surprised. "The only person who calls me Benjamin is my dad," he said. "Everyone else calls me Benny."

"Hi, Benny. I'm Nina."

"I know."

"Oh." I regretted sitting there and I was about to get up and go back to my seat when he sat up and leaned forward so that his head was close to mine. He had a mint in his mouth and I could smell it on his breath, hear it clicking against his teeth when he spoke.

"People keep telling me that I should meet you. Why do they say that?"

I felt like he'd just turned a spotlight on, and shined it directly in my eyes. What was I supposed to say to that? I thought for a second. "It's because no one else wants the responsibility of having to be friends with either of us. It's easier on them if we just become friends with each other. It's their way of pawning off the job. And they can still feel good about themselves for doing a good deed by hooking us up."

He looked contemplatively down at his feet, the enormous black snow boots splayed on the mat in front of him. "Sounds about right." He stuck a hand in his pocket and pulled out a tin and offered it to me. "Mint?"

I took one, put it in my mouth, and breathed in deep. Everything tasted so fresh and clean, our breath commingling in the freezing air of the bus, that I felt brave enough to ask the obvious. "So, *should* we be friends?"

"That depends."

"On what?"

He looked back down at his feet, and I

noticed that flush creeping up his neck from below his scarf. "If we like each other enough, I suppose."

"And how will we know that?"

He seemed to like this question. "Well, let's see. We'll get off the bus together in Tahoe City and go get a hot chocolate at Syd's and make some obligatory small talk about things like where we moved here from and how much those places sucked and how much we hate our parents."

"I don't hate my mom."

He looked surprised. "What about your dad?"

"Haven't seen him since I was seven. So I guess you could say I hate him, but it's not exactly based on any current relationship."

He smiled. It transformed his face, from a collection of unsettled features in awkward juxtaposition — freckles, beakish nose, enormous eyes — to something pure and joyful, almost childlike with beauty. "OK. See, look, we're getting somewhere already. So yeah, we'll go to Syd's, and after about fifteen or twenty minutes of conversation we'll either be bored to tears because we have nothing of interest to say to each other — in which case you'll probably make some excuse about homework and ditch me, and we'll spend the rest of the year avoiding each other in the halls, because: *awkward* — or we'll find enough to say to each other to repeat the

106

process a second time, and perhaps a third, thereby proving all of our classmates right. At which point we'll have done *our* duty as responsible citizens, by making them feel good about themselves. A win-win."

The conversation was so heady, so grown-up and frank, that it was making me feel dizzy. Teenagers I knew didn't talk like this; they tiptoed around unspoken truths and let the unsaid mean whatever they most wanted it to mean. Already, I felt like the two of us had joined some secret society that none of our classmates would understand.

"So what you're trying to say is that you want to go get a hot chocolate," I said. "With me."

"Actually I prefer coffee," he said. "I figured you for the hot chocolate."

"I prefer coffee, too."

He smiled. "See, there's something else. Maybe there's hope for this friendship after all."

We got off the bus in town and walked along the slushy sidewalks to a café on the main road. I watched him lope along in his giant moon boots, the scarf wrapped up around his chin and his woolen cap pulled over his forehead so that only four inches around his eyes were showing. He looked over and caught me staring at him and blushed again, and I realized that I liked how he wore his emotions on his skin. How easy it was to read him. There were snowflakes catching in his eyelashes and I found myself wanting to reach out and wipe them away. Something about us being here together felt completely natural, as if we'd already played through to the end of a game and had declared ourselves both winners.

"So why were you on the bus today?" I asked as we stood in line.

"My mom had another one of her meltdowns and couldn't pull it together to pick me up."

He said this so casually that it shocked me. "Meltdown? Like, what, she called the front office crying and told you to take the bus?"

He shook his head. "It was my dad. And I have a cellphone."

"Oh." I tried to act as if this was totally normal, as if I'd encountered lots of kids with personal cellphones in my lifetime. I wanted to pluck at him for the details of his world; pull out feathers until I could glimpse the naked shape beneath. "And he didn't offer to send, like, a driver or something?"

"You're awfully interested in my means of transportation. Kind of a boring subject, if you ask me."

"Sorry. I just didn't take you for a bus kind of guy."

He looked at me, something sad flickering across his face. "So you know who my family is, I take it."

I felt myself blushing now. "Not really. Sorry, that was presumptuous of me." I'd never had a conversation with a rich person before. Were you supposed to gloss politely over the luxuries that they enjoyed and pretend you just didn't see them? Wasn't their wealth as obvious a part of their basic identity as their hair color, or ethnic background, or sports ability? Why was it rude to bring it up?

"No," he answered. "It's a fair assumption. And we do have a driver, but I'd kill my parents if they tried that. It's bad enough . . ." He let this thought trail off, and I could see suddenly that the wealth that he wore was as alienating for him as my transient life was for me.

We were at the front of the line now, so we ordered coffees. When I went to pull out my change purse Benny put his hand on my arm to stop me. "Don't be ridiculous," he said.

"I can afford a cup of coffee." I felt myself bristling, suddenly wary, wondering what he knew about *my* background.

"Of course you can," he said, and quickly pulled his hand away. Then he drew a nylon wallet from his back pocket and extricated a single, crisp, hundred-dollar bill. "But why waste the money when you don't have to."

I stared at the hundred-dollar bill, trying not to act like an idiot, and yet I couldn't help myself: "Your parents pay your allowance in *hundreds*?"

He laughed. "God, *no.* They don't trust me with an allowance, not anymore. I stole this out of my dad's safe. He uses my birthday as the combination." And then he offered me a big, conspiratorial smile. "For someone who thinks he's so much smarter than everyone else, he's really pretty stupid."

Looking back at the beginning of our friendship now, I remember it as an awkward time, simultaneously sweet and bitter, as the two of us stumbled around the vast differences in the ways we'd been raised; finding common ground mostly in our mutual disaffection. We were a strange, mismatched pair. We began hanging out after school once or twice a week. Some days, I'd see the taillights of the Land Rover accelerating past me as I shivered at the bus stop by myself. But increasingly I'd find him there waiting for me inside the bus shelter, extra hand warmers in his backpack that he'd silently give to me as we huddled in the cold. In town, we'd go to Syd's and do homework together. He loved to draw, and I'd watch him doodle comics of the other customers in his notebook. Eventually we'd walk down to the snowy lakeshore and watch the wind whip the water into froth.

"So, are you taking the bus with me because you want to or because your mom is having meltdowns all the time?" I asked him one day in February, as we sat on a snow-covered picnic table, nursing rapidly cooling coffees.

He broke an icicle off the edge and gripped it in his glove like a weapon. "I told her she didn't have to pick me up anymore and she was relieved." He examined the pointy end of the icicle and then pointed it toward the water like a magic wand. "She's doing this thing she does sometimes, where she doesn't like to leave the house."

"A *thing*?"

"Kind of, just, loses her equilibrium. First she'll start making scenes in public — you know, screaming at valets and getting speeding tickets and going on spending sprees at Neiman's. And then after my dad finally loses it on her, she'll climb in bed and won't want to get out again for weeks at a time. It's part of the reason why we came up here in the first place. Dad thought that a change of scenery would be good for her, you know, get her out of the city and away from all the" — he put his gloved hands up and jerked his fingers in derisive air quotes — " 'pressure' of society life."

I thought of the woman who was barely visible behind the wheel of the Land Rover — her hands sheathed in leather gloves, her head swallowed up by the fur of her parka's hood. I tried to imagine her swathed in silk and diamonds, drinking champagne for breakfast and spending afternoons being pampered at the spa. "I had no idea that going to parties

111

could be so hard. I'll remember that next time I get invited to a ball."

He laughed and made a face. "Mostly I think Mom was just embarrassing Dad by being so weird all the time." He hesitated. "We both were. Besmirching the good Liebling family name. So he dragged us up here to the musty old ancestral estate for a time-out. Like naughty children. *Behave yourself or I'll make you stay here forever* is pretty much the message. My dad's a bully: If he doesn't get what he wants at first, he'll just threaten you until he does."

I thought about this. "But wait. What did *you* do?"

He jabbed the icicle into the snow, leaving perfect circular stab wounds. "Well, I got kicked out of school, for a start. I was giving Ritalin to my classmates. They decided that made me a drug dealer. Even though I wasn't actually taking money for it. I figured it was a public service." He shrugged.

"Wait. Slow down. You're on Ritalin?"

"They have me on *everything.*" He frowned at the whitecaps on the lake. "Ritalin, because I was sleeping too much and not paying attention in class and so they figured ADD. And then a lovely cocktail of antidepressants because I spend too much time in my room alone and apparently that means I'm moody and antisocial. Apparently if you don't like to

112

participate in things you *must* be mentally ill."

I thought about this. "Then I guess I'm mentally ill, too."

"Which explains why I like you." He smiled, then ducked his head as if to disguise it. "I'm pretty sure they both just wish I was more like my sister. *Vanessa* does everything she is supposed to. Debutante and prom queen and captain of the tennis team, then shipped off to Dad's alma mater so that they can brag about her at parties. She'll get married young and push out a few heirs for them and look pretty in the family photos." He made a face.

"She sounds awful."

He shrugged. "She's my sister." He was quiet for a moment. "Anyway, I'm pretty sure my dad is afraid I'm going to end up being *weird,* like my mom, so he's trying to knock it out of me before it's too late. And my mom puts all her efforts into fixing me so that she doesn't have to face the fact that she's the one who really needs to be fixed."

I sat there next to him on the picnic table, wondering what to do with this information. I was unaccustomed to these sorts of confessional friend moments, when the curtain finally gets drawn back and you see what's really going on behind the scenes. We sat there, watching our breath puff into clouds and then melt away.

"My mom is careless," I found myself saying. "She's careless and she does stupid things, and when she fucks up she runs away. And I know she's got good intentions, at least when it comes to me — all she wants to do is protect me — but I'm tired of having to deal with the fallout. It's like *I'm* the adult in our relationship."

He studied me, thinking about this. "At least your mom isn't trying to change who you are."

"Are you kidding? She's decided I'm going to be some sort of super-scholar-rock-star-president-CEO. You know, no pressure. I just have to overcompensate for all her failings as a human being and be everything she couldn't be herself. I'm supposed to reassure her that *her* life choices haven't completely destroyed mine." I chucked the cold contents of my coffee cup into the snow below us and stared down at the brown splashes against the white, surprised by myself. I immediately felt guilty for what I'd said, like I'd betrayed her somehow. And yet, deep inside, I felt something rise in me, a dark and bitter nut of resentment that I'd never before acknowledged. I savored it, let it fill me. Why *was* my life like this? Why couldn't my mom bake cupcakes and work as a receptionist at a veterinary hospital or a nursery school? Why did it feel like I'd somehow been royally screwed by circumstance, that I hadn't had a fair shot and probably never would?

114

I felt something on my back. It was Benny's arm, creeping tentatively across the space between us to rest gently along my spine. Something approximating a hug, without quite going all the way. The padding of our down parkas insulated us from each other, so thick that I couldn't even feel the warmth of his body cocooned inside all those layers. I leaned my head on his shoulder and we stayed that way for a while. It was beginning to snow again and I felt the flakes landing on my face and melting into tiny cold droplets.

"It's not so bad here, though," I said finally.

"No," he agreed. "It's not so bad."

Why were we drawn to each other? Was it simply a lack of other options, or was there something innate about our personalities that connected us? I look back now, over a decade later, and wonder if we came together not because of our similarities but our differences. Maybe the foreign nature of our respective life experiences — each arriving from the far end of two extremes — meant that we couldn't really compare and contrast and find ourselves lacking. We came from such disparity already that all we *could* do was draw closer. We were kids, we didn't know any better.

So that's one way of answering the question. Another way: Maybe first love is merely the inevitable emotional fallout of finding the first person who seems to give an honest shit about you.

By early March, our routine — bus, coffee, beach — had started to wear thin. The temperature had dropped, due to a polar freeze blowing through, and the picture-book snowscape had hardened into crusted ice. On the sides of the roads, the plowed mountains of snow were black and filthy, a reflection of the general emotional state of the locals as they dragged their way through the third month of winter.

One afternoon, on the way into town, Benny turned to me. "Let's go to your house today."

I thought of our cabin, the spangled fabrics pinned to the walls and the thrift store furniture and the chipped Formica of the kitchen table. Most of all, though, I thought of my mother, of the fuss she'd make over Benny. I imagined Benny watching her get herself ready for work, the hot whiff of steam from her shower and the shriek of the blow-dryer. I thought of the fake eyelashes my mom peeled off after work and left on the coffee table in the living room. "Let's not," I said.

He made a face. "It can't be that bad."

"Our place is tiny. My mom will be all up in our business." I hesitated. "Let's go to yours instead."

I waited for the sideways look, the one that

116

would let me know I'd crossed a line. But he just flashed me a quick smile. "Sure," he said. "Just promise me you won't freak out."

"I won't freak out."

His eyes were sad. "Yeah, you will. But that's OK. I forgive you."

This time, when we got to Tahoe City, instead of lingering in town, we changed buses and headed down the West Shore. Benny grew more and more animated the closer we got to his house, his limbs sprawling in every direction as he launched into an inscrutable lecture about comic book styles I'd never heard of.

And then, abruptly, he said, "OK, here," and jumped up, signaling to the driver that we wanted to get off. The bus obligingly shuddered to a stop and ejected us out onto the icy road. I looked across the street at an endless-seeming river-rock wall, high enough to block the view, topped with iron spikes. Benny dashed across the road to the gate and punched a code into a box. The doors swung open for us, creaking as they scraped across the ice. Once we were inside, the afternoon grew suddenly quiet. I could hear the wind in the pine needles, the creak of the trees under their heavy mantle of snow. We trudged along the driveway until the mansion reared up before us.

I'd never seen a house like it before. It was the closest I'd ever come to a bona fide castle;

and even though I knew it wasn't *that,* exactly, it still gave off a foreign gravitas. It made me think of flappers and garden parties and shiny wooden boats speeding across the lake, and servants in uniforms serving up champagne in flat-bottomed crystal glasses.

"I don't know what you thought I'd freak out about," I said. "My house is bigger."

"Haha." He stuck out his tongue at me, pink and raw against his cold-flushed cheeks. "You should see my uncle's place in Pebble Beach. This is nothing compared to that. Plus it's so *old.* My mom is always complaining that it's ancient and musty and she's gonna redecorate, but I think it's a lost cause. The house just wants to be what it is." And then he ran up the steps and threw open the front door like it was just a normal house.

I followed him in and stopped just inside the entry. The inside of the house — well. My only comparison point, at that stage in my life, was the grand casinos of Las Vegas: the Bellagio, the Venetian, with all their gilt-veneered frippery, gargantuan tributes to trompe l'oeil. This was something far different: I didn't know anything about the things surrounding me — the paintings, the furniture, the objets d'art cluttering the sideboards and bookshelves — and yet even in the gloom of that dark, cold entry I could tell that they glowed with authenticity. I wanted to touch everything, to feel the satin finish on the mahogany table and the distant chill of the porcelain urns.

From where I stood in the foyer, the house unfurled in every direction: a dozen doorways through which I glimpsed formal rooms and endless hallways and stone fireplaces so big you might park a car inside. When I looked up, to the ceiling that towered two stories above me, I could see wooden beams hand-stenciled with intertwining gold vines. The grand staircase that curled along the far wall was carpeted in scarlet and illuminated by an enormous brass chandelier dripping with crystal teardrops. Wood gleamed from every surface, carved and paneled and inlaid and polished until it almost looked alive.

Two portraits hung on the walls on either side of the grand staircase, giant oils of a man and a woman standing stiffly in formal wear, each staring disapprovingly at the other through the gilt of their respective frames. The paintings were the kind of thing that I'd look back at now and pinpoint as emerging from a certain, worthless era of portraiture — early-twentieth-century remnants of the Sargent school — but at the time I assumed they must be valuable artwork. WILLIAM LIEBLING II and ELIZABETH LIEBLING, the paintings read, on tiny brass placards just like in a museum. I imagined the woman — Benny's great-grandmother? — sweeping through these rooms in her wide skirts, the swish of satin across waxed floors.

"It's nice," I managed to say.

Benny poked my shoulder, as if making sure I was really awake. "It's not. It's a robber baron's lair. My great-great-grandfather, the one who built this shit heap, got sued for refusing to pay the architect and the builders. Not because he didn't like the house or couldn't afford it; just because he was an asshole. When he died his obituary said he was 'scrupulously dishonest.' My dad has that clipping framed in the library. He's proud of it. I think he's, like, my dad's role model."

I felt like we should be whispering. "Is he here? Your dad?"

He shook his head. The foyer, with its soaring ceilings, had diminished Benny, dwarfing even his distinctive height. "He's mostly here on weekends. He goes down to the city during the week in order to, you know, sit in his fancy office with views over the Bay, and foreclose on factory workers who just lost their jobs."

"Your mom must hate that."

"That he's not here? Maybe." He looked glum. "She doesn't exactly tell me anything."

"*She's* here, right?" I wasn't sure if I wanted her to be home or not.

"Yeah," he said. "But she'll be up in her room, watching TV. And if she thinks you're here she definitely won't come down, because that will mean she has to actually get dressed." He dropped his backpack at the bottom of the grand staircase and then peered up to see if the noise would generate any activity upstairs. It didn't. "Anyway, let's go see what's in the kitchen."

I followed him to the back of the house, to that kitchen, where an elderly Latina woman was hacking away at a pile of vegetables with an enormous chef's knife. "Lourdes, this is Nina," he said as he squeezed past her toward the fridge.

Lourdes squinted at me, wiping hair out of her face with the back of her hand. "Friend from school?"

"Yes," I said.

Her wizened face broke out into a toothy smile. "Well. You hungry?"

"I'm fine, thank you," I said.

"She's hungry," Benny retorted. He threw open the fridge and rummaged around, emerging with half a cheesecake. "OK if we eat this?"

Lourdes shrugged. "Your mama won't. It's all yours." She turned back to the mountain of vegetables in front of her and renewed her attack. Benny grabbed two forks from a drawer and then walked out another door, and I floated behind in his wake, still feeling stunned. We emerged into a dining room, with a long dark table polished to a shine so high that I could see my reflection in it. A crystal chandelier hung overhead, piercing the gloom with shattered rainbows. Benny looked at the formal table, the cake held aloft in one hand, and hesitated.

"Actually, I have a better idea. Let's go out to the caretaker's cottage."

I had no idea what this meant. "Why do we need the caretaker?"

"Oh, we don't actually *have* a caretaker anymore. Not one who lives on the property. It's just, like, a guesthouse for when people come for weekend visits. Which happens, like, never."

"So what are we going out there for?"

Benny smiled. "I'm going to get you stoned."

And so a new after-school ritual was established: The bus to his house, two or three times a week. Then the kitchen, for snacks, and out the back door, which emptied us onto yet another porch overlooking what was usually the summer lawn, this time of year just a vast field of white. We'd trudge through the snow, matching our feet into the snow prints we'd made in the days before, until we arrived at the caretaker's cottage hidden at the edge of the property. Once we were inside, Benny would light up a joint, and we'd lie there on the musty brocade couch, smoking and talking.

I liked being stoned, the way it made my limbs heavy and my head light, the opposite of how I usually felt. I particularly liked being stoned with Benny, and how it seemed to blur the boundaries between us. Lying on opposite ends of the couch, our feet tangling in the middle, it felt like we were part of one continuous organism, the pulse of the blood in my veins matching his, an energy passing between us where our bodies touched. I wish I could remember what we talked about, because it felt at the time like what we were discussing was so vital, but really it was just the silly prattle of fucked-up teenage kids. Gossip about our classmates. Complaints about our teachers. Speculation about the existence of UFOs, of life after death, of bodies floating at the bottom of the lake.

I remember feeling something growing in that room, the relationship between us blurring in a confusing way. We were just friends, right? So, why, then, did I find myself looking at his face in the sideways afternoon light and wanting to press my tongue to the freckles along his jawline to see if they tasted like salt? Why did the pressure of his leg against mine feel like a question that he was expecting me to answer? Sometimes I would startle out of my stoned reverie and realize that we'd been quiet for a long minute, and when I looked over at him I would see him watching me through those long lashes of his, and he'd blush and look away.

Only once in those early weeks did we

encounter his mother. One afternoon, as we slipped through the foyer on our way toward the kitchen, a voice came piercing through the leaden hush of the house. "Benny? You there?"

Benny stopped abruptly. He gazed blankly at some point on the wall next to the portrait of Elizabeth Liebling, a careful expression on his face. "Yeah, Mom."

"Come in and say hello." Her words seemed to be lodged in the back of her throat, as if the sounds had gotten trapped there and she wasn't quite sure if she should swallow them back or just spit them out.

Benny tilted his head at me, in silent apology. I followed him as he trudged through a maze of rooms I'd never been in before until we landed in a room lined with floor-to-ceiling bookshelves. A library, presumably, complete with uninviting, jacket-less tomes; it looked like they'd been glued into position decades earlier and not moved since. Hunting trophies hung across the wooden paneling — an elk's head, a moose, and a stuff bear standing erect in the corner, all of them with bereft expressions that suggested their resentment at this indignity. Benny's mother sat on an overstuffed velvet couch in front of a fire, her legs tucked up under her, surrounded by an avalanche of interior design magazines. Her back was to us, and she didn't bother to turn around when we came into the room, so that we were forced to navigate the couch and stand before her.

Like supplicants, I thought.

Up close, I could see that she was actually quite striking; her eyes, large and damp-looking, overwhelming a small, fox-like face. Benny's red hair must have come from her, but hers was more of a russet color now, and smooth, like the mane of an expensively groomed horse. She was thin, so thin that I thought I might be able to pick her up and snap her in half over my knee. She wore a pale silk jumpsuit of some sort, with a scarf tied around her neck, and it looked like she'd just gotten back from a fancy lunch at a French restaurant. I wondered where one even *had* a fancy lunch up here.

"So." She put a magazine down and peered up at me. "I take it you are the voice I've been hearing around the house. Benny, are you going to introduce us?"

Benny shoved his hands deeper into his pockets. "Mom, this is Nina Ross. Nina, this is my mother, Judith Liebling."

"Nice to meet you, Mrs. Liebling." I held out a hand and she stared at it with wide eyes, in faux astonishment.

"Well, *someone* here knows their manners!" She reached out with a soft, limp hand, gave mine a quick squeeze, then dropped it almost immediately. I could feel her taking me in, even as she continued flicking rapidly

125

through the pages of her magazine: the fading magenta streaks in my hair and thick black liner rimming my eyes, the stained parka with someone else's phone number already inked into the tag, the moon boots with duct tape covering the split in the toe. "So, Nina Ross. Why aren't you out on the ski slopes with the rest of your classmates? I thought that was the *thing to do* up here."

"I don't ski."

"Ah." She studied a photo spread of a fancy New York apartment, folded the corner for future reference. "Benny is an excellent skier, did he tell you that?"

I looked at Benny. "You are?"

She nodded when he didn't. "We've been vacationing in St. Moritz since he was six years old. He used to *love* it. He's just trying to make some sort of a point by refusing to do it now that we're actually living in the snow. Aren't you, Benny? Skiing, rowing, chess, all those things he used to love and now all he wants to do is sit in his room and draw cartoons."

I could see the cords in Benny's neck, straining. "Mom, cut it out."

"Oh, please, honey, have a sense of humor." She laughed, but it didn't strike me as a very joyful laugh. "So, Nina. Tell me about yourself. I'm very curious."

"Mom."

His mother was staring at me, head cocked

126

slightly to the side, as if I was a particularly interesting specimen. I felt like roadkill in her gaze; frozen in place, somehow compelled to stand there forever until she ran me over entirely. "Um. Well, we just moved here last year."

"We?"

"My mother and I."

"Ah." She nodded. "And what brought you all the way up here? Your mother's work?"

"Sort of." She waited, expectant. "She works at Fond du Lac."

Benny finally lost his patience. "For God's sake, Mom. Stop prying. Leave her alone."

"Oh fine. *Pssht pssht.* Shame on me for wanting to know the tiniest thing about your life, Benny. Anyway, go. Go sneak off to wherever you two sneak off to every after-noon. Don't mind me." She turned back to her magazine, snapping through three pages in quick succession, so fast that I thought they'd tear right out. "Oh, Benny, you should be aware that your father will be back for din-ner this evening and that means family meal." She gave me a meaningful look as if to say, *You are not invited, please take the hint and be gone before dark.*

Benny, already halfway out the door, hesi-tated. "But it's Wednesday."

"Yes, it is."

"I thought he wasn't coming back until Friday."

127

"Well" — she picked up a magazine — "we talked about that and he's decided he wants to be up here more. With us."

"Terrific." His words were drowning in sarcasm.

She looked up at this, and her voice dropped to a warning growl. "Benny."

"Mom." He mimicked the tone in her voice in a way that made me uncomfortable. Was this normal, to be so rude and condescending to your mother? But she seemed to take it in stride, kissing the tips of her fingers and flapping them in Benny's general direction. She reached for a fresh magazine and began rapidly flipping pages. We'd been dismissed.

"Sorry about that," he said as we made our way toward the kitchen.

"She wasn't *that* bad," I ventured.

He grimaced. "You must be judging on a curve."

"But she's up and out of bed. And your dad's coming home. That's all good, right?"

"Whatever. None of it really matters." But the way his features contorted suggested to me that it did matter, far more than he was willing to let me know. "What it means in reality is that he'll make an appearance for the meal, because she's woken up enough to lay down the law, and then he'll vanish off to wherever he goes in the evenings. He doesn't stick around. Because she doesn't really want to spend time with him, either. She just wants him to come when called, so she can prove she has some agency in their relationship."

Benny had done a lot of therapy, I was starting to understand. "Why don't they just get divorced?"

He offered a small, bitter pill of a laugh. "Money, silly. It's always about money."

For the rest of that afternoon, he retreated into himself, as if he couldn't stop chewing over his mother's behavior. I thought of it, too; the way she flicked through the pages of the magazine, as if compelled by some impulse she couldn't control. We smoked pot and then he drew in one of his notebooks while I did homework, sometimes feeling him studying me from the other end of the couch; and I couldn't help wondering if seeing me through his mother's eyes had damaged the picture he had of me. I left early that afternoon, well before dusk; and when I arrived back at home and found my mother in the kitchen, making macaroni with her hair up in curlers, I felt a warm pulse of gratitude.

I gave her a hug from behind. "My baby." She turned in my arms, and squeezed me into her bosom. "What's this about?"

"Nothing, really," I murmured into her shoulder. "You're OK, right, Mom?"

"Better than ever." She pushed me back so she could examine me, traced the edge of my face with a pink-manicured finger. "And what about you? School is going well, right? You like it? You're getting good grades?"

"Yeah, Mom." I was, despite the afternoons I was spending getting stoned with Benny. I *liked* being challenged by my homework; I had grown to love the school's progressive atmosphere and the teachers who engaged us with ideas instead of just handing out multiple-choice tests. Over six months in, and I was already getting mostly As. My English teacher, Jo, had recently pulled me aside and handed me a brochure for a summer program at Stanford University. "You should apply next year, after junior year. It could really give you a leg up getting into college," Jo had said. "I know the director, and I could give you a personal referral."

I'd slipped the brochure onto my bookshelf and every once in a while, I'd pull it out and study the kids on the cover, in their matching purple T-shirts and radiant smiles, backpacks laden with books and arms slung around each other. Of course it was too expensive; and yet for the first time, *that* life felt like it was within reach. Maybe we'd find a way.

My mother was beaming. "Good. I'm so *proud* of you, baby."

Her smile was so genuine, so truly *pleased* by my smallest of achievements. I thought of Judith Liebling. Whatever my mother's faults may be, she certainly wasn't cold. She would never belittle me; I would never come up short. Instead, she'd put *everything* on the line for me, over and over again. And now we had made our nest here, safe and warm against the elements. "Why don't you call in sick tonight and we'll stay home and watch a movie?" I asked.

Distress crossed her face. "Too late for that, baby. The manager loses his mind when someone misses a shift. But I'm off work on Sunday, why don't we go down to the Cobblestone and see what's playing in the theater there? There's a James Bond film, I think. We could get pizza beforehand."

I dropped my arms. "Sure."

The timer on the stove went off and she darted away to drain the macaroni. "Oh, and don't worry if I'm late tonight. I offered to do a double." She gave me a radiant, dimpled smile as she maneuvered the pot to the sink, steam blurring her features. "Keeping us in macaroni!"

One day in mid-April, I looked around and realized that spring had arrived. The mountain peaks were still capped with icy crusts but down at lake level rain showers had wiped out the last of the snowdrifts. With the new season, Stonehaven felt like a different house entirely. Daylight savings had arrived, and now when we got there in the midafternoon the house was still bathed in sunlight that filtered through the dappled pines. I could finally see the green lawn spreading like a blanket from the mansion to the lakefront, as it revived itself from its winter hibernation. Violets materialized along the paths, planted by an invisible gardener. Everything about the house felt less ominous, less oppressive.

Or maybe it was just that I felt more comfortable at Stonehaven now. I no longer felt intimidated when I walked up the steps of the mansion; I started flinging my back- pack down next to Benny's at the base of the stairs as if it belonged there. I even encoun- tered Benny's mother once, drifting like a pale ghost through the empty rooms with a vase in each hand. She was in a rearranging phase, Benny informed me, tugging the furniture from one side of the room to the other and back again. When I said hello, she just nodded and wiped her cheek with the back of her forearm, leaving a gray smear of dust.

One Sunday morning, at the beginning of spring break, my mother and I walked down to Syd's to get bagels and coffee. As we waited for our order — my mother flirting with the genial bearded manager — I heard Benny's voice lifting over the other custom- ers', calling my name. I turned and saw him behind me in line, standing with a girl I'd never seen before.

I walked toward him, studying the strange girl. She didn't look like a local. She was as polished and golden as an Oscar statuette:

132

hair, nails, makeup, everything buffed to a pale gleam. She wore only a Princeton sweatshirt and jeans, and yet I could still feel the money wafting off her in a way that it never did off Benny: something about the flattering cut of her denim, the bright flash of the diamond tennis bracelet under her sweatshirt cuff, the smell of the leather from her purse. She looked like a cover model for an Ivy League catalog, bright and clean and forward-looking.

She was studying the phone in her hand as I walked over, oblivious to the noise of the café. Benny flung an arm over my shoulder, his eyes flicking back and forth between us. "Nina, this is my sister. Vanessa, this is my friend Nina."

The older sister, then. Of course. I felt conflicting emotions tug at me — wanting to be liked by her, wanting to *be* her; the knowledge that I never *could* be, and finally the knowledge that I shouldn't *want* to be her and yet I did anyway. She looked like the Future that my mother imagined for me; and her presence made me realize how very far away that really was.

Vanessa glanced up then, finally noticing that her brother had his arm around someone. I saw something flash across her big green eyes at this realization — surprise, and maybe delight — and then all that fell away as she studied me further. She was well mannered, there was nothing so obvious as an up-and-down glance, and yet I could tell immediately that she was one of those girls who measure. Everything about her was deliberate and watching. I felt her adding up the sum of my parts, calculating my value, and finding it too low to be worthy of engagement.

"Charmed," she said unconvincingly. And then, just like that, she was done with me. Her eyes slid back down to her phone. She took a step backward and away.

My face burned. I could see, maybe for the first time, that everything about my appearance was *wrong:* I wore too much makeup, poorly applied; I wore clothes that were supposed to conceal my hips and stomach but instead just looked baggy; my hair wasn't edgy and cool, it was just fried from drugstore hair dye. I looked cheap.

"Is this a school friend of yours?" My mother was suddenly beside me. I was grateful for the distraction.

"I'm Benny," he said, and gamely stuck out a hand to her. "Delighted to meet you, Mrs. Ross." A sharp flicker of surprise on my mother's face — I wondered if it was the first time anyone had ever addressed her as *Mrs.* — and then it was gone. She took his hand, shook it formally, hung on to it for a half second too long until Benny began to blush.

"I'd love to say that I've heard all about you," she said. "But Nina has not been forthcoming with information about her new friends."

"That's because I don't have many," I said. "Just this one." Benny met my eyes and smiled at this.

"You could have at least let me know you had a lovely new friend and that he had a *name.*" She dimpled at Benny. "I bet you tell your parents all about *your* friends."

"Not if I can help it."

"Well, then. Us parents should all get together and commiserate. Compare notes." My mother rolled her eyes, but I could see her take careful measure of the way Benny was smiling at me, the faint flush I could feel on my own cheeks. There was a moment of awkward silence, and then my mother looked around.

"Now, where's the creamer? I can't drink this stuff without a ton of sugar," she said. "Let me know when you're ready to go, Nina." She stepped toward the coffee bar at the end of the counter, a polite masquerade. There, she made a great show of fussing over the sugar dispenser, as if we weren't just three feet away. I silently thanked her for her discretion.

But Benny and I just grinned silently at each other until we reached the front of the line, Vanessa trailing just behind us. "Coffee for me and a cappuccino for my sister," Benny said to the barista.

135

"Soy," Vanessa said, still not looking up from her phone.

Benny rolled his eyes. "Yeah, you can ignore that part." He fished a hundred-dollar bill out of his wallet. Vanessa finally looked up from her phone long enough to notice what he was doing. She lunged forward and grabbed his wrist, examining the money in his hand.

"Jesus, Benny, are you stealing from the safe again? One of these days Dad is going to notice and then you're going to be in deep shit."

He shook her hand off. "He has a million dollars in there. He's never going to notice that a couple hundred bucks are missing."

At this, Vanessa's eyes shot over to me, and then away again. "Shut *up,* Benny," she hissed.

"What's up your *butt* today, Vanessa?"

Vanessa sighed and threw up her hands. "Discretion, baby brother. Learn some." She was intentionally not looking at me now, as if she believed that disregarding my presence would somehow make Benny's gaffe vanish from memory. The phone in her hand began to vibrate. "Look, I've got to take this, I'll be back in a sec. Don't forget we have to stop by the airstrip so I can look for my sunglasses." She spun and left the café.

"Sorry. She's usually not so rude. Mom is making her go to Paris with us instead of let-

136

ting her go to Mexico with her friends, so she's in a *mood.*"

But I'd already moved on from Vanessa's dismissiveness, my mind instead wrapping itself around the vision of a million dollars in a dark vault inside Stonehaven. Who kept that much money just sitting around in cash? What would it look like? How much space would it take up? I thought of heist movies I'd seen, robbers filling duffel bags with bright green stacks of bills; I imagined a bank vault hidden inside of Stonehaven, a giant round steel door with a lock that took two people to open. "Your dad really keeps a million dollars in your house?"

Benny looked uneasy. "I shouldn't have said anything."

"But what for? He doesn't trust banks?"

"Yeah, but it's not just that. It's in case of an emergency. He always says it's important to have cash at the ready, right? If shit hits the fan and everything falls apart and you need to just *go.* He keeps some in our house in San Francisco, too." He offered this casually, as if it was completely normal to need a seven-figure reserve. *For what?* I wondered. *In case you need to flee a zombie apocalypse? An FBI raid?* The barista handed Benny his coffees, and when he turned back to me that familiar red flush was creeping up his neck. "But look, can we not talk about my dad's money?"

137

I could tell by the expression on his face that I had broken an unspoken agreement between us: I was to pretend that I didn't know he was rich, and even if I did know, that I didn't care. And yet, there it was: a million dollars lying around "just in case" and an airstrip where a private jet was waiting to whisk them off to Paris, two signposts marking the gulf that lay between us. I looked over at my mother standing by the creamers in her worn Walmart parka and thought about how she watched men throw away tens of thousands of dollars every night at the gambling tables, as if it were meaningless paper.

And I realized, with sudden clarity, a second intention behind my mother's life choices, the ulterior motive behind her (formerly!) thieving ways. We lived with our faces pressed up against the glass, looking through it at those who had so much more, watching as they so casually rubbed our faces in their privilege. Especially here, in a resort town, where the working class bumped up against the vacation class with their $130 ski-lift tickets and luxury SUVs and lakefront estates that sat empty 320 days a year. Was it any wonder that people on the wrong side of the glass would eventually decide to take a hammer and break it, reach through and take some of it for themselves? *The world can be divided into two kinds of people: those who wait to have things given to them and those who take what they want.* My mother certainly wasn't the kind of person who would passively gaze through that glass, hoping that she would eventually make it to the other side.

Was *I*?

Of course, I know the answer to that question now.

But on that day: "I'm sorry," I said to Benny, stricken with guilt, unwilling to open up this whole can of worms lest I drive him away.

"That's OK, it's no big deal." He squeezed my arm, oblivious to my inner turmoil. "Look, we're flying out tomorrow, but we'll hang out as soon as I'm back from Paris, right?"

"Bring back a baguette for me," I said. My cheeks hurt from smiling.

"You bet," he said.

Benny was back on the bus on the first day of school after spring break, twitchy and wired, as if the spring weather had infected him with some sort of nervous giddiness. He jumped out of his seat when he saw me climb aboard and waved two baguettes over his head as if they were swords.

"Baguettes for mademoiselle," he said proudly.

I took a baguette and tore off a piece. It

was stale, but I ate it anyway, touched by the gesture and yet also acutely conscious of the fact that the millionaire's son had brought me pennies' worth of bread (again, in the back of my mind, a flash of green bundles in a dark, hidden safe). Of course, I reminded myself, the real value was that he'd listened, and thought of me, and brought me what I'd asked for. That was what was really important. *That* was the kind of person I was. Right?

And yet.

"Jesus, I'm glad to see you." He flung an arm over my shoulder in a way that felt strangely definitive. I could tell that something was going on with him, something I couldn't quite read. "Sanity at last."

"How was France?"

He shrugged. "Spent most of my time sitting around eating pastries while I waited for my mom and my sister to finish shopping. And then my dad would lose it when we got back to the hotel and he saw how much they'd bought. Thrilling stuff."

"Pastries and shopping. Oh yeah, *awful. I* spent my holiday boning up on biological individuality in the town library. Bet you're jealous."

"Actually, I am. I'd rather be *anywhere* with you than with my family in Paris." He squeezed my shoulder.

There it was again, that strange new flicker of resentment — Paris sounded awfully thrilling to me, he could at least have the good grace to appreciate his luck. But it sounded like he really believed that I was more interesting than a vacation in France, and who was I to dismiss that compliment?

We ate the baguettes, a carpet of stale crumbs spreading out below us, until we got to the gates of Stonehaven. But once we were inside the property, Benny didn't launch himself up the steps of the house. Instead, as we walked up the drive, he grabbed my sleeve and tugged me to the left, into a stand of pines on the side of the house.

"What's going on?"

He put a finger to his lips and pointed at an upstairs window. *Mom,* he mouthed.

I didn't understand what he meant by that, but I followed him through the pines and down a dirt path that took us around the edge of the property before depositing us at the caretaker's cottage. Once inside, he marched into the tiny kitchen where we kept our snacks and pulled a bottle out of a cabinet. He held it up for me to examine: vodka, expensive-looking stuff, from Finland. "My pot stash is gone," he said. "But I stole this from my dad's liquor cabinet."

"Gone? You smoked it all?"

"Nah. My mom did a room raid before we went to France. She found it under my bed and flushed it down the toilet." He looked abashed. "I'm in the doghouse. Actually,

141

you're not even supposed to be here. They forbade me from seeing you. That's why we didn't go inside the house."

I put two and two together: His curious bravado, the way he threw his arm around my shoulders on the bus like I belonged to him — it was all a middle finger to his parents. "What you're saying is . . . they blame me. For the pot. They think I'm a bad influence because, what, my hair is pink? And I don't ski?" A hot bubble of self-righteous anger rose inside me.

He shook his head. "I told them it had nothing to do with you. Problem predates you. They know that. They're just being . . . overprotective. Irrational. As usual. Fuck them."

The vodka bottle was still hanging between us, a totem of some symbolic transition, or of rebellion, or maybe apology. Finally, I reached out and grabbed it. "Is there juice? I'll make screwdrivers."

"Shit, no. Just vodka." He blushed when he met my eyes and I thought of a term that I had read before in a book — *liquid courage.* I unscrewed the cap of the bottle and lifted it to my lips and took a swig. I'd sipped at my mother's martinis before, but this was a proper, showy gulp. It burned; I choked. Benny reached out and whacked my back as I spluttered.

"I mean, I *was* going to offer you a glass

142

but . . ." He took the bottle from my hand and lifted it to his own lips, convulsing when the liquor hit his esophagus. Vodka dribbled out of the side of his mouth and he wiped it away with the sleeve of his T-shirt. His eyes were watering and red, and as they met mine we both started laughing.

The vodka lit up my stomach; it made me wired and punchy and hot. "Here," he said, handing it back to me, and this time I swallowed down a good inch before coming up for air. Five minutes of this and we were drunk and giddy, and I was tripping on the chairs in the dining room and laughing from the lightness in my head. When Benny grabbed me to stop me from falling and spun me around, I finally screwed up my courage and kissed him.

I've been kissed, all these years on, by so many men, almost all of them better kissers than Benny. But the first kiss is the one you always remember; and even now I can break that kiss down in detail. How chapped his lips were, but also how softly they gave way. The way he kept his eyes closed even when mine were open, and the way that made him look so serious and intense. The terrible sound of our teeth clicking against each other as we jockeyed for position; him stooping to pull me up to his face as I stood on my tiptoes, balancing myself against his chest. How when we stopped for a moment we both gasped for air as if we'd been underwater the whole time.

I could hear his heart as I rested in his arms, galloping so hard that it sounded as if it might race straight out of his chest and through the door. It slowed as we stood there for a while, adjusting to this new reality. "You don't have to do this out of pity or something," he whispered into my hair.

I pulled back, smacked him in the arm. "I kissed *you,* stupid."

His eyelashes fluttered, his eyes as soft and watching as a deer's. I smelled the vodka on his breath, like sweet gasoline. "You're beautiful and smart and tough and I don't get it."

"There's nothing to *get,*" I said. "Stop thinking so hard. Let me like you without second-guessing it."

But maybe he had a point. Nothing is ever as pure as it seems at first glance; there is always something more complicated to be found if you peel back the unmarred surface of pretty things. The black silt at the bottom of the pristine lake, the hard pit at the center of the avocado. I can't help wondering now if I kissed him as a kind of statement of intent; a way of putting my mark on him. His parents were going to forbid me to see him, they thought I was a bad influence? Kissing him was my way of saying to his parents, *Fuck you, he's mine. You don't get to win this one. You may have everything else in the world but I*

144

have your son.

Maybe that's why I felt so sure of myself as I took his hand and led him, stumbling, to that dormered bedroom with its creaking bed. Maybe that's why I let the fire of the vodka light me up with a boldness I didn't recognize in myself; why I abandoned myself so readily to the tugging and prodding, the clothes on the floor, the tongues against flesh. To the piercing, momentary pain; the gasp and thrust of it all. To the path forward into my future.

And yet, however tainted our motivations might have been at the time, what happened to us that day — and in the weeks that followed — felt pure. The cottage was ours, and the things that we did there, hidden inside its walls, seemed to belong to some kind of liminal space. At school, our relationship remained the same — racing past each other in the hallways on our way to class, occasionally eating pizza together at lunch, never really touching, although our feet sometimes found each other under the cafeteria table. Even on the bus to his house, as I felt the electric anticipation building, we still didn't play out the typical boyfriend-girlfriend roles. There was no hand-holding, no doodling initials on each other's forearms in blue ballpoint pen or sharing a single soda with two straws. Nothing was articulated out loud, nothing assumed. Only once we got to the cottage did everything shift, as if it had taken us that long — the better part of a day, plus a half-hour bus ride — to find the confidence to step into our insurgence.

"So who's the boy?" my mom asked one evening, as I stumbled through the door just before dinner, everything askew. I could still smell Benny on my skin and I wondered if she had smelled him, too, a pheromonal red flag signaling adolescent lust.

"What makes you think there's a boy?"

She stood in the doorway to the bathroom, pulling curlers from her hair. "Baby, if I know anything about anything, it's about love." She considered this for a second. "Make that sex, actually. You're using protection? I keep condoms in the upper drawer of my night-stand, you can take as many as you need."

"Jesus, Mom! Stop. Just say something like *You're too young* and leave it at that."

"You're too young, baby." She raked her fingers through her curls to soften them, and then shellacked them back into place with hair spray. "Fuck, I was thirteen, so who am I to talk? Anyway, I'd like to meet him. Invite him for dinner sometime."

I thought about this — should I confess that it was the boy she met at the café? Or maybe she already suspected, and was waiting for me to tell her. But I felt strangely reluctant to bring Benny back with me across

146

the Rubicon that divided our two worlds. It felt dangerous, as if something critical might be broken in the process. "Maybe."

She sat down on the toilet and tentatively massaged the toes on one foot. "OK. I think this is where I'm supposed to give you a lecture, so here goes. Sex — it can be about love, yes. And it's wonderful when it's that, and God, baby, I hope that's what you've found. But it's also a tool. Men use it to prove a point to themselves, about their power to take what they want. You're just the first rung on the ladder of their world domination. And when *that's* the kind of sex you're having — which is most of the time — you got to make sure that *you're* using it as a tool, too. Don't let yourself be used up by them, all the time believing it's some kind of equal relationship. Make sure you're getting just as much out of it as they are." She shoved the swollen foot into a shoe and stood, wobbling a little on her heels. "Pleasure, at the very least."

I hated how this made me feel. My relationship with Benny wasn't transactional, I was sure of it. And yet my mother's words lingered there in the air between us, injecting poison into my pretty picture. "Mom, that's a really antiquated view of sex."

"Is it?" She studied herself in the mirror. "From what I see every night at my work, I would say it's not." She caught my eyes in the reflection. "Just, baby — be careful."

"Like *you* are?" The words came out sounding more spiteful than I meant them to.

Her blue eyes blinked rapidly, as if trying to rid themselves of an irritant. A flake of mascara. A flotsam of regret. "I learned my lessons the hard way. I'm just trying to save you from having to do the same thing."

I softened; I couldn't help myself. "You don't have to worry about me, Mom."

She sighed. "I don't know how not to."

The last day that I ever saw Benny was a Wednesday in mid-May. There were only three weeks left in the school year, and we were in the midst of finals; I hadn't seen him in almost a week while I crammed for my tests in a last-ditch effort to bring a last few B pluses up to As. When he showed up on the bus and sat beside me that last day, he handed me a piece of paper. It was a portrait of me, carefully inked on thick linen. He'd imagined me as a manga character in a tight black costume, the pink fringe of my hair whipping out behind me, strong legs leaping through the air. I clutched a sword in one hand, dripping blood; and below my boots was a fire-breathing dragon, cowering in fear. My dark eyes gazed out from the page, shiny and huge, challenging whoever looked back to *just try it, fucker.*

I studied the picture for a long time, seeing myself as Benny must have seen me: as a kind of superhero, stronger than I really was, capable of rescue.

I folded it and put it in my backpack and then wordlessly took his hand. He smiled to himself as he wove his fingers between mine. The bus coughed its way along the lakeshore, warm spring air leaking through the cracked-open windows.

"My mom's in San Francisco for the week," he said as we approached his neighborhood. "She had to go down to the city to get her meds adjusted. Guess she rearranged the furniture one time too many and my dad finally got a clue." He tried to laugh but the noise that came out sounded like the pained squawk of a dying seagull.

I squeezed his hand. "Is she going to be OK?"

He shrugged. "It's just the same thing over and over again. They'll dope her up and she'll be back and we'll go through it all again next year." But then he closed his eyes, his lashes vibrating against his pale skin, belying his blasé. And I thought of Benny's own cocktail of meds, the way they kept his lips cracked and dry and his pulse thumping erratically, and I wondered if he ever worried about how much of his mother he had inside him.

"Does that mean we have the house to ourselves?" I imagined finally going upstairs at Stonehaven and getting to see Benny's bedroom, which remained as mysterious to me as it had on the day we met. I'd still only ever seen the parlor, the hallway, the kitchen, the dining room, the library — a handful of Stonehaven's forty-two rooms, and (I could see now) a reminder of how much I wasn't really welcome there.

He shook his head. "Remember? I'm grounded. They don't trust me with just Lourdes. So my dad's up here while Mom's down there. Convenient for them both, I guess." He frowned. "If his car is in the driveway we'll have to be extra sneaky, OK? He pays closer attention than my mom."

But his father's Jaguar wasn't in the driveway; only Lourdes's mud-splattered Toyota, discreetly parked under the pines. And so we once more sauntered through the house as if we owned it, stopping in the kitchen to pick up a pair of Cokes and a bag of popcorn before going out to the caretaker's cottage. There, we sat on the steps, our legs hooked over each other's, watching a flock of geese that had landed on the lawn. Occasionally we'd toss a kernel of popcorn and a brave goose would creep toward us to gobble it down, eyeing us warily. They grazed and honked, pooping dark pellets all over the beautiful green grass.

"So. Bad news." Benny's voice broke the silence. "My parents are sending me to Europe this summer."

"What?"

"Some kind of reform camp in the Italian Alps where I can't get in trouble. You know, *fresh air* and *physical exertion* and all that stuff that will magically turn me into the boy wonder they want me to be." He flung another piece of popcorn at a goose and it flapped its wings in protest. "I guess they think *European* air is somehow more restorative than *American* air." He looked over at me. "I'm flunking three subjects, you know. This is, I guess, their last attempt to fix me up before they give up on me forever."

"Maybe if you ace your tests they'll let you stay?"

"Unlikely. Both that I'll ace the tests and that it will make a difference. I can't cram and get As the way you do. I can barely even read for five minutes, for chrissake. Why do you think I like comic books so much?"

I thought of my own summer. I'd landed a minimum-wage job at a river-rafting company in Tahoe City, loading and unloading the rubber boats that clotted the Truckee River from Memorial Day to Labor Day. This prospect sounded even more unappealing now that he wouldn't be there waiting for me after work. "Shit. What am I going to do without you?"

"I'll get you a cellphone of your own and then I'll call you every day."

"Nice. But still not the same."

We sat in the sun in silence for a while, looking out at the lake. The boats weren't out

151

yet; the light that dappled the surface of the water was blinding against all that blue. Eventually Benny kissed me and his lips felt sadder than usual, like we were already saying goodbye for the summer. And when he pulled back for a moment he kept his eyes closed and said, almost as a murmur, "I love you." And, heart racing, I echoed his words back. It felt like we had everything we needed, right there, forever; and that with these words we would somehow conquer all of the things in our way.

It was the first and last time I ever felt pure, unadulterated joy.

We moved into the cottage, and then to the bed. We shed our clothes en route, discarding T-shirts and socks like Hansel and Gretel's breadcrumbs. In the bedroom, the dim light glowed across his milky skin, and I traced the red freckles on his chest before climbing on top of him. At this point, after a dozen trysts, we'd figured out how we fit together; there was less of the awkward bumping of elbows and knees and more of the thrill of discovery. How it felt when you touched *there,* or were touched *here;* what this body part might do when in contact with that one. A children's science experiment, but with so much more at stake.

And *that* — the shocking heat of his mouth on my breast, the damp slide of his stomach against mine — was why we didn't hear his father enter the cottage. We were so absorbed with each other that we didn't have time to scramble for cover until he was already in the doorway, his bulk blocking out the light from the living room. And then Benny's father's hand was on my arm and he was yanking me off of his son, and I was shrieking and grabbing for a sheet to cover myself while Benny was exposed on the bed, blinking and stunned.

William Liebling IV. He looked just like the photos I'd seen — a big, bald man in an expensive suit — except that in person he seemed so much larger than life, even bigger than Benny. He must have been in his sixties, but he wasn't at all frail; instead, he had that air of gravitas and power that comes with inherited money. And unlike the pictures that I'd seen, the opera photos where he looked so benignly at ease, his face was beet red and his eyes were burning coals inside puffy folds of skin.

He ignored Benny, who was scrambling out of the bed with his hands covering his groin, and addressed me instead. "Who are you?" he barked.

I felt damp and exposed. My heart was still on fire in my chest, my flesh still suffused and sensitive; I couldn't reconcile everything racing through me. "Nina," I stammered. "Nina Ross." My eyes darted to Benny, who was tripping over his giant feet as he grabbed

153

at the boxer shorts he'd abandoned on the floor. He inched toward the doorway, his eyes fixed on the jeans lying on the floor of the hallway.

Mr. Liebling turned and barked at Benny. "Stop right there." He turned back to me and examined me for a long time. "Nina Ross." He rolled the name in his mouth, clearly committing it to memory, and I wondered if he was the kind of dad who would call my mother to complain. Probably. Or maybe Benny's mom would do the honors. I imagined my mom telling them both to go fuck themselves.

Benny had succeeded in getting his underwear on and he stood hunched there near the doorway, his thin arms covering his naked chest. "Dad . . ." he began.

His father whirled around and lifted a finger in the air. "Benjamin. Not. A. Word." He turned back to me and tugged on the bottom of his suit jacket to straighten it. This seemed to calm him. "Nina Ross. You will leave now," he said coolly. "And you will not come back here. You will leave Benjamin alone from now on. Do you understand?"

I could smell something in the air, pungent and sharp: It was the anxiety pouring off Benny as he watched me with a helpless expression on his face. He looked shrunken and young suddenly, like a little boy, even though he had at least a half foot on his

154

father. I felt a surge of emotion, a desire to protect him from everything that might break him. I thought of the Nina in Benny's drawing, the superhero with the dripping sword. My heart wasn't racing anymore; I felt calm as I tucked the sheet tighter around my torso. "No," I heard myself saying. "You can't tell me what to do. We love each other."

The muscles in Mr. Liebling's face twitched, as if jolted by an electric shock. He stepped close to me and leaned in, voice dropping to a hoarse bark. "Young lady, you don't understand. My son *cannot handle this.*"

I looked over at Benny, hunched in the corner, and for a stinging second I wondered if his father was right. "I know him better than you do."

He laughed then, a mirthless, condescending sound. "I am his *father.* And you" — he measured me with his eyes — *"you* are nobody. You are *disposable."* He pointed to the door. "You'll leave now, or I'll call the police and have you removed."

He turned to Benny, and ran a hand over his bald pate, as if testing the shape of his skull. "And you. You will be in my study in five minutes, fully dressed. Yes?"

"Yes," Benny said, his voice almost a whisper. "Sir."

His father examined him for a long minute, his eyes running over his son's long loose

155

limbs and concave chest; and then a little sound came out of him, like a sigh, and I could see something deflate inside him. "Benjamin," he began, reaching out a hand to his son. Benny flinched. His father stopped, midgesture, and rather than leaving the hand hanging there in midair, he instead ran his hand over his pate again. Then he turned and walked out the bedroom door.

We waited until we heard the cottage door slam and then we grabbed for our clothes, scrambling to get dressed as quickly as we'd gotten ourselves undressed. Benny wouldn't meet my eyes as he yanked his sweatshirt back over his head and tied on his sneakers. "I'm sorry, Nina," he kept saying over and over. "I'm so sorry."

"It's not your fault." I put my arms around his waist but he just hung there limply, as if his spine had snapped inside him; he turned away from me when I tried to kiss him. And I knew then that, even though I'd stood up to his dad, Benny certainly wasn't going to. No matter how much he pretended to hate his family, if he had to choose between them and me, it wasn't going to be a contest. I was not a superhero, slaying dragons for him; I was *nobody*. It felt like a mirror that I'd been gazing into had shattered, and now all that was left was tiny fragments I had no idea how to reassemble.

He didn't hold my hand as we trudged back

along the path to Stonehaven. He didn't hug me when I turned right to go around the house and he turned left to go up the steps to the kitchen porch. He just closed his eyes tightly, as if trying to see something hidden inside his head, and then he said those words once more, barely audibly — "I'm sorry, Nina" — and just like that we were done.

So then: finals and June commencement, which at North Lake Academy meant that the entire student body spent the last day of school down at the lake, kayaking and water-skiing and barbecuing tofu dogs on the dock of someone's private beach. I'd only glimpsed Benny a few times in the intervening weeks — a gaunt figure I'd spy sloping through the halls in the distance, as my throat seized up with Pavlovian longing — and I lay in bed at night imagining how we might finally get to talk at the party. How he'd see me sitting on the beach and come over and cry and apologize; and I'd of course forgive him and we'd embrace and then we'd be back together forever. The end.

But Benny didn't come to the beach party at all, and so instead I spent the day lying in the sand next to Hilary and her friends, listening to them talk about their summer lifeguarding jobs, and trying not to cry.

At one point, Hilary rolled over so that she was facing me, and propped her head up on one hand. "So hey. Where's your boyfriend today? Off on his family's yacht or something?"

"Boyfriend?" I repeated dumbly.

She gave me a knowing look. "Give it up, girl. Everyone knows. You're not that sly." She smiled. "I *knew* you two would hit it off. From the start."

I lay back on my beach towel and squeezed my eyes shut so hard that I saw red fireworks behind them. "He's not my boyfriend," I said. "We broke up."

"Oh. Shit. That sucks." She flopped over onto her stomach and loosened her bikini strings. "Hang out with us this summer. I'll find you someone better. That's the good thing about being a lifeguard, it's easy to meet guys."

Any thoughts I might have had about this dubious plan — becoming a beach bum, making Hilary my new BFF and hooking up with the sunburned summer kids — vanished when I got home that afternoon. The minute I turned the corner to our house, I could see it: my mother's hatchback, packed to the gills with boxes and Hefty bags. I walked up the driveway and stood there, staring through the windows at the jammed back seat. I could see my patched-up moon boots, pressed up against the glass. And I couldn't stop myself anymore: I began to cry, big hideous sobs of despair at how everything could go from wonderful to awful in just a few weeks.

Eventually my mother came outside and approached me, her arms extended for a hug. "I'm sorry, baby. I really am."

I sidestepped her, swiping at my nose with the back of my arm. "You *promised.* We'd stay until I graduated."

She looked like she might cry, too. "I know I said that. But it's not turning out how I hoped." Her hands worked at the bottom of her shirt, rolling it and unrolling it. "It's not about you, baby. You kept up your end of the bargain. It's just . . ." She hesitated.

The expression on her face stopped me. "This is about Benny, right?"

Tears were pooling at the corners of her eyes, but she didn't deny it. "Nina . . ."

"They called you, didn't they? His parents, the Lieblings? They called you to tell you that he and I were *involved*? They told you to keep me away from him because I'm not *good* enough for their son."

I looked at her and she wouldn't look back at me, just kept rolling and unrolling the hem of her shirt as her ruined mascara ran in rivulets down her face. And as I stood there watching her, my entire life packed into a pitifully small number of boxes, I *knew.* They'd driven us out of town. To the Lieblings, we were just trash, a minor nuisance in the way of their world domination, and therefore we had to go. And because they

159

were rich, they had gotten their way.

I wondered about the strings that they had pulled, in order to get us to leave. Because how else could they have forced my mom to give up a job, a home, her daughter's glorious Future? They'd strong-armed, they'd threatened. That was the Liebling way, Benny had already told me as much: *My dad's a bully: If he doesn't get what he wants at first, he'll just threaten you until he does.* A call of complaint to North Lake Academy, my scholarship yanked. A well-placed word at my mother's job, threatening her livelihood. How easy it must have felt for them to take away the little that we had. After all, we were insignificant to them.

I felt my mother's arm creep around me. "Don't cry, sweetheart. You don't need him. You have *me,* and that's all you need. You and I, we are the only people we can trust," she whispered, her voice breaking. "Besides, you are better than anyone I have ever met. You are better than their horrible son."

"Then why are we letting them get away with it? We don't have to let them do this to us," I insisted, growing frantic. "We shouldn't let them have what they want. We should *stay.*"

My mom shook her head. "I'm so sorry, baby. But it's too late."

"What about the Ivy League?" I managed. "What about Stanford summer school?"

160

"We don't need a fancy private high school for that." She straightened, squeezed my arm, turned to the car as if something had been decided without me. "You'll do well wherever we go, if you just apply yourself. That was my mistake. We never needed to come here in the first place."

And so we moved back to Las Vegas, and I started my junior year at yet another enormous, concrete institution. And maybe my mom was right that I didn't need a private high school to excel, but our year at Tahoe had also broken something critical inside me: the ability to believe in my own potential. I knew now who I really was: a nobody, disposable, destined for nothing.

After Tahoe, my mother lost her footing, too. The first few months that we were back in Vegas, she was giddy, going on shopping sprees for our new apartment and speculating that our ship was about to come in. But by that winter, she'd gone grim and silent, once again disappearing to the casinos at night; and this time, I knew that she didn't have a waitressing job. Eventually, she was arrested for credit card fraud and identity theft. She went to jail, and I went into foster care until she got out six months later. When she was freed, we moved to Phoenix, then Albuquerque, and finally Los Angeles.

Despite all the disruption, I managed to

rise far enough above the underserved herds at my subpar schools to gain admittance to a middling liberal arts college on the East Coast; but not high enough for the Ivy League, not high enough to qualify for scholarships. Still, I was determined to get as far away from my mother's life as possible, even if it meant turning down the local junior college and taking on student debt. I went off to get a BA in art history, still so blindly in thrall to Stonehaven that I didn't think much about career viability. Inevitably, I emerged four years later in a worse state: even more broke, underqualified and lost. The bright shiny Future — the one in the Princeton sweatshirt, the one on the cover of the Stanford summer school catalog — was not for me after all.

The Lieblings stole all that from me, and I never forgave them for it.

For a long time I hoped that I was wrong about Benny; I hoped that he wasn't like his family after all, and just needed to be reminded who he really *was.* For a while, after we first arrived back in Las Vegas, I wrote letters to him; rambling thoughts about loneliness, stories about my depressing new school, little observations underlined by a silent plea to let me know that I still mattered. After a few months of this, I got a postcard in the mail: a photo of the boathouse at the Cham-

162

bers Landing pier, and on the back a single sentence, in a childish scrawl: *PLEASE STOP.*

So was my mother right? *Was* my entire relationship with Benny a transaction, a failed power grab between two fundamentally unequal people? Was I just covetous of Benny's life and hoping to take a piece of what he had? And was he just trying to assert his dominion over another human being, trying to live up to the example his ancestors had set? Maybe what we experienced never was love; maybe it was always just about sex and loneliness and control.

In a different sort of story, I would have saved that portrait that Benny drew of me, the one where I looked like a manga character; and I would have tenderly pulled it out for inspiration in moments of self-doubt, as proof that I was *somebody* after all. But the reality is that I burned that picture in the fireplace of our Tahoe cabin before we drove out of town that last day. I sat there with a poker and watched the edges of the portrait blacken and curl; watched the fire lick at those confident eyes and the sword-wielding hand, until all that was left was ash.

In a different story — one with a kinder, gentler protagonist — I also would have looked Benny up some years later and we would have commiserated and grown close, maybe rekindled a friendship that transcended what had once driven us apart. But again, that's not this story. And while it's true that I followed the Lieblings' doings from a distance — I knew when Judith Liebling drowned in a boating accident, not long after I got that horrible postcard; I knew when Vanessa Liebling became an Instagram celebrity; I knew when William Liebling IV died — I never bothered to reach out to Benny. Why should I, when he'd never reached out to *me* to explain why he'd so easily abandoned me? I was angry at him for so long that it became an essential part of my being, an ache that sat at the pit of my stomach, the tender genesis of all my rage at the world.

And yet. When I ran into Hilary on the street in New York a few years later, and she let it drop that Benny had been diagnosed as schizophrenic — that he'd been sent home from Princeton after he attacked a girl on his floor and then ran naked and raving through his dorm — I was surprised when the pang that I felt was not of vindictive rage but of pity. *Poor Benny,* I thought, as Hilary prattled on about how he was living at some fancy institution near Mendocino, how someone from school had visited him and he was basically a vegetable now, drugged out of his mind.

And then, tearing up — *Poor us.*

So maybe I did still love him after all.

As for the rest of the Lieblings — for them, I had nothing but hate.

8.

Vanessa, Vanessa, Vanessa. Does she feel it, as I walk across the cobbled drive toward her — something electric in the air, a premonitory tingle? Her intuition warning her that something about me — my poised, rehearsed, yoga-instructor walk; the toothy grin slapped across my face — isn't quite right? Does she find herself fighting a strange urge to board the windows, take in the lawn furniture, lock the doors tight, and hide in the basement?

I doubt it. I am a category 5 hurricane coming her way, and she has no clue.

VANESSA

9.

Stonehaven. I never imagined I'd someday live in this monstrous heap. Growing up, it was the albatross that hung around the Liebling family neck: an estate so firmly attached to our name that it was impossible to imagine *ever* letting it go. It felt like Stonehaven had stood there on the West Shore forever, an anachronistic stone monolith that rejected any attempts to dress it up as something new. The house had been passed to the firstborn son of five generations of Lieblings, which meant that someday it would belong to my little brother Benny — not to me.

Toxic patriarchy! you might be thinking. *Fight against the injustice!* But honestly, I wanted nothing to do with the place.

I have hated Stonehaven since I was six years old and first came up here for Christmas. My grandparents, Katherine and William III, had mandated that the extended Liebling family spend the holiday at Stonehaven, so we all slowly rolled in one snowy

December afternoon, the wheels of our town cars leaving muddy tracks along the drive. Grandma Katherine (never Kat, or Kitty, but Katherine, always with the emphasis on that first *ah*) had brought in a decorator for the family gathering and, honestly, she had quite *de trop* taste. When you walked in the front door of the house you were assaulted with the holiday. Swags and garlands hanging off every cornice, poinsettias brandishing their poison petals from the centerpieces. A tree that brushed the ceiling, drooping with silver ornaments and gold tinsel. Full-sized Victorian Santas that lurked in dark corners, their faces frozen midchortle, and scared the stuffing out of me.

The whole house smelled of fresh-cut pine boughs, a medicinal smell that made me think of murdered trees.

My grandmother was a great collector of European decorative arts, the more gilded and elaborate the better; though my grandfather preferred chinoiserie. (Previous ancestors had dabbled in eighteenth-century American, Jacobean, French Revival, Victoriana.) So Stonehaven was full of delicate furnishings balanced on spider legs, and precious objects rendered in bone-thin porcelain. The house was a giant slap in the face to the very *concept* of childhood.

My grandmother sat all of the cousins down on the day we got there. "There will be no running inside Stonehaven," she warned us all sternly. Benny and I were perched side by side on a silk-covered sofa in the drawing room, sipping chocolate from child-sized teacups. Grandmother Katherine's silver hair had been shellacked and teased until it was as stiff and shiny as the ornaments on the tree; she wore a pink Chanel suit that dated back at least two decades. My mother (*Maman,* she liked us to call her, though Benny refused) paced silently behind her, tugging on her diamond studs, chafing at being sidelined here. "There will be no throwing of balls, or wrestling, or playing of wild games. Do you understand me? In my house, little children who do not follow the rules get spankings." My grandmother peered over her bifocals at the children. We all squirmed under her gaze, and nodded.

And then I forgot. (Of course I forgot! I was *six.*) In the third-floor bedroom where I was supposed to sleep with my baby brother, there was a glass-fronted cabinet full of darling porcelain birds. I was immediately besotted with a pair of bright green parrots, their black eyes like little beads. At my family's mansion in San Francisco, everything in my bedroom was solely for my entertainment — no one got upset if I smeared makeup on my Barbies or fed puzzle pieces to the dogs — and so of course I assumed that these birds were toys that had been put there for *me.*

171

That first night, I pulled one of the parrots from the cabinet and set it next to the bed where I slept, so that it would be the first thing that I saw in the morning. Instead, as I slept that night, a decorative sham slid off the bed, taking the parrot down along with it. When I woke up at dawn, there was no bird, just a pile of shards on the floor.

I burst into tears, which woke Benny up, and then he started wailing, too. Maman soon appeared in the door with her silk robe wrapped tight against Stonehaven's chill, blinking blearily.

"Oh God. You broke a Meissen." She nudged a shard of green porcelain with her toe and made a face. "Gaudy little baubles."

I sniffled. "Grandmama is going to get mad at me."

My mother stroked my hair, gently tugging out the tangles. "She won't notice. She has lots of them."

"But it was a pair." I pointed to the cabinet, where the remaining parrot was peering inquisitively through the glass, as if looking for his dead friend. "She'll see there's only one left. And then she'll spank me."

Benny wailed some more in the bed beside me, sallow and sulky. Mother swept him up with one arm and perched him on her hip, and then swanned across the room to the cabinet. She threw the glass door open and reached in to grab the remaining parrot, plac-

172

ing it on the palm of her hand. She balanced it there for a moment, and then tipped her hand slightly, so that the bird fell to the floor and shattered. I shrieked. Benny whooped with excitement.

"Now we both broke one, and she won't dare punish me, which means she can't punish you, either." She came back and sat on the bed next to me, wiping the tears from my face with her soft white hand. "My beautiful girl. You are not going to be spanked, ever. Do you understand? I will never let that happen."

I was stunned silent. My mother disappeared and a few minutes later came back with a broom and a dustpan — I remember thinking that they looked so *unlikely* in her hand — and swept the shards into a bag that she then spirited away. My grandmother never came into the bedroom that Christmas (she avoided us altogether, for the most part) and so as far as I know she never noticed that the birds were missing. Benny and I spent most of the rest of the trip outside with our cousins and our nannies, building igloos until we were pink with cold and our snow pants were soaked through, but at least there we were safe from the dangers that lurked inside the house.

So yes, I hated Stonehaven. I hated everything that it represented to me: honor and expectation, all that formality, the noose of history dangling just over my neck. I hated it when my grandmother made a grand gesture over Christmas dinner, as she peered down the table at the children, and murmured, "Someday all this will be yours, children. Someday you will be the caretakers of the Liebling family name." It didn't make me feel big at all, this legacy that had been handed to me; instead, it made me feel tiny under its looming shadow, as if I was insignificant in comparison to its sprawl, as if I could never *possibly* live up.

I was never supposed to be Stonehaven's caretaker and yet somehow here I am anyway. Hooray. Life is ironic, no? (Or maybe I should say *bittersweet, unfair,* or just plain old *fucked-up.*) Some days, as I wander these rooms, I feel the echoes of my ancestors inside myself: as if I am another in a line of elegant hostesses, keeping the clocks wound while I await my callers.

More often, though, I wonder if I am Jack Torrance, and this is my Overlook Hotel.

A few months back, not long after I moved in, I came across an appraisal document for those parrots. They were valued at $30,000 for the pair. Reading this, I thought of Maman gently tipping her hand: Did she know that she was throwing $15,000 in the trash? *But of course she did,* I realized, *and she didn't care.* Because *nothing* was truly valuable to her except for me. Benny and I — *we* were her Meissen birds, precious objects she wanted to guard behind glass. She spent her life protecting my brother and me from spankings, until the moment when she died. And sometimes I feel like life has been beating us both senseless ever since.

10.

I know what you're probably thinking: *Look at the spoiled rich girl, all alone in the great big house, trolling for our sympathy when she doesn't deserve any of it.* You feel so smug, looking at me! And yet you also can't seem to look *away* from me. You follow me on my social media accounts, you swipe up to study my links, you watch my YouTube fashion tutorials and *like* my travelogues and read every Page Six mention you can find. You can't stop yourself from clicking on my name even though you tell everyone that you hate me. I *fascinate* you.

You need me to be the monster so that you can position yourself in opposition to me and feel superior. Your ego requires me.

And there's another thing, though you would *never* admit this out loud: When you look at me, you also think, *I want what she has. Her life should be mine. And if I were given the resources at her disposal, I would do*

it all so much better.
Maybe you're not so wrong.

11.

I sit at the window of Stonehaven's front parlor, waiting to greet the couple that's making their way through the twilight toward me. The torrential rains of the morning have slowed to a light drizzle that sparkles like glitter in the lights along the drive. I'm as wired as a teenager on Ritalin, wound up by the prospect of human interaction. (*Giddy! Practically buoyant!*) I'm pretty sure I haven't spoken to another human being in two weeks, other than to tell the housekeeper, in broken Spanish, that she can't keep ignoring the dust on the windowsills.

When I woke up this morning, I could feel that the black funk that had weighed on me for most of the year had lifted. In its place, a familiar *fizz* and *pop,* as if something inside me had been set on fire and was crackling back to life. I could see everything *so clearly* again.

I spent the morning washing my hair and dyeing the roots back to blond with a bottle of Clairol that I found in the grubby grocery store in town (beggars can't be choosers). I gave myself a mani-pedi (ditto), applied a trio of Korean face masks, and then spent an hour digging through boxes until I unearthed the perfect *Lounging in the Manor* outfit: jeans and a black designer tee, a blazer in garnet velvet with a gray hoodie underneath. Chic, yet approachable. I snapped a selfie and uploaded it for my Instagram followers. *This is what "dressing up" looks like in the mountains! #lakelife #mountainstyle #miumiu*

I tore through the rooms of Stonehaven, cleaning up abandoned wineglasses and plates sticky with crumbs; hid the piles of laundry in the bedroom, straightened the fashion magazines strewn across the tables in the parlor (and then reassessed, and tossed them altogether). I arranged, and then re-arranged, a little tableau of snacks in the kitchen, until I thought I might cry from the stress of it all. (To calm my nerves, I reread that day's inspo from my own Instagram feed, a Maya Angelou quote I'd found online: *Nothing can dim the light which shines from within.*)

Then I sat in the front window with a bottle of wine, and waited.

By the time I see their lights coming up the drive, I've nearly finished the bottle of wine. When I jump up I realize that I'm actually quite tipsy. (Déclassé, as Maman always said, while she primly poured herself an exact half glass at dinner.) I am quite skilled at deception, though. Four years of documenting my every move online has trained me in the art of looking sober (insert: *happy/thoughtful/ excited/contemplative*) when in fact I am very much not.

So I dash to the door, take a breath to chase away the dizziness, slap my face once — *hard* — and then step out onto the front portico to greet them, my cheek still burning.

There's a winter chill in the air, a layer of damp that clings to the stones of the house. I've grown so thin that even my size 0s feel loose on me — cooking for one is just too depressing, and besides the grocery store is so *far away* — so it feels like the cold is penetrating straight into my bones. I stand shivering in the shadows as their car picks its way carefully along the slick drive. It's a vintage BMW with Oregon plates that are splattered with mud from the highway. The car slows down a hundred yards out. It's hard to make out their faces through the mist and the evening shadows, but I just know that they're craning their heads to take it all in. Of course they are. The pines, the lake, the mansion — it is *so much,* so much that it sometimes hurts me to even look out the window. (Those are the days that I just climb back in bed and take three Ambien and pull the covers over my head. But that's neither here nor there.)

Then their car pulls forward and parks, and I can suddenly see them clearly through the windshield. They're taking their time, laughing about something, which stirs up a nest of longing inside me. Even after a whole day of driving together, they're in absolutely no rush to escape each other's company. Then she leans across the car and kisses him, long and hard. It goes on and on. They must not see that I'm there, and suddenly it's rather awkward that I'm spying on them like some sort of Hitchcock voyeur.

I step backward into the shadows of the overhang, thinking I'll slip back inside and just wait for them to ring the bell. But then the passenger door flies open, and she steps out.

Ashley.

It's like the chilly forest has come to life around her. The silence to which I've grown so accustomed is shattered with a blast of music from the car stereo. (The climactic aria of some opera that Maman surely would have recognized.) Even from twenty feet away, I can almost *feel* the close, car-heated air still clinging to Ashley's skin, as if she's brought her own personal ecosystem with her. She stands with her back to me and flexes, a smooth little yoga stretch with palms to the sky, then turns and catches me standing there watching her. If this bothers her, she doesn't show it. Instead, she smiles at me with mild pleasure, as if she's used to being observed. (And of course she is: She's a yoga instructor! Her body is her *raison d'être.* Something we share, I suppose.)

There is something feline about her, something poised and watching: Her dark eyes scan the space around her, as if measuring the distance necessary to leap. Her hair is a glossy pelt, pulled back into a long tail, and her skin is a smooth olive that absorbs the light. (Perhaps Latina? Or Jewish?) She is unsettlingly pretty. Most of the beautiful women I've known over the years would flaunt this — the hair, the face, the body would all be enhanced, amplified, and exposed — but Ashley wears her looks as casually as the faded jeans that grip her curves. It's as if she couldn't care less about being stared at.

So of course I'm staring. ("Stop *staring,*" I hear Maman in my head. "You look like a trout when you gawk like that.")

"You must be Vanessa!" She's halfway toward me, extending her hands to grip mine. And then suddenly I am being pulled into a hug, and my face is buried in her hair, which smells of vanilla and orange blossom. The heat of her, pressed against me, is disarming. Something blooms inside me: When was the last time I was hugged? (For that matter, when was the last time I was even *touched*?

I've barely even masturbated in months.) The embrace goes on for a half second longer than I expect — Am I supposed to pull away? My God, what's the protocol here? — and when she finally draws back, I feel flushed and hot and a little bit dizzy.

"Ashley, right? Oh *wonderful*. Oh *thrilling*! You made it!" My voice is shrill, almost squeaky, and far too gushy. "Was the drive just *awful*? All this rain. It's been relentless." I hold up a hand above us, ineffectively shielding her from the drizzle.

"Oh, I love the rain," she says with a smile. She closes her eyes and inhales, her nostrils flaring. "It smells so fresh here. I've been sitting in a car for nine hours, I honestly could use a bit of cleansing."

"Haha!" I trill. (*Oh for God's sake, stop it,* I tell myself.) "Well you'll get lots of that here. Rain, I mean. Not cleansing. Though why not both, I suppose?!"

She looks a little baffled by this. I'm not quite sure what I mean, either.

There's a clatter in the driveway, the sound of suitcases being dragged across paving stones and then bumping up the stairs of the portico. I look over Ashley's shoulder and suddenly I am gazing straight into the eyes of her boyfriend.

Michael.

It's startling, the way he's looking at me. His eyes are a pellucid blue, so pale and

183

transparent that it feels like I'm seeing clear into the center of his mind, where something glints and shines. I flush: Am I staring again? *Yes.* But he's also staring intently back at me as if he can see inside me, too, and is seeing things that I didn't intend to reveal. (Did he know I was just thinking of masturbating?) I feel the blush rising up through my neck, and I know that I must be the color of lobster bisque. I wish I'd worn a turtleneck.

I recover, extend a formal hand. "And you're Michael?" He takes it, responding with a little bow of his own and a funny wry smile.

"Vanessa." It's a statement, not a question, and once again I have that *strange* feeling that I have just been identified, that he knows something about me that hasn't been spoken at all. Do I know him? It seems unlikely — isn't he an English professor, from Portland?

But then — does *he* know *me*? It's quite possible. I am, after all, a little bit famous, and being Internet-famous is the opposite of traditional fame: Instead of being put on a pedestal, like a rock star or movie star, being an Internet star means that you must always be *just* within reach of your fans. Special, yes, but approachable; giving the illusion that your life is within clawing distance if one is just ambitious enough. That's half the appeal. In New York, strangers would often come up to me at restaurants and speak to me as if we were old friends, as if a few liked photos and a handful of comments meant we were besties. (Of course I was always gracious and friendly no matter how unnerving the encounter, because: *approachable.*)

But Michael, in jeans and flannel, hair a little unkempt, doesn't strike me as someone who would follow fashion social media. In fact, when I looked him up online, I couldn't find his Instagram account at all. He's an *academic,* that's what Ashley's email had said; so, perhaps not surprising. Academics don't go in for that thing so much. In person, too, he gives off an air of sober intellect; and so I feel the need to check myself. I don't want to come off as *frivolous.*

(Maybe I'll tell him I'm reading *Anna Karenina*?)

And yet. I've learned over the years to reserve judgment about what goes on underneath the surface of other human beings. How many times have I stood and chirped giddily for the camera, flipping my hair around like I'm in front of an industrial fan and grinning like a circus emcee, when inside all I wanted to do was drink a bottle of Drano? The ability to convincingly perform *authenticity* is perhaps the most necessary skill set for my generation. And the image you exude must be *compelling,* it must be *brand-positive,* it must be *cohesive* no matter how fractured your internal dialogue might be, because otherwise your fans will sniff you out as a fraud. I gave a lecture about this at a social media conference called FreshX last year and 250 aspiring influencers (who all looked like variations of *me*) dutifully wrote it down; and as they did, I felt like I was witnessing my own doom.

Michael and Ashley are standing in front of me on the steps, looking expectant. I return to myself — to *elegant hostess* — and smile.

"Come on in," I say. "You're probably starving. I have a little snack in the kitchen, and then I'll show you to the cottage."

And I throw open the doors to Stonehaven, and welcome my guests inside.

I can tell immediately that they are taken aback by Stonehaven: the way they stop, just inside the door, and stare up to the ceiling twenty feet above us (hand-stenciled with an old family crest, as Grandmother Katherine used to point out to her visitors). The grand staircase unrolls its scarlet carpet like a feverish tongue, the crystal chandelier trembles overhead, my Liebling ancestors gaze coolly from the oil portraits that line the hall. Michael drops the suitcases on the inlaid mahogany floor with a little *thunk* and I wince at the thought of the divots this will leave in the wood.

"Your house . . ." Ashley says, emotion naked on her face. She gestures with a finger as if drawing a circle around the foyer. "You didn't mention *this* in the rental listing. Wow."

I turn and follow her gaze up the stairs, as if seeing it all for the first time. "Well. You know. I didn't want to advertise it. Might attract the wrong kind of people."

"Oh, of course. A lot of creeps and weirdos on the Internet," she says, her lips twitching up into a smile.

"I've encountered a lot of them," I say. Then, realizing — "Oh, I hope you don't think I mean you."

"Oh, we're bang-on the wrong kind of people, true enough." Michael carefully wipes his hands on his jeans, rocks back on the heels of his sneakers.

Ashley gently squeezes his arm. "Stop it, Michael. Don't scare her."

I've just noticed something else. "You're English," I say to Michael.

"Irish, actually," he replies. "But I've been in the States a long time."

"Oh, I *love* Ireland. I was in Dublin just last year." Was I? Or was that Scotland? It's all a blur, sometimes. "Where is your family from?"

He makes a funny little dismissive gesture. "Small village you wouldn't have heard of."

I lead the way through the grand foyer and into the formal parlor. Ashley's gaze flicks with disinterest across the objects we pass, as if she is unconcerned about the opulence of

187

her surroundings; but I can see something alert in her eyes. I wonder what Stonehaven looks like to her; I wonder what her own upbringing was like. Probably modest, judging by her dirty tennis shoes and her generic-brand performance fleece. Or is she one of those trustafarian types, whose bohemian appearance belies the size of their pocketbooks? She isn't *gawking,* which suggests she's comfortable with money (a relief, honestly). I can't quite put my finger on who she might be; and yet every time I glance her way she is smiling at me, which is really the most important thing.

She rests her fingertips gently atop an inlaid sideboard, some ancient monstrosity that my grandmother always said was the most valuable piece in the house. "So many antiques," she murmurs.

"I know, it's a lot, right? I just inherited the house. Sometimes it feels like living in a museum." I laugh, as if the house is just a quaint bauble that shouldn't overwhelm them.

Ashley spins to look at me. "It's *stunning.* You should feel very lucky to live with such beautiful things. What a glorious privilege." In her voice I hear a rebuke, but she's still smiling so I'm not sure what to think of the contrast between her words and her face.

I don't think *anything* in this house is beautiful. Valuable yes, but most of it is hideous. Sometimes I dream of living in a minimalist white box with floor-to-ceiling windows and nothing to dust. I try to muster up the proper enthusiasm. "Oh, it's so true! I don't even know what half of this stuff is, but I'm afraid to sit on most of it."

Michael is hanging back, studying everything with anthropological curiosity. He stops in front of an oil of one of my distant great-aunts, a grande dame in tennis whites, posed with her greyhounds. "You know what, Ash? This house reminds me a bit of the castle. This one in the painting here, she even *looks* like my great-grandmother Siobhan."

This stops me. "Which castle?"

Ashley and Michael exchange a glance. "Oh, Michael comes from old Irish aristocracy," Ashley offers. "His family used to have a castle. He hates to talk about it."

I turn to him. "Really? Where? Would I know it?"

"Not unless you have an encyclopedic knowledge of Ireland's thirty thousand castles. It's some moldering old heap in the north. My family sold it when I was a child because it cost too much to keep up."

This explains it then; the strange tug that I felt earlier, as if there was some kind of invisible cord tightening between us. *He's from even older money than me!* It's a relief to hear, as if I've been wearing a formal dress and might now shrug it off and put on cashmere sweatpants. "Well, then, you must understand what it's like to live in a place like this."

"I certainly do. A curse and a privilege, right?" He's torn the thoughts straight out of my mind. I feel light-headed. We look at each other, faint smiles of mutual understanding on our faces.

"Oh, yes, exactly," I breathe.

And then Ashley puts a hand on my arm, in that oddly intimate way. Is this what yoga teachers do? Touch a lot? It's presumptuous, but I think I like it. Her fingers are warm through the velvet of my jacket. She frowns. "Is it really that awful to live here?"

"Oh really, it's not so bad." I don't want to come off as unappreciative, not to a yoga teacher, for God's sake; not to a woman whose Facebook photo is captioned *Without inner peace, outer peace is impossible.* (I thought about cribbing this for my own Instagram feed, but what if *she* looked *me* up and saw it and knew that I stole it from her? So I used a Helen Keller quote instead.)

"And you're living all alone? You don't get lonely?" Her eyes are dark pools of sympathy; they peel away at the veneer of happiness I thought I was projecting.

"Well, a little, yes. A lot, sometimes," I say. "But hopefully not anymore now that you're here!" I laugh lightly, but this is perhaps a little too close to honesty for comfort. I need to shut myself up, but the words just keep bubbling out of me like water out of a faucet that I can't quite control.

I shouldn't have drunk that wine.

My eyes keep sliding over to Michael, each time noting another tidbit to add to the portrait I am assembling in my mind. The way his hair curls darkly around his neck, overgrown in a manner that suggests that he has more important things to think about than haircuts. The dry skin of his lips, which hover languorously in a wry curl of a smile. The soft burr of his accent, which wraps itself like a snake around the consonants that drop off his tongue. I could swear he's making a conscious effort not to look at me, and I tear my own focus back to Ashley instead.

Ashley doesn't seem to notice any of this. She runs her finger along the marble edge of a credenza. "All I can think of is the *cleaning,*" she says. "It must be a full-time job. For three people. You don't have a live-in staff? Aren't those servants' quarters that I saw out there?"

"Just a housekeeper, she comes once a week. But she doesn't clean all of it, just the rooms I'm using, for now. I'm just letting the whole third floor go, and the outbuildings — no one's lived in them for years. Half the bedrooms are shut up, too. Honestly, why bother dusting my great-great-grandfather's hunting trophies? Creepy old relics that no one wants, and I'm supposed to care for them forever just because a relative I never met once shot a bear." Am I talking too much? I think I'm talking too much, but they are gaping at me as if intrigued, so I just keep going. Stonehaven is freezing and yet I'm so hot that I can feel the sweat trickling under my arms and dripping down the sides of my T-shirt. "That kind of stuff just *has to go.* Maybe I'll just give it all away to charity!! Use it to feed hungry children!"

And then we are in the kitchen, where I have pulled out one of my mother's favorite afternoon tea services and placed it on the table by the window. It makes for a pretty tableau (in fact, I have already popped a photo of it up on Instagram: *Tea for three #tradition #soelegant*), and yet I wonder if it was overkill: the flowers, the fancy china, food enough for a small army. But we sit without ceremony, and then Ashley is laughing with pleasure as she bites into a scone, and Michael is turning my mother's teacup in his hand, studying the mark on the bottom with interest. They are handsy with each other and chatty and familiar with me, and I don't even have to think about how to keep the conversation rolling because they are doing all the work themselves.

I can feel Stonehaven filling up with life, like the wine in my cup (which Michael has slowly, carefully filled to the brim); and as I sip at it and laugh at their jokes I feel the

192

desperation ebbing away from me.

I am not alone I am not alone I am not alone anymore, I think, the words thrumming along with the pulse of my racing heart.

But then, with a clatter of luggage and a blast of cold air, they are off to get settled in at the caretaker's cottage and suddenly I *am* alone again. I have failed to make a plan with them. I should have invited them to dinner with me! I should have invited them to go hiking! A Tahoe tour, a movie night — Why did I just let them disappear off into the night, leaving me here by myself? Why didn't they invite me? (So much for my *light shining from within.*)

When they are gone, I spend three hours looking at photos of puppies on Instagram and weep.

12.

There are winners and losers in life, and not a lot of space for anything else in between. I grew up secure in the knowledge that I had been born on the right side of that equation. I was a *Liebling.* That meant that I had been conferred with certain advantages, and while there would always be those who would want to take that away from me, I started from a high enough perch that it felt there wasn't any danger of tumbling all the way down.

Right from the very beginning, right from my very inception, I was lucky, because I never should have existed. Maman had been informed by her doctor, mid-pregnancy, that she suffered from severe preeclampsia, putting both her and me at high risk of mortality. He advised my parents not to bring me to term — tossed around phrases like *hemodynamic instability* and *ethical termination.* He suggested abortion.

My mother refused. She forged ahead, through all forty weeks, and delivered me anyway. She bled so much during delivery that they thought she was a goner. When she finally came out of her coma in the ICU, the doctor told her it was the stupidest decision he'd ever seen a woman make.

"I would do it again, in a heartbeat," she used to tell me, as she swept me up in a perfumed hug. "I would do it again, because you were worth dying for."

Maman loved me that much.

My brother, Benny, was born via a surrogate three years later. So I was the only of her two children that came directly from my mother's womb, and although she insisted that this meant nothing to her — that we were both "her babies" — I could always feel that she loved me more. I was her golden girl, the child that could turn her mood from darkness to light. (*Your smile is my sunshine,* she would say.) Benny couldn't do that. He was always retreating to his bedroom, his emotional state as heavy and gray as the fog that hung over the Bay. I think Benny reminded my mother too much of the things she hated about herself, as if he somehow reflected and amplified all of her own flaws.

Maman came from an old French family; one that came to the States for the Gold Rush but had lost most of its fortune in the intervening years. It was the Lieblings who had the *real* money, riding the real estate tide that built California. My mother met my father

— the eldest of three brothers, and a man eighteen years her senior — at her own debutante ball in 1978. There's a photo of them dancing in the ballroom of the St. Francis, my father towering over my mother, his feet swallowed up by the cotton-candy swirl of her skirts. (Pale rose Zandra Rhodes: Maman always did have exquisite taste.)

There's always an implicit negotiation in marriage, right? I assume, in their case, it was his riches and power in exchange for her beauty and youth — but they also loved each other, I *know* they did. You can tell by the way they are looking at each other in that photo, the delight on my mother's face as she looks up to meet my father's intensely protective gaze. Something changed along the way, though. By the time Benny and I were in high school, they'd started living separate lives: my father in a glassed-in Financial District office, alongside the brothers and cousins that made up the Liebling Group's board; my mother in the parlor of our mansion, holding court with her socialite friends.

I grew up in San Francisco, a place where everyone knew who the Lieblings were. My family's name was in *Fortune,* we had a street named after us in the Marina District and owned one of the oldest houses in Pacific Heights (Italianate, quite stately, though not as big as Danielle Steel's). When my last name came up in conversation I could see how everything shifted. How people tilted in toward me, suddenly that much more attentive, as if hoping that some of what *I* had might rub off on *them.* Smarts mean a lot in the world, and good looks mean even more — my mother, with her closet of couture and her endless low-carb diets, had taught me that much — but money and power are, of course, the most important of all.

That was the lesson I took away from my father.

I remember visiting my father on the top floor of the Liebling Group office tower, on Market Street near the Ferry Building, when I was still small. He perched me on one knee and my brother on the other, and spun in his chair so that we were facing out the wall of windows. It was a clear, windy day, and out on the chop of the Bay the sailboats flew south toward the salty flats of the Peninsula. But my father wasn't interested in what was happening on the water. "Look at this," he said, and gently pressed our foreheads against the glass so that we could gaze straight down the side of the building. Fifty-two stories below, I could see people scurrying along the sidewalks, clots of tiny black specks, like iron filings being drawn along by an invisible magnet.

I was dizzy with vertigo. "It's a long way down," I said.

"It is." He sounded pleased to hear this.

197

"Where is everyone going?"

"The vast majority? Nowhere important. Just hamsters spinning on their wheels, never quite getting ahead. And that is the great tragedy of existence." I looked up at him, puzzled and concerned. He kissed the top of my head. "Don't worry. That will never be a problem for you, cupcake."

Benny squirmed and whined, more interested in my father's fountain pens than the life lesson that was being conveyed. I felt sorry for all those little ants down there; a faint tug of guilt that circumstance had placed them there, waiting for someone to step on them like bugs. But I also knew what our father was trying to tell us. We belonged *up here,* Benny and I; we were safe with him in the heights.

Oh, Daddy. I trusted him so much. His bulk was the bulwark that defended us all against life's vicissitudes. No matter how much Benny or I lost control — no matter what self-destructive whims I might obey (Dropping out of Princeton! Financing indie movies! Modeling!) — he was the person who reeled us back inside the gates of his protectorate before it was too late. And he always did; until suddenly, at the most critical moment, he *couldn't.*

They say DNA is destiny. And probably this is true for those with gifts coded in their genes: say, a rare beauty or intelligence, the ability to run a four-minute mile or dunk a basketball, or perhaps just an innate cunning or insatiable drive. But for the rest of the world, those born without some obvious *greatness,* it's not your DNA that will get you ahead; it's the life you were born into. The opportunities you were (or weren't) handed on a silver platter. It's your circumstances.

I am a Liebling. I inherited the very best circumstances of all.

And yet, circumstances can change. The natural trajectory of your life can be utterly disrupted by one unexpected encounter, setting you so wildly off course that you're not quite sure if you'll ever find your way back to the path you were on.

For me, it's been twelve years, and I'm *still* trying to find my way back.

Growing up, I knew what was expected of me. Private school and debate club and tennis team, boyfriends whose last names graced buildings in downtown San Francisco, grades that were good enough (but — let's be frank — boosted *just a tad* by Daddy's generous donations to my schools). It's true that I struggled occasionally with what my parents called "impulse control" — like the time I borrowed Maman's Maserati, got drunk, and crashed it, or the time I threw my tennis racket at an unfair judge at the junior nationals. Still, for the most part, I knew how to play my role and hit those benchmarks. Nothing I did couldn't be fixed with a dimple, a smile, and a check.

My brother was the one who was irreparable. By the time I was in high school, it had grown clear that Benny was — as Maman delicately put it — "troubled." When he was eleven, my mother found a notebook hidden under his bed with elaborately drawn pictures of men being disemboweled by dragons and their faces melting off, so she sent him off to a psychiatrist. He flunked all his classes, scribbled on his locker, was bullied by his schoolmates. At twelve, they put him on ADHD medication, then antidepressants. At fifteen, he got kicked out of school for giving his meds to his classmates.

I was in my senior year of high school then, a month away from graduation, already sleeping in a Princeton T-shirt. (Legacy, *bien sûr.*) The night that Benny got expelled for passing out his Ritalin at school, I could hear my parents shrieking at each other in the music room downstairs — a room they sometimes picked for their fights because it was supposedly soundproofed, without realizing that their voices actually carried through the mansion's heating ducts. Lately, they'd been shrieking a lot.

"Maybe if you were ever *here* he wouldn't

feel the need to do stupid, reckless things in order to get your attention. . . ."

"Maybe if you weren't such a mess yourself you would have noticed that something was wrong with him before it got to this point."

"Don't you dare make this about me!"

"Of course it's about you. He's just like you, Judith. How do you expect him to get his shit together when you refuse to do it your-self?"

"Oh that's rich, coming from you. . . . You don't even want me to start on your shit! Your addictions are going to destroy us all. Women and cards and who knows what else you're hiding from me."

"For fuck's sake, Judith, you've got to stop letting your imagination get away from you. How many times do I have to tell you that it's all in your head? You are *paranoid,* it's part of your illness."

I crept down the hall and knocked on Benny's door and didn't wait for him to answer before I slipped inside. He was lying on the floor in the exact center of the area rug, arms and legs spread-eagled so that he looked like a pale, scrawny version of da

Vinci's Vitruvian Man. My brother hadn't slipped comfortably into adolescence; it was as if his growing body had outstripped the child that he still was, and left him rattling loose inside this strange, oversized vessel. He lay there, staring blankly at the ceiling.

I sat down on the rug next to him and tugged my skirt over my knees.

"I don't get it, Benny. You had to know that was against school rules. What did you have to gain from it?"

Benny shrugged. "Kids are nicer to me if I give them drugs."

"You know, there are other ways to make people like you, stupid. Like, maybe make an effort sometimes? Join the chess club. Spend your lunchtime actually talking to people instead of sitting in a corner drawing creepy pictures in your notebook."

"Well, it's a non-issue now."

"Oh, please. Dad will offer to build the school a new auditorium or something and everything will be forgiven."

"No." It alarmed me, how limp and motionless he was on the rug, how affectless his voice was. "Dad wants us to move to Tahoe. They're going to send me to school up there. Some progressive academy that's going to turn me into Paul Bunyan or something."

"Tahoe? How ghastly." I thought of that huge, cold house on the West Shore of the lake, cut off from everything I considered

202

civilization, and I wondered what leverage my father had over my mother to convince her to move there. Since my father had inherited the house the previous year, we'd been up only once, to go skiing over spring break. Maman spent most of our stay wandering around the rooms, gingerly touching the spindly old furniture with a pinched expression on her face. I knew exactly what she was thinking.

Benny's arms and legs swept slowly up and down the nap of the rug, like he was making a snow angel. "Not really. I hate it here anyway. Can't be any worse up there. Probably better. The kids at our school are so full of themselves."

I watched my brother scratching at the crop of pimples that had recently erupted, red and angry, on his chin. They matched the color of his hair, which made them even more obvious. My oblivious brother didn't realize how much harder he was making life for himself; he seemed determined to shrug off all the advantages that came with being *us.* Back then I still believed that Benny's issues were mostly of his own design, like he could just choose to stop sitting in his room drawing cartoons and acting weird, and then everything would be OK. I didn't understand yet.

"You don't give anyone a chance," I said. "And stop scratching your pimples or you'll get scars."

He gave me the middle finger. "Anyway you're going to be off at college, so stop acting like you give a shit where we live."

I ran my own hand across the nap of his rug. It was thick blue pile that the decorator had put in to disguise the ink stains from Benny's abandoned Sharpies. "Maman's going to go crazy up there."

He sat up suddenly and looked at me fiercely. "Mom's already crazy. Didn't you know that?"

"She's not crazy, she's just moody," I said quickly. And yet, there *was* a whisper at the back of my mind, an awareness that her moods went beyond your average midlife ennui. Benny and I never really discussed our mother's swings but I saw him watching her sometimes, as if her face were a weather vane and he was using it to predict the coming storms. I did the same thing, awaiting the moment when the switch inside her would flip from *on* to *off.* One day she'd be picking me up at school in the town car, her eyes lit with excitement, calling through the window. *I made appointments for facials* or *Let's go to Neiman's* or, if she was feeling really heated, *I'm dying for some decent French, we're going to take the plane to New York for dinner.* And then, the next day, her rooms would go silent. I'd arrive home from tennis practice or a study session to an ominous stillness in the house, and would find her lying in bed, with

204

the drapes drawn shut. "I have a migraine," she'd whisper, but I knew that the medications she took weren't for headaches at all.

"Maybe Tahoe won't be so bad," Benny said hopefully. "Maybe it'll be good for Mom. Like . . . a spa retreat or something. She loves those."

I imagined Benny and Maman rattling aimlessly around Stonehaven, trapped inside those stone walls, and it sounded like the exact opposite of a spa retreat. "No, you're right," I lied. "It'll probably be good for her." Sometimes you have to pretend that a bad idea is a good idea because you have no control over the outcome, and all you can do is hope that adding your false optimism to the pile might tip the scale in the right direction after all.

"She loves to ski," Benny offered.

"So do you. And you're better at it than I am."

Even though Benny had turned into this strange creature, oozy and crusty and fuzzy, his room smelling like spunk despite the housekeeper's best efforts, I couldn't look at him without thinking *baby brother.* Without thinking of the way he used to climb into my bed as a toddler and make me read him picture books, his soft little body pressing warm and needy against mine. Our parents loved us both but they loved me a tiny bit more because I was easier to love, and some part of me felt guilty about that; like, it was my job to make up for what he was missing.

So I adored him unconditionally, my little brother. I still do. Sometimes, I think it's the best thing about me. Certainly, it's the only thing that doesn't feel *hard.*

That day, I reached out and placed a hand on the back of Benny's neck, wondering if he still gave off superhuman heat, the way he had as a child. But he twitched at the sensation, and my hand slid off.

"Not anymore," he said.

And so I went off to Princeton, pretending that my family's move to Lake Tahoe wasn't the end of the world.

Of course, it was. Wealth is a Band-Aid, not an inoculation; and if the disease runs deep enough, it will cure nothing at all.

I threw myself into life at Princeton — social clubs, academics, parties. I fit right in, at least when it came to the social milieu (the classwork was a different story). I spoke to my mother weekly, and my brother occasionally, and nothing they said seemed alarming. Mostly, they sounded bored. I flew in for Christmas at Stonehaven — the formidable annual gathering of cousins and great-uncles and family friends with Fortune 500 surnames — and found everyone in a festive mood. We skied. We ate. We opened gifts. Everything felt normal enough; even Stone-

206

haven seemed more welcoming than it did in my childhood memories, jammed with relatives, the kitchen ejecting a steady stream of baked goods and hot drinks. I flew back out again, reassured.

Then it was March. I had just gotten home from a dorm party late one night when my phone rang. I almost didn't recognize my brother's voice: It had dropped an octave since we last spoke, and it sounded like a man's, as if he had become a completely different person in the space of a few months.

"Doofus, it's one in the morning," I said. "Time zones, remember?"

"You're awake, aren't you?"

I lay back on my bed and examined the tiny chips in my manicure. "What if I wasn't? What's worth waking me up for?" But inside, I already knew.

Benny hesitated, dropped his voice to a whisper. "Mom's doing that thing where she doesn't want to get out of bed anymore. Like, as far as I can tell she hasn't left the house in a week," he said. "Should I do something?"

What was there to do? Her moods changed, they had always changed, but they had never broken her entirely; she always came back. "Talk to Dad?" I offered.

"He's never here. Only on the weekends, if he makes it up here at all."

I cringed. "Look, I'll deal with it."

"Really? Awesome. You're the best." I could

almost feel his relief flooding the line.

But it was midterms and I was desperately behind in my classes so I didn't have the bandwidth to properly address the drama back home; the thought of my mother's storm cycles, endlessly repeating themselves, exhausted me. So "dealing with it" meant giving my mom a call, a half-hearted test probe: *I'm going to ask if you are doing OK and please give me the answer I want to hear.*

And she did. "Oh, honestly, I'm fine." She snipped off her syllables with neat, patrician bites; I heard my own voice mirrored in hers, the lack of *California* in our accents. (No valley drawl in my family; no surfer slang for us!) "It's just a little tiring, all this snow. I'd forgotten how much *hassle* it is."

"What are you doing with yourself? Are you bored?"

"Bored?" There was a slight intake of breath on the other end of the line, a hiss of annoyance. "Not at all. I'm working on ideas for redecorating this place. Your grandmother had such *awful* taste, so baroque and kitsch. I'm thinking of flying out an appraiser and putting some of it up for auction. Selecting some pieces that are more appropriate to the period of the estate."

It should have been reassuring, but I could hear it in my mother's voice, the stutter of exhaustion, the effort it was taking her to sound lively and alert. A miasma hung around her, of thick inertia. And by the time I came home for spring break a month later, she'd slipped into the next phase in the cycle: the hyperactive one. I felt it in the air the minute I stepped inside Stonehaven: the cool crackle of tension, the brittle edge to my mother's movements as she passed from one room to the next. My first night in town, the four of us sat around the formal dining table for dinner and my mother chattered away at high speed about her redecorating plans while my father tuned her out completely, like she was a static channel on the TV. Before dessert was even served, he'd pulled his phone out of his pocket, frowned at a message, and excused himself from the table. In a minute, the headlights from his Jaguar illuminated Maman's face through the window, as he headed down the drive. Her eyes were dilated and unseeing.

My brother and I gave each other meaningful looks across the table. *Here we go again.*

The next morning, Benny and I escaped Stonehaven with the excuse that we were going to get coffee in town. As we stood in line at a café, I kept sneaking glances at my brother. He held himself with a strange new confidence, his shoulders straighter, as if for once he wasn't trying to disappear. It appeared that he had finally learned to wash his face, and his acne was clearing. He looked *good,* and yet there was something distracted

209

and aimless about him that I couldn't quite put a finger on.

I was jet-lagged and distracted myself, which is probably why I didn't pay much attention to the girl that Benny was talking to at the café. She had materialized in line in front of us, an unremarkable teenager in ill-fitting clothes that failed to disguise her heaviness, and thick black makeup that masked whatever natural prettiness lurked underneath. Her hair was pink, a home dye job; I had to look away to avoid staring at the mess she'd made of herself. Her mother, hovering nearby, was her physical opposite: blond, overtly sexy, and trying too hard. *Benny's poor friend needs a makeover and some self-esteem, and clearly her mom isn't the one to give it to her,* I thought idly, and then my phone began to vibrate with messages from friends back East. So it wasn't until they'd already left that I glanced at my brother and noticed the expression on his face.

He took a sip of his coffee, then dropped the cup back on the saucer. "What?" He stared back at me.

"That girl — What was her name? You *like* her."

He flushed. "Who said that?"

I pointed at the top of his shirt, where red splotches marched upward from his chest to start their onslaught of his face. "You're

210

blushing."

He put a hand on his neck, as if this might conceal the pink. "It's not like that with us."

The café's windows were fogged with steam. I peered out to see if I could catch a better look at the mystery girl, but she and her mother had already disappeared around the corner. "So how is it, then?"

"I dunno." He smiled to himself, and slid down in his chair so that his legs stuck out into the aisle, blocking the path of everyone walking by. "She's smart and she doesn't take shit from anyone. And she makes me laugh. She's not like other people. She doesn't care who our family is."

I laughed. "That's what you think. Everyone has an opinion about our family. Some people are just better at hiding it."

He scowled at me. "And you like that, don't you, Vanessa? You like people paying attention to you because you're rich and pretty and your family is supposedly *important,* don't you? Honestly, though, don't you ever want people to look at you and just see a person, instead of a *Liebling*?"

I knew the correct answer was *Yes, of course.* But the truth was that I didn't. I *liked* hiding behind the name Liebling. Because honestly, what would people see if they did look past it? A girl of no particular ability, no particular brilliance, no particular beauty; someone fun to have at the party but not

211

someone *meaningful.* A person skating on top of the successes of the people who had come before her. I knew that about myself: I knew I didn't have something powerful inside me, something compelling me toward greatness. I had only *good enough.*

(Oh, you're surprised by this little streak of self-awareness? Just because I'm rich and pretty and Internet-famous doesn't mean that I haven't spent my time loathing myself. More on this later.)

What I did have: a name that meant that this didn't matter, in the grand scheme of things. I could earn a 3.4 GPA and *still* get into Princeton, because of my family. So yes, I *liked* being a Liebling. (Wouldn't you?) The only person in the world whose impression of me wasn't ever going to be the least bit impacted by my last name was the person sitting next to me, the person who shared that name. Benny.

"Whatever, doofus. If you think she's so great, maybe you should ask her out." I put down my cappuccino and leaned in. "Seriously. If you like her, make a move. She wouldn't be hanging out with you all the time if she didn't like you, too."

"But Mom says —"

"To hell with them. What do they have to do with it? Please. Just . . . kiss her if you like her. I guarantee she'll be into it." What I didn't say: *Of course she'll be into it, she'll be kissing a millionaire! Even if she pretends that's not an aphrodisiac, I promise you it's got an appeal that she is not immune to.*

He squirmed a little. "It's not that easy."

"It *is* that easy. Look — have a drink first, sometimes that helps. Liquid courage."

"No, I mean, it's not so easy because I'm grounded. As of two days ago. Mom and Dad said I'm not allowed to see her anymore."

"Wait, why?"

He spun the empty cup in the saucer and it splattered dregs of coffee across the chipped café table. "They found my pot stash and blamed it on her. They think she's a bad influence."

"And? Is she?" I reconsidered the girl's black clothes, heavy makeup, the pink hair. It was true she didn't exactly give off that *wholesome-Tahoe-mountain-girl* vibe.

"They don't know her at all." When he looked at me his eyes were strangely luminous, his pupils huge, like he might be able to see things that I couldn't. I remembered his frailty then — that he could be easily broken, just like our mother. My brother was teetering on a knife's edge; all it would take was a push in the wrong direction and he could end up tumbling off.

But I thought I knew the right direction! Oh, I was so *proud* of myself. A girlfriend, an *amour fou*! That would normalize him in a way that my parents' overprotectiveness would not. *Look at me,* I thought. *Giving my brother real advice, something that might actually help him function in the real world and get out of his messed-up head.* I thought I could help him in a way that our well-intended but clueless parents could not. I thought I knew how the world worked for kids like us.

I was so *very* wrong.

Benny ended up taking my advice and kissed his little friend. He kissed her and then, apparently, he fucked her. Good for Benny, right? Except that our father caught him in the act and my parents both completely lost their minds. And my brother was shipped off to a summer camp in Italy, from which he sent me morose postcards: *Who knew Italy could feel like prison?* And: *I swear I'm never talking to Mom and Dad again.* And then, as the summer progressed, longer letters that were more disturbing. *Do you ever hear voices talking to you when you're lying in the dark and trying to fall asleep? Because I'm wondering if I'm going crazy or if it's just some kind of coping mechanism because I am so fucking lonely here.* And then, toward the end of summer, a letter on thin blue paper that was written entirely in Italian. I do not speak Italian. I wasn't even sure it was Benny who had written it because the handwriting was so cramped and strange, except that it was his signature at the bottom.

I was pretty sure he didn't speak Italian, either.

I was back in San Francisco at the time, for my first summer break. I had assumed that Maman would also be there with me, but she vanished not long after I arrived, off to a spa in Malibu where they hiked five hours a day and ate only liquefied vegetables and did colonics instead of facials. She was supposed to stay for two weeks but she ended up staying for six. When she came back home, just two days before I was heading back to Princeton, she was as thin as death, her eyes popping from her tanned skull. "I feel absolutely *amazing,* like all the filth from living was just *sucked* out of me, like I've been *purified,*" she gushed, but I could see how jittery her hands were as she pressed carrots into her fancy new juicer.

I found Daddy in the library, poring over earnings statements. "I think Mom needs medication."

He gazed at me for a long minute. "She takes Xanax."

"Yeah, I don't think that's helping, Dad. I don't think the spa retreats are healthy for her, either. She needs real professionals."

He looked down at the papers in front of him. "Your mom will be OK. She gets like this sometimes, and then she bounces back. You know that by now. Telling her she needs

215

a therapist will just upset her more."

"Dad, have you looked at her? She's *skeletal*. And not in a good way."

My father pushed aside the top paper with the tip of his finger in order to glance at the file underneath. I'd read online that my father's position at the Liebling Group was tenuous; that my uncle — his younger brother — had just attempted a boardroom coup. The stress was visible in the pouches under my father's eyes and the furrow bisecting his brow. But he sat back in his chair, as if he'd settled something. "Look. We're going back up to Stonehaven next week, after your brother gets back from camp. Lourdes is an excellent cook, she'll make sure your mother is eating. It's good for her to be up there. Quiet and calm."

I hesitated, wondering if I should bring up Benny's alarming letters. What would my parents do, put him on yet more drugs, or — worse — send him off to some reform school? Maybe he *did* need help, but it also struck me that Benny had been through enough already — isolated in Stonehaven, shipped off to Italy, his friends monitored by Maman. Maybe he just needed to be left alone, to feel *loved* for once. I stood there before my father, undecided; but before I could say anything my father rose from his chair. He reached across the space between us and wrapped me in a rare hug, folding me into his chest. He

216

smelled like starch and lemons, a whisper of whiskey on his breath.

"You're a good daughter," he said. "Always looking out for our family. You make us proud. And it's a relief to know that we don't have to worry about you." He laughed. "God knows we have enough to worry about with your brother."

I could have said something about the letters then. I didn't. Because in that moment it felt like the biggest betrayal to my brother would be to set myself up in opposition to him. The easy child and the difficult child. I couldn't do that to him again.

So back to Princeton I went, and that was the last I ever saw of my mother. Eight weeks later, she would be dead.

My mother died on the last Tuesday of October. I still hate myself for letting the weeks before her death slide by; for failing to note the fact that she wasn't calling me to check in. But I had a new, all-consuming boyfriend; and then I dumped him; and then there was another; and then my grades were tanking (again) because of the boys; and then I needed a distraction from all *that* so I organized a weekend trip to the Bahamas. When I returned, tanned and just a little spun out, it finally occurred to me that my mother was MIA. Even then, it still took me a few days to rally myself to pick up the phone, as if I was afraid what might be waiting for me on the other end of the line.

Her voice, when she finally answered the phone, sounded like a cloudy day, flat and affectless and gray. "Your father has been having an affair." She was as matter-of-fact as if she was informing me of the outcome of an opera board meeting.

Downstairs in my dorm, a party was going on, Eminem blasting so loud that the floor under my feet was vibrating. I wasn't sure I'd heard her correctly. "Daddy? Are you sure? How do you know?"

"There was a letter. . . ." She swallowed the end of the sentence, mumbled something I couldn't hear.

Girls were shrieking with laughter down the hall. I covered the phone with my palm and screamed out the door, *"Shut up shut up SHUT UP!"* There was a sudden, resounding silence, and then I could hear them giggle. *Vanessa Liebling has lost her shit.* I didn't care.

An *affair.* But of course: *That's* why he'd been spending his weekdays in San Francisco, instead of at Stonehaven with his family. Maybe that's even why he'd moved them to Stonehaven in the first place — to keep them separate from his mistress. Poor Maman. No wonder she'd been such a wreck for so long.

I wasn't shocked, though; *of course* I wasn't. My father was hideously ugly, objectively speaking; but that wasn't what mattered to some women. Power is its own aphrodisiac. And the lure of taking what already belongs to someone else — even *more* powerful. Most of my mother's friends had already gone through a society divorce, their husbands now married to much younger women (*gold-diggers/trophy wives/ tacky whores*) while they resettled themselves in Four Seasons penthouses with generous divorce settlements.

So of course Daddy had affairs; it was an inevitability.

"Is Daddy there right now?" I asked.

She laughed, and it was a terrible sound, like stones rattling inside an empty box. "Your father is *never here,* darling. He sent us up here to rot, your brother and me, up in this awful house where we can't embarrass him anymore. Like, what's that novel? *Jane Eyre.* We're the mad relatives he's shut up in the attic. He thinks *my* family is the one with the bad genes but let's talk about his —"

I cut her off. "Is he in San Francisco?"

"I think he's in Florida," she said, sounding uninterested. "Or maybe Japan."

Now it was Snoop Dogg on the stereo downstairs, singing in his nasal, soporific drawl. "Maman, can I talk to Benny?"

"Oh, I don't think that's a good idea."

"What do you mean?"

219

"Benny's not himself."

"Not himself *how*?"

"Well." A pause. "To start he says he's vegan now. He says he won't eat anything with a face. Apparently he's conversing with the meat on his plate."

I thought of his letters. *Oh God, everything is going to hell out there.* "I'm going to come home, OK?"

"No," she said darkly. "You stay there and focus on your studies."

I wanted to reach through the phone and wrap my arms around her until she sounded like herself again. "Maman —"

"Vanessa. I don't want you here." Her voice was chilly.

"But, Maman —"

"I love you, darling. Now, I've got to go." She hung up.

Sitting in my dorm room, listening to the revelry all around me, I wept. I'd been excommunicated. My mother had always wanted me; I was *all* she wanted. How could she shut me down like that? How could she take away my home?

In retrospect, I can see what she was doing: She wanted to wound me in order to keep me away. Because she must have already known then, what her plan was: How she was going to untie our yacht, the *Judybird,* from the dock and drive it toward the exact center of the lake the following morning right after

220

Benny had gone to school. How she would drop anchor and then put on her silk bathrobe with the enormous pockets, pockets that she would weigh down with a half-dozen first-edition law books that she took from the library. How she would jump off the boat into the chilly, choppy water, and drown there.

She didn't want me there for all that. Even in the end, she wanted to protect me.

I should have seen it then. I should have realized *when it mattered* what she was trying to do. Instead of doing what I did — calling my father at his office in San Francisco (he was doing business in Tokyo, his assistant told me) and leaving messages for Benny (also unanswered) — I should have booked a flight home right away. As it was, it took me far too long to finally work myself up into a panic and get on an airplane to Reno. By the time the town car deposited me at Stonehaven, my mother had been missing for almost a day.

They found the *Judybird* floating in the center of the lake, a few hours after I arrived in town. My mother's robe was tangled in the rudder. She hadn't made it to the bottom at all, but had drowned within arm's reach of the surface, one strong kick away from life.

So, *now* do you feel sorry for me after all? Not that I'm pandering for your sympathy (OK, maybe I am, just a little; isn't *any* shared story just a cry to be understood?), but if nothing else makes me human, I think a dead mother certainly will. In the end, we are all our mothers' children, no matter how saintly or evil they might be; and the loss of their love is the earthquake that cracks your foundation forever. It's permanent damage.

And then, amplifying *that:* suicide. Yes, yes, of course, it's part of a *disease,* but still, a mother's suicide leaves you with a whisper of self-doubt that will never, ever go away. It leaves you with questions whose answers will never be satisfying.

Was I not worth living for? What's wrong with me that my love wasn't enough for you? Why didn't I know the thing to say that would have made you want to live again? Why didn't I get to you sooner, and talk you out of it? Was I in any way responsible for what you did?

Twelve years on, and I still wake up in the middle of the night, panicked, with these questions echoing through my mind. Twelve years on, and I'm still terrified that her death was somehow all my fault.

Maybe I should have confronted my father about his affair, but in the months after my mother's death, he was so despondent that I couldn't bring myself to ask. And besides, there were other, more pressing issues: the fragile state of Benny, for example, who could barely be dragged out of the house now, and refused to go to North Lake Academy entirely. (Sometimes when I lurked outside his door I could hear him holding low conversations with someone who wasn't there.) Someone had to decide what to do with the *Judybird,* which was now dry-docked in the boathouse, a hideous reminder. Someone needed to pack up Stonehaven, where no one now wanted to be, and move us back to our Pacific Heights house. This also meant that someone needed to find a new school for Benny, one that would overlook his precarious psychological state.

I was in no shape to do any of that. It felt like I'd been driving on high speed and suddenly I'd crashed and come to a complete stop. Some mornings I woke up and looked out at the lake and thought of my mother jumping over the edge of the *Judybird* and felt the same dark tug.

My father's brother and sister-in-law arrived, with toddlers and nannies in tow, to help address the mess left in my mother's wake; and my mother's personal secretary was assigned to the crisis; but even then I couldn't make myself go back to school. I took the rest of the semester off from Princeton and spent my afternoons sitting in the study with Benny, blinds drawn, watching *West Wing* reruns in silence. Eventually, a friend of my mother's located a boarding school in Southern California that specialized in "equine therapy," as if all Benny needed was a vigorous horseback ride to shake off both his grief and his incipient madness. It seemed as good an idea as any.

We left Stonehaven in early January. On our last night there, Lourdes cooked lasagna. My father, Benny, and I sat and ate in the formal dining room, with the crystal and the silver, our first proper meal as a family since my mother's death. Lourdes cried as she served us.

My father cut his lasagna into perfect squares and forked them one by one into his mouth, as if eating was a chore that had to be endured. The skin under his eyes sagged like deflating balloons; dry red crescents framed the side of his nose, chapped from blowing.

Benny glowered at my father across the table, not touching his meal. And then: "You killed Mom," he blurted.

My father's fork stopped in midair, cheese strings dangling from the tines. "You don't mean that."

"Oh, I do," Benny said. "That's what you do. You destroy people's lives. You destroyed mine, and then you destroyed Mom's. Your business, everything you do, is about leeching the life out of other people."

"You don't know what you're talking about," my father said quietly to the lasagna.

"You were having an affair," Benny said. He pushed his plate away from him and it knocked over his water glass. Liquid slowly spread across the table toward our father's plate. "Mom killed herself because you cheated on her."

My father reached out with his napkin and carefully lay it across the puddle of water. "No, your mother killed herself because she was ill."

"You made her ill. This place *made* her ill." Benny stood. He threw a long spindly arm out and swiped it through the air, as if trying to chop Stonehaven in half. "I swear to God, if you ever drag me back here after tomorrow, I'm going to burn this fucking place to the ground."

"Benjamin, sit down." But Benny was already gone; we could hear him galloping heavily across the wooden floors, before he was swallowed up by the depths of the house. My father picked up his fork again and carefully tucked a piece of lasagna into his mouth. He swallowed like it hurt, and then looked across the table at me. There was a grim satisfaction in his expression, as if he'd been waiting for weeks (*years!*) for someone to hit him, and the blow had finally come. Now he was relieved it was over and he could move on.

"It will help your brother to not be here, I think. This place reminds him too much of

225

your mother."

I swallowed against the thick lump in my throat. Then, after a minute, I asked the question I had been afraid to ask for months: "The other woman — Are you still with her?"

"God, no! She meant nothing." He weighed the silver fork in his hand. "Look. I was not always a good husband to your mother, I know. We had our issues, just like any married couple. But you need to believe me that I did my best to protect her. I knew she was . . . fragile. I did what I thought was best for her." He pointed the fork at me. "Just like I try to do what's best for you and your brother."

I could see my father studying my face, trying to measure how much anger I was harboring against him. And maybe I was angry (*I was! I was so angry*), but I'd already lost one parent. I couldn't bear to lose two. It was easier to direct my fury toward the faceless mistress, the opportunistic *bitch* in her San Francisco flat who tried (and succeeded!) to tear our family apart.

"I know, Daddy," I said. I stabbed at my lasagna, splattering marinara sauce across the white china, imagining his mistress's guts splashed across my plate.

He watched me eviscerate my lasagna for a moment, alarm in his face. Then he put his own fork down on the plate and aligned it with the edge of his knife. "We have to keep up appearances, cupcake. We're Lieblings. No one gets to see what's in our basement and no one ever should; there are wolves out there, waiting to drag us down at the first sign of weakness. You can never, *ever* let people see the moments when you're not feeling strong. So you'll go back to your life and smile and be your charming self, and move forward from this." He looked up at me, and for the first time since my mother's suicide, there were tears in his eyes. "But no matter what, you should know that I love you. More than anything."

We left Stonehaven the following morning, leaving behind rooms cloaked in dustcloths, the windows shuttered tightly against the elements. A fortune of gleaming antiques and priceless artwork, a veritable museum that would be locked up and left in limbo for the next decade. I'm not sure why my father never sold Stonehaven — maybe out of some deference to Lieblings past, a sense of duty to the unbroken chain of our ancestry — but he didn't. And none of us ever went up there again, not until the day I showed up last spring with a moving truck in tow.

My mother's death broke something essential in the rest of us, and the next few years unspooled with one crisis after another. I returned to Princeton and promptly flunked a half-dozen classes; I was put on academic probation and forced to repeat my sophomore year. Meanwhile, back in San Francisco, the Liebling Group was contending with the market crash. As the value of its real estate holdings plummeted, my father was ousted as chairman of the board in favor of his younger brother.

But it was Benny who was in the worst shape of all. *Poor Benny.* He had squeaked by at boarding school (maybe the horses *did* help) but by the time he arrived at Princeton, his disease had started to take over his mind. I would spy him on campus sometimes, wearing head-to-toe black, flying through the crowds of students like a disoriented crow. He had finally reached his full height of six-six, but he bent himself almost in half as he scurried, as though this might make him invisible. I heard through the grapevine that he was doing a lot of drugs, hard stuff: meth and cocaine.

Just a few months into his fall semester, Benny's roommate moved out abruptly. When I went to visit the room myself I understood why: Benny had covered his side with disturbing pen-and-ink drawings, mazes of black scribbles that suggested an ominous tunnel, with the eyes of monsters hidden in the shadows. They papered the wall from floor to ceiling, Benny's nightmares come to life.

I stood looking at these, fear knocking dully in my chest. "Maybe keep these in your notebook next time?" I suggested. "Try not to creep out the new roommate?"

Benny's eyes flew back and forth across the images, as if they were a puzzle he was still trying to solve. "He couldn't hear them," he said.

"Hear *what*?"

His eyes drooped at the corners; purple bruises darkened the patches of freckles under his eyes. Disappointment colored his face. "You don't, either, do you?"

"Benny, you need to see the school therapist."

But Benny was already back at his desk, with a fresh pen and paper in his hand. I could see deep black scratches in the surface of the desk, where he'd scribbled so hard that it went all the way through the paper. When I let myself out of the room I stood out in the hallway for a long time, panicked, on the verge of tears. Normal kids crossed back and forth in the hall before me, on their way to football games and concerts; they skirted past Benny's room, as if the very door itself were infectious. It broke my heart.

I called the campus medical center and asked to speak to a doctor. Instead, I got a harried-sounding nurse. "Unless he does something to harm himself, or threatens another student, there's not much we can do," she told me. "He has to come to us of his own volition."

Two weeks later, the campus police were called to Benny's dorm in the middle of the night. He'd walked into the room of a girl who lived down the hall from him and climbed into bed with her in the dark. He wrapped his arms around her, as if she was a teddy bear, then cried and begged her to protect him against some *thing* that was coming to get him. She woke up screaming. He ran off into the night. When the authorities finally found him, he was naked and raving in the bushes outside the library.

The psychiatric ward at the hospital diagnosed Benny with schizophrenia. My father flew in on his plane and retrieved him to take him back home to the Bay Area. I cried when they left me behind in New Jersey, but before he boarded the plane my father pulled me in close and hugged me. He breathed in my ear, so that my brother couldn't hear. "You need to keep it together now, cupcake."

I didn't.

Did I mention before that I dropped out of Princeton? Not my finest moment. But I was on the verge of failing anyway, and there was an engineering student I'd met who was starting up a dot-com that needed financing. I had that trust fund just *sitting* there so I thought, *I'll be an investor! An entrepreneur! Who needs college anyway?* Daddy would forgive me for dropping out when I proved my business acumen, I figured; he'd be *so proud* when I made my first million on my own.

Anyway. It didn't end well, but that's a different story.

That year was the beginning of my brother's long decade of recovery and relapse: manic wanderings through the streets of San Francisco that would end in back-alley methamphetamine binges; months of seeming normalcy punctuated by suicide attempts. A phalanx of psychologists calibrated and recalibrated his drugs, failing to get the balance right; often, he'd refuse to take them altogether because they made him feel dull and drowsy. Finally, my father committed him to a luxury residential psychiatric care facility in Mendocino County: the Orson Institute.

By that point I'd given up on the dot-com and moved to New York City, but I would visit Benny at Orson whenever I came back to California. The facility was outside Ukiah, a woodsy area in the Mendocino coastal range full of meditation retreats and clothing-optional resorts where aging hippies lounged in mineral-crusted hot springs. The Orson Institute was a pleasant enough place, a big modern facility with rolling lawns and views over the hills. There were only a few dozen patients, who spent their days doing art therapy, tending to an impressive vegetable

231

garden, and eating gourmet meals cooked by Michelin chefs. This was where families like ours stashed problem relatives — anorexic wives, grandfathers with dementia, children who liked to set things on fire. Benny fit right in.

The medication they gave Benny made him spacey and soft. His belly protruded over the elastic of his sweatpants now. His primary daily occupation was wandering the property in search of insects that he would capture in plastic baby food jars. His suite was decorated with drawings of spindle-legged spiders and shiny centipedes, but at least the monsters that he doodled were real now, and they didn't talk back to him. Even though it broke my heart to see him so defanged, I knew that at least here he was safe.

I sometimes wondered what had misfired in Benny's brain, and how much of his illness he had inherited from our mother. Was her faulty wiring the same as his? As we took walks around the Orson Institute grounds I would watch my brother aimlessly ambling, purposeless, going nowhere, and experience a pang of guilt: Why him and not me?

(And then, accompanying this, a dull twinge at the back of my brain, a nagging question: What if it *was* me, too, and I just didn't know it yet?)

Driving away, though, what I usually felt was simple rage. I knew — I know it now —

that schizophrenia is a disease, written into the brain from birth. But there had to be some alternate version of Benny's life where none of this happened; where he was a normal kid, maybe with some mood swings (like me!), but at least able to function in the world. Surely the trajectory of his life was not supposed to be *this,* just as my mother's suicide should never have occurred.

I called Benny's doctor at the Orson Institute, and posed my question to him. *Why Benny? Why now?*

"Schizophrenia is genetic, though there can also be exacerbating external factors, too," he said.

"Like what?" I asked.

I could hear him shuffling papers in the background. "Well, your brother was quite a drug user. And drug usage doesn't *cause* schizophrenia, per se, but it can trigger symptoms in people who are susceptible." Hearing this, the timeline started to snap into place: Benny's first psychotic episodes coincided with the period at Tahoe when he started doing drugs. The bad news girlfriend — what was her name? *Nina.* My mom had been right, after all. I'd given him terrible advice that day: I should have warned him away from her instead of encouraging him. (*Amour fou,* crazy love — Jesus, what had I been thinking?)

Oh God, maybe it was even *my fault* he'd

ended up so ill. After all, I was also the one who didn't flag Benny's behavior to my parents sooner, who didn't tell my father about the Italian letters or drive Benny to the Princeton therapist myself. My fear of hurting Benny had just let him hurt himself.

Sometimes, as I flew back across the country from the Orson Institute, I would imagine an alternate life for us. A life in which my parents had stayed in San Francisco, and my brother had found some kind of therapeutic school before it was too late, and my father hadn't had an affair. A life in which the isolation of Stonehaven hadn't hurtled both my mother and brother over a cliff that they never managed to climb back up. Maybe it was possible that all *this* — the schizophrenia, the suicide — could have been avoided (or at least mitigated!). Maybe my mother would still be alive and my brother's issues would be manageable and my father would be stable and we would all be *just fine*. Happy, even!

An optimistic fantasy, of course, but one that grew in power as the years ground on: the lost possibility of an alternate universe, one that spun correctly on its axis, one that hadn't been knocked off kilter by forces I couldn't quite comprehend.

13.

Modern culture loves to fetishize risk, as if the norm for *everyone* should be deviating from the norm. (Saith Oprah, patron saint of inspo quotes: *One of life's greatest risks is never daring to risk.*) Spend enough time with any bestselling biography and you'll come to the conclusion that greatness is practically guaranteed if you just do something reckless and wild. But what most people don't like to dwell on is that risk is really only an option if you've had some luck first.

For a while, I had all the luck I needed. One of the greatest luxuries of growing up with money is that you have the freedom to be impulsive: If you fail, there's always that trust fund there to cushion your fall. So I took a lot of *risks* in the first few years after I dropped out of Princeton. Unfortunately, none of them took me particularly close to greatness — not my attempt at film financing (two flops, lost $10 million), not the handbag line I designed (out of business within a year), not the tequila brand that I backed (partner went rogue with the money). Only bankruptcy.

By the time I met Saskia Rubansky at a gala in Tribeca — a benefit for a pediatric leukemia foundation to which my family regularly gave generously — I was, as I put it at parties, *in between projects.* I kept an office in SoHo and I'd told people I was an "Internet innovations expert" but that mostly meant spending my days surfing the Web and looking for inspiration. My father would occasionally fly in from San Francisco to check on me. He'd sweep into town and make proclamations about how I was "clued in" and "on the bleeding edge," but I could tell by the way he so loudly proclaimed my genius to anyone who would listen that he was overcompensating. I could smell the disappointment wafting off him, see it in the way he failed to meet my eyes.

Then again, how could I blame him? Maybe Benny was drifting along in exile at the Orson Institute, listless and lost, but I had no clear agenda for my life, either, and also no good excuse.

I felt anchorless. In a city of eight million, I had few close friends, although I had countless *petit amis,* the people I rubbed up against out and about on the society circuit. And I went out a lot. Manhattan was a Candyland of cocktails and tasting menus, galas and art

openings, parties on the roof decks of midtown penthouses. Dates with trust fund kids
and hedge fund managers.

That, in turn, necessitated *shopping*. Fashion quickly became a kind of armor for me, a
way to gird myself against the ennui that
sometimes threatened to leak out and drown
me. I lived for the serotonin hit that came
with a new outfit: a dress straight off the
runway, a perfectly draped scarf, shoes that
made people stare on the street. Bill Cunning-
ham clothes. *That* was my true joy. I drained
my trust fund allocation down to the last few
pennies every month on Gucci and Prada and
Celine.

All this is to say — I was primed and ready
for Saskia Rubansky's sales pitch.

The leukemia benefit that night was in a loft
with views over Lower Manhattan. Waiters
with trays of canapés circulated, delicately
stepping over the skirts that trailed along the
parquet floor. Candles flickered in candela-
bras and plumes of pale chiffon hung overhead. Broadway stars did a step-and-repeat
for photographers in front of a wall of white
roses, hands cocked on the hips of their
donated dresses.

In a sea of well-coiffed women in couture,
Saskia stood out. It wasn't that she was prettier than anyone else (in fact, underneath the
airbrushed foundation she had a pinched,

small-featured face), or that she was that much better dressed (though her red-feathered Dolce & Gabbana was one of the best in the room). It was that she had a dedicated photographer following her, soberly documenting her every move. As she worked the room, she tossed her balayaged hair over her shoulder and laughed with her chin tilted toward the ceiling, cutting her eyes at the photographer at the precise moment when he clicked the shutter. *Who was she?* I wondered. Clearly, a celebrity of some sort. Maybe a South American pop singer? A reality TV star?

Eventually I found myself standing next to her in the powder room, where half the women at the party were refreshing their lipstick and patting their underarms with linen towels. Saskia's photographer had been relegated to the corridor outside the bathroom, and Saskia puffed out a little sigh as she examined herself in the mirror, as if releasing some pent-up pressure in preparation for another onslaught of attention. She caught me watching her in the mirror and smiled sideways.

I turned to study her profile. "I'm sorry, but should I know who you are?"

She leaned closer to the mirror and blotted her lips with a tissue. "Saskia Rubansky."

I ran the name through my mental registry of society names and came up empty. "I'm sorry. I'm drawing a blank."

She tossed the tissue toward the trash can and missed, left it lying there on the floor for someone else to retrieve. I caught the eye of the bathroom attendant and flashed her an apologetic smile on Saskia's behalf.

"It's OK," Saskia said. "I'm famous on Instagram. You've heard of Instagram?"

I *had* heard of Instagram. I'd even set up my own account, although I had only a dozen or so followers (Benny was one), and had yet to figure out its true purpose. Pictures of my new puppy, what I was eating for lunch: Who cared? No one, judging by the number of likes I was getting. "Famous for doing what?"

She smiled, as if the question was a silly one. "For doing *this*." She made a delicate circling gesture with her wrist that took in the dress, the hair, the face. "For being me."

Her cool self-assurance shattered me. "How many followers do you have?"

"One-point-six million." She turned slowly to regard me. The sweep of her gaze took in my dress (Vuitton), my shoes (Valentino), the beaded clutch (Fendi) lying on the vanity. "You're Vanessa Liebling, right?"

Later, I would come to learn that Saskia's real name was Amy. She was from a solidly middle-class Polish family in Omaha, had escaped to New York to get a degree in fashion design. She'd auditioned for *Project Runway* four times, but never got picked.

Instead, she started a "street fashion" blog that slowly morphed into an Instagram feed. A year in, she turned the camera around so that instead of photographing fashionable strangers, she was documenting her own flashy outfits, and her following skyrocketed. She'd practically invented the term *Instagram fashion influencer.*

Saskia changed clothes, on average, six times a day, and had not paid for her own clothing in years. She billed herself as a "brand ambassador" — for woven sandals, for sparkling water, for moisturizing lotion, for Florida resorts, for whoever would pay her to breathlessly promote them while posing in designer dresses. She flew around the world on private jets that were chartered by her sponsors. She wasn't quite rich, but on Instagram you'd never know the difference.

Another thing about Saskia: She had not landed here by accident. Her appearance at this society gala was the outcome of years of careful study: of fashion, of course, and marketing, but also of the names that appeared in Page Six and *Vanity Fair* and the New York Social Diary. She knew when it would be useful to thrust herself into a frame, who might serve as another rung on the ladder she was climbing. She had fame; she wanted the *respect,* the kind that she thought someone might get from proximity to someone like me. She'd pegged me from the moment I walked into the party.

Honestly, you have to give the girl credit for her balls.

"You should give it a whirl, too, it's fun, and you get all kinds of shit for free. Clothes, trips, electronics, I even got sent a fucking *sofa* last week." She said this with a kind of bemused blasé. "You're on Instagram, right?" I nodded. "Yeah, and you already have a brand. You know — old-money name, prestige lifestyle, people go crazy for that, American royalty and all that bullshit." She threw her lipstick back in her clutch and clicked it shut with a definitive little *snap,* as if something between us had already been decided. "Look, I'll tag you in some of my posts. We go out a few times together, you'll hit fifty thousand followers within the month. You'll see."

Why did I leap at her suggestion? Why did I plug my number into her phone so she could call me the next day and make plans to meet for salads at Le Coucou? Why did I follow her out of that bathroom and then pose with her by that wall of roses, champagne raised and laughing at some joke no one had actually uttered, while her photographer snapped away?

Oh, I'm sure you've already figured it out by now. I wanted to be *loved.* Don't we all? Some of us just choose more *visible* ways to seek it than others. My mother's love was gone; I needed to find that same gratification

241

elsewhere. (So a therapist once told me, at $250 an hour.)

But there were other reasons, too. Saskia's confidence knocked me off my feet. I was a Liebling, *I* was supposed to be the one sitting in the catbird seat, and yet ever since the day my mother plunged over the edge of the *Judybird* I'd felt . . . unmoored. There were nights when I woke up barely able to breathe, battling the familiar, panicky feeling that I'd somehow screwed *everything up forever;* that I was an abject failure notable only for my name. That without *that* I might just disappear off the face of the earth without a trace. I'd spent most of my twenties seeking something that would solidify my existence in the world, and what Saskia did — well, it seemed wholly within my capabilities. I could prove that I was good at *something.*

Or maybe it was just that Saskia's cool superiority made me feel the need to beat her at her own game.

Or maybe it was just as simple as *Why the hell not?*

Regardless: When I woke up the next morning, I discovered that she'd tagged me in a series of photos (*New bestie! Girls' night out, helping sick kids, so much fun! #dolceandgab bana #leukemia #bffl*). In just eight hours, I had gained 232 new followers.

And with that, I found my *something.*

242

■ ■ ■ ■

I couldn't tell you exactly how I went from a few dozen Instagram followers to a half million. One day, you're uploading photos of your dog wearing sunglasses; and the next you're being flown to Coachella on a private jet with four other social media It Girls, twenty suitcases full of wardrobe changes provided by a major fashion website, and a photographer to document the moment when you nonchalantly twirl your Balmain dress *just so* while pretending to eat an ice cream cone.

That Balmain moment will be liked by 42,031 strangers. And looking at the comments (*Beauty! — YAAS SLAY — Vanessa I adore U — SUCH A BABE*) you will feel more substantial than you've ever felt in your life: as if you really *are* that glamorous, jet-setting fashion queen with an army of friends and no self-doubt whatsoever. You are admired — *adored,* even — beyond your wildest imagination. You're living the *V-Life;* everyone wants to be you but only the very lucky few will come even close.

If you play out a role long enough, can you become that person without even realizing it's happened? This happier, more evolved person you are pretending to be — can they just inhabit you? Every day, as you put on a show for a worshipful audience of hundreds of thousands (or, heck — even just one other person), when does the performance stop being a performance and just become *you*?

I'm still waiting to find the answer to that question.

Several years passed like this, a blur of fashion shows and late-night dinners at caviar restaurants and rides across Lake Como with rich men whose names I had no reason to remember. Once I hit 300,000 followers I finally told my father what I was doing, which didn't please him one bit. "You're doing what?" he barked, when I tried to explain the term *Instagram influencer.* The mottled pink skin at his temple wrinkled with consternation; his nostrils — which had grown veined and corpuscular with age — flared like those of an enraged bull. "I didn't raise you to just live off your trust fund. Vanessa — that's really not wise."

"I'm not," I protested. "It's a real career." And it *was*! At least, if you judged it by the sheer amount of effort it required: My growing audience was voracious, demanding original content eight, nine, ten times a day. I'd hired a pair of social media assistants whose primary job was to identify Instagramable outfits and locales, before the influence-aspiring hordes found their way to them and turned them into middle-America clichés.

But as for profitability . . . the truth was that I was getting paid more in merchandise than I was in actual cash, and the cost of a staff adds up *fast.*

My new friends were a quartet of social media stars. Besides Saskia there was Trini, a bikini model descended from German nobility; Evangeline, a celebrity stylist whose fashion signature was that she never, ever removed her sunglasses; and Maya, originally from Argentina, famous for her live makeup tutorials and boasting more followers than all of us combined. We were frequently invited to do things as a pack: Fashion houses would fly us to Thailand, to Cannes, to Burning Man, where we were wined and dined and spent our days gallivanting around picturesque locations in sponsored "looks." These girls understood the odd pace of the documented life: Spontaneous moments that had to be replicated over and over until they were captured correctly. Pretending to take a sip of espresso, but never actually drinking it because it would ruin your lipstick. Ten minutes to walk across fifty feet of grass.

I had made dutiful study of Saskia's talents: learning from her how to swan and preen like an exotic bird when performing even the most mundane tasks, how to twiddle with my hair as I talked to the camera so that I wouldn't look inert, how to tilt my head to disguise the soft flap of my weak chin. Exclamation points in your captions were important, I learned; as was a gushing appreciation of the wonderful things in life; and so my persona online was upbeat, excited, #*blessed.* I took up the practice of live video fashion feeds, panning the camera up and down my body, all the while reciting in a practiced voice: "The shoes are Louboutin, the dress is Monse, the bag is McQueen!" The words in my mouth were a mantra, a security blanket that protected me from the world that existed beyond the tinted windows of my town car, the things I didn't want to see.

I loved everything about this new life, the whirlwind of activity that kept me spinning from morning until night: fashion shows, exotic vacations, music festivals, shopping expeditions, magazine galas, film openings, pop-up restaurants. Social media was an emotional roller coaster that I was eager to board every day. It made me feel *alive,* the way each new post (and its response) sparked tiny emotions into billowing flames of gratification. And yes, I'd read all those doom-and-gloom features written by the Boomer scolds; I knew that to *them* I was little more than a rat pushing a lever, waiting for my next endorphin hit. Did I care? *Bien sûr que non.*

I had regular followers, who I knew primarily by their Instagram handles and the emojis they favored. My own personal *community*! When the low moments came around now,

I'd just cruise through the comments on my posts, sending smiles and kisses, basking in the superlatives. *Obsessed. Dying. Covet. Gorgeous. Everything. Need. Love.* Nothing in my new world was half-felt; everything was observed to the extreme. *Everyone* was a bestie.

After a few years of this, though — perhaps inevitably — the constant high began to wear off. And my pendulum moods returned: A week of parties in São Paulo would be followed by a week in which I couldn't get out of bed. I'd come home from a dance club, look at the twenty-eight posts documenting my *#epic* evening, and burst into tears. Who *was* that woman, and why didn't I feel as happy as she looked? Sometimes, when riding on a gondola in Venice or walking down a street in Hanoi, I would study the local people, living their simple private lives; and even though I knew they struggled in ways I couldn't fathom, I wanted to weep with jealousy. *Imagine the freedom in being invisible like that!* I would think. *Imagine not caring whether anyone cares!*

Sometimes, when I was alone, lying in a dark hotel suite in a foreign country or listening to the insomniac hush of a private jet's air filters, I would even wonder, *Isn't there more than this? Have I forgotten what it feels like to be in the moment? Who is watching me and do they honestly care about me at all?* A storm cloud descending to ruin the picnic. As I was slipping off to sleep, I'd tell myself, *Maybe tomorrow I will turn the Internet off forever. Maybe tomorrow I will give everything away. Maybe tomorrow I'll become a better person.*

But then the sun would rise on another day and Gucci would invite me to preview a line of sequined bomber jackets (so *now*!) and someone would offer to fly us all to their vacation home in Barbados and fifty thousand strangers would tell me how amazing I was. And all that melancholy would pass like the temporary squall that it was.

And then, a few years in, I met Victor.

I was thirty by then, with a growing awareness of my own expiration date: My following had plateaued at just over a half million, and there were now a dozen girls a decade younger who had leapfrogged past me into the limelight. Increasingly, as I was walking around my neighborhood, I would find myself gazing wistfully at the babies that I passed. Their mothers smiled knowingly as they looked at me over their strollers, the sidewalks clearing before them, as if they knew a universal secret that I had somehow missed myself. They had love they could trust to last, forever: a child's love.

I recognized that curious tug — the itchy

248

longing for soft, pliable flesh — for what it was. My biological clock, perhaps, but more than just that: I wanted to build a whole new *family,* to replace the one that had been lost. That's what I had been missing; *that* was what was going to dispel my nagging ennui. I needed a baby, and soon. Maybe two, or three.

It's hard to date when you're in a different city every week, but I made a concerted effort, and eventually I met someone at a party. His name was Victor Coleman. His mother was a senator from Maryland and he worked in finance, so on paper he was everything that an eligible bachelor should be, an excellent potential father of future children. On camera, he also excelled — his face chiseled and shadowed like a classic sculpture, the perfect Nordic sweep of his wavy blond hair — although at first I found I wanted to keep him mostly to myself, rather than letting my ravenous community devour him in the comments.

Where he didn't excel: in bed. We fumbled drily in the dark, reaching for each other but never quite mastering the proper grips. Our relationship was perfectly easy in all other ways, though, our tastes and routines well aligned. We did wonderfully mundane things together: walks with my dog, Mr. Buggles; brunch over Sunday Styles; TV in bed. It felt like what I think love must feel like.

Victor finally popped the question, during a morning stroll through springtime Central Park. He got down on one knee in the grass — "Vanessa, you are so vibrant, so full of life, I can't think of a better partner" — but I could barely hear his words because of the high-pitched buzz in my ears.

I chalked this up to adrenaline.

"Oh, good *call,* girl," said Saskia, when I told her that I'd gotten engaged. We were sitting together in the waiting room of a Palm Springs spa, waiting to get stem cell facials after a long morning of posing in crocheted bikinis by pools we didn't dare swim in. Our photographer slumped over her laptop nearby, dutifully photoshopping zits and bulges to make us look twenty-five percent prettier than we actually were. Saskia clapped like an eager child. "Oh! This gives you a whole new narrative line. Wedding dress shopping, flowers, picking the venue. And of course, we'll throw an engagement party! Invite all the big names on social media, so it goes wide. Your fans are going to go bonkers. And think of the sponsors."

It was at this moment that I realized that I hated Saskia a little bit. "Wrong response," I said. "Try again."

She stared blankly at me. She'd recently gotten mink eyelash extensions and they were so long that she had to open her eyes extra wide to see through them. She looked like a stunned alpaca.

"Congratulations?"

"That's better."

"OK, grumpy. You know I'm happy for you. I didn't realize I had to say it out loud."

"I'm getting married because I love him, not because it'll make a good Insta-story," I said.

She turned quickly away to smile at the approaching beautician but I could have sworn I saw her roll her eyes. "Of course you are." She squeezed my hand and then stood. "Now please tell me that I'll get to pick out the bridesmaids' dress? I'm thinking we talk to Elie Saab."

But of course, Saskia was right, and the posts about my engagement were among the most popular of my career. My following started to creep up again. At first Victor was obliging, letting me bring my photo assistant along on our tours of the reception rooms at Cipriani and the Plaza. But at our cake tasting, when I asked him to pretend to pop the red velvet in my mouth, already imagining the caption I might use (*Practicing for the big day! #wed dingcake #nosmashplease*), he suddenly balked. He glanced sideways at my latest photo assistant, Emily, a twenty-two-year-old NYU grad who was poised with her camera at the ready. She smiled encouragingly at him.

"I feel like a trained seal." He grimaced.

"You don't have to do it if you don't want to."

"Why do *you* have to do it?" He stuck a finger into the frosting of a chocolate-raspberry mousse cake, dug around a little, and then sucked it off his thumb.

I was struck dumb by this. He'd never expressed doubts about my career before. "You know the answer to that question."

"I just think . . ." He hesitated, slowly withdrawing the thumb from his mouth. He wiped it clean on his napkin, and lowered his voice so Emily couldn't hear. "I just think you can do more than this, Vanessa. You're smart. You have resources at your fingertips. You could do anything you want to do. Make the world a better place. Find something you're good at."

"This is *exactly* what I'm good at," I told him. And to prove this point I pulled the cake toward myself, and artfully moved it toward my lips, offering a perfect sly expression — *I'm so cool and down-to-earth, I'm not even thinking about the calories in this thing* — for Emily to capture.

The red velvet was too sweet. The sugar burrowed painfully into my molars.

Our wedding date was five months away when my father called to tell me he was dying: "Advanced pancreatic cancer, cupcake," he said. "The doctors say this is it. I've got weeks, not months. Any chance you can come home?"

"Oh God, Daddy. *Of course.* Oh God."

He was uncharacteristically subdued on the other end of the line. "Vanessa — I just want to say it now — I'm sorry. For . . . everything."

My eyes were dry but I couldn't breathe. I felt something sharp and insistent tug at my center of gravity, ready to drag me downward. "Stop it. There's nothing for you to be sorry about."

"Things might get hard but do not doubt your strength. You're a *Liebling.*" There was a thin, pale wheeze on the other end of the line. "Don't forget that. You need to push through, for Benny's sake. And your own."

I flew back to San Francisco and collected Benny from the Orson Institute and we settled into the mansion in Pacific Heights for a swift but agonizing deathwatch. My father's organs were failing fast. He slept all day, drugged up on morphine, his body so puffed and bloated that I was afraid he would pop if I hugged him hard. While he napped, Benny and I careened aimlessly through the house we grew up in, touching familiar surfaces with the lingering fingers of impending loss. Our childhood bedrooms, unchanged since our mother's suicide, remained shrines to the people our parents once believed we would become: my Princeton banner and tennis trophies, Benny's ski medals and chess set. The family we were *before.*

My brother and I kept watch over our dying father together. One night, as he grunted and whimpered in his sleep — fighting death with all the force with which he fought life — we sat side by side on the couch and watched TV reruns from our youth: *That '70s Show* and *Friends* and *The Simpsons.* When Benny drifted off, numbed with exhaustion and meds, he slipped sideways until his head rested on my shoulder. I stroked his shaggy red hair, as if he were still my baby brother, and felt profoundly at peace despite it all.

I wondered what my brother was dreaming about, or if the medications he took robbed him of dreams altogether. And then I wondered if the loss of another parent would set Benny off again. If it did, who would I have to blame this time?

"Don't be afraid," I whispered. "I'm going to take care of you."

He opened one eye. "What makes you think that I'm the one who needs taking care of?"

And then he laughed so that I knew he was joking, but something about this unsettled me anyway. As if Benny recognized something inside me that was also inside himself, something that had been inside our mother: how close I was teetering to that edge.

Our father died abruptly, slipping away with

a soft rattle of his chest and a convulsion of his limbs. I had assumed we would have a *moment* before he died — the movie deathbed scene, where my father would tell me *how proud* he was of me — but in the end he wasn't lucid enough. Instead, I gripped his frail hand until it grew cold in mine, wetting both with my tears. On the other side of the bed, Benny rocked back and forth, arms wrapped tightly around his chest.

The hospice nurse tiptoed back and forth, waiting to nudge us toward the inevitable next steps: doctor, funeral director, obituary writer, lawyer.

At a loss, I did what I knew how to do best: I tugged my phone out of my pocket and took a photo of our still-entwined hands, something to document this final thread of connection before everything was irretrievably gone. Almost without thinking, I uploaded this to my Instagram, *#mypoordaddy*. (Thinking without thinking: *Look at me. Look at how sad I am. Fill this hole with love.*) Within seconds, the condolences started rolling in: *So sad 4 U — what a touching photo — Vanessa DM me for virtual hugs.* Kind words from generous strangers, but they felt about as personal as the letters on a movie marquee. I knew that within seconds of commenting each person had already moved on to the next post in their feed and forgotten me.

I shut the app down, and didn't open it again for two weeks.

We were alone now, Benny and me. We only had each other.

Victor flew out for the funeral and held me while I cried; but he had to fly back immediately in order to attend a political fundraiser for his mother, who was being groomed as a VP candidate for the upcoming presidential election.

I was still in San Francisco, dealing with my father's estate, when Victor called me a week later. After a few minutes of benign small talk, he dropped his little bomb: "Look, Vanessa, I've been thinking, we should call off the wedding."

"No, it's OK. My father wouldn't have wanted me to postpone. He would have wanted me to go on with my life." There was an uncomfortable silence on the other end and I realized that I had misunderstood. "Wait. You're kidding. You're dumping me? My father just died and you're *dumping me*?"

"The timing, I know . . . it's bad. But waiting would have made it worse." His voice was strangled. "I'm really sorry, Van."

I had been sitting on the floor in my parents' bedroom, sorting through old photo albums; when I stood up a cascade of pictures came tumbling out of my lap. "What the hell? Where is this coming from?"

"I've just been thinking," he began, and then he stopped. "I want . . . more? You know?"

"No." My voice was ice, it was steel, it was fury. "I don't. I don't know what you're talking about *at all.*"

There was another long pause. He was in his office, I was sure, because I could faintly hear the cacophony of Manhattan below outside his window, the taxis bludgeoning their way through the midtown traffic with their horns. "That photo, of your dad's hand after he died?" he finally said. "I saw that on your feed, and it made me go cold. That this was going to be our life, you know? Everything out there on the table for the world to see. Our most private moments on display, being monetized as clickbait for strangers. Because I don't want that."

I looked at the photos scattered around me. There was one of newborn Benny just days home from the hospital. I was three years old, and carefully holding him in my tiny lap as my mother leaned protectively over us both. She and I had intent expressions on our faces, as if we were both aware that the line between life and death is just a matter of a slip of the wrist. "This is coming from your mother, isn't it? She thinks I'm bad for business, for some reason. Too much in the public eye?"

"Well," he said. Through the line I could

hear an ambulance siren, and I couldn't help but think of the person trapped inside it, approaching death as the ambulance went nowhere in the rush hour gridlock. "She's not wrong. Vanessa, your lifestyle . . . it's just . . . The optics are bad. A trust fund kid who's famous for traipsing around the world in expensive clothes — it's not so relatable. With all the talk of class warfare right now . . . I mean, you saw what happened with Louise Linton."

"Dammit, I'm *self-made*! I did this all *myself*!" (And yet, even as I was screaming this into the receiver, I remembered with a twinge of guilt the monthly trust-allocation check sitting on my desk in Manhattan.) "So, what, your mom thinks it wouldn't do for her son to be seen running around with an heiress on private *jets* even though she would've taken my dad's money for her campaign in a heartbeat? Hypocrite. Don't you see? People are angry at us when really they would trade their lives for ours in an instant if given the opportunity. They want to *be* us; they would *kill* to climb aboard a private jet. Why do you think I have a half-million followers?"

"Whatever, Vanessa." He sighed. "It's not just my mom. What if I decide to go into politics, too? It's been bothering me for a while. Your work, your life, it just feels . . . shallow. Empty."

"I've built a community," I said hotly.

"Community is a vital part of the human experience."

"So is reality, Vanessa. You don't actually *know* any of those people. All they do is tell you how great you are. There's nothing authentic about any of it, it's just the same predictable posturing day in and day out — parties and outfits and *oooh* doesn't she look cute sitting on the steps of that four-star hotel. Rinse, repeat."

This cut uncomfortably close to the bone. "So, what now?" I snapped. "You work in *finance,* Victor. Don't tell me about shallow. So somehow when I'm out of the picture you're going to become an enlightened human being? You're going to quit your job and start building latrines in Mozambique?"

"Actually." He cleared his throat. "I *did* just sign up for a meditation course."

"Oh *fuck you!*" I screamed, and threw the phone across the room. And then I tugged the engagement ring off my finger, and flung it after the phone. The ring rolled into a corner and when I went to look for it a few days later, it had vanished entirely. I was pretty sure the cleaning crew took it.

Good, I thought. *They can have it.*

The next week, my father's will was read. Of course Daddy didn't leave Stonehaven to my brother. Why would he leave the estate to someone who vowed to burn it to the ground?

259

No, the house was to be *my* burden now: Five generations of our family's *stuff,* the Liebling legacy, and I was now its caretaker.

But Stonehaven was also a gift, I soon learned. Because when I finally went back to New York, I couldn't muster up any enthusiasm for *V-Life* anymore. Rather than organizing trips and shoots and looks, I holed up in my apartment, eating salted caramel gelato and bingeing on Netflix. My posts grew few and far between. The golden rule of influencing is *Don't bum out your audience,* but I didn't have it in me to smile. Saskia and Trini and Maya sent me concerned texts — *You aren't posting much, are you doing OK? What's going on? Worried about U XX* — but of course I knew from their feeds that they were continuing their lives without me. A new girl — a twenty-one-year-old Swiss pop star named Marcelle — had taken my spot in their jet to Cannes.

Mr. Buggles was run over by a taxi on the way to Bryant Park.

My followers started to get crabby about the lack of posts; and then, they started to unfollow me. Increasingly, instead of basking in the adulatory comments on my posts, I found myself focusing on the nasty ones: *Get over yourself bitch. Where's UR ring, did U get dumped? Haha. You think you're cool because you're rich, why don't you sell that ugly dress and donate the money to refugee children?* On social media it's all or nothing: lavish praise or appalled outrage; sycophants or trolls. Caption-and-comment culture in all its brevity leaves out the middle ground, where most of life is found. So I *knew* I shouldn't pay attention to this empty noise, shouted by those who knew nothing real about me, but I still couldn't help myself. Why did they loathe me so much, a total stranger? Did they think I was breathing such thin air up here that I couldn't feel pain?

With every new insult, Victor's words came echoing back to me: *It just feels . . . shallow.* I thought of my father's face, his words when I told him what I was doing: *That's not a career, cupcake, that's just a shiny toy that's going to get old real soon.*

Maybe they were right.

I couldn't help but wonder: *Were* people just following me in order to hate me? I never meant to be the personification of privilege; I was only ever doing this because it made me feel good about myself. And it didn't anymore. I looked at the heaps of clothing in my closet, unworn dresses with five-figure price tags still hanging off them, and felt ill: How did I become this person? Because I didn't think I wanted to be *her* anymore.

I was done with *V-Life.* I needed to get out of New York and do something new. But what?

And then it hit me one sleepless night: *Stonehaven.* I'd move there, really set myself the goal of becoming someone *at peace with the world,* someone balanced and self-assured. (The embodiment of those inspirational quotes I threw up sometimes, to fill the gaps in my feed: *Some daily inspo, guys! #mother teresa #serenity #kindness.*) I would breathe life into Stonehaven, make it a place that was habitable and appealing again, a home that my children (someday) would actually want to visit. I could remodel (or at least redecorate!), erase the taint of tragedy, start the Liebling story anew! Bonus: It would lend itself to a whole new social media narrative: *Vanessa Liebling moves to her family's classic Tahoe estate in order to find herself.*

I called Benny to tell him what I was going to do. He was silent. "You know I'm not going to visit you there, Vanessa. I can't be in that place."

"I'll come visit you instead," I said. "Besides, it's just for the short term. Until I figure out the next thing."

"You're being awfully impulsive," he said. "Think about it for a second: It's a *terrible* idea."

I *knew* I was clutching at straws; but straws were all I had. Within the week, I'd packed my entire life into boxes, including the wedding dress that I never had a chance to wear;

fired my staff; and terminated the lease on my Tribeca flat.

Saskia and Evangeline threw me a going-away party on a Chinatown rooftop, with a DJ and half of Manhattan in attendance. I wore a silver minidress that Christian Siriano had designed just for me and I dispensed kisses and invitations to visit *the family estate.* I made it sound like the Hamptons, only better. "We'll come out this summer!" Maya trilled. "I'll bring the girls and we get sponsors and we make it a whole week get-a-way, like, spa retreat, yes?" I didn't have the heart to tell her that there were no spas near Stonehaven, no SoulCycle studios, no restaurants serving avocado toast. But Saskia seemed to have figured that out on her own: At the end of the party she hugged me as if she was saying goodbye to me forever.

I couldn't get away fast enough.

A moving truck arrived the next day and hauled my life away. I snapped a last photo as the truck lumbered off, rattling uneasily along the cobblestones, and uploaded this to Instagram: *And so I begin a new journey! "Every great dream begins with a dreamer" — Helen Keller. #sotrue.*

Later, I would discover that Victor had liked this image, and I would wonder what he liked about it: the positivity, or the departure.

Stonehaven was like a time capsule when I

arrived. Nothing had changed since the day we left, years earlier: The furniture was still covered in white cloths, the grandfather clock in the foyer was stopped at 11:25, the tins of foie gras in the pantry had expired in 2010. There was no dust and the property had been well maintained, thanks to the caretaker and his wife who, until my father died and the bills began going unpaid, had been living in a cottage on the far edge of the property. Still, as I walked through the dark, lifeless rooms, I realized I'd moved into a crypt. Everything cold to the touch. Everything inert.

Sometimes, as I moved through the house — throwing off dustcloths, examining bookshelves — I thought I felt the ghost of my mother. There was a soft dent in the sofa in the library, on the cushion where she liked to sit, and when I settled myself into the groove she left behind, there was a prickle at the back of my neck, as if someone had blown gently on the hairs there. I closed my eyes and tried to remember what it felt like to have Maman's arms around me, but what I felt instead was a cold knot in my belly, the grip of skeleton fingers rising from the grave to grab at me.

At one point I found myself in the guest bedroom where the Meissen birds still sat frozen in their cabinet, waiting to be set free. I picked one out — a yellow canary — and turned it in my hands, remembering how my mother tipped her hands and let that parrot shatter. I wondered if my mother identified with these trapped birds. I wondered if her suicide was a kind of escape, not just from the pain of her failed marriage and troubled child, but from a cage she'd felt locked inside.

I won't let this house kill me, too, I thought, and then gave myself a little shake, to toss off this morbid thought.

It didn't help that I was so alone. Tahoe City was not so far on the map, but it felt like a world away; I wasn't sure how to go about making friends on this quiet stretch of the West Shore. People come and go in Tahoe; the lights in the vacation homes along the shoreline flick on one week and off the next. At the general store up the road, the locals buying their coffee and the *Reno Gazette-Journal* looked right past me, assuming from my New York clothes and the Mercedes SUV parked out front that I was just passing through.

And so I spent my days alone, milling through the rooms of Stonehaven, feeling increasingly like a bird in a cage myself. I'd pace the property, shoreline to road and back again, walking in circles until my calves ached, never seeing a soul. On warm days, I'd walk down to the end of the dock, where the water-skiers turned the glassy water into chop, and dutifully upload smiling bikini selfies: *Loving my #lakelife!* On bad days, I'd stay in bed, blinds closed against the light, scrolling through my own Instagram archive: thousands upon thousands of photos of a strange woman who shared my name. *Social media feeds the narcissistic monster that lives within us all,* I would think to myself. *It feeds it and grows it until the beast takes over and* you *are left outside the frame, just looking at images of this creature, like everyone else in your feed, wondering what it is that you birthed and why it's living the life you wish you had.*

Sometimes, even I could be terribly self-aware.

One morning, while out on a walk around the property, I pried open the wooden doors of the old stone boathouse and found myself staring up at the *Judybird.* My father had never bothered to sell it after all, so there the yacht still hovered on its hydraulic lift, a few feet over the surface of the lake. The caretaker had kept the boat fueled, the battery fresh; but it still looked forgotten there, a forlorn beached whale. The cover was filthy with spiderwebs and bird droppings from the swallows that rustled in the eaves overhead.

I stood on the wooden ramp beside the boat, the cold water lapping at my sneakers, and put my hand up to touch its side, as if I might be able to feel the ghost of my mother in the fiberglass. The boards of the dock groaned and gave under my feet, weak with rot. And for a moment, just a brief one, I wondered what it would feel like, *really,* to drive the *Judybird* out to the middle of the lake and just jump in the water, my pockets full of stones. Would it be a kind of relief? As if in a dream, my hand reached for the switch that would lower the yacht back down to the water.

And then I jerked it away. *I am not my mother; I don't want to be.* I turned and left the boathouse, locked it behind me, and vowed never to go inside again.

Summer arrived, the lake filling with boats; tourists clogging the roads. At Stonehaven, nothing changed. And then, one day, as I walked from the dock back toward the house, I noticed the empty caretaker's cottage. I stopped to peer in the window: I'd never been inside. I was surprised to see that it was still fully furnished, clean and neat as a pin. Something ignited inside me, an idea suddenly coming to life: *Here it is, the answer to my problems.* I could rent out the cottage! Why not? It would bring *life* to the property, since God knows I might lose my mind if I didn't find someone to speak to besides my housekeeper. It would give me a focal point, inside the unspooling nothing of my current life.

Two weeks later, my first JetSet.com guests arrived, a young French couple who liked to sit at the edge of the water and drink wine all day. The wife had a guitar and as the last light passed over the lake she sang old pop songs in her dreamy, lisping lilt. I sat with them, and as we talked about the places we loved in Paris, I felt a strange nostalgia for the life I was living just six months ago. Vanessa Liebling, globetrotter, fashionista, brand ambassador, Instagram influencer. Did I miss being that person? Maybe a little. But my mood lifted with their presence, and as we sang *When I'm Sixty-four* together I felt that I was getting a glimpse of a new, more *centered* person I might actually be able to become.

The French couple were followed by married retirees from Phoenix, a group of German men biking their way across the Sierras, three moms from San Francisco up for a girls' weekend, and a taciturn Canadian woman with a suitcase full of romance novels. *Normal* people, living *normal* lives. Some of my guests were antisocial, but others were eager for a local tour guide, and so I took them hiking in Emerald Bay, to outdoor concerts beside the lake, to the Fire Sign Café for eggs Benedict and hot cocoa. This filled my days with some sort of purpose and took the edge off my solitude. Plenty of material for my photo stream. The days flew by.

But when summer came to a close so did

the rental bookings. And as the empty days returned, so did the dark whisper in the back of my head: *What now? What are you doing here? How long can you keep this up? Who are you really and what are you doing with your life?*

One day in early November, I woke up to a query in my inbox from "Michael and Ashley." *Greetings!* the message said. *We're a creative couple from Portland, looking for a peaceful place to spend a few weeks, maybe longer? Michael is taking some time off from teaching to write a book, and I'm a yoga instructor. We're on a little sabbatical from life and your cottage looks perfect for us! Is it available? We're new to JetSet so we don't have any reviews yet, but we're happy to tell you more about ourselves if you'd like!*

I studied their photo for a long time. In it Ashley was standing right in front of Michael and he had one arm wrapped around her shoulders, leaning his chin on her head as they both laughed at some private joke. They looked intelligent and attractive and grounded, like models in a Patagonia ad. I was immediately drawn to them, the easy confidence in their smiles, their happiness together. He was, I noticed, quite handsome. As for *her:* I plugged her name into a search engine and, after sifting through a thousand

269

other Ashley Smiths, eventually came across her website: *Ashley Smith Yoga Oregon.* There she was, sitting on a beach in the lotus position, her eyes peacefully lowered and hands extended to the sky. *"We need to learn to want what we have, not to have what we want," teaches the Dalai Lama. I believe that my role as a teacher — and a human being! — is helping people come to this awareness, and in doing so find their peace within. Only internally can we locate the validation that we spend so much of our lives seeking elsewhere.*

It was almost like it was written *just for me.* I zoomed in on the photo to study her closer, admiring the serenely knowing expression on her pretty face. She looked like the kind of person I was trying to become; the one I pretended to be in my social media feed. I wondered what *I* might learn from her.

I felt something lift inside me: my heartbeat, winging back to life. And so I clicked *Accept,* without thinking twice about it.

The cottage is available, and you can stay as long as you like, I wrote back. *Looking forward to getting to know you better in person!*

14.

There she is.

Ashley is practicing yoga out on the lawn, softly backlit by the early morning sun. Steam rising off her skin; her yoga mat spread out like a tongue lapping at the lake. Yoga's never been my *thing* — I always preferred the obliterating burn of boot camp or spin class — but as I watch Ashley out there, working through her Sun Salutations, I realize that this is another thing that I should change about myself. It looks so *centering*. From where I stand in the kitchen window, Ashley appears to be swimming through the air, just one leg kick away from taking flight.

And — Oh! The light is perfect for a photo, and it's been at least twelve hours since my last post. (How far into obsolescence have I fallen in that time?) I pull out my phone and frame a shot of Ashley, her serene face silhouetted by the lake, her body bent into a triangle with fingers thrust to the sky. I upload this to my feed: *My very own backyard*

warrior. #yoga #sunsalutation #goodmorning.
Maybe I should have asked her permission, but how identifiable is she really? And why would she mind, anyway? This is what she does for a living, it's good brand awareness. I hit refresh until the first *likes* materialize, wait for the dopamine kick that will thrust me back into the land of the living. *There.*

Then I stand watch in the window, hypnotized, for nearly half an hour, as she rolls through her asanas and finally finishes up with a Shavasana. She lies flat on the dewy grass so long that I start to wonder if she's fallen asleep. But then she stands, abruptly turns around, and once again, she's caught me watching her. She must think I'm some sort of stalker. (I *am* some sort of stalker, I suppose.)

I wave at her. She waves back. I make a "come here" gesture. She gathers up her mat and walks to the back door, where I meet her with my cup of coffee in hand.

She dabs sweat from her forehead with what I recognize as a bath towel from the caretaker's cottage. Then she smiles at me, revealing a charmingly wonky left incisor. "Sorry about that, I should have asked if you'd mind if I did yoga on your lawn. But the sunrise was so glorious, I couldn't resist. The day was calling to me."

"Not at all," I said. "In fact, I was just thinking that I should join you tomorrow."

Too late, I realize that this sounds pushy, presumptive.

But she smiles. *"Absolutely."* She points to the mug in my hand. "Can I beg a cup of coffee off you? We don't have any in the cottage."

"Of course!" I am unduly pleased. "You don't have to beg."

She steps into the house, and there it is again, that warm penumbra that surrounds her, the *life* of her, the *glow* of her. When she enters my space it feels like an electric shock, heating me back up.

"Michael doesn't do yoga with you?" I putter around the kitchen, fiddling with the fussy Italian coffee machine that I haven't quite mastered.

She gives a low laugh. "I think that if I woke him up this early he would literally bite my head off." She takes the coffee from me and sips it, smiling at me over the rim. "Let's just say that yoga is my thing, not his."

"Ah." I refresh my coffee and then stand there, awkwardly, trying to come up with something to say. When was the last time I attempted to befriend someone? What does one even *talk* about? I think back to my friends in New York — Saskia, Evangeline, Maya, and Trini, my constant companions and partners in visibility. We were together so much and discussed so little. Our conversations mostly revolved around brand names

273

and diet trends and restaurant recommenda-
tions, which at the time felt like a relief — to
just skate along the surface of things without
having to think about the darkness below —
but now I see as a symptom of the dreaded
shallow. When my father died, they sent texts,
but didn't pick up the phone. Maybe that
was the moment that I realized that my
friendships were like the thin crust on a
frozen lake, a barrier blocking the way to
anything deeper.

Maybe Ashley intrigues me because she is
my only friend option at the moment, but
there is also something about her, the way
she seems to be connected to something
meaningful, that I find refreshing. As she
walks through the kitchen of Stonehaven,
lightly touching the surfaces as if testing them
for solidity, she doesn't seem to register my
curiosity about her. Does she know that I am
looking at her as a buoy to cling to, one that
might keep me from drowning?

*Please don't hate me. I know there are so
many things about me to hate. That I am vain
and superficial and privileged; that I haven't
done more to make the world a better place;
that I focus on my family's sorrows rather than
those of society at large. That instead of actually being a good person I have focused on
looking like a good person. But isn't that the
best way to start? From the outside, in? Show*

me what else I should do.

"Want to go sit down in the library?" I blurt. "It's warmer in there."

She lights up. "Lovely!"

I usher her into the library, perhaps the least forbidding room in the house. I've got a fire going, the couch is soft, all those books speak of weightiness. I sit down, leave room for her on the cushion beside me. But Ashley hesitates in the doorway, flicks her eyes across the bookshelves as if looking for something, before gingerly depositing herself on the couch. I wonder whether she is worried about transferring the sweat from her yoga pants to the velvet of the couch. I want to reassure her that I don't care.

She is staring across the room with an odd expression, as if riveted, and I follow her gaze and realize that she's looking at the framed family photo on the fireplace mantel. "Oh, that's my family," I offer. "Mom, Dad, little brother."

She barks out a little nervous laugh, as if embarrassed to be caught in the act. "You look . . . close."

"We were."

"Were?" She is still studying the photo. Something flickers across her face again. She comes and sits down next to me.

"My mother died when I was nineteen. She drowned. My father died earlier this year." I realize that I haven't said this out loud in

275

months, and unexpectedly the grief wells up inside me and I'm sobbing. Big heaving gasps of woe. Ashley turns to look at me with wide eyes. *Dear God. She'll think I'm a basket case.* "God, I'm so sorry. I didn't realize I was still so raw about that. It's just . . . I still can't believe my family is gone."

She blinks. "What about your brother?"

"He's a mess, so he's not much help. Jesus, I'm so sorry, bawling all over you like this."

"Don't apologize." I can see conflicting emotions flickering across her face — *Is she repulsed? Have I screwed it all up?* — but then they settle and smooth into something soft and reassuring. Her hand stretches across the couch to rest on top of mine. "How did your father die?"

"Cancer. It came on very quickly."

I see her swallow. "Oh. How terrible."

"It is," I say. "It's got to be the most agonizing way you could die — slowly, like that, just *eaten up.* It was like the cancer just stole him and then left his body to die for weeks and weeks. And I had to just sit there *watching this,* wanting him to die so that it could all be over and he'd be out of pain, but also begging him to live for just a little while more, for *me.* "

I am about to go on, but then I realize that she looks a little stricken, and so I stop myself. Her hand grips tighter onto mine. "It sounds awful," she says hoarsely, near tears herself, and I'm surprised and touched that my father's death is making her feel so emotional, too. She must be an empath (another thing I am not but *should be*).

Tears are gathering in the folds of my nose and I need to wipe them away, but I'm unwilling to break the connection of our hands so I let them drip freely. They rest on the velvet nap, tiny puddles of woe.

"I am very . . . alone . . . right now." My voice is small.

"I can't even imagine." She is quiet for a moment, and then: "Or, maybe I can imagine." Something in her voice has abruptly changed, her speech more tentative, as if she doesn't quite trust the words coming out of her mouth. "My father is gone, too. And my mother is . . . ailing." Our eyes meet and there is something painful and sharp that passes between us, an unspoken understanding that can only be shared by those of us who have lost parents too young: How dreadful it is to live in a world without them.

"How did your father die?" I ask.

She looks away for a moment, and when she looks back there is a wistful blankness in her eyes, as if she is excavating an old memory from deep in the recesses of her brain. She slips her hand from mine. "Heart attack. It was very sudden and really devastating. He was such a . . . kind and gentle man. A dentist. We were really close. Even when I moved out for college he would call me every day. Other dads didn't do that." Her shoulders rise and fall, almost theatrically, as if shaking off a memory. "Anyway. As I like to say: *Inhale the future, exhale the past.*"

I like this. I inhale, and exhale, but still feel like crying. "What about your mother?"

"My mother?" She blinks fast, as if unprepared for the question. Her hand falls to the nap of the couch, and she rubs it, hard. "Oh, she's lovely."

"What does she do?"

"What does she do?" She hesitates. "She's a nurse. She likes taking care of people. Or, she did, until she got sick."

"So you got that from her."

She's leaving little scratches in the velvet but I don't have it in me to ask her to stop. "Got what?"

"The caretaking. Yoga — it's a healing profession, right?"

"Oh, yes. Right."

I lean in closer. "It must be terribly fulfilling, spending your life trying to help other people. You must sleep quite well at night."

She looks down at her hands, curved into the cushion, and laughs softly. "I sleep well enough."

"Yoga teaches us to cure what need not be endured and endure what cannot be cured." It comes out before I can think twice. "I saw

278

that on your Facebook page."

"Oh yes, of course. I think that was . . . Iyengar?" She gives me a funny look. "You looked me up online?"

"Sorry, should I have pretended that I didn't? I mean, you've got to figure these days that everyone is doing it. You found *my* Instagram feed, I assume?"

Ashley's eyes have clouded over; they are dark and inscrutable. "I don't really do social media. When you're documenting everything you do, you stop living life for yourself and start living it as a performance for others. You're never in the actual moment, just the response to the moment." She hesitates. "Why? Should I look at your Instagram?"

"Oh." I realize I've made a terrible gaffe, but now I have no choice but to flounder ahead anyway. Why did I bring this up? She's unlikely to be impressed; rather the opposite, and *Oh God, she's right.* "I'm kind of an Instagram lifestyle celebrity, actually. My feed's about being inspired by global culture. You know, manifesting dreams and creativity. Through fashion. Though I've pivoted lately, to be more about nature and spiritual fulfillment." I have just served up a word salad, oily with empty meaning. She will surely see right through it and realize that there's nothing there.

She is back to smiling, though; bright and toothy, revealing that wonky little incisor. (I

279

wonder why her father, the dentist, never bothered to fix it for her.) "That sounds *fascinating.* You'll have to tell me more about it sometime." I am so jaded from my years of *faking it* in photos that, of course, I wonder if her smile is just a front; perhaps I put her off with the tears and the social media bragging, and she is just good at hiding it. And then her smile wobbles; her nostrils flare slightly. "Oh my goodness. You're being polite and not saying anything but I just smelled myself and I desperately need to take a shower."

She rises abruptly, and I want to grab her hand and drag her back down to the couch. *Stay with me, don't leave me alone again.* But I obediently rise and follow her toward the door.

As we pass the fireplace she suddenly pauses in front of the family portrait, and places a finger on the glass. Right under my father's head, fingernail against the proud smile on his face.

"What was he like, your father?" The way she says this makes the question sound like a test. I hesitate before answering. I think of his infidelity and his gambling and his carelessness; but also how he tried so hard to compensate for the loss of our mother, how much he loved me and Benny despite our faults. I remember the smile on his face as he proclaimed to anyone who would listen that I was a *genius.*

280

"He was a good man," I say. "He always tried to protect us, especially from his own mistakes. He sometimes made bad decisions in the process, but he had good intentions."

Her head lists slightly to the right, as if trying to see the photo from another angle. "I suppose that's what parents do. I suppose as their children we'll forgive anything that they do in the name of their love for us. We have to do that, so that someday we can forgive ourselves for doing the same." She looks at me, but I look away, not liking to think about this too much.

We bustle back through the cold halls toward the rear of the house. We're almost to the kitchen when Ashley stops.

"I forgot my yoga mat in the library!" she cries, and turns back, jogging down the hallway and disappearing into the depths of the house. I stand there, waiting for her, for what feels like an ungodly long time. When she returns — the mat under her arm — her face is flushed and pink with some emotion and she won't meet my eyes. I wonder: *Has she been crying?* Perhaps I was prying too much, digging into wounds that were too fresh. She slides past me in the hall, moving too fast toward the door; I feel like she might be about to slip away for good.

I grab her hand, and stop her in her tracks. "I'm so glad we talked like this," I say. "I'm going to be honest, I haven't really had a lot

281

of girlfriends in my life. All this" — I make a vague gesture with my free hand, taking in Stonehaven but also the entirety of my life — "has made it difficult. And with my career and all, I've grown more used to public proclamations than personal confessionals. There's less on the line, you know? It's easier. But this is what I *need,* I think. Honesty. Does that make sense? Anyway, I'm sorry if I've overwhelmed you."

We're still standing in the dim hallway, next to a marble console where a decorative clock ticks out the hour with a silvery peal of chimes. Ashley blinks at me, and in the gloom it's hard to read her expression. "It's fine. Really. I'm sorry that you've had such a . . . rough year."

Impulsively, I give her a hug; inhaling the yeasty smell of her, the tackiness of her warm skin under my hand. She stiffens, as if startled, but then I feel something give way inside her. Her hands creep around my back, gripping the bony wings of my scapulas as if looking for leverage with which to climb.

"Thanks so much for listening," I whisper in her ear. "I'm so *happy* that we're going to be friends."

■ ■ ■ ■

NINA

■ ■ ■ ■

15.

She thinks that we are *friends.*

Her arms around me are like a vise; naked longing drips from every syllable of her sentence; her breath in my ear is sweet and rank. The narrow hallway, cold with stones; the metronymic claustrophobia of that ancient, ticking clock. I feel like I'm going to choke. I feel like I might choke *her.*

She clutches me tighter, willing me to hug her back; and despite my loathing I remind myself that I am not Nina, I am *Ashley,* and of course *Ashley* would hug her. *Ashley* is full of love and understanding and forgiveness. *Ashley* feels pity for this sobbing, jittery, wreck of a girl, this newly orphaned basket case. *Ashley* is a far better person than I.

So *Ashley* reaches around Vanessa's narrow little body — she feels like naked bones swaddled in cashmere — and hugs her back.

"Of course we're friends," I murmur. Something clicks at the back of my throat.

And I smile, as I think of what I just put in her library.

16.

Vanessa is not quite what I expected.

I realize this as soon as she comes into focus, standing there on Stonehaven's porch, half-hidden in the gloom. She is so *small*. In my mind, she has always loomed much larger — of course, I've spent so many hours studying her that she expanded to occupy my entire imagination. But in person, she is just a slight thing, dwarfed by the great tree-trunk pillars of her family's ancestral home. It feels as if the porch might close around her and swallow her whole, history eating her alive.

She moves toward me as I step from our car and turn to greet her, readying a smile. And then she stops abruptly, peering at me. For a moment, I am gripped by the irrational fear that she might have somehow recognized me. But the likelihood of this is remote: Why would Vanessa remember a friend of Benny's that she barely lifted her head to acknowledge twelve years ago? Besides, even if she did, *that* Nina — baby-faced, chubby, a pink-haired alterna-girl in shapeless black — bears little resemblance to the coiffed, toned Nina I've since grown into. And even less resemblance to *Ashley,* in all her athleisure glory.

Vanessa is wearing jeans and a hoodie under a blazer, all of such a cut that the price paid for them is evident in the drape of their folds. Her sneakers are pristine white, as if someone has recently gone over them with bleach and a toothbrush. But although she is groomed to perfection — hair falling loose around her shoulders, makeup done with a precision hand — something feels off. The color of her blond highlights is a little too brassy. I can see the puffiness under her eyes. Her hip bones are like blades, the jeans hooked over them and billowing loosely around her thighs.

"You're sure that's not the housekeeper?" Lachlan murmurs from behind me.

"It's Vanessa."

"Not what I expected," he says under his breath. "What happened to *V-Life?*"

"We're in Lake Tahoe, not the Hamptons. What did you expect? Diamonds and couture dresses?"

"Basic personal hygiene. Is that too much to ask?"

"You're the worst kind of snob." I march away from the car and toward the porch, contorting my face into a rictus of surprise, as if I've only just now spied her standing there on the porch. "Oh! You must be Vanessa?"

"Ashley, right? Oh *wonderful.* Oh *thrilling!* You made it!"

Her squeal of faux excitement makes me cringe. *Good grief,* I think. *Nothing about this woman is sincere.* I walk up the stairs and she approaches me, and suddenly we are right up against each other. There's an awkward moment, and I can tell she's unsure of the proper protocol: Is she supposed to shake my hand or hug me? *Always take control of the situation; lead, instead of being led* — a lesson Lachlan taught me when we first started at this game. So I reach in quickly, and press my cheek against hers in an affectionate embrace, squeezing the tops of her arms. *Ashley* the yoga instructor would be completely at home with physical contact, accustomed as she is to poking and tugging at sweaty, Lycra-clad bodies.

"Thank you for inviting us into your home," I say, close to her ear. I can sense her quivering in my embrace like a captive starling; a musky smell of something wild coming in waves off of her.

As we exchange pleasantries, Lachlan comes up behind me, a suitcase in each hand. Vanessa is still close enough that I can see something change in her as she takes him in;

289

her body going still, like a deer sensing an approaching predator. She pulls away, plucks at the cuff of her blazer, eyes fixed on him as he lopes leisurely toward us. I turn to see that Lachlan has unleashed his biggest, most laconic smile.

So that is how it's going to go, I think to myself.

I remind myself that it's all for show. Nothing is real here, not even me. We're all just facades and fakery.

I've probably spent less than an hour total inside the walls of Stonehaven in my life — my time here was mostly spent in the cottage — and yet the house has always loomed large in my imagination.

This house was where I learned the meaning of *social class* and *legacy,* what it meant to own furniture that cost more than a car, what it meant to have portraits of your ancestors hanging over the mantel. Walking into Stonehaven, at age fifteen, I understood for the first time that family money like that is a gift of permanence — not just that you'd never have to worry about the daily scramble for basic subsistence, but that you'd exist as a link in an unbroken chain that extended far into both the past and the future. Coming from a family of two, a family without a real home (or even a real name, for that matter), I pined for that kind of anchor. I'd listen to

Benny complain about his family — *predatory stuck-up assholes* — and seethe with jealousy even as I soberly nodded in agreement.

Stonehaven changed everything for me. It gave me something to long for, and also something to resent. It demonstrated for me the size of the abyss between my life and that of the people who ran the world. It awoke an interest in beauty that still stays with me; it was why, when I had to choose a college major, I checked the box next to *art history* rather than something more practical like *economics* or *engineering.* It awakened in me a rage that I haven't quite managed to rid myself of, all these years later.

Nothing about the interior has changed since I was last here. Apparently no one has attempted to update the décor in the intervening years, and the mansion feels frozen in time. The same polished sideboard sits in the foyer, displaying a pair of Delft baluster vases; the same hand-painted rose-print wallpaper hangs in the sitting room, now slightly yellow with age; the same moon-faced grandfather clock ticks away the minutes on the landing. Portraits of the Liebling ancestors still gaze sternly down from the walls.

In my memories, Stonehaven is enormous, like a castle from a fairy tale; and yet as I stand in the foyer for the first time in twelve years, I realize that it isn't nearly as big as I've remembered it being. It's impressive, certainly, but the past few years in Los Angeles's mansions have spoiled me. The rich these days prefer glass, unimpeded views, a bare minimum of confining walls, the vast empty acreage itself being the real luxury. Stonehaven is from another era. It is warren-like, its rooms built to conceal the scurrying of servants and polishing of silver and smoking of cigars. The house has a dark, claustrophobic quality; the rooms are cluttered with more than a century's worth of furniture and objets d'art, the remnants of five generations of Lieblings with divergent tastes. Other than the bones of the great house itself, everything feels mismatched, unconsidered.

And yet. The house is imposing in a way that no modernist goliath could ever be. It feels alive, like it has a heartbeat of its own, secrets mortared in with the stones.

As I stand there in the foyer for the first time in twelve years, I feel like I am fifteen again. A nobody, from nowhere, with nothing. I am stunned silent. Vanessa is babbling on about the history of the house while Lachlan circles the edges of the room, peeking through the doorways to scrutinize the sitting room and the formal parlor. I know what he's doing: Looking for a likely spot for a hidden safe. Behind a painting, probably, or inside a closet, maybe set into the floor under a rug.

As for me, I gaze at the beautiful things around us, ones that I recall from all those years ago, and make a mental inventory. Those Delft chinoiserie jars, gaudy objects that I remember studying as a kid while listening to Benny's tirade about robber barons — the pair would go for $25,000. I hadn't known that back then, but I certainly know it now. That grandfather clock? I'll need to look closer, but I suspect it is an eighteenth-century French piece, and worth at least a hundred thousand.

Lachlan is standing in front of a painting of some stuffy old matron with fussy dogs. "You know what, Ash? This house reminds me a bit of the castle," he begins, just like we practiced in the car on the way up the mountain. This is where I'm supposed to casually let it drop that "Michael" is "Irish aristocracy"; but before I've even gotten my line out, Vanessa has already seized on Lachlan's words.

"Which castle?" She is suddenly alert and straining with excitement, like a trout thrashing at the line.

Lachlan offers his vague enough answer. (We've done our research: There are, in fact, a dozen or so castles owned by O'Briens.) Vanessa's entire body seems to relax as she leans toward him, relief naked on her face: "Well, then, you must understand what it's like to live in a place like this."

"I certainly do. A curse and a privilege, right?" Lachlan's eyes flick over to me, a smug little smile on his face: *This is going to be easy.*

"Oh *yes,* exactly," she sighs, and I want to smack her. A *curse?* To be given all this, with zero effort of your own; to own all these glorious treasures that no one else gets to see — and call it a *curse?* She is privilege, and only privilege. How *dare* she.

"Is it *really* that awful to live here?" I prod. I want to hear her whine some more, to bolster my hatred of her. It will make this so much easier. But something about the expression on my face gives her pause. She blinks, her face stuttering with alarm.

"Oh really, it's not so bad," she murmurs.

Lachlan is giving me a look of death over Vanessa's shoulder. I realize that I am coming off as unsympathetic, even judgmental, not exactly *Ashley*-like. I soften my tone, blink hard so that my eyes mist over with something approaching empathy. "And you're living all alone? You don't get lonely?"

"Well, a little, yes. A lot, sometimes. But hopefully not anymore now that you're here!" Vanessa laughs a little too hard, a frantic high note that vibrates the vases on the table. She glances over to see if I've noticed this, with a look of neediness so obvious that it's like she's just flipped the switch on a neon sign.

She *hates* being here by herself, I suddenly understand. She's lonely, yes, but that's only part of it. Is it possible that she loathes this place? Are Lachlan and I here to frighten off the ghosts of her past?

Despite myself, I wonder what they might be.

The kitchen stretches along the left rear of the house, a sprawling room designed during the era of cooks and kitchen maids and mistresses who never entered the kitchen. The years have clearly seen some attempt to turn it into a more modern kitchen — the cooking fireplace now houses a decorative arrangement of white birch logs and a Viking stove has been installed against one wall. A kitchen island the size of a boat anchors the room, its wooden top appealingly nicked and stained with age. Gleaming copper pots hang from a rack over the center island, polished to a shine. But all the counter surfaces are bare, as if emptied and staged for a real estate showing, and it's hard to imagine anyone cooking in that enormous space, let alone whipping up meals for one on that eight-burner stove.

A long breakfast table has been pushed along the wall below a row of picture windows that overlook the lake. This is set with an elaborate spread: plates of pastries and cookies, a cluster of bone china teacups, an embossed tea service in polished silver, a crystal carafe of wine, freshly cut flowers. It's all so pretentious, so ludicrously over-the-top, that it almost feels like a weapon, intended to make us feel small before her.

Lachlan catches my eye and raises an eyebrow. *La-di-da.*

"I know, I went a little overboard, but I couldn't help myself, but it makes no sense to just let this stuff get *dusty,*" Vanessa says as she herds us toward the table. She laughs nervously, and picks up a teacup, turning it in her hands. The porcelain is so thin it's nearly translucent, painted around the edges with a decorative motif of a bird. A warbler or a sparrow or a starling — Who am I kidding, I know nothing about birds. "This was my mother's favorite china, she always insisted that we use it every day instead of saving it for special occasions." Her eyebrows shoot upward in sudden alarm. "Oh, but I don't mean to give you the impression that you're *not* a special occasion! Anyway, half of it is gone at this point because we broke it. I have wine, too, I wasn't sure if you drink, so just let me know which you'd prefer."

She is twittering like a bird on speed and I just want to tell her to stop it. I am starting to wonder if she isn't a little bit . . . unhinged.

"I'll have wine," I say.

She is visibly relieved. "Oh good, me, too."

Lachlan is standing at the table, just staring

out the windows because he can finally see it properly: the lake, spreading out before us. The rain clouds are clearing and the last of the setting sun is leaking through them, with shafts of pale light illuminating the surface of the lake below. The water is steel gray and jagged — not the serene dark blue you find on the postcards for sale in Tahoe City, but something darker and more ominous. I know the lake well so I am prepared for its cold, imposing beauty, but Lachlan is momentarily riveted by the sight. I wonder whether he had been expecting something smaller, something rinky-dink and benign: pleasure boats and fishing docks and lifeguards playing reggae.

"Have you ever been to Tahoe before?" Vanessa is still cradling the teacup in her palm, as if it's a small pet.

I sit down at the table and reach for a scone, to avoid meeting her eyes. "Never."

"Oh, really? Well, I guess it's not very convenient to Seattle. That's where you're from, right?"

"Portland, actually."

She shakes her head, as if Portland and Seattle might as well be the same place for the amount of appeal each holds for her. "So the thing about Tahoe . . ." she continues. "Most people come in the summer. Or for ski holidays. This time of year, it's pretty quiet. I have to warn you that there's not a whole lot to do, really, unless you're into hiking and mountain biking." She seems to be relaxing a little, and her voice starts to develop a patrician little drawl, her words growing more arch. "I hope you weren't expecting something a little more lively. And as for the restaurant situation — this is the land of burgers and zucchini fries." The expression of revulsion on her face makes me wonder how she is surviving without her usual diet of caviar and bone broth garnished with twenty-four-carat gold leaf. Maybe this explains why she is so thin.

"We came especially *for* the quiet," Lachlan says as he sits down next to me. "I'm on sabbatical from my teaching job so I can work on a book. So my idea of heaven is a little room with a beautiful view and no one around to bother me while I write." He laughs. "Except for Ashley, of course. Because she never bothers me. And besides, Ash *is* a beautiful view."

I am surprised the treacle in his voice isn't sending Vanessa into diabetic shock. "He says that now, but ask him again in the morning before I've had my coffee."

Lachlan reaches for my hand and I stroke his forearm with my fingers. Such a happy couple, such a *well-adjusted* couple, so supportive of each other. We've inhabited similar roles, on previous jobs, and I can't say I mind it, my arm's-length lover suddenly behaving like a model boyfriend. A thread of comforting conventionality in this bizarrely unconventional life I've come to lead. I look at Lachlan and see the mirth in his face and match it with my own, and for a moment, in the midst of our grift, I feel a lift of elation that we are in this together, the heady frisson that comes with precision teamwork. Maybe this is a strange kind of attachment, but it's something we both understand. Vanessa is watching us smile at each other, and I wonder what she sees.

"So, Michael, you're a writer!" She perches on a chair across from us. "I *love* to read. I just finished *Anna Karenina*! What do you write?"

Lachlan and I have gone around and around on this one for a long time. It was important, I thought, to actually have a portfolio of pages ready; but ones that sound off-putting and obscure, so that she won't ask to read them. Lachlan scoffed at my efforts. "The woman doesn't read anything other than the labels on her clothes. Do you really think she's going to ask to see pages of my manuscript?"

Now he fiddles with his napkin, frowns. "Oh, a little poetry here and there. And I'm working on a novel. Kind of an experimental thing, you know, visceral realism, in the vein of Bolaño." He delivers this convincingly enough, although I know he'd never heard of Roberto Bolaño before I fed the name to him two days earlier.

Her smile tightens. "Oh. Wow. I don't even know what those words *mean.*" She begins to worry the edge of her cuff again, picking threads loose with her fingernails. I wonder if the pretension was a mistake. I've learned over the past few years that rich people believe that their wealth is the result of some intellectual or moral superiority; when you pop that bubble and suggest that they might not be so smart or special after all, you're headed for trouble. Better to reassure them of their position at the top of the chain by showing the proper deference.

I lean across the table toward her. "Want to know a secret? I don't either, and I've been listening to him talk about this book all year." It hurts a little, to pretend that I'm so dim.

She laughs. Equilibrium settles across her face again. "And you're a yoga instructor? I mean, I can tell. You look so . . . *fit.*"

I am not particularly fit, actually; it's amazing what the power of suggestion will do. "Well, yes. But I believe that yoga is really more about the balance of the mind, not just the balance of the body."

If she realizes that I'm just regurgitating clichés skimmed from self-help websites, she doesn't show it. "I *love* that," she gushes. "Maybe you can give me a private lesson while you're here. I'd pay you, of course. What do you charge?"

How like the rich to assume that everyone around them is for sale. I wave away the suggestion. "Oh, please. It would be my pleasure. Really, I'm grateful for any opportunity to share my practice." I lean in conspiratorially. "That's how Michael and I met, actually. He came in for one of my classes."

"It turns out I wasn't that into yoga after all. But I was *very* into the teacher." Another line that Lachlan workshopped with me on the drive up.

Vanessa laughs as Lachlan picks up the wine and waves it in her general direction. She looks around and murmurs, "Oh damn, I forgot wineglasses."

"Your mother said to use the teacups, right?"

She hesitates for just a second, and holds her teacup out. He pours in a splash of red wine, and then another, and another, until the cup is perilously close to brimming over and spilling onto her jeans. She waits, patiently, for him to stop, the saucer quivering in her hand, her eyes fixed on the rising liquid. A neat turning of the tables by my Lachlan. He stops a millimeter shy of the brim and smiles at her.

"Do you take sugar?"

She stares at him for a minute and then laughs, a startling, coquettish trill; tosses her hair just so, as if a camera might be trained on her. "Do I *look* like a two-lumps kind of girl?" Her chest rises a bit, her eyes open theatrically wide, as if preparing herself for a photo. *This is the Vanessa from* V-Life, I think: performative, moving from *moment* to *moment* without much consideration of the space in between.

Lachlan glances at me and then back at her. It is obvious to both of us what she is looking for; she wants a *like* right about now, and even if there is no convenient heart emoji to click on, there are other ways to give her the approval she seeks. "Two lumps at the least," Lachlan says, his eyes narrowing, the faintest hint of a dimple visible at the edge of his smile. "At the *very* least."

She blushes then, a pink flush that rises up her neck in a manner so familiar that I am stopped cold. Maybe it is this sweetly childish reaction, or maybe it's the wolfish expression on Lachlan's face, but I am suddenly ill at ease. He is so cool, Lachlan is; why do I feel so hot? This woman is *my* enemy, not his. *I'm* the one who should be stiffened with the steel of righteous conviction. But her flush, it reminds me so much of Benny — of the way he flushed when he looked at me, puppy love written in pink across his chest.

But the woman before me is not Benny. She's not in love with me, just herself. She's a privileged brat, a *Liebling,* a member of the family that filled my pockets with poison and set me along the path that led me here. It's *her* fault, really, that I'm here at all.

And so I smile innocently, lift the cup of wine to my lips, and drain it in one gulp.

17

The caretaker's cottage still nestles in the pines on the edge of the property, on a bluff over the lake, surrounded by ferns. We follow Vanessa, now tipsy, down the dark path (although, of course, I could have walked this way blindfolded) and then watch politely as she turns on the lights and shows us how to operate the heater. That done, she remains standing in the cottage's living room for an awkward minute, as if waiting for an invitation.

"Well," she says finally. "I'll let you get settled."

Once she is gone, Lachlan turns to survey the room. "Well," he says, "pretty posh accommodations for the caretaker."

The cottage is cramped, and smells slightly like must, but this is mitigated by the fire that someone (Vanessa's housekeeper, presumably) has set in the stone fireplace. There is a bottle of wine sitting alongside a bowl of waxed apples on a table in the dining nook, and fresh flowers on the mantel above the fireplace. Personal touches designed to disguise the fact that the cottage is clearly a depository for furniture that has been ejected from the main house over the years. The cottage, I now see, is a glorified storage facility for five generations of antiques collectors. In the living room, an embroidered silk couch from the 1980s is paired with Craftsman Stickley chairs, and framed by a Pennsylvania Dutch sideboard and an Art Deco secretary. In the dining nook sits a mahogany table with claw feet that is far too large for the space; its chairs bump up against the walls. Dusty paintings hang on the walls, a collection of crystal bowls are piled on the bookshelves, and two giant porcelain urns (yet more chinoiserie) flank the fireplace. And yet something about this ad hoc collection makes me smile: Nothing is contrived, just lost objects seeking attention and love.

I walk through the cottage, examining furniture, registering the memories that rise as I do. There is the sofa where Benny and I used to lie on opposite ends with our bare feet pressed up against each other as we drew and studied. There is the kitchen stove, an old Wedgewood, where we would roast marshmallows over the burners using monogrammed silver forks, and then shove the scalding sugar into our mouths. There is the garnet-colored crystal bowl that we used as an ashtray, still black with pot residue.

This cabin was the entirety of our little personal universe, a place where we fit in a world where we otherwise didn't. Or, at least, it's where I *thought* I fit in it, until his family dragged me out and showed me exactly how I didn't belong.

I sit down at the table in the dining nook, rubbing my finger across the scars in the wood: a series of circular marks in the finish, faded water rings. Could that be from the beer cans we set down here, years ago, when Benny and I would smoke joints at this table and bitch about our families? How easy it is to be careless when you're young and ignorant of the permanence of damage.

Lachlan throws himself down in the chair next to me and unscrews the top on the bottle of wine. He studies the label on the bottle and then picks at a price tag with his finger: $7.99. "Well. She didn't exactly dig up the wine cellar on our behalf," he says.

"We're commoners. She probably thinks we won't know the difference."

"She thinks *you're* a commoner. *I'm* landed gentry, remember? You should feel lucky to be in my presence."

I pick up the bottle and press my lips to the rim, tipping it so the wine rolls down my throat. It's warm and sweet, but it will do the job. "At least she's trying to be friendly."

"More than friendly. Did you see how

much makeup she was wearing? She didn't do that for you, darling." He tilts his head, considering something. "But she's rather pretty, if you scraped all that slap off her face. Has a Grace Kelly patrician blonde thing going for her."

I don't like the expression on his face at all, like he's about to bite into a particularly enticing bonbon. I take another gulp from the wine bottle. "Can we just focus on the plan now, please?"

And what *is* the plan, you may be wondering.

In our luggage, buried beneath a stack of poetry books and my old yoga mat, we have packed a dozen tiny spy cameras. Each is the size of a screwhead, and yet they are capable of streaming high-definition video from Stonehaven to our laptops in the cottage, a few hundred yards away. What was once cutting-edge technology, now available online for $49.99.

The cameras are to be planted in inconspicuous hiding spots inside Stonehaven, where we might be able to track Vanessa's movements and pinpoint the location of the safe. The safe is most likely to be in her bedroom, or perhaps a library or an office. We'll have to find excuses to get into those rooms, however we can. The closer we can get to Vanessa, the easier this will be.

It's not that there aren't other valuable targets within the walls of Stonehaven: Just the grandfather clock that I saw in the parlor would cover six doses of my mother's cancer medication. And yet, as long as Efram is missing in action, we lack a fence for antiques. The money in Vanessa's safe is a better bet. Easier to smuggle out, easier to liquidate.

Once we've located the safe, sussed out its contents, and taken measure of the security system, we'll check out of the cottage and go somewhere else for a while. We'll hunker down somewhere nearby and let a few more renters come through the cottage, erase ourselves from Vanessa's memory, delete our trail from the Internet. And then, six weeks or so later, maybe over Christmas if she leaves to visit her brother, we'll go in and take it all.

I close my eyes and an old, familiar image rises in my mind: a dark vault, stacks of green bills bound with paper bands and luminous with promise. So much rides on luck, of course: that the code hasn't changed, that the cash is still there. But I just *know.* The Lieblings were both paranoid and lazy. I remember how Benny talked about the money in the safe, as if it was simply *understood* that everyone needed a seven-figure emergency fund: William Liebling had surely passed his neuroses on to his children. After all, we inherit our parents' habits — good and bad — along with their genes.

I let myself imagine what else we might find in the safe, once we get it open. Gold coins? Jewelry? The diamonds I saw fastened around Judith Liebling's neck in the photo from the San Francisco Opera opening: Vanessa surely inherited that, along with the rest of her mother's jewelry collection. Likely they are in there as well, tucked in velvet boxes alongside the cash.

Don't get greedy. Just this once, am I allowed to ignore all my own rules?

Lachlan and I sit there, drinking and scheming, until the wine is gone and we are tipsy and exhausted. I am in desperate need of a shower, so I grab my bag and take it to the bedroom. I throw open the door and then find myself standing in the doorway, unable to go any farther.

Because there it is, the bed. A great four-poster monstrosity, dulled from years without polishing, but still a piece grand enough for a princeling. Probably it was, once. It is also the bed where I lay as Benny peeled off my jeans, tugging them awkwardly over my calves, while I kept my eyes riveted to the painting on the wall. The bed where I lay waiting for him to take his own clothes off, my body shaking from fear and desire and strange roiling emotions I didn't know how to name.

Poor Benny. Poor me.

I wonder what Benny would think of me, if he could see me now. Not much, probably; but then again, I suppose he never really did, not once that flush of puppy love had faded away and his family reminded him who I really was.

Lachlan has come up behind me, I can feel his breath on my neck as I stare into the bedroom. "Bringing back memories?" he says.

"Yeah." I choose not to elaborate. Because something about this adult lover that I have now — so modern and cunning and slick with deceit — feels like a rebuke to that first, naïve, tender love I so briefly experienced here in this cabin. This is the person I've become, a stranger to the child Nina who once trembled in the arms of a skinny teenage boy. No, the Nina I am now has never been in this cottage at all.

He wraps his arms around me from behind, crossing them over my chest, drawing me in, close to him. "I lost my virginity to my babysitter," he whispers into my ear. "Emma Donogal. I was thirteen and she was eighteen."

"Jesus. That's child molestation."

"Technically, I suppose, but at the time it felt like the greatest thing that had ever happened to me. Her breasts had already been a fixture in my wet dreams for years. Lovely Emma. I had a fixation on older women for a long time, because of her."

310

I spin in his arms to look up at his face, surprised by the wistful tone in his voice, but he looks amused more than melancholy. He laughs at the expression on my face, and then kisses my forehead and rests his chin in my hair. "Of course, younger women are lovely, too. Don't worry." And I wonder, not for the first time, if he ever had a thing with my mother. He splits the difference between us — a decade between us both — and God knows my mother has seduced her own fair share of younger men over the years. I am afraid to ask.

Lachlan was the one who found my mother, three years back. He'd come to pick her up for a poker game and discovered her collapsed in the bathroom, head gashed open on the edge of her sink. Lachlan took her to the hospital for stitches, which turned into an MRI and an overnight stay for further testing. The two of them had been developing a con together — what it was, they never told me; but needless to say, it never happened. Instead, Lily's cancer happened.

I wouldn't have known if Lachlan hadn't gotten my phone number from my mother and called me in New York City. He was just a strange disembodied voice on the end of the line back then, a barely detectable burr of an accent. "I think your mother needs you here. It's cancer," he'd said. "But she's too stubborn to ask. She doesn't want to disrupt your life."

My life. I don't know what my mother had told him I was doing out there in New York, how she still dreamed my Great Future had manifested itself, but it certainly wasn't the life I was actually leading. After graduating from my third-tier college with a BA in art history and six figures in student loan debt, I'd headed to New York, thinking I'd find a job at an auction house or a Chelsea gallery or an arts nonprofit. It turned out that those jobs were few and far between and, I quickly discovered, reserved for those with *real* connections — parents on the museum board, family friends who were famous painters, influential mentors from their Ivy League colleges. The only job I could find was as the third assistant to an interior designer whose specialty was redecorating luxury vacation homes in the Hamptons.

At that point, I was still determined to get as far away from my childhood as possible. I'd groomed myself until I looked like a facsimile of the woman I aspired to be, I was slim and shiny in my fast fashion. But when Lachlan called, I was also impossibly broke, living on falafel and ramen, and sharing an apartment in Flushing with three other women. I scurried about New York and the Hamptons, one of thousands of underpaid and overqualified young women similarly scurrying, sourcing fabric for custom curtains and arranging for Italian settees to be craned into penthouse windows and, most of all, fetching *venti macchiatos* for my boss. I was fluent in the language of *bone* and *ivory* and *eggshell*. I memorized the contents of Sotheby's auction catalogs and the names of the oligarchs who bought $60 million paintings and fourteenth-century gold-inlaid secretaries. I spent my days monitoring workmen as they hung hand-painted wallpaper that the homes' owners — society matrons, hedge fund wives, Russian billionaires — would immediately demand be ripped down because *it just didn't feel right.*

My job, I knew, was a dead end. And yet, there were those moments when I would be alone in one of those enormous houses, alone with all of those beautiful *things,* and I could pretend that it all belonged to me. I'd come face-to-face with an Egon Schiele drawing hanging on a wall in a bathroom, or would run my hands along a seventeenth-century card table, hand-inlaid with mother-of-pearl marquetry, or sit on the very same Frank Lloyd Wright armchair that I'd studied in an architectural design course. Objects that transcended all of *this,* objects that had endured centuries of indifferent owners, objects whose enduring mystery and beauty lived in opposition to the ephemeral nature of our digital age. These things would still exist when I did not, and I counted myself fortunate to be able to have time with them at all.

Nearly a decade had passed since my mother had told me it was time to focus on my Future, and yes, I'd managed to get an education — an education into the way the one percent lived, a way I would never be able to live myself. It was like sitting in the front row of a Broadway show and longing to join all the action on the stage in front of me, but realizing that there was no stairway to get me up there, too.

So when the strange voice on the other end of the line informed me that my mother needed me in Los Angeles, I quit my job on the spot. Within the day, I'd packed up all my cheap black dresses, given the key back to my roommates, and was on a plane to California. I told myself at the time that I was leaving New York purely out of responsibility for my mother — I was all she had, *of course* I would go take care of her — but wasn't I also fleeing my own failure?

And when I got off the airplane there was a man standing there waiting for me, suit jacket slung over one shoulder, ice-blue eyes roving across the faces of the people coming in until they snagged on mine and stayed there. A faint smile on his face, so impossibly handsome: I felt a little lift of hope at the sight of him, matching the accelerated thrum of my pulse. "You look just like your mother," he'd said, as he gently pried the suitcase from my hand.

"We're nothing alike," I'd retorted, still clinging to the last residue of that Great Future I'd once been so sure I had.

And yet, as I stand here in the cottage at Stonehaven three years later, I know that my mother and I are more alike than I ever imagined.

18.

And so it begins.

The next morning, at an hour when the light is still pallid and anemic, I drag a mat out to the great lawn and conspicuously run through a yoga routine. The lake is a confrontational gray, and the frigid November air penetrates my workout clothes; I'm shivering even as I sweat. I've done plenty of yoga over the years, but never quite like this, like I have something to prove. My body balks at the unnatural exertions, the unnatural hour. And yet there is also something about being out there under the pines that feels clean and elemental. The crisp air that smells of green: It brings me back to my childhood, and the way that Tahoe felt like an oasis to me.

Sun Salutation and Half Moon, Wild Thing and Side Crane. Toes clawed into my thigh, hands lifted to the sky: I imagine eyes watching me from both the cottage and the main house, and feel powerful under their gaze. An earth goddess; or at the very least, a good enough fake.

When I'm done, I roll up the mat and do a few showy bonus stretches and then turn around to face Stonehaven. Vanessa is standing at the French doors that lead from the kitchen to the garden, watching me through fogged windowpanes. She steps quickly back, as if embarrassed to have been caught spying on me, but I wave at her before she can vanish, and walk toward the house. When I'm a few feet away, she pushes the door open and stands there with an awkward smile on her face. She's wearing pink silk pajamas topped with a fuzzy cashmere cardigan, her hands wrapped around another one of those porcelain cups.

"Sorry about that, I should have asked if you'd mind. But the sunrise was so glorious, I couldn't resist." There is sweat trickling down the side of my face; I dab at it with a towel.

She tugs her cardigan around her body with one hand, tucking it tight against the draft. "I'm impressed. I only just woke up."

"I'm an early riser. The dawn is the best time of day. Just so quiet and full of promise." This is a lie. At home, I'll stay in bed until noon if given the chance. But sleep eluded me last night; something about being back in the caretaker's cottage, the claustrophobia of all those memories. Every time I drifted off I would dream of a hulking figure, reaching

317

out to yank me from under the covers, and I would wake with my heart in my throat. Then I'd lie there in the dark, listening to Lachlan's soft snores beside me, wondering who I was and what I'd done, why I was back here of all places. Thinking also of my mother back in Los Angeles, slowly being eaten away by cancer while she waits for me to return with the money for her cure; remembering also how beautiful she once looked in that blue sequined cocktail dress, her face pink with laughter.

Around four A.M. I finally gave up on sleep altogether and went to the kitchen to study yoga tutorials on my laptop.

Now Vanessa takes a sip of her coffee. She is pale and drawn without the heavy makeup she was wearing yesterday, as if someone took an eraser to her features overnight; and I realize how much of her beauty is yet another illusion. "Maybe I should join you tomorrow . . . ?" she says. The sentence trails off into a tentative question mark.

"Of course!" I wait for an invitation to come inside and, when it doesn't come, I gesture at the cup in her hand. "Can I beg a cup off you?"

She looks down at her hands, as if surprised to discover that there's something there. "Coffee, you mean?"

"We don't have any in the cottage," I say pointedly. "I'm a horror in the morning if I don't have caffeine." *This* is true. Already I feel myself tallying up the truths and the untruths I'm telling her and I wonder how soon I'll start mixing them all up. She's still standing there as if she doesn't understand what I'm talking about. "We don't have any coffee in the cottage. We haven't had a chance to do a grocery run."

"Oh! Of course. No need to beg, I should have offered." She smiles and pulls the door open wider and steps back. "I've got a pot in the kitchen. Come in."

Compared to the closeness of the caretaker's cottage, Stonehaven is freezing, despite the efforts of the ancient furnace that I can hear creaking and huffing below the polished wooden floorboards. I follow her into the kitchen, where an Italian coffee machine is keeping a pot of coffee warm. "I'm still figuring out how to use this thing," she says as she pours me a cup. "I lived in New York for so long that I started to believe that coffee only came from bodegas."

I know for a fact that Vanessa Liebling does not get her coffee from bodegas; that the coffee she drinks generally sports elaborate latte art and fussy little garnishes and is served at outdoor cafés in Greenwich Village or Le Marais. (Her coffee habits have been well documented on her feed.) I suppose she thinks that identifying with the common people who buy crappy coffee in paper bags

319

will somehow make me like her more. I would hate her less if she owned up to her privilege, instead of pretending that she's slumming it with me.

Smile, I remind myself. I need access to Stonehaven; I need her to like me. But as the two of us stand here, awkwardly lobbing lies at each other, it feels impossible that any kind of connection — false or not — might be forged between us. We politely sip at our coffees, smiling nervously at each other, until Vanessa finally breaks the silence.

"So Michael doesn't do yoga with you?"

"Oh God, no. He'd murder me if I tried to rouse him that early." A semi-truth.

She nods as if she can relate to this sentiment. "Do you want to . . . sit down? We could go in the library. It's a little warmer in there."

The library. I can still see Mrs. Liebling sitting on that velvet couch, design magazines stacked in slippery piles around her. "That would be lovely. Otherwise I'll be creeping around the cottage trying not to wake Michael up."

Vanessa tops up our coffees and I follow her into the library. It's all as it was the last time I was in here — the bereft moose, the jacketless tomes, the green velvet couch, all looking a little worse for the wear. Vanessa throws herself down in a corner of the couch where the nap is particularly flattened and she tugs a blanket over her feet. I follow her lead but find myself stopping in front of a photograph in a silver frame that's displayed prominently on the mantel over the fireplace. It's a portrait of the Lieblings that I've never seen before, one that must have been taken a year before I met Benny because there's Vanessa at the center in a maroon cap and gown, graduating from high school. Her parents flank her, her mother in a pristine yellow day dress with a silk scarf around her neck and her father in a bespoke suit with a matching yellow pocket square. I am taken aback by the broad, genuine smiles on their faces, the wholesome nature of their obvious parental pride; in my memory, they are both scowling, joyless fiends with pointed teeth.

Benny stands on the edge of this pretty troika, awkward in a button-down shirt and a polka-dot bow tie, the only one whose smile looks forced. He looks a little younger than he was when I met him, his cheeks full and downy, his ears too big for his face. He hasn't yet had the final growth spurt that will propel him into the land of giants, and his father still towers over him. He is just a child, I realize with a start. *We were just children.* A piano chord chimes inside me, in a poignant minor key. Poor Benny. Despite myself, I wonder how he's doing in that institution.

"Your family?" I ask.

A brief hitch of hesitation. "Yes. Mom,

321

Dad, little brother."

I know I should let it go, that I'm poking at an anthill with a short stick, but I can't help myself. "Tell me about them," I say. I throw myself on the couch across from her. "You guys look close."

"We were."

I can't stop looking at the photograph even though I know I'm staring, and when I glance over at Vanessa, she is watching me. I can't help it: I blush. I want to ask about Benny but I am afraid that something in my voice would give me away. "Were?"

"My mother died when I was nineteen. She drowned." Her eyes flick over to the window, with its view of the lake, and then flick back to me. "My father died earlier this year."

And then she bursts into tears.

I freeze.

I remember when I came across the news clipping during one of my Google searches, years ago: JUDITH LIEBLING, SAN FRANCISCO ARTS PATRON, DROWNS IN BOATING AC-CIDENT. The article was light on details of her death, but heavy on lists of the philanthro-pies she'd been involved in: not just the San Francisco Opera, but also the de Young Museum, Save The Bay, and (somewhat poi-gnantly) the Mental Health Association in California. I'd had a hard time reconciling the benevolent society do-gooder in the ac-companying photos — standing alongside the mayor, red hair flying loose, smile wide — with the judgmental recluse I'd met at Stonehaven. *She got her just deserts,* I'd thought, before closing the page down. This was before I knew that Benny had been diagnosed with schizophrenia; I didn't spend much time thinking about how the loss of her would have affected the family she left behind.

But as I listen to Vanessa sob, it occurs to me that the Liebling children have perhaps experienced more than their fair share of tragedy. I think of the photo of Vanessa's dying father's hand and even though that image pissed me off — it felt exploitive, like she was using his death to troll for attention: *Look at how* sad *I am!* — now that I'm sitting next to her, I am uncomfortably aware of how genuine her grief is. Both parents gone and a brother in an institution. If I were a better person I would feel sorry for this bereaved woman sitting next to me and reconsider my plans for her, but I'm not. I'm shallow and I'm vindictive. I'm a *bad* person not a good one, and as I battle through this unwelcome pang of genuine empathy I force myself to think instead of the safe. I look around the room and wonder if it's in here: Hidden behind a panel of books in that bookshelf? Under that pastoral oil painting of some Liebling ancestor's prize horse, a beast with oversized haunches and a cropped tail?

But beside me, Vanessa is still weeping —

murmuring "I'm sorry" — and I can't help it, I reach over and place my hand on hers. Just to make it stop, I tell myself, and yet there's a hollow feeling in my chest that I can feel filling up with sorrow for this semi-stranger that I am planning to rob. "How did he die?" I can't think of anything else to ask.

"Cancer. It came on very quickly."

Oh God. The last thing I wanted to hear; I do not want to identify with her, in any way. "How awful," I manage limply as she launches into a harrowing description of her father's dying weeks that evokes my own worst nightmares.

"I'm very . . . alone . . . right now," she gasps. Why is she telling me these things? I want her to stop talking. I want to hate her, but it is hard to hate her when she is dripping tears on my hand.

"I can't imagine," I say lightly, hoping that will end this train of conversation, and gently tug my hand away. But something about the way she looks at me when I say this, as if the only thing she wants in the world is to be understood, makes me rethink my answer. Because dammit, I *do* understand. I think of Vanessa's photo of her dying father's hand and I see my own mother's shriveled hand; I imagine the choking silence of our house if the cancer takes her before I can save her. I know that if she dies this time I will be *alone alone alone* forever. Just like Vanessa. And my

324

eyes mist over and my mouth falls open and I hear myself saying, "Or, maybe I can imagine. My father is gone, too. And my mother is . . . ailing."

Her tears stop and she looks at me with bald eagerness in her face. "You, too? How did your father die?"

I scramble for an answer, because I know the proper one is not *Oh, he's not dead, my mom just chased him off with a shotgun after he hit me one too many times.* Instead, I imagine an alternate past for myself, a doting father who played Uno with me instead of drinking tequila until he passed out, a dad who threw me in the air not to make me scream but to make me laugh. "Heart attack," I offer. "We were really close." I find myself choking up at the thought of this imaginary father, the purity of his love for me, the safety I feel in his strong arms.

"Oh, Ashley, I'm so sorry." She's not crying anymore. She's giving me this *look* and I feel a little sick to my stomach knowing that I now truly have her exactly where I want her: She thinks we are sisters in our struggles.

I can't afford to start believing that, too.

I have never done a job like this. I've never moved so fully into someone else's life, infiltrated their home and coerced them to be my *friend.* Most of my cons have taken place in the dark, under the cover of intoxication: parties, nightclubs, hotel bars. I've grown quite good at pretending to like someone that I secretly loathe. It's easy when it's four o'clock in the morning, and your mark has just consumed a liter of Finnish vodka, and you don't have to look past their repelling facade. But this — *this* is a whole different beast. How do you rebuff someone who is genuinely trying to connect with you? How do you look them in the eye over a cup of coffee, for God's sake, and hold yourself at arm's length?

It's easiest to judge from a distance. That's why the Internet has turned us all into armchair critics, experts at the cold dissection of gesture and syllable, sneering self-righteously from the safety of our screens. There, we can feel good about ourselves, validated that our flaws aren't as bad as *theirs,* unchallenged in our superiority. Moral high ground is a pleasant place to perch, even if the view turns out to be rather limited in scope.

But it's much harder to judge when someone is in your face, human in their vulnerability.

Ten more minutes of making small talk with Vanessa — spinning lies about my mother, my yoga career, my powers of healing (*Hello, I am Saint Nina!*) — and I am so drained that I can barely see straight. It's time to get to the *point* of all this. Finally, I beg off, saying that I need to shower, and let Vanessa lead me down the hall and back toward the rear of the house.

When we're almost at the kitchen, I halt abruptly. "I left my yoga mat in the other room," I chirp, and dash back down the hall before she can stop me.

Back in the library I softly, silently, fish a camera the size of a pencil eraser from the hidden pocket in the waistband of my leggings. I scan the room and then sidle over to the bookshelf I'd noted during our conversation, one built into the corner with an angle that takes in the sweep of the room. I tuck the camera between two faded volumes — *I, Claudius* and *The Richard D. Wyckoff Method of Trading in Stocks* — and position it just *so,* and then step back to examine my handiwork. The camera is invisible unless you're specifically looking for it. I grab my yoga mat from under the couch, where I discreetly kicked it while we were talking, and slip back out into the hallway.

I jog back, flushed and breathless. Vanessa is waiting for me exactly where I left her.

"You found it."

"Under the couch." She's staring at me, and I wonder, *Does she know?* But of course she doesn't. She has no clue. The adrenaline that flushes my body makes me feel more alive and righteous than an entire hour of asanas did. *This is going to work. This is why I'm here.*

So when she throws her arms around me and hugs me, it takes me a minute to realize that she is not celebrating my small victory, but is instead anointing me as her new confidante. "I'm so *happy* that we're going to be friends," she breathes in my ear.

She thinks that we are *friends.*

In her arms I am Nina and then I am Ashley and then I am Nina again, my identity as amorphous and shifting as a cloud caught in the wind. Too much of this and I may lose my grip on myself.

"Of course we're friends," Ashley murmurs into Vanessa's ear.

I still hate you, Nina thinks.

And then both of us hug her back.

Back in the caretaker's cottage, Lachlan is sprawled on the couch with his computer in his lap, surrounded by pastry crumbs. He looks up at me when I come in. "You could have brought me a cup of coffee, at least."

"There's a Starbucks in Tahoe City, be my guest," I say. I throw myself down on the couch next to him and pick up a half-eaten scone from the coffee table. It's stale. Famished, I eat it anyway.

Lachlan fiddles with his keyboard. "I was watching you out there, and you know, you're not that bad at yoga. Maybe you should consider it as a career option, if all this doesn't work out."

"Do you have any idea how much a yoga teacher makes?"

He peers over the top of his glasses. "Not enough, I take it."

I think of my mother's cancer treatments, mentally calculating how many $30 classes I would need to teach in order to pay for them. "Not nearly enough."

"Check it out," he says, and swings his laptop around so I can see what he's been tinkering with. It's the live feed from the camera that I just hid in Stonehaven's library. The quality of the image is bad — it's grainy and dark — but the angle is just right, so that we can survey all three walls of the library and the space in between. The taxidermized bear hulks menacingly by the fireplace. The space heater glows in the corner. Lachlan and I watch together as Vanessa sweeps back into the room — still in the silk pajamas — and throws herself down on the couch. She sinks down into the pillows and pulls her phone out of her cardigan pocket, scrolling rapidly through it. I can tell without even seeing her screen that she is going through her Instagram feed.

"One camera down, fair play," Lachlan murmurs. He reaches over and cups my cheek in his hand: "I knew you could do it, my love."

I watch Vanessa's blank face, lightly illuminated by the glow of her screen. *Flick. Flick. Flick.* She types a few words. *Flick. Flick. Flick.* I wonder if this is what she does all day: studies what everyone else is doing everywhere else, and decides if it's worth liking, as she holds it up for comparison with her own life. How pathetic. The vulnerable, agonized Vanessa of before is gone; from here, she is once again a blank and empty vessel that I can observe with contempt. It's almost a relief.

"She googled Ashley," I say. "She quoted my own fake Facebook account back to me. Do you think we were careful enough?"

He turns his eyes back to the screen. "She's going to see what she wants to see. She's thick as a plank, and vain to boot."

I am giddy, the heat of victory still pulsing through my body; the dried sweat from my yoga workout sticky between my thighs. A week or two of this, and we'll have all of our cameras exactly where we need them to be. And then it will be easy to bait our mousetrap and wait for Vanessa to walk right into it.

We might be back in Los Angeles by the end of the year. By January, my mother could be partway through her new cancer regimen and on the path to remission. And then — Christ, if we get enough from that safe, I may never have to do *this* ever again. What a relief it would be; to stroll away from here and straight out into a whole new life, all debts paid off, and a bit more to spare. The Lieblings could at least, finally, give me *that.*

I try not to think of the policemen standing watch over my Echo Park home, waiting for me to return so they can arrest me; or of the bills piling up in my mailbox; or of my dying mother lying in a hospital by herself, with no one to hold her hand. I try to remain steady in my belief that this horrible, tainted mansion — the same one that tore my life apart — will be the place where everything is magically glued back together again.

On Lachlan's laptop, Vanessa is still scrolling through her own tiny screen. The unbearable sadness of watching someone else's life reduced to a screen on a screen makes me look away, my stomach twisting with sour distaste. *What are we about to do to this woman?* The thought bubbles up, unbidden: *We should leave, now.* It is a familiar feeling: this nagging sense that I've been looking at the world through a tilted mirror, and that if I were to turn it around and look at myself I would be horrified by what I saw.

I am good at what I do, but that does not mean that I always enjoy what I do. My ability to weave lies, to try on new identities, to stir and deceive — yes, I love the adrenaline kick and vindictive high of it all. But I also sometimes feel it sitting at the bottom of my stomach, a sweet thick secret that sickens even as it thrills. *How can I do this? Should I do this? Do I love this or hate this?*

The first time I ran a grift with Lachlan (a coke-addled action-film producer with a history of sexual harassment and a rare set of Pierre Jeanneret chairs worth $120,000), I fell ill for three days afterward. Vomiting all night, a shakiness that kept me abed. It was as if my body was purging some toxin that had infected it. I swore I would never do it again. And yet when Lachlan called me up for another job a month later, I could feel that the toxin was still there: a hot compulsion, a throb along my veins that made me feel faint. Perhaps it was in my blood.

This, certainly, was what Lachlan believed. "A natural-born con, you are — but of course you would be. It's in your genes," he'd said, after we finished that first job together. *So this is what my mother feels when she runs a successful con,* I'd thought. Maybe it wasn't so bad. After a lifetime of running away from my mother's life, it was almost a relief to give up, turn around and run toward it.

And yet, I hadn't gone looking for the grift; the grift had come looking for me.

The day that I arrived back in Los Angeles, Lachlan took me straight from the airport to the hospital to see my mother. I hadn't visited her in almost a year, and I was shocked by her appearance: the brown roots darkening her blond hair, the dark circles under her eyes, the false eyelashes peeling away at the corners of her lids. She was gaunt, her skin loose and sallow. The ghost of her beauty still clung to her, but in the months since I'd last seen her she'd gone from looking like someone who could have her way with the world, to looking like someone who'd been decimated by it.

"Why didn't you tell me?"

She reached out and took my hand in hers. I could feel her bones clicking together in my grip and it was excruciating. "Oh, baby. There was nothing to tell. I've been feeling bad for a while but it just didn't seem *that* bad."

"You shouldn't have waited so long to see a doctor." I blinked away tears. "You might have caught it before stage *three.*"

"You know I hate doctors, baby." This seemed disingenuous. More likely: My mother had the barest minimum of insurance, and was afraid of what the doctor would tell her, and this was why she'd ignored her symptoms for so long.

I looked across the bed at Lachlan, as if he might have some insight into the situation, and he caught my gaze and returned it steadily. "So," I said. "How do you know my mom?"

333

"From the poker circuit. She's a sharp one, your mum."

I regarded him warily; noting, again, the crisp cut of his suit, the knowing bite to his smile, his lupine good looks, and a watch as expensive as the ones my mother liked to steal. "The poker circuit" — I knew this was where my mother trolled for marks. Was he a mark, himself?

"Has she been like this for long? Why didn't one of you think to call me sooner?"

Lachlan shook his head, offering a faint smile of apology. "Your mum is a force," he said, and reached out to smooth the blanket over her legs. "She does what she wants to do. And she puts on a good front, as I'm sure you know."

My mother beamed up at him with all the wattage she could muster and yet I could see the bravado in her smile, the panic creeping into the spidery lines around her eyes. She looked old suddenly, far older than her years. I thought of what the doctor had told me, of how weak she already was and how fast the cancer could advance. "Yes, she's good at faking it."

My mother squeezed my hand. "Don't talk about me like I'm not here," she chided. "I'm a little sick. I'm not brain dead. *Yet.*" I hated the way she laughed at this.

Lachlan studied me from across the hospital bed. "You know, your mother has told me a

334

lot about you."

"She didn't tell me anything about *you.*" I looked down at my mom, who dimpled guilelessly back at me. "What has she been saying?"

He pulled up a chair and settled himself down in it, crossing his left leg over his right. There was a languid quality to him, as if he was slipping through cool water. "That you've got a degree in art history from a fancy college," he said.

"Not that fancy," I retorted.

He was running a thumb along the pale skin of my mother's inner arm where it lay on the blanket, gently, like a father caressing a sleeping child. I felt something stir inside me, a desire to feel that finger pressed against my own flesh. "That you know lots about antiques. That you've spent the last few years making expensive houses look nice. That you are in frequent proximity to rich people. Billionaires. Hedge fund types."

"This is interesting to you for some reason?"

"I could use someone like you. For some work I've been doing. Someone with a discerning eye." I could feel Lachlan's assessing gaze, studying me, and I suddenly understood: He was a con, just like my mom. That explained his coolheaded demeanor, the invisible power he seemed to wield over my mother. *How close to legitimacy was he skat-*

ing? I wondered. Whatever his game was, it was clearly working for him.

My mother struggled upright in the bed and shook a finger at him. "Lachlan, stop it. Leave her alone."

"What? You can't blame me for asking. You've spoken so highly of her."

"Nina has a *career.*" My mother's smile shone up at me from the bed. "My bright girl. She has a BA."

The way she pronounced those two letters, as if they were a magic spell that was going to protect us both, nearly broke me. I was glad my mother had never seen me fetching soy lattes for my boss, had never visited my sad Flushing apartment or witnessed me polishing a billionaire's gilded bidet. "I'm weighing some options while I'm out here, but thanks," I lied to Lachlan. "I'm not sure that your line of work is my cup of tea."

"What makes you think you know my line of work? So presumptuous." His smile undercut his indignation, and I saw that he had teeth that were white but lopsided. I thought of my own crooked teeth, the result of being unable to afford dentistry as a child, and wondered if we had that much in common. I found myself smiling back at him, despite myself. He stood, and patted my mom's hand. "I have to run."

"You're not leaving?" My mother's eyes were open suddenly, and pleading.

"You know you can call me if you need anything at all, Lilybelle." He leaned over my mother and pressed his lips gently against her forehead, as if she were a tiny precious thing that might break under undue pressure. I wanted to build a wall of steel around my heart, a defense against this man, but something about the tenderness in that kiss moved my defenses. I wondered how long he'd been taking care of my mom, and if it had been a hustle on his part. If there had been anything in it for him, I couldn't see what it was. My mother was broke and broken; she had nothing to give. He seemed genuinely fond of her.

"He's a good man," my mother whispered to me. She clutched my hand. "A real softy, underneath it all. I don't know what I would have done without him."

Maybe that's why, as he left the room, I accepted the piece of paper that he slipped me, the one with his phone number on it, "In case you change your mind," he whispered in my ear. Maybe that's why I didn't throw the paper away, but tucked it into my wallet.

On the day that my mother and I left the hospital, with a fistful of prescriptions and a chemo schedule in my purse, Lachlan's phone number was still there. It was there when I got to my mother's Mid-City apartment and discovered the squalor in which she'd been living; it was there when the first hospital bill arrived, a five-figure abomination; it was there when my mother vomited blood after her first chemo treatment, and I understood that her care was going to be a full-time job for the foreseeable future. It was there when I got rejected for jobs at two dozen local art galleries, museums, and furniture shops.

I hadn't been around to take care of my mother over the last few years, and I was determined to make up for it; but I had no clear way to live up to this task. My mother had no safety net: *I* was supposed to be her safety net, and yet I had none of the things she needed most. No money, no job, no friends, no prospects. Only debt and determination.

On the day that I withdrew the last fifty dollars from my bank account in order to pay my mother's gas bill, I found Lachlan's number in my wallet. I fished it out with two fingers and looked at it for a long time — at the crisp boldness of his neatly inked digits, definitive against the stark white bonded paper — before dialing. I thought about the little shiver of desire I'd felt as he pressed his lips up against my ear. When he answered, and I told him who I was, he didn't even hesitate, as if he already knew exactly why I was calling.

"I was wondering how long it would take for you to wise up."

I steeled myself. "Here's my rule: only

people who have too much, and only people who deserve it."

He chuckled. "Well, of course. We take only what we need."

"Exactly." I felt a little better already. "And once my mom is healthy again, I'm out."

I could almost hear him smiling. "OK, then. How much do you know about Instagram?"

19.

The next morning I run through the same routine — yoga on the lawn — and wait for Vanessa to show up with her mat in tow. An hour of asanas later and my muscles are shaking with fatigue, but no Vanessa. I do my cobras facing the house so that I can watch the windows, but there is no movement behind the curtains. When I take a casual stroll around the property on my way back to the cottage, I see no signs of life at all. The big wooden garage doors are closed tight and the lights in the windows are out. A battered sedan has materialized in the driveway, but even though I linger nearby, I don't catch sight of the person who drove it.

I go back to the caretaker's cottage and pull up the library feed. After a while, an older woman drifts into frame, her hair scraped back into a ponytail, an old-fashioned feather duster in the pocket of her apron. Presumably the housekeeper. I wonder, with some concern, if she will find the hidden camera, but she ignores the shelves of books entirely. Instead she listlessly moves a few things around on the coffee table, plumps up the pillows on the couch, and drifts back out of frame.

Vanessa passes through the library twice after the housekeeper leaves, but she never stays in the room. She just wanders through, looking like she's lost, looking like she can't quite figure out where she's headed. The phone firmly clutched in her hand, like a child's well-worn stuffie.

Lachlan comes and looks over my shoulder. "What a useless human being," he says. "Does she do nothing at all? Does she even have a *mind*?"

Something about his tone makes me sour; I find myself feeling oddly protective. "I wonder if she's depressed." I study the somnambulant cant of Vanessa's walk. "Maybe I should go ring her doorbell again, try to cheer her up."

Lachlan shakes his head. "Make her come to us. Don't want to come off too eager, yeah? Puts us in the power position. Don't worry, she'll come 'round."

But she doesn't. Two more days pass in the same restless routine — yoga on the lawn, walks around the property, lunch at the general store a mile up the road. We spend most of our time in the cottage, pretending

341

at our writing retreat. Lachlan has scattered books and papers around the room in case Vanessa shows up at the door, but mostly he sits at his laptop, binge-watching true-crime TV shows with an absorbed expression on his face. I've brought a pile of novels — I'm working my way through the Victorian era, starting with George Eliot — but there are only so many hours in the day that one can read before one starts to feel like one's mind is literally melting inside one's skull. The minutes drip past like a slowly leaking faucet and I wonder how long we're going to have to stay cloistered inside the manufactured heat of these three rooms.

On the fifth day of our stay, I drive into Ta-hoe City to stock up on groceries at the Save Mart. Afterward, I linger in town, where the bustle and activity is an antidote to the deathly stillness of Stonehaven. I go to Syd's for a bagel, even though I'm not hungry, and find that little has changed in the last dozen years. The fairy lights that hang over the hand-chalked menu have been replaced with fluttering flags, and the flyers pinned to the bulletin board advertise a fresh round of teen-age babysitters and lost dogs. But the pony-tailed manager is still there, his hair gray now, his belly soft. He doesn't recognize me, which is to be expected, but is also unsettling, as if I was always invisible but I only just discov-ered it.

I order a coffee and then walk down to the picnic bench on the beach where I used to sit with Benny. I think about the turns of the last twelve years until it's unbearable, and then I pack up my trash and drive back to Stonehaven.

When I return to the cottage, I find it empty and cold. There's no sign of Lachlan; his coat and sneakers are missing. I go and stand outside on the lawn, looking up at the lights of the mansion, wondering if I should knock on the door. But something holds me back. Instead, I sit by myself in the gloomy cottage, my mood brooding and sour.

Lachlan blows back through the door a few minutes later, electric with excitement. "Jaysus." He exhales. "She's a bit of a mental case, that one."

"I thought you said we should let her come to us." There's a petulant note in my voice; I realize that I do not like having been left out. Or is it that I'm jealous that he got back inside Stonehaven when I did not? Or even — a curious thought — that I'm eager to slip back into *Ashley's* skin, so simple and good and free of inner turmoil?

"Ran into her when I was taking a walk, didn't I? She invited me in." He shrugs off his jacket and flings it at the couch. "I got one more camera hidden, but she was on me like a hawk, so that was it."

"Where?"

"The games room."

I didn't even know there was a games room in Stonehaven — though of course there would be, a mansion like Stonehaven would always have been intended as a monument to leisure. When Lachlan loads up the camera, it shows a billiards table, a wooden bar with upholstered chairs and dusty decanters of Scotch, and a wall of old golf trophies. The far wall is hung with antique swords, at least three dozen of them, framing a pair of ornately engraved pistols hung in a position of pride above the fireplace.

"It's not a games room, it's an *armory*. Jesus. What the hell were you doing in there? Playing checkers?"

Lachlan frowns. "You're in a *mood.*"

"What'd you two talk about?"

"Just some mild flirtation. Discussion about my family's castle and so on. She likes me."

"She likes both of us," I say. "But I'm not sure that's helping much. At this rate, we'll be here all year."

"I set the bait," he assures me. "Just sit tight. She'll take it."

And he's right. Early the next afternoon, there's a clatter outside the door to the cottage. Lachlan and I freeze, and stare at each other. He shuts down the video he's watching, and I gather myself, take a breath, turn myself into *Ashley.* When I open the door with a bright smile on my face, Vanessa is standing there in hiking pants, her face carefully made-up, designer sunglasses balanced on top of a mass of glossy, blown-out hair. She looks like a model in an advertisement for vitaminwater and I instinctively want to slap the sunglasses right off the top of her head.

"*There* you are!" I say instead. I reach out and fold her into another hug; press my warm cheek against her cold one. I pull back, give her a look. "Are we still going to do yoga together? I was so looking forward to that. I've been out there every morning, without you."

She flushes. "I know. I've had a cold. But I'm feeling better now."

"Maybe tomorrow, then." I lean against the doorframe. I notice that she's holding a backpack in her hand. "You going somewhere?"

Her eyes skitter over my shoulder to Lachlan, still lying on the couch surrounded by papers. "I'm going for a hike to Vista Point. And I thought maybe you guys would want to come." When he doesn't look up from his laptop, she turns back to me. "The weather report says that a winter storm's coming, in the next day or two. So this might be your last chance. To hike."

"I'd love that," I say. I turn to Lachlan. "Honey? Take a break?"

Lachlan slowly tears his eyes away from the screen, his eyebrows furrowed, as if his mind has been engaged in deeply intellectual internal debate and he resents being dragged back to the mundane present. If I didn't know that he was just watching reruns of *Criminal Minds,* I would almost be convinced myself.

"I'm in the middle of this —" he says.

Vanessa blanches. "Oh, you're writing. I'm sorry, I didn't mean to interrupt."

"Oh, no, it's fine. A hike, eh?" He sits up and stretches, and his T-shirt rises up a bit, exposing a toned expanse of stomach. He offers us both a dazzling smile as if he couldn't be more thrilled by the idea, even though I know that *hiking* is on the bottom of the list of things he enjoys, flanked by *taxes* and *rom-com movies.* "I wouldn't mind stretching my legs. I was struggling with that paragraph anyway."

Twenty minutes later we are in Vanessa's car, a Mercedes SUV so new that it still smells of the factory in which it was assembled. We drive south along the lakeshore, passing weather-beaten motels with neon vacancy signs out front, a shingled general store advertising sub sandwiches and cold beer, A-frames with covered boats in their driveways, away from the multimillion-dollar vacation homes and into the hush of the national forest. Vanessa is gushy, almost manic, as she peppers us with facts about the places that we pass.

"We're coming up to the estate where they filmed *The Godfather Part II,* although it's all condos now. See, out past that boat? That's where Fredo gets murdered."

"Down that driveway is Chambers Landing, a pier with a historic bar, it's been around since 1875, though now it's mostly full of frat boys getting loaded on Chambers Punch cocktails."

"There's a charming little Scandinavian mansion up ahead, it looks like something straight out of a Norwegian fjord. My great-grandfather used to play pinochle with the owner, back during the Depression."

I remember some of these stories from when I lived here as a teenager. Every place has its lore, but Tahoe clings particularly tightly to the time when it was more exclusive, more glamorous; when it was more than just an overpriced weekend ski getaway for San Francisco's tribes of tech bro millionaires. I stare out the window at the forest flying past and think that it's nice to be in the mountains, away from the toxic bustle of urban life, the glittering lights that advertise desire. I imagine bringing my mother up here, to recover from her disease. The fresh air might be therapeutic; certainly it would be good for us both to get away from city life.

And then I remember that once Lachlan

and I leave here, along with Vanessa's money, we'll never be able to come back again.

Lachlan and I listen intently to Vanessa's patter, interjecting little appreciative comments at all the right moments, acting like eager tourists on an all-inclusive sightseeing tour. "You must really love it up here," Lachlan finally says.

His observation seems to surprise her. She grips the leather steering wheel as she leans into a tight turn, the corner of her glossed lip anchored between two perfect white teeth. "I didn't choose the place, it was chosen for me," she says finally. "I inherited it. It's not about love, it's about honor. But yes, it's awfully lovely up here, too."

She accelerates until she's flying around the curves on the road, and flips on the radio. An old Britney Spears song comes on. In the back seat, Lachlan groans. "You don't like Britney?" Vanessa asks nervously, then turns to me. "What do you guys listen to?"

What *would* a yoga teacher listen to? Indian sitar? Whale song? Jesus, too clichéd. I wait too long to answer. Her hand hovers over the knob, ready to change it.

"I really only listen to classical and jazz," Lachlan interjects from the back seat, sensing my struggle. "Growing up in the castle in Ireland, that's all we had around. Records, yeah? Not even a CD player. My grandmother Alice was a close friend of Stravinsky's."

I suppress a laugh. He's overreaching with the faux aristocratic intellectualism. I reach over and turn the music up, just to annoy him. "He's a *snob,*" I whisper to Vanessa. "Top Forty is fine."

Lachlan jabs my shoulder, hard. "I prefer the term *aesthete.* I'm sure you would understand that, Vanessa? You seem like a woman of discriminating taste."

"I have to confess, I know nothing about jazz."

Lachlan settles back in his seat and props a foot on the console. His sneakers are brand-new and blindingly white and far too trendy for a poet-professor. A detail he didn't consider. "I didn't mean jazz necessarily. It just strikes me that you're an artistic type. You have that air about you. Surrounding yourself with fine things. You have an *eye.*"

Vanessa blushes, rather pleased with herself. She believes in his bogus flattery, the vain fool. "*Thank* you! Yes, that's true. But I still like Britney."

"There you go." I flash Lachlan a *look.* "If you're seeking a fellow snob, you're not going to find one with her. We're not changing the station. Right, Vanessa?" I reach across the seat and grip her forearm possessively and she glances at me and smiles happily. She's enjoying us fighting over her. We've inflated her ego to dirigible size so that she can float, self-satisfied, above us.

Lachlan throws his hands up. "I'm outnumbered. I give up."

But the debate is moot now because Vanessa suddenly veers right into a parking lot and screeches to a stop at the bottom of a trail. "Here!" she chirps.

We peel ourselves from the car, accept granola bars and water bottles from Vanessa's pack, then start up the trail. It's a dirt path, just a few feet wide, winding up through the pines. The trees are dense enough to block out the sun, and as we climb it grows dark and damp, the air smelling of moss and earth. It's so quiet here that the only thing I can hear is the breeze in the tops of the trees, the creak and groan of ancient wood wavering in the wind, the crackle of pine needles under our feet.

The trail is steep and I find that I'm struggling. My muscles are sore from all those yoga workouts and I'm not used to the altitude and soon I'm regretting having come. Lachlan moves slowly, picking his way across each rock and stick as if he's afraid to get his shoes dirty. Within minutes, he's fallen woefully behind. Vanessa stays with me, glued so tightly to my side that my hand keeps banging into hers. I notice that she's got welts all over the backs of her hands.

Halfway up, we come to a clearing with a

view overlooking the lake. Tahoe spreads out before us in all directions, today the inkiest of blues, the water rippling like a harp that's just been strummed. Overhead, cumulus formations tunnel toward the heavens and below us the dense pines march, green with glory, into the horizon. There's something familiar about the view, and I suddenly realize why. I climbed up here once, with Benny. We stood here at this same vista, stoned, staring out at the span of blue. I remember feeling like the world was unfurling itself before us, as deep and unknowable as the lake itself. I remember feeling the urge to fling myself into the void and let it embrace me in its chilly oblivion.

I stop. I am wordless, panting, and there are shooting pains in my calves.

Vanessa turns to look at me. "Everything OK?"

"Just taking it all in. I think I might stop for a minute and" — I reach for *Ashley* — "meditate."

She peers at me curiously. "Meditate? Here?"

"This is exactly where one should meditate, don't you think?" I say a little archly.

She smiles nervously. "I wish I could do that but my mind doesn't ever shut up for long enough. It's like, I try to quiet everything and instead my brain just *overflows* like one of those volcano experiments kids do in

351

elementary school, with the bubbles frothing everywhere. How do you *do* that? Turn it all off?"

"Practice."

"Oh? Like how?" She looks at me expectantly, waiting for more.

Good Lord, she's persistent. I've never meditated in my life. "Just —" I go still, close my eyes, and try to look like my mind is empty. I hear her feet shuffling in the pine needles, moving restlessly in circles. Maybe she'll go away and let me rest here for a bit.

But when I open my eyes, she's standing there with her phone out, pointing it at me, studying the screen with a practiced eye. She cups her hand to examine the results, then starts to type. And immediately I understand what she's doing: She's uploading a photo of me to her Instagram feed. Oh sweet Jesus: *That cannot happen.*

"No!" I fly at her and snatch the phone from her hand, as fast as a striking snake. Sure enough, there I am, in portrait mode, my eyes closed, the sun soft on my face. I look . . . peaceful. The unfinished caption reads *My new friend Ashley is.* Despite myself, I want to know how she was going to finish the sentence: What *is* Ashley? I delete the photo and shut Instagram down as Vanessa stares at me, her eyes huge and unblinking. "Sorry to be such a stickler but . . . I'm a very private person. I know social media is your thing,

but I'd really rather not have you post photos of me online."

"I'm so sorry. I didn't know. I just assumed . . ." She quivers; I've wounded her. I almost feel bad. "It's just, it was such a good shot."

I'm quivering, too — *close call* — as I gently press the phone back into her hand. "How would you know? It's really my fault. I should have said something earlier. Don't worry about it, OK?"

She backs away from me, her eyes frantically looking at anything but my face. I've frightened her, or worse. "I should go retrieve Michael," I say. "He's probably wandering around lost."

"I'll wait here," she says.

I trudge back down the trail. Lachlan is a quarter mile back, leaning against a tree, just staring at his shoes. He frowns when he sees that I'm alone.

"Where's Vanessa?"

"Up a ways, waiting."

He reaches for my water bottle and frowns when he realizes that it's empty. "Showing off your athletic ability, eh, *Ashley*?"

"At least I'm making an effort, *Michael.*"

"What were the two of you nattering on about, anyway? I thought I heard you shouting."

I don't see the point in telling him about

353

the photo; it's been deleted, anyway. "Oh nothing. She wanted me to teach her how to meditate."

He snorts. "I'm sure you had *lots* to offer. Look, all this *hiking* shite — it's not helping us. I'm going to press her to invite us over for dinner. We'll get her a little drunk, then ask her for a tour of Stonehaven — *the whole house* — and we can drop the rest of the cameras. It'll be easier with both of us there, so one of us can distract her."

"OK." I look back up the trail. "I should go back up."

"Nah. She's probably up there taking self-ies, the shallow cunt."

I shove him, harder than I mean to. "Stop it. That's horrible."

He gives me a strange look. "Jaysus, Nina. When did you start being such a softy? Do you actually *like* her now? I thought she was your sworn enemy." He frowns. "How many times have I told you not to get emotionally involved?"

"I'm not. I just object to your language. It's misogynist."

He leans in, pressing himself against me, whispering in my ear. "The only cunt I like is yours." His lips, damp and cool and salty, find mine.

"You're awful," I mutter, pushing him away.

But he nestles his nose into my neck and nibbles the nerve there until I gasp and writhe. "Cunt cunt cunt."

Over his shoulder I see Vanessa coming down the trail toward us. She notices us embracing and stops just on the other side of the pines: Does she think I can't see her? I watch her over Lachlan's shoulder, feeling his lips buzz my clavicle, my sweat seeping through my shirt. I can see that she is riveted by the sight of us, even as she takes a polite step backward. And then her eyes finally creep up to meet mine and she freezes, and we are just looking at each other with a strange, cool understanding; even as Lachlan's hands move under my damp T-shirt to cup my breast. I can see her measuring my desire, like a tourist in front of a museum exhibit. I see her own raw longing reflected back. It feels oddly intimate, as if *we* are the two people sharing this moment, and Lachlan isn't even there.

Finally, she blinks and vanishes back into the woods. I close my eyes and kiss Lachlan back until my skin is vibrating and my pulse is singing along with the wind in the trees.

When I open my eyes again, Vanessa is standing right beside me. I startle, and jump away from Lachlan. "Oh, there you are!" I cry. Vanessa's features are pinched with annoyance. She looks from Lachlan to me and then back again. *She doesn't like it when we're not focused on her,* I realize.

Lachlan runs a hand slowly across his lips,

looking rather smug. "Ah, that's good, yeah?" he says. "The team has reassembled itself. No casualties."

Vanessa turns to me. "What happened to you?" she demands. "I thought you were coming back to get me."

I'm surprised by the sharp tone in her voice. Is this still about the photo? Or is this sexual jealousy? How much *has* Lachlan been flirting with her? I make myself sound meek, apologetic, unthreatening. "My leg cramped up. Sorry."

She tilts her head, looking baffled. "Really? I'm surprised. I mean, you're a yoga instructor, right? And I barely move off my couch most days. Funny that."

"Different muscle groups," I offer.

"Well, I'm knackered, myself," Lachlan interjects. "But we should crack on, shouldn't we? That storm cloud is looking rather ominous."

"The temperature has dropped. I'm freezing," I say. And I know I shouldn't, but I can't help it. Just to prove a point, I grab Lachlan's arm and drape it over my shoulder. "Warm me up, honey."

Vanessa watches this interaction with measuring eyes; but then they swiftly clear, as if a wind had just chased off a cloud. "Oh, Ash, here — take my sweatshirt." She tugs it over her ponytail and then thrusts it at me.

I disentangle myself from Lachlan and yank

it over my head. The sweatshirt is thick and soft, and warm from her body. It even smells like her, like expensive lotion and lavender sachets; her presence on my body makes me feel disoriented, as if the boundaries between the two of us have grown thin. I wish I hadn't taken it. But I smile because that's what Ashley would do. "You're so sweet."

"It's nothing," she says. The dimples are back. And it seems like that unexpected fissure has been all smoothed over; but I also note, as we start back down the hill, that with the act of giving me her sweatshirt, she succeeded in pulling Lachlan and me apart.

20.

I've just climbed out of the shower when the rain starts. I stand naked and damp in the tiny bathroom, listening to the ominous hammering on the roof. I do not want to go to Stonehaven for dinner. I want to light a fire and curl up with a book and let the storm howl outside. But that's not an option, of course: This is the opportunity we've been looking for since we arrived here. (And in the end, it had been so easy! A suggestion from Lachlan in the car after the hike — "Should we have dinner at yours, tomorrow?" — and like that it was done, planned.)

But I feel unsettled, and I'm not sure why. I stare in the mirror and I try to summon up *Ashley* but all I see is a woman with dripping hair and circles under her eyes, exhausted by the effort of being too many people all at once. Dutiful daughter, partner and girl-friend, teacher and huckster, and friend and fraud; and where am *I* in all of that?

Lachlan peeks his head into the bathroom,

already dressed in a cashmere sweater and crisp new jeans. He looks me up and down. "Is that what you're wearing? Because clothes with pockets would be more practical. Unless you plan to hide a camera up your fanny."

"Very funny."

By the time we've filled our pockets with the cameras and strategized a game plan for the evening (Lachlan will distract by flirting, I will plant the cameras), the storm has landed with full force. When we open the door to the cottage, the wind catches it and flings it backward against the doorjamb so hard I think it might splinter. Slicing rain needles my face as we run up the path toward the beckoning lights of Stonehaven. I'm drenched before we've made it halfway to the porch.

Vanessa is waiting for us with martinis in hand; the flush in her face suggests she might already have had one herself. I wipe the rain from my eyes and take a quick gulp of my drink. It is strong, and briny with olive juice. "My goodness, you pour a strong drink." I cough.

Vanessa looks worried. "Should I have made something else for you? Matcha tea? Green juice?"

"Oh, no. It's delicious." I smile at her, take another sip; but inside I'm kicking myself. *Would* Ashley drink martinis? Oh God, I am off my game. Too late now. I take another sip, a bigger one, let it play along my nerves and take the edge off.

Vanessa is making some kind of French stew — no formal dining room tonight, judging by the plates set out on the table — and the kitchen smells like garlic and boiling wine. She flits from pot to pot, flinging in spices, adjusting flames with a practiced hand, talking a mile a minute.

"The trick to authentic coq au vin is that you need to use an old rooster. But you can't believe how bad the butcher here is; nothing free range at all and definitely no roosters, so I had to make do with some breasts. And of course, you must use a French wine, a Beaujolais . . . or perhaps a burgundy. Braise for four hours if you can, but I think six is even better, more is more, right? Haha!"

So she can cook; color me surprised. I remember Lourdes slaving away in this kitchen, making food that Benny's mother never ate: Was Lourdes the one who taught Vanessa to cook?

Lachlan follows closely behind her, peering into pots and asking her about knife technique, cloyingly solicitous. I sit by myself at the kitchen table, sipping my martini in silence, growing irritated. As far as I know, Lachlan knows nothing about cooking, but I am perennially surprised at his ability to make shallow knowledge sound deep. I'm already feeling swimmy from the gin, and the smell of charred fats is making my stomach turn.

Finally I interrupt Vanessa as she's explaining her browning method to Lachlan. "Any chance we could get the grand tour of Stonehaven? I'd really love to see the rest of the house."

Vanessa wipes a strand of hair from her eyes with the back of her hand, glances at the nearly empty glass in my hand. "Sure. I'm just finishing up here, so maybe after dinner. Looks like you're done with that martini — Want some wine? I opened a Domaine Leroy that I found in the wine cellar. It was a bit dusty, so hopefully it won't have gone off."

"Domaine Leroy! What a treat. I had one when I stayed at Holkham Hall, with the Earl of Leicester. Do you know him? No? Well, his wine cellar was extraordinary. *Legendary,*" Lachlan gushes, his eyes popping open. *The Earl.* Please. He is so transparent that I can't quite believe she's buying all this. But I smile and nod as if I know what this means, too, even though I purchase my own wine from the ten-dollar section at the local liquor store. Vanessa whisks a decanter to the table, along with our dishes, and pours us each a glass. Lachlan swirls it dramatically and takes a sip. "Ach, Vanessa. We don't deserve wine this nice."

"Of course you do." She is clearly quite pleased with herself for impressing him. "If

361

dinner with friends isn't deserving of a good wine, I don't know what is. I mean, otherwise I'm going to be drinking this all by myself, and wouldn't that be a shame?"

"I can't object to that." Michael raises his glass. "To new friendships."

She gazes back at him, a little teary, and I wonder if she's going to get emotional on us again. I feel woozy; my appetite for this is waning and I wish we were back in the cottage. I have no energy to be Ashley tonight. Maybe I've just had too much gin.

Lifting my glass takes more effort than it should. "And to *you*, Vanessa. Sometimes the universe brings you together with someone that you just feel like you were *meant* to know." It sounds like a sufficiently Ashley-ish empty sentiment.

Vanessa smiles at me, her eyes flickering wildly in the light from the candles. "To the *universe*, then. And unlikely meetings. The wine — you like it?"

Maybe I'm just not a connoisseur, but the wine tastes like gasoline to me. I murmur something vaguely appreciative, and then turn my attention to the plate of food in front of me: chicken swimming in grease, a spooling mass of mashed potatoes that are pink around the edges from where they've soaked up the oily juices; asparagus spears, limp and doused in anemic yellow aioli. I take a small bite of potato, feeling light-headed, and my stomach immediately gives a violent protest.

There's a faint sheen of sweat on my forehead — When did it get so hot in here? And the light from the pendants over the table is painfully bright. I push my chair back to get some air and the movement makes my intestines convulse. I realize that I'm about to vomit.

"Where's the bathroom?" I manage.

Vanessa is riveted by the sight of me: I must be a mess. She stands up from her chair and points toward the hallway, saying something that I can't catch as I stumble from the room. I barely make it into the powder room in the hall before regurgitating the pale remains of my lunch. What did I eat? Oh yes, a tuna sub from the market down the road. It was crusted around the edges, oddly fishy, I should have checked the expiration date. The bathroom spins, cold marble against my knees, porcelain against my cheek, a sour stench clogging my esophagus.

I heave, and heave again, until all that's left is bile that burns on the way up.

There's a soft knock at the door and then Lachlan is standing there above me. He crouches down beside me, gently pulls my hair from my face and holds it in his fist. "What's going on?"

"The tuna sub, I think." I turn back to the toilet and retch once more.

"Jaysus. You got a bad dose of it, didn't you.

363

Glad I had the turkey, yeah?"

The toilet has an old-fashioned pull chain that I can't even reach high enough to flush. Instead, I slide down until my face is resting against the marble and close my eyes. "I can't do this tonight," I mutter. "Let's call it off."

Lachlan pulls a square of toilet paper from the roll and dabs at my forehead with it. "That's OK, I can handle this myself. Just give me the cameras. You go back to the cottage and I'll stay here."

"She'll think it's strange you're not coming back to take care of me. Bad boyfriend. Unlikable."

Lachlan rolls up the toilet paper and squeezes it in his hand into a tiny little wad, and then pitches it toward the garbage can. "Actually, I think she'll be happy to get some one-on-one time with me. Just tell me not to come with you. Make a little fuss. You don't want to spoil Vanessa's evening, you're being so thoughtful and considerate, yeah yeah yeah."

"Fine, whatever." I push myself upright, feeling feverish and dizzy. Lachlan helps me back to the kitchen, where Vanessa is waiting for us at the table, wide-eyed with alarm, her glass of wine still untouched as if she's been too concerned about me to even drink.

"Ashley needs to rest, we're going to have to go back to the cottage to give her a lie-down." We have stopped at the table and

Lachlan gently lets go of my waist, taps my back as if to say, *Go on.* I'm afraid that if I open my mouth again I might vomit all over the table.

"No, you stay here," I manage. "Don't waste all that beautiful food Vanessa cooked. A shame. It would be."

Vanessa shakes her head. "Oh, no no, Michael, that's OK. Ashley needs you."

"I'm fine," I gasp. I am not fine. "I'm just going to sleep."

Lachlan gazes at me with a magnificently wrinkled brow. "Well. If you insist. I won't stay long. You're right. A shame to waste all this."

I'm already at the door, lurching as fast as I can toward the relief of the cold wet air, so I don't get to see Vanessa's reaction to this — whether she smiles with delight about him staying or frowns with alarm about me. At this moment, I couldn't care less: I head off into the dark, and the rain on my face makes me think of my mother's cool hand on my forehead. And as I stumble toward the cottage the years fall away until I am a child in the dark, looking for relief, calling for my mama.

Back in the cottage, I crawl into bed but I can't sleep. My body shakes with fever; my guts convulse every time I lift my water glass to clear the terrible taste in my mouth. I make the trip from bed to toilet and back again a half-dozen times, until something finally breaks inside me and I start to cry. I am dehydrated, hollowed out, so alone. Why did I even come here? I find my phone folded in the sheets, sticky with the sweat from my hands, and dial my mother.

"Mom," I say.

"My baby!" Her voice is like a warm bath, like lavender salts, cleaning the rot out of my head. "Are you OK? You sound strange."

"I'm fine," I say. Then, "Actually, I'm not."

Alarm sharpens her voice, brings her words into focus. "What happened?"

"Food poisoning."

There's a momentary silence, and then a soft cough. "Oh, darling. That's it? That's not so bad. Drink some ginger ale."

"There's none around here," I say, letting myself indulge in childish petulance: the unfairness of it all. I realize that my mother doesn't know where "here" is, but she is making little comforting sounds on the other end of the line, and doesn't ask for details. "I'll be OK. I just needed to hear your voice."

There's a faint tinkling sound in the background, ice swirling in a glass. "I'm glad you did. I've been missing you."

I hesitate, afraid to ask: "Have the police been 'round again?"

"Once," she says. "I didn't answer the door and they went away. And the landline keeps ringing, but I'm not answering it, either."

My brain spins, feverish and faint: *What do they have on me? What if they track me down here? Can I ever go home again?* But of course I will go home. I *have* to. "How are *you*?" I ask. "How are you feeling?"

She coughs again, a muffled sound, as if she's trying to hide it in her sleeve. "I'm OK. No appetite, though, and I've got that bloat again. Mostly I'm just so *tired* all the time. It's like, you finish a marathon and you're exhausted and you look up only to realize you've just landed at the starting line of *another* marathon, and you have no choice but to start running again. You know?"

Another wave of cramps passes through me but I try to ignore them, stoic in the face of my mother's greater suffering. "Oh, Mom," I whisper. "I should be there with you."

"Absolutely not. You take care of yourself for once, OK?" she says. "Dr. Hawthorne has been very nice, he wants me coming in after Thanksgiving to start treatment. A first round of radiation. And then the new protocol. But maybe I shouldn't. . . . I don't know."

"Jesus, Mom, why wouldn't you?"

"But, Nina — the *cost.* I don't know where you are — and I'm not going to ask, darling. I know all about plausible deniability — but you're clearly not minding your antiques store here, so . . . How are we going to come

367

up with the money? It's going to be a half-million dollars, once you add in the radiation and the fancy drugs and the doctor visits and the home care and the hospital stay. I talked to my insurance company again, they still refuse to cover anything but basic chemo. Said this was an 'experimental' protocol they won't approve." Another muffled cough, her voice going fainter, as if this conversation has fatigued her. "But I can just do chemo. It will probably be fine."

"No," I say. "Chemo didn't work the first time around. So you'll do whatever the doctor is recommending you do. I'll have the money by the end of the year. Maybe even sooner. All of it. Just — do what he says. Start the protocol."

She is quiet on the other end of the line. "Honey, I hope you're being careful, whatever it is you're doing. I hope I taught you that much. You should always be thinking three steps ahead."

I try to say something reassuring but something horrible is happening in my gastrointestinal tract that requires urgent attention. I gasp a goodbye to my mother and stumble to the bathroom for another round at the toilet, and then collapse into bed and fall, feverish, to sleep.

I dream that I am at the bottom of Lake Tahoe, swimming frantically through the freezing water toward a faint light above, my lungs bursting as the surface keeps receding away. There is someone swimming up there above me, a black shadow against the blue, and I'm trying to call for help but then I realize that they aren't there to help me. They're there to keep me from surfacing. When I finally startle awake I am slicked with sweat and disoriented. But my stomach is no longer twisting in knots, although I still feel shaky and queasy.

I lie in bed listening to the storm howl around the cottage. The rain has turned to hail, and it rattles the windows so violently that I wonder if the glass will break. When I reach for my phone and look at the time I see that three hours have passed. Where is Lachlan? What are they doing?

Eventually it crosses my mind that I can easily get the answer to this question. I rouse myself from bed and stagger into the living room to find Lachlan's laptop, and then collapse on the couch and boot it up.

When his computer leaps to life I see that there are now eleven live camera feeds on his desktop. One I recognize as the downstairs office, anchored by a presidential desk. One camera is in the upstairs foyer, angled just so, to take in the sweep of the halls. Other feeds display the library, and the games room, gazing over the billiards table; plus the front parlor, and a few other rooms I'm not familiar with. A final feed shows what must be the master bedroom. I study this last one closely: I've never seen the master suite of the house. It is as dark and grand as the rest of Stonehaven — a canopy bed draped in scarlet linens, a formal settee upholstered in velvet, an armoire the size of an army tank. Brass greyhounds flank the stone fireplace, motionless watchdogs staring balefully at the bed across the room. It is a room designed for a fin de siècle oligarch with pretensions of royalty.

There's only one jarring note in this museum-ready tableau: the brown packing boxes that line the far wall, stacked three high and at least a dozen boxes deep. I zoom in and peer at the labels hand-printed on the sides in neat black Sharpie: *Dress coats: Celine & Valentino. Skirts — Pleated. Clutches & Minibags. Light sweaters. Misc. Louboutin. Silk blouses.* Two things immediately occur to me: First, that Vanessa's wardrobe could easily fill an entire clothing boutique, and would probably fetch a small fortune in an online consignment shop. Second, that Vanessa has lived here for months now, and apparently still hasn't unpacked.

I watch the feed for a minute, waiting for Lachlan or Vanessa to cross the screen, but they never do. They must be in the kitchen. The rest of the house is as empty as a tomb.

What is Lachlan finding to talk about with her for three straight hours? I find myself wishing that we'd splurged for the cameras with an audio feed, so I could at least hear echoes of what's happening out of view.

Eventually I drift off on the couch. I'm not sure how long I've been asleep when I startle awake to see Lachlan looming above me. His breath is fungal and sweet; I can smell the wine on him. "I placed them all. All the cameras," he says, swaying slightly, and I realize that he's drunk.

"I saw," I say. "Enjoyed yourself, I see?"

"Don't be jealous, darling. It's a bad look on you." He meanders off toward the bedroom, ricocheting off the furniture that crowds the room.

I sit up, his laptop still on my lap. "Don't you want to take a look at the feed?"

"In the morning," he calls. "I'm knackered."

I listen to him bumping around the cottage, swearing at the antiques, and then the thump of his body collapsing in bed. Deep, rattling snores come from the bedroom. The cottage creaks and groans as the night grows cold, and I think of the coming storm.

After being woken up by Lachlan, I find I can't fall asleep again. And so I open the laptop and pull up the feed. There's Vanessa, moving about her bedroom as if she's searching for something. She disappears into the

371

bathroom and then comes back out and stands at the end of the bed staring at it for a long time. I can't figure out what she's looking at. She wears underwear and a camisole, through which I can practically count her ribs; little crescents of undereye face masks are stuck below her eyes, making her look ghoulish. Finally, she climbs in bed and picks up her phone on the table next to her and flicks through it. But then she changes her mind. She turns off the light and lies back, staring at the ceiling, motionless.

She is tiny in that enormous four-poster, like a doll in a human-sized bed. I wonder if she can feel all the dead Lieblings that have slept there before her. *She should really get a new bed,* I think. I watch as her chest slowly lifts and falls; and then lifts and falls a little faster, with odd little hitches; and then Vanessa lifts her hands to cover her face and I realize that she is crying. At first it's just a gentle weeping, but soon her body starts to heave and convulse with gut-wrenching sobs. Her blond hair spills across her pillow as she writhes with abandon, believing herself alone there in the dark. I have never witnessed such raw despair.

I feel disgust then, but not for her. I imagine looking at myself from the outside, as if someone is watching *me* on their own private feed of my life. And what I see is a pathetic voyeur, spying on a woman in her most private moment. An emotional vampire that uses a stranger's sadness to fuel her own loathing.

How did I become a person who lives in the shadows, who looks at the world and sees only targets and marks? Why am I cynical instead of optimistic; a taker instead of a giver? (Why aren't I more of an *Ashley,* really?) I hate myself suddenly, and the small, petty person I've become; it's a hate more powerful than I ever felt for the Lieblings and their ilk.

They didn't do this to you. You did this to yourself, I think.

I close down the video feed, telling myself as I do that I will not look at it again. I want this whole endeavor to be over. I want to be back home in Echo Park with my mother. I want to make enough money from this job that I never have to do this again. I want this, and I also want so much more — to have a fresh shot at being the person I once thought I could be, the one with the bright Future.

Right before the feed shuts down, Vanessa's hands fall away and her face is suddenly visible, pale and shadowed against the scarlet linens. I can barely make out her features in the dark, but something about her face gives me pause. Because I could swear, in that half second before the image blinks out, that Vanessa isn't crying at all.

Vanessa is laughing.

21.

The rain has turned to snow overnight. When I wake up and go to the window in the living room, I see a half foot of powder on every surface, softening our view. Thick and silent the snow falls, in perfect dime-sized flakes. The great lawn has vanished, buried under a familiar blanket of white.

I haven't seen snow like this in years, and I find myself standing on the stoop in my pajamas, sticking out my tongue. Lachlan comes up behind me with a cup of tea in his hands, a comforter wrapped around his shoulders. He is haggard and hungover; the soft skin under his eyes puffy and wrinkled. He looks his age for once — a man now running up against forty — which comes as a shock.

"You're letting all the cold air in," he says, and then looks at what I'm wearing. "Christ, Nina, you're going to freeze to death if you're not careful." He pulls me in under the comforter with him, trapping the heat of his body against me. He smells sour, like old sweat and stale breath.

"Do you think we'll be snowed in?" I ask.

"Let's hope not." He wraps the comforter tighter around us and shivers. "After I moved away from Dublin I swore I wouldn't live anywhere cold ever again. I was always cold when I was a kid. My parents could never afford the heat and so every winter we'd freeze. I guess they hoped that with eleven kids shoved in three bedrooms, we'd survive off body heat alone." He looks gloomily at the snowflakes coming down. "I'd be doing my homework with gloves on so I wouldn't get frostbite in my own goddamn living room. My teachers always gave me bad marks for handwriting."

What I want to tell him is that snow feels hopeful to me, in its purity. That I remember looking out at this same vista as a teenager, and feeling like I'd wandered into some kind of fairy-tale wonderland. That maybe *I* could be happy up here, in different circumstances. But I say none of those things. Instead I slide out from under his arm and slip back inside the warmth of the cottage. "No time for sentimentality," I say. "Let's get started."

A little while later, I trudge across the field of white to Stonehaven. My boots break through the fresh crust of snow, exposing the flattened grass beneath as snowflakes melt in the prints

375

that I leave behind. I climb up to the back porch and have to knock three times before Vanessa finally shows up at the door. She blinks at me, her eyes bloodshot and puffy, a quavering smile plastered across her face. Clearly, she also had too much to drink last night.

"You're feeling better already?" Surprise is naked on her face. "That was fast."

"It passed quickly," I say. "The body is a mystery sometimes, isn't it? Even when you spend your life trying to understand it, it can still do things that surprise you."

"Oh!" Her brow wrinkles, parsing this. "What do you think it was? Food poisoning?"

"Probably the tuna sub I had from the deli down the road."

"Oh God, if you'd asked me, I would have warned you off those sandwiches. They have very suspect refrigeration there." She's still standing there staring at me as if she can't believe I'm standing upright. "Well, we missed you at dinner."

"I felt terrible to miss it, after all the effort you put into it. I hope you'll offer a do-over." I smile.

She looks over my shoulder, in the direction of the cottage, and I can feel her mind go through some calculation — the value of company versus the effort required to entertain again so soon. "Sure," she says.

"When?"

Her eyes flutter, surprised by my sudden pushiness. "Tomorrow, I guess."

"Great." I nudge my toe in the door. "Look, can I come in and dry off for just a second? I have a favor to ask of you."

Inside, the kitchen looks like it was the scene of a violent crime. There are dirty pots and pans strewn across the counters, crimson splashes of braising liquid along the back-splash tiles, wineglasses with gritty scarlet residue dried in the stems. The remains of last night's meal are still on the table: plates of congealing stew in yellow puddles of fat, silverware with crusts on the tines, white napkins marked with lipstick, a green salad wilting in a pool of dressing.

"Looks like you had fun last night," I say.

She regards the mess with a curious sweep of her head, as if it was left there by someone else. "The housekeeper was supposed to come this morning to clean it up, but she got snowed in." Something about the way she says this suggests that the housekeeper is to blame for the weather. She picks up a half-empty wineglass from the counter and moves it five inches closer to the sink, as if this is as much cleaning as she can muster.

"I'll send Michael over to do the dishes. He helped make the mess," I say, delighting in exactly how much Lachlan will hate this idea.

"Oh God, please don't do that. It'll stop snowing soon, I'm sure. The snowplow will be around eventually." She looks out the window at the lake and winces at the light reflecting off the snow, then drops into a chair. "You said you had a favor to ask?"

I pull out a chair next to her, take a breath, make myself become *Ashley.* "So, I'm not sure if Michael told you this already — he can be so *private,* sometimes. . . ." I offer her a shy little smile. "But he asked me to marry him. We're engaged."

She stares at me dully for a split second, as if on time delay. And then her face lights up, and she lets out an ear-piercing squeal. It's so over-the-top, she sounds like a parody of herself. Truly she can't be *this* excited for us. "*Tremendous! Fantastic!* He did *not* tell me! How wonderful!" She leans in close, dank morning breath in my face, hands clutched to her bosom as if overtaken with joy. It's all a bit much. "Oh, tell me everything. Where, and how, and oh, show me the ring!"

"The first night we got here, on the steps of the cottage actually. We were outside looking at the full moon over the lake and he got down on one knee and . . . well. You can imagine." I slowly pull off a mitten and push my left hand out for her to examine. Sagging off my ring finger is an Art Deco engagement ring, a cushion-cut emerald shocker the size of my thumbnail, surrounded by diamond baguettes. If it were real, it would be worth at least $100,000. It's not real. It's an excellent

378

fake that my mother slipped off a drunk woman's hand at the Bellagio many years ago. It's rattled around my jewelry box ever since, coming in useful in moments like this.

Vanessa grabs my hand and makes little cooing noises. "Vintage! An heirloom?"

"It belonged to Michael's grandmother."

"Alice." She gently rubs a thumb over the stone.

It takes me a minute to recognize the name. "Right, *Alice.* And I love it. I mean, it's gorgeous." I hold my hand up to admire the sparkle, and the ring knocks against my knuckle. "But see? It's far too big and it won't stay on my finger. I'm afraid to wear it until I can get it resized. And even then, between you and me, I'm a little shy about wearing something so ostentatious. . . ." I muster up a blush. "Honestly I'm a pretty understated person. It's not like I can wear this when I'm teaching. If it were up to me, I'd just donate it and get something smaller."

"Oh, I'm *sure.*" She nods, all serious, as if she can relate, although I know from Instagram that there is no rock that would be too big for Vanessa Liebling.

"Anyway, I also hate just leaving it sitting there in the cottage. I guess I'm paranoid, but the cottage feels so exposed. . . ." It seems ludicrous to suggest that robbers will be prowling the snowy lakeshore in the dark, but she frowns, as if seriously considering the possibility. I hope I haven't just scared her into installing a better alarm system. "Anyway, I was wondering — Do you have a safe here?"

She lets go of my hand. "A safe? Yes, of course."

"Would you mind, terribly, keeping my ring there, for safekeeping, while we're staying here?" And I slip the ring off my finger and drop it into her palm before she has a chance to think about it. Her hand instinctively closes around it, like a baby clutching a toy. I cover her fist with mine, and give it a gentle squeeze of appreciation. "It would really make me feel better to know it's somewhere where I don't have to worry about it. I've never owned anything this nice. And I just feel . . ." I hesitate. "Well, I feel like I can trust you."

Her eyes drop down to our two hands, clasped softly together around what she believes is my most precious possession. "I totally understand." When her eyes rise to meet mine, I'm surprised to see that they are damp with tears. *Here we go again. Why is she crying this time?*

But then I remember the engagement ring she posted on her *V-Life* feed, the radiant smile on her face as she peered through her fingers at the camera. *Guys: I have news.* That ring is gone now; yet another line in the ledger of poor Vanessa's personal tragedies.

380

What happened? I wonder. Maybe it's because I'm still playing at *Ashley,* or maybe it's because some humanity inside me wants to connect with the humanity inside her despite it all; either way, I feel compelled to ask.

"You were engaged earlier this year, right?" I ask softly.

She looks startled. "How did you know that?"

"Your Instagram."

Her mouth falls open slightly and her thoughts seem to go inward. It looks like she's trying to summon up a speech she's prepared, an inspirational quote that will demonstrate how resilient and introspective she is. But for some reason it won't come. Her hand unclenches, revealing my ring in her palm; she rolls it back and forth so that it catches the light, an oddly possessive gesture for a ring that doesn't even belong to her. "He didn't like my lifestyle very much," she finally says, watching the ring sparkle. Her voice has changed, flatlined. "He wants to go into politics like his mom and he decided I was a hindrance to his life goals. My 'optics' were bad. Unseemly for a public servant to be seen on a private jet, especially in the current environment. Comes off as shallow. So." She shrugs. "I can't say I blame him."

This is not what I had expected to hear. I figured, infidelity, maybe drug problems —

something sordid and contemptible. I am surprised, too, to discover that she's got a modicum of self-awareness. *Shallow?* I would never have imagined that word coming out of her mouth. "He waited until you were engaged to decide this?"

"He decided to dump me two weeks after my father died."

I am not so heartless that I can't feel the barbarism in this. I lean in closer. "Anyone who would do something like that doesn't deserve your time. Not that it's any consolation, but it sounds like you dodged a bullet, in the long run." I mean it, too. "So, that's why you left New York?"

"That's why I moved here," she offers. She looks around the ravaged kitchen. "I needed a change of scenery and up popped Stonehaven, at what seemed like the right moment. Daddy left it to me, and I thought . . . maybe it would be comforting, to be back here, in our old family home. I thought it was serendipity." She looks back at me and I see that her eyes have gone as flat and cold as the lake outside. "Turns out, I forgot that I hate this house. *Terrible* things happened to my family in this house." The words drop from her mouth like shards of ice. "Stonehaven is just a shrine to the tragedy that is my family: Everything bad that happened to my mother and father and brother started here. You know my brother is schizophrenic? It started here.

And my mother committed suicide here."

I'm startled into silence by this new Vanessa: not the weepy, needy depressive from the library; nor the giddy hostess, out to please; but a new one, cold and angry, bitterly cognizant. And — her mother committed suicide? This is news. "My God. Suicide?"

She stares at me curiously with those flat green eyes, as if seeking something in my face. For once, it's not really an effort to look empathetic. Then she looks down, and shrugs. "It wasn't in the papers of course. Daddy made sure of that."

A boating accident. That was what the newspaper said. I'd never thought to wonder about how a middle-aged woman might die in a boating accident on a yacht. What I want to ask is, *Why did she do it?* But I know that this isn't an acceptable question, this isn't what *Ashley* would ask. "She must have been very troubled," I say softly, remembering the brittle, patrician woman on the couch in the library with a pang of sudden doubt. What else didn't I see that day? "I'm so sorry. I had no idea."

"Why would you?" She gives her shoulders a violent little shake. "Why would anyone? I'm Vanessa Fucking Liebling. I'm *hashtag blessed* and don't you know I know it. I'm not allowed to complain or feel pain, or I'm unappreciative of what I've got. I'm supposed to spend my life doing penance for my own

383

good fortune. No matter what I do, even if I give it all away, it will *never* be enough for some people. They'll always find a reason to hate me." She stares at the ring in her hands, turning it to catch the light. "And maybe they're right. Maybe I *am* fatally flawed; maybe I *am* somehow less worthy of empathy."

Despite myself, despite everything, I feel a prick of genuine pity for her. Is it possible that I've been too judgmental? That my distaste for her is misplaced, and Lachlan and I have picked an undeserving target this time? After all, she wasn't the Liebling who dragged me naked out of bed that day; she wasn't the Liebling who drove my mother and me out of town. She barely even knew I existed. Maybe it's unfair of me to blame the sins of the parents on the child.

She's looking at me expectantly, as if waiting for me to offer up soothing words, an Ashley-like prescription for serenity in the face of tragedy. But I can't make myself do it. "Give it all up," I say instead. My voice sounds different, harsher; and I realize, it's because it's *me.* "This place is toxic to you? You're tired of judgment? Then *get out,* leave it all behind. You don't need this place. Give up Stonehaven and go start over somewhere where you have no baggage. Turn off the cameras and live in peace. But Jesus, you have to *pull it together.* And stop asking other people to tell you that you're worthy. Why do you care what they think, anyway? *Fuck them all.*"

"Fuck them all?" I see hope cross her face, possibility dawning in her eyes. And then they slide up to meet mine. "You're kidding, right?"

I realize that I'm perilously close to blowing my cover. What am I trying to prove? "I'm kidding." I reach for an anodyne platitude, something Ashley might say. "Look, it sounds like you've had a really challenging year. You should consider self-care. I can give you some mindfulness exercises, if you like."

"Mindfulness exercises." She stares at me, as if astonished by the suggestion. "What is that?"

"It's like, spiritual cleansing." I know it sounds pathetic; I would hate this advice if it was given to me. "You know, being *present.*"

She pulls her hand from mine, and I can see that she regrets having spoken at all. "I *am* present," she says flatly. She pushes back abruptly from the table. "Anyway. I'll put this ring in the safe now. Is there a box?"

"A box?" I realize my mistake — of course, it would have come in a velvet box. "Shoot, I left it in the cottage."

"That's OK," she says. "Wait here."

She vanishes from the kitchen and I hear her move through the house. I listen carefully for her footsteps, but the house swallows the

385

sounds of her movements. I can't even tell if she's gone upstairs. I sit there at the kitchen table, heart racing, and hope that we dropped the cameras in the right locations. There are forty-two rooms in this house, and only a dozen cameras.

She returns a few minutes later and stands over me. "Done," she says. She seems to have recovered herself while she was gone; her hairline is damp, as if she's splashed water on her face.

I stand. "I can't thank you enough, really."

"Oh, it's *nothing*. The *least* I could do for a friend." Her voice has returned to that breathy, patrician lilt. "Just let me know when you need it back."

I want to drag the other Vanessa back, the darkly bruised cynic that I just glimpsed underneath this shallow, featherlight phony. I reach out and take her hand in mine. "Seriously," I say. "I'm sorry that you're not happy here. You really should think about leaving."

She blinks at me, then slips her hand out of my grip. "Oh, I think you took my words the wrong way. I'm sure I'm back here for a reason. In fact," she says, showing twenty-two of her perfect white teeth, "I *know* I am."

When I get back to the cottage, shaking snow out of my hair, I find Lachlan sitting at the dining table. The laptop is propped open in front of him, live video feeds streaming across

386

his desktop. When he sees me at the door, he kicks his legs up onto the chair next to him and leans back, grinning.

"Bingo," he says. "The safe is behind a painting in the office."

22.

Three adults — a blond woman, a dark couple — sit in the dining room of a mountain mansion, a lonely trio anchoring one end of a table built for twenty.

The table is set for a formal multicourse meal. Bone china plates edged in gold filigree are stacked like Russian nesting dolls, each layer awaiting its course. Monogrammed silver cutlery marches up one side of the china and down the other. Cut crystal stemware reflects prisms in the light of the overhead chandelier. The room smells of woodsmoke and the roses in the arrangements on the sideboard.

The blonde, their hostess, has pulled out all the stops.

She is wearing a green chiffon Gucci dress likely intended to bring out the color of her eyes, but the couple, uncomfortably, are in casual denim. They had not anticipated a meal this grand. They had not anticipated the caterers scurrying about the kitchen, the uniformed woman pouring the wine, the housekeeper waiting to sweep up their crumbs and crusts. Something has changed over the last forty-eight hours since a meal was previously on offer here, but neither of them knows why the blonde suddenly feels the need to impress.

But the conversation is friendly and animated, steering clear of topics that might be sensitive (politics, family, money). Instead, they talk about zeitgeisty subjects with which they are all familiar: the latest critically acclaimed television shows, celebrity divorces, the merits of the Whole30 diet. The wine flows, the soup arrives; the wine flows some more, and here comes the salad. They are all getting tipsy, although if you pay attention you might notice that the couple are sipping their wine much more slowly than the blonde. Occasionally, the couple's eyes meet across the table, and then skitter quickly away.

The main course — a winter-citrus salmon dish — has just been set on the table when the meal is interrupted by the sound of a ringing telephone. The dark-haired woman scrabbles in the pocket of her jeans, fishes out her cellphone, and studies its screen with a frown. Conversation briefly stops as the woman answers the call. She mouths a word to her dinner-mates — *Mom* — and they nod, understanding. As she stands up from the table she gives a helpless shrug of apology, and then she steps out of the room, talking to the person on the other end of the line.

The two people remaining at the table smile awkwardly at each other. The blonde looks down at the perfectly plated dish — *Should they wait?* — but the man tears into the food as if he's starving to death and so eventually the woman relaxes, too, and picks up her fork. The brunette's salmon cools and congeals on her plate.

Meanwhile, she walks quickly through the mansion, through cold, dark rooms that feel even darker the farther she gets from the sound and activity in the dining room. She keeps chatting loudly on her phone until she is a safe distance away, and then she abruptly drops the pretense. The call was a fake, of course. There are apps for that.

The woman finds herself in the mansion's front parlor, where disapproving dead plutocrats peer down from their portraits, then she cuts through the drawing room and into the office. The office is at the base of the round turret that anchors the center of the mansion, and so the room is circular, with curving walls of inlaid wooden bookshelves. Each shelf nook lovingly displays a singular object: a celadon urn, a porcelain cow, a globe lamp, a curlicue boudoir clock. The desk, a lake of polished mahogany, is bare except for an old-fashioned pen-and-ink set and a framed silver photo of a mother and two young children, taken some decades earlier.

The woman walks to the desk, and turns in a slow circle, studying the room. She focuses in on a painting on the wall across from the desk: an oil depicting a British hunting scene, a pack of dogs chasing a fox through the heather. She moves closer to examine it. The painting juts out from the wall by a telling hair, and the gilt of its frame has worn slightly thin in one spot. The woman pulls a pair of latex gloves out of her pocket and slips them on before grasping the frame in the same place. When she gives it a gentle tug, the painting swings away from the plaster, revealing the safe behind it.

The woman pauses, carefully listening, but the house is quiet except for the occasional peal of laughter, like a needle piercing the silence. She studies the safe. It's the size of a television, as big as the painting that covered it, and fairly modern, with an electronic keypad. Although not *too* modern; nothing that's been recently updated.

With gloved hands, the woman carefully punches in a birth date, one that she recently looked up in an online database of birth certificates: 062889. She waits, listening for the click and release of the lock. Nothing happens. She tries again, three more variations on the same date, in quick succession — 061989, 280689, 198906 — but still nothing happens. She presses an ear to the safe's metal surface to listen, like a safecracker in an old-fashioned heist movie, but even if there was something to hear she wouldn't know what to listen for. Her fingers stab at the keypad, growing frustrated. She has read enough about safes to know that she will get only five tries before the safe detects foul play and cuts off any further attempts.

She collects herself, shakes her hands, tries one more time: 892806.

The safe lets out an electronic whine of complaint. The bolts release with a metallic clunk. The door goes slack under the woman's hands, and she pulls it open and peeks into its dark interior.

It's empty. The safe is empty.

I peer inside in disbelief. There's the fake Art Deco engagement ring, right at the front of the safe. Vanessa has put it in a small silver bowl for safekeeping, and in the dim light it looks like a sad bauble that's been forgotten in a soap dish. Behind it, there's nothing. No bundled stacks of cash, no velvet-lined jewelry boxes, no coins in precious metals.

I feel faint. It was all for nothing.

But no — that's not true, the safe isn't *quite* empty. Tucked in the back of the vault is a sheaf of papers and a stack of expandable file folders. I gently lift out the latter and pry them open to peek inside. But it's just documents, many of them yellow with age. I shuffle through them — stacks of business papers, house deeds, government bonds, birth certificates, assorted legal ephemera that I don't have the time or interest to parse through. Probably these pages contain an interesting historical document of Stonehaven and its inhabitants, but there's nothing of value to me.

I place the file folders back the way they were, and then carefully slide the stack of loose papers to the front of the safe. Again, there's nothing there of value. It's just old letters.

Still, I quickly riffle through them, just to be sure; and as I do, one of the letters catches my eye. It's a handwritten note on lined three-hole paper, the kind you find in children's binders across America. The handwriting is a woman's, carefully penned in ballpoint ink.

Something inside me stops. *I know that paper. I know that hand.*

I tug the letter out from the pile and hold it under the light of my smartphone flashlight. *You're imagining things,* I tell myself, as I start to read. But it feels as if a snake has wrapped itself around my chest and is starting to squeeze.

October 15, 2006

William —

I know you thought this was all over when I left town, but guess what? I've changed my mind. I've realized that my silence came too cheap. I'm worth more than what you gave me last June.

As you know I have proof of our affair — photos, receipts, letters, phone records. I'm now offering to sell these to you for $500,000. I'm including examples of the photos that I have, so you know I'm for real. If you choose not to pay me $500,000, I'll send them to your wife instead. And then I will send a copy to the investors on your board. And then I will send a copy to the newspapers and gossip websites.

You have until November 1 to get the money to my account at Bank of America.

You owe Nina and me that much.

Sincerely,
Lily

The snake that is winding around my chest tightens until it stops my breath, and the whole room spins.

Bells are pealing inside my head; but no, it's just the boudoir clock chiming out the hour. Nearly eight minutes have passed since I left the dining table. I shove the letter back in the safe, hiding it in the middle of the stack of papers; then close and lock the safe with trembling hands. I move blindly back through the dark house, following the sound of voices, trying to make the pieces of my history fit neatly back together again, but I can't. Nothing makes sense. Or maybe it's that everything suddenly does.

My mother. I picture her as she was back then, a bombshell in a blue sequined dress; and then I picture her in William Liebling's sagging, fleshy arms. I shudder.

I need to talk to her. I need to *see* her.

Eventually I stumble back into the dining room, blinking in the sudden wash of light, the heat from the fireplace. Two sets of eyes fix on me and I wrench my mouth up into what I hope is a calm, reassuring smile. But Lachlan can tell something is wrong. When he looks at the expression on my face the muscles in his jaw tighten, almost imperceptibly, into a mask of alarm.

Vanessa doesn't seem to notice. "There you are! Michael was just telling me about his novel, I'm *dying* to read it. Maybe I can get a sneak peek?" She dimples at Lachlan and when he fails to respond immediately, she quickly recalibrates and turns her gaze on me. She frowns. "Wait, Ashley, is everything OK?"

The smell of the salmon fills my nose and makes me want to gag. The candles on the table sputter with the draft that I brought in with me. I study Vanessa, wondering if she knows about the letter, feeling exposed and tender. Vanessa looks back at me wide-eyed, as groomed and guileless as a pedigreed house pet. And then I remember: I'm *Ashley.* Even if Vanessa had come across the letter in her father's records, there would be no reason for her to connect the "Lily" in the signature with the woman who stands before her. I wrap myself in Ashley's protective quilting. I quiver bravely and I improvise.

"It's my mom," I say. "She's been hospitalized. I have to go home."

Lachlan is furious. He paces the perimeter of the living room, the veins popping in his neck, hands raking his curls into a tangle of static frizz. "Christ, Nina — empty? Where the fuck *is* everything, then?"

"I don't know," I say. "Hidden somewhere else, in all likelihood. A different safe. Or a safety-deposit box. Or a bank."

"Fuck *me.* You were *so sure.*"

"Excuse me, but it's been twelve years. Things change. We knew it was a long shot."

"You never said it was a long shot. You said it was a sure thing. Our big play."

I want to throw a chair at him. "At least the code still worked so that I was able to get in to the safe and see."

He flings himself down on the couch, look-

396

ing grim. "So now what?"

"Well, it's not like this place is lacking in valuables. There are pieces in that house that are worth hundreds of thousands of dollars. That grandfather clock. I'll come back and do an inventory, come up with some options. We won't leave empty-handed."

He draws his face into a pucker of distaste. "It's just so much more of a hassle. Finding a way to get it all out of here. Finding another fucking fence to sell it. We only get a fraction of its value once they take their cut. This was supposed to be the big easy score, and now once again we're talking small potatoes." He glares at me. "And what the hell is all this about going to visit your mom?"

"It helped with the story, it made the phone call more plausible." I can tell that he doesn't believe me, but there is no way I'm telling him about the letter. Besides, what bearing does it have on what we're doing here? None. Though I feel like something has shifted; as if the pool of moral certainty in which I've been swimming for all these years has suddenly drained and I'm looking around at my barren surroundings, wondering where the hell I really am.

I sit down next to him and put a hand on his leg. He ignores it. "Look, I *am* worried about my mom. We agreed that I'd be able to go home and check on her. That's why we stayed in California, remember?" He's still

397

silent. "I'll only be gone a few days."

"Vanessa will expect me to leave with you. I'm your fiancé now, remember?"

"No, you stay here and work on a plan B. I'm sure you can muster up a convincing reason why you have to stay behind. Tell her I didn't want you to interrupt your writing. Tell her my mom isn't that sick, after all."

Outside, the snow keeps falling, carpeting the cottage in silence. The ancient thermostat ticks and ticks and then catches, blasting us with a current of scorched heat. Lachlan scowls and tugs his sweater over his head.

"Christ, Nina," he mutters. "What am I going to do while you're gone? I'm going crazy here already."

I shrug. "You're a big boy. You'll figure something out."

23.

I drive to Los Angeles the next morning. First, the slow grind over the snow-tossed summit, tires struggling to bite the road, the windshield splattered with soft brown slush. Then down through the rain-slicked valley, where clots of cars push their way through the mist. Farther south I drive through miles of farmland, dormant for the winter; and finally over the velvet hills of the Grapevine, soft with shadow. It takes nine hours, and yet it feels as if I blink in Lake Tahoe and I blink again and I am parking in front of my bungalow in Los Angeles.

Inside the cottage, it smells like sweet decay. My mother's perfume, lingering and stale; or maybe it's the spray of lilies weeping bruised petals over there on the sideboard. The cottage is dark, the damp night pressing in through the seams in the warped wooden windows. I've been gone only a few weeks and although I know that isn't enough time for my mother to have gone radically downhill, I find myself holding my breath, wondering if I will find her supine on her bed, shrunken, already too far gone.

But then there's a sound from the kitchen, and the door swings open and my mother is there, backlit by a rectangle of yellow light. She must not see me at first in the gloom of the house, because she sways silently toward me, a pale wraith in a moon-satin nightgown.

"Mom," I say, and a horrible sound comes from the ghost's mouth. There's a crack, and the sound of shattering glass, and then the light blinks on overhead. And there my mother stands, frozen by the light switch, surrounded by glittering shards.

"Jesus, Nina. What are you doing creeping around the house like that?" Her voice is sharper than I expect, shaken. She takes a tentative step backward, her toe nudging glass aside to find a clear spot among the floorboards.

"Here, don't move, you'll cut yourself." I rush past her toward the kitchen to get the dustpan and broom. When I return, she's still standing motionless, her body vibrating with tension. I peer up at her as I sweep the bits of glass into the pan. She is pale, a faint sheen of sweat on her brow, and I swear she is thinner than she was just a few weeks ago. Signs of the lymphoma settling back into her system. I chide myself for not having called her doctor to expedite her treatment. She shouldn't be waiting another week for radiation, she needs it *now.*

The ramifications of that empty safe are growing real to me, now that I'm home: I've returned with empty pockets, not a penny to cover my mother's medical costs. *One dose of Advextrix = $15,000 = one Delft vase sold on the black market.* I imagine Stonehaven's treasures, sitting there forgotten in those cold rooms. I need to go back and take a second look. *The grandfather clock, two of the chairs from the living room, some of the silver . . .* As I sweep up shards, I mentally walk through the rooms of Stonehaven, putting price tags on the furniture, comparing them to the value of my mother's life. Surely, Lachlan and I can find a way to smuggle some of it out and sell it without Efram; there must be other fences we could use.

We'll have to take too much, though. It will be riskier than anything we've ever done before. How will we get it all out of Stonehaven? How will we manage to avoid getting caught in the process?

We'll figure it out, I tell myself. We have to. I have no other ideas.

I'm afraid to look up and meet my mother's gaze, afraid that she'll see the failure written across my face.

My mother's hands are on my shoulders, tugging me up from the floor. I stand and realize that my jeans are soaked from whatever was in her glass: gin, it smells like.

"You shouldn't be drinking alcohol," I say. "Not if you're about to start radiation therapy."

"What, it's going to kill me?" She laughs, but I can tell that she's self-conscious, her lashes fluttering, her hand clutching at the gap in her robe.

"It could kill you faster."

"Don't judge me, darling. I've been lonely. It's been so quiet here without you, I needed something to do with myself. It makes the time pass quicker." She pulls me into a hug, presses her cool face against mine; I can smell her primrose lotion, the medicinal gin on her breath. "I'm so glad you're back."

She stands back and studies my face. "You've been spending time outside, I can tell. You forgot to put on sunscreen." But she doesn't ask exactly where I've been; I can feel that careful calculation on her part. Her eyes slide over my shoulder and into the darkness of the room. "Is Lachlan with you?"

"Here's not here."

"But he came back to L.A. with you?"

"No."

"Oh." She wobbles now toward the living room, her hand clutching at the furniture as she passes. I can't tell if she's weak or if she's a little drunk. Perhaps both, I think, as she flicks on a lamp and collapses onto her couch. The cushion puffs out a small sigh, the springs creak in protest. I sit beside her and tip sideways, let myself slide toward her lap until my head is resting there, like a child. Only now do I realize how exhausted I am. I feel like myself for the first time in weeks. Her hands settle in my hair and smooth the frizzed strands.

"My baby. What brought you home?"

"I missed you," I whisper.

"Me, too." I wish I could hug her tight but I'm afraid of breaking her; she feels like a blown egg underneath me, fragile and empty. I pick up her hand and press it against my cheek. "Darling," she says slowly. "Are you sure it's safe for you to come back? I love to see you but maybe you shouldn't be here. The police."

In my haste to get to her, I had almost forgotten about this; but it seems immaterial at the moment, a vague danger pulsing somewhere at the back of my mind.

"Mom. I have to tell you where I've been," I say. "I've been up at Lake Tahoe."

And I feel it, immediately, how she changes beneath me, how she stiffens, how her breathing suddenly catches and shifts. When I sit up and look at her face I can see her eyes, flickering back and forth, looking for a safe place to settle. She is trying as hard as she can not to look at me.

"Mom." I keep my voice gentle even though

the urgency inside me is fizzing and popping as it struggles for escape. "I've been staying at the Lieblings' house. At Stonehaven."

My mother blinks. "Who?"

She used to be such a good liar, my mother; she might still be convincing to a stranger, but I know better. "Don't bother pretending you don't know who I'm talking about," I say. "And I have some questions."

She reaches toward the coffee table as if she might find a glass there, but her hands grab blindly at nothing. Finally she pulls them back into her lap and wraps them in the cord of her robe. She does not look at me.

"Mom," I say. "You have to tell me what happened, back when we lived there. Between you and William Liebling."

Her eyes come to rest on the blank screen of the television, just beyond my shoulder. The room is silent except for the ragged whistle of her breath in her throat.

"Mom? You can tell me. It was all a long time ago. I'm not going to be angry." Except that I *am* angry, I realize. I am angry because there is a secret that was kept from me, one that set the frame through which I have viewed the world for the last decade. I'm angry because I thought we were close — the two of us a united front against the world — and I'm suddenly realizing that we're not. How much of my life has been a fiction that she wrote for me?

I sit back in the couch and fold my arms, watching her reaction.

She keeps her eyes on the blank screen, her jaw resolutely set.

"OK, let's try it this way." I'm losing patience. "You were having an affair with William Liebling when we were living up at Tahoe, right?"

Her eyes flicker to me. Her voice is barely a whisper. "Yes."

"You met, I'm going to guess . . . at the Academy? At Back to School night?" Faint amusement flickers across her face and I realize my mistake — school events would have been Judith's domain, not William's. I guess again: "No, you met at the casino. The high-roller room? He came in to gamble and you served him drinks."

She's blinking too rapidly, and I can tell that I'm right. "Nina. Please. Don't. Just let this go, it's really not important."

"But it is, Mom." I study her, thinking. "What was your plan?" She shakes her head slowly, her eyes fixed on me, assessing, waiting to see how much she can still keep from me. "Identity theft? Credit cards?" She shakes her head again. "OK, what then? What was the deal?"

"No deal," she says defiantly. "I *liked* him." She wraps the cord of her robe tightly around her hand, until her palm is turning white.

"Bullshit," I say. "I *met* him, Mom. He was an asshole. You didn't *like* him."

She gives me a wry smile. "Well, I certainly *liked* that he was paying our bills."

I remember now, the way our money troubles abruptly stopped that spring; how I attributed that to the tips in the high-stakes rooms at the Fond du Lac. Still, I don't quite buy it. Bilking a business tycoon out of a few hundred bucks for the heating bills? She would have aimed higher than that.

"But what else?" She hesitates. "Come on. You were running a con on him, right?"

There's a wicked twinkle in her eye, and I can tell that she's dying to tell me despite it all, that she's *proud* of herself for some reason. Her lip twitches into a smile. "Fake pregnancy. I was going to threaten to keep it, scare him a little so that he'd pay me off to get rid of it and go away."

I want to cry. What a tawdry and sad scam. "But how? Wouldn't you need a fake pregnancy test and an ultrasound?"

"There was a girl I worked with at the casino, she was knocked up and needed cash. She gave me the urine, in case he wanted me to pee on a stick to prove it to him. And she was going to go to a clinic, pretend to be me, get an ultrasound with my name on it. I was going to give her five thousand dollars when it was all done."

I finally snag on a word she's been using:

was. "But you didn't go through with it."

"Things . . . changed. Unexpectedly." She sighs.

I am mentally running through those months in my head; remembering the silk scarf that appeared around her neck, the nights that she arrived home at dawn because of "late shifts" at the casino, the subtle change in the color of her hair. And then something else horrible occurs to me. "Did you know about me and Benny when all this was going on?"

She shakes her head. "It started before I knew about you two. And I never *really* knew for sure, darling. You never told me, you were so . . . elusive. Such a teenager, with your secrets. When I met Benny that day, at the café, I *suspected* — the way the two of you looked at each other — but I didn't *know.* It wasn't until . . ." She stops.

"Until the Lieblings called you? When they drove us out of town?"

"No." She is quiet for a moment. "At Stonehaven . . ." Her eyes have gone dark and distant again. At *Stonehaven*? And then I understand, with sickening clarity: The day that Benny's father caught us in the caretaker's cottage, what had he been doing out there anyway? Had Lourdes given us up, told him where to find us? Or had he been headed to the cottage for a discreet assignation of his own? "You were with William Liebling that

407

day, at Stonehaven, right? When he caught me and Benny in the cottage together. *You were there.*"

She blinks. Her eyes are filling with tears.

"Oh God, Mom." I feel ill. I imagine my mother cowering in the bushes outside the caretaker's cottage, listening to William Liebling berate me. I remember how it felt to be naked and vulnerable in front of a strange, powerful man — *You are nothing,* spat into my face — and I'm suddenly furious that she didn't come into the cottage to defend me. I stand up from the couch and pace back and forth in front of the coffee table. "Why didn't you stop him?"

Her voice is so small I can barely hear her. "I was ashamed. I didn't want you to know that I was with him."

This stops me for a minute. "Why were you even *there*?"

She goes quiet again.

"Oh, for God's sake, Mom. Enough with the twenty questions. Just tell me."

She stares at the cord wrapped painfully tight around her hand. She winches it even tighter, then releases it. When she speaks again, her voice is slow and deliberate, as if she's measuring out each word with a teaspoon.

"His wife was out of town," she begins. I nod, remembering. "He brought me there, to the cottage. It was the first time I had been to Stonehaven, but he wouldn't take me into the main house. I was going to tell him that day. That I was pregnant. I had a test with me and my friend's pee in a cup, in case he didn't believe me. But he opened the door to the cottage . . . and right away we could hear you." Her voice cracks a little. "I ran back outside and I thought he would follow, but he didn't. So I hid, and waited. But, darling — I swear. I didn't know it was you in there." Her imploring eyes seek out mine. "Until he came back out and was so *mad.*"

"At me?"

Her throat works up and down. "At *us.* He thought . . . you and Benny . . . that you and I were in it together. A team. Targeting his family. He was *paranoid.* And there was no way I could pretend to be pregnant after *that.*" There's something flat and accusatory in her voice, and I realize with a start that she might actually blame *me* for stepping in the way of her con. "Anyway, that was it. It was over. He dumped me."

"And made us leave town." There's a long silence. "Right? Mom? That's why we moved so suddenly? He forced us out of Tahoe because he wanted to break me and Benny up." But even as I'm asking, I know that this isn't true; this was *never* true. I remember my mother's caginess the day that we left, the way she was so reluctant to elaborate about what the Lieblings had done to drive

409

us from town. Not to protect *me,* but to protect herself.

Her head tilts up to look at me. Her eyes are blurred with tears. "We needed money. Nina . . . the bills. Without him — I couldn't. . . . It was too *hard.*"

I sit heavily on the sofa, which groans beneath me and releases a faint puff of dusty air. Of course. The letter: *My silence came too cheap. I'm worth more than what you gave me last June.* "We left town because you *black-mailed* him? God, no wonder Benny wouldn't speak to me after that!!"

"Nina." She huddles in the corner of the couch, shrinking into herself. "I'm sorry about Benny. But your thing with Benny — it wouldn't have lasted."

"What was the trade, Mom?" I'm yelling at her, and I'm sure Lisa can probably hear me all the way in her house next door, but I can't stop the anger that is pouring out. "What did you demand from him?"

A tear spills from her eye and worms through the soft crevices of her hollow cheek. "I said . . . I'd tell his wife about our affair. I had photos, compromising ones I'd taken just in case, when we . . ." She trails off. "Anyway, I said I'd leave town, if he paid me off. That you'd leave his son alone."

I think back to the day that I came home to the packed car, and my mother's apology: *It's not turning out how I hoped.* A lie. And I also understand for the first time that we *weren't* driven out of town by a vengeful family who thought we weren't as good as they were. Instead, we fled, tail between our legs, because my mom was incapable of going straight after all. Because she was *greedy. She* sent us into exile, not them.

So I guess they were right: We *weren't* as good as they were, not at all.

"How much, Mom?" I ask. "How much did he give you?"

Her voice is barely audible. "Fifty thousand."

Fifty thousand. Such a pitiful sum, really, for selling out your daughter's future. And I wonder what my life would have been, had I stuck it out in Lake Tahoe, in the warm embrace of West Lake Academy and its progressive ideals. If I hadn't walked away from that year thinking myself a failure, a reject, a nobody.

"Jesus, Mom." I sit there on the couch with my head in my hands for a long time. "And then you sent a letter. A few months later, when we were back in Las Vegas. You blackmailed him for more money, a lot more, half a million this time."

She looks startled. "How do you know that?"

"I saw the letter you wrote him. It's still in the safe at Stonehaven."

411

"You *saw* it? In Stonehaven?" Her words are phlegmy, stuck in her throat, and in the middle of all this revelation I realize that my recent sojourn at Stonehaven is the one thing I haven't fully explained. "Wait — Nina —"

"I'll explain later. But, Mom — you black-mailed him *again*?"

She turns slowly to gaze at me, her expression vague and distant, as if she's looking at me from the bottom of an aquarium. "I tried. He never answered."

Of course he didn't. I can still vividly recall the Vegas apartment where we retreated after Tahoe, a tiny shoebox with a tub that didn't work and a kitchen that smelled of mold. If my mother had a half million in her pocket, she would have moved us to a penthouse at the Bellagio and blown through the money in six months. "And that's it? You just gave up?"

"Well, I saw in the paper . . . about his wife. That she died." She looks hard at me. "I figured, I'd lost my opportunity. Plus I felt a little bad for him then."

"But apparently you didn't feel so bad for *me* when you yanked me away from the only place I'd ever been happy." I know I sound bitter.

"Oh, sweetheart. I'm so sorry." The effort of our conversation seems to have depleted her. She closes her eyes and vanishes back into herself. I watch as another tear forces its way from below her closed lids and darts

412

down her face, until it lands at her chin and clings there, wobbling precariously. I can't help it — I reach out and gently take it off with my fingertip. It hangs there, a tiny prism reflecting the room, and the two of us in it. Then I wipe my mother's chin dry with the cuff of my sleeve, tenderly, like a baby. Because that's what my mother is, I see. It's what my mother always was: a child, unable to take care of herself, unable to take care of me, lost in a world that no one adequately trained her how to navigate; a child too small to see over the horizon to where the consequences of her actions awaited her.

This is the great horror of life: that mistakes are forever, and cannot be undone. You can never truly go back, even if you want to retrace your steps and take another route. The path has already disappeared behind you. And so my mother forged blindly ahead, doubling down, hoping that she might miraculously emerge in a better place even as the decisions she'd made guaranteed that she would end up exactly where she is: a cancer-riddled con artist with nothing to her name, and no one except her daughter to care about her existence.

Her eyelids suddenly fly open again. "The safe at Stonehaven," she says as if finally registering what I said. "You were in their safe?" She leans forward, a burning spark in her pupils.

413

I realize then that my charade is finally up. Because my mother knows — has *always* known — what I've been doing for the last three years: She never believed for a second that I was a legitimate antiques dealer, somehow floating all *this* on the resale of an occasional Heywood-Wakefield sideboard. It's time to come clean, to her and myself. I'm Nina Ross, daughter of Lily Ross, a grifter, a talented sham. I am what the world made me. I can't trace my steps backward, either.

I lean in and whisper, "Mom — I got into Stonehaven. Vanessa, the older Liebling kid, Benny's sister? She lives there now. I walked right into her life. She opened the door and invited me in. I got in and I broke into her *safe.*"

And as I say this, I feel a little swell of emotion — of pride of accomplishment, because my mother was a small-time grifter and I'm sure she never imagined something quite so audacious and bold. But something about this emotion twists inside me, and I realize that there's vindictiveness hidden in there, too, because what I also want my mother to know is that I have become the person she never wanted me to be, and it's *her fault.*

I don't know what I expect to see in my mother's face, but it's not what I'm seeing: Curiosity? Or confusion. I can't quite tell. "What else did you find in the safe?" she asks.

Of course, I think. My mother, always the opportunist at heart, would want to know what I got.

"Nothing," I say flatly. "It was empty."

"Oh." She stands up abruptly, a little wobble in her knees but she holds herself steady on the arm of the couch. "And Lachlan — is he still there?"

"Yes."

"Are you going to go back?"

That's the question, isn't it? And for a moment, a brief beautiful moment, I imagine that I *won't.* That instead of getting in the car and driving back up to Stonehaven to finish my con, I will drive to LAX and get on a plane and fly . . . God knows where. That I will hand my mother the little money left in our bank account, tell her that she's on her own this time, and let her deal with her cancer herself. That I will release myself from my past, and let myself be free.

Who will I be if I'm not taking care of my mother anymore? If nothing else, I know that I no longer want to be the person I am now. I imagine myself packing up this house, leaving Los Angeles in my rearview mirror, finding someplace quiet where I can start fresh. Someplace green and serene and full of life. The Pacific Northwest. Oregon, Ashley's home. A place where I really *could* become her (or at least a facsimile). Maybe that wouldn't be so bad.

And what of Lachlan? I wonder. But I already know what I will do, I've known it for some time. I don't need him anymore, and I don't *want* him, either. I think of him still up there with Vanessa, and experience a painful twinge of conscience. *I'll call him off,* I think. *I'll find some excuse to get him out of Stonehaven and out of Vanessa's life.* An olive branch invisibly proffered to my oblivious nemesis. Or is she my nemesis anymore? Over the last ten days she has evolved for me: She is no longer a caricature on whom I can hang all my resentment, but a human being who has cried on my shoulder. She has her flaws — she is shallow, certainly; she has committed the sins of blind entitlement and conspicuous consumption — but she doesn't necessarily deserve what we were about to do to her. Especially now that I know the Lieblings are *not* at the root of everything bad in my life, not in the way that I once believed.

But I don't have the chance to make the call to Lachlan, or the drive to LAX, because at that moment the doorbell rings.

My mother turns to me, her face gone white. "Don't answer it," she hisses.

I stand frozen by the couch, just a few steps away from the front door. I can hear footsteps on her porch, at least four feet shuffling against the creaking boards. I am so close that I can see breath fogging the front window when someone cups their hands against the

416

glass and peers inside. My eyes meet those of a policeman; he holds my gaze, mutters something softly to the person still knocking at the door.

"Run," my mother whispers. "Just leave. I'll take care of this."

"I can't *just leave.*"

What is it I'm feeling as I drift toward the front door, like a magnet drawn to its inevitable polarity? Is it self-awareness, that I finally see the consequences of my actions, and am ready to face them? Is it fear, about the future I am headed toward? Or is it a curious kind of relief, that this may not have been the path I would have chosen, but at least I am about to be free of the path I was on?

I wrench the door open as my mother squeals in protest.

On my doorstep are two policemen in full uniform, hands draped loosely over their guns even though their trigger fingers are poised and at the ready. One has a mustache and one does not, but otherwise they could be twins, and they are looking at me with cool distrust in their eyes.

"Nina Ross?" the one with the mustache asks.

I must have answered in the affirmative because suddenly they are reading me my rights, and one of them is unclipping handcuffs from his belt and the other is grabbing my arm to spin me around. I'm trying to argue and my voice is so panicky and frantic that it doesn't sound like my own; and then over that we all hear a terrible shrieking moan from behind me in the living room, like the wail of a wounded beast. It's my mother. Everyone stops.

I turn to the mustache. "Please, sir, let me have a moment with my mother, she's got cancer and I'm her primary caregiver. I promise I'll go willingly if I can just have a minute with her."

They look at each other and shrug, but the mustache releases my arm and follows me into the living room. He hovers as I hug my mom, who has gone stiff and soundless, as if the scream has emptied her entirely. I put a hand on her face to calm her.

"It's OK, Mom. I'll be back as soon as I can. Call Lachlan and tell him what happened, OK? Tell him to come bail me out."

She twitches in my grip, her breath coming fast and frantic. "This is wrong. How did this happen? We can't — you can't."

"Don't go anywhere, OK?" I kiss her on the forehead and smile, as if I'm just going on a little vacation, nothing at all to worry about. "I love you. I'll be in touch as soon as I can."

Her face twists. "My baby."

The detective tugs on my arm, dragging me out the door, as my mother gasps soft words

418

of love in my direction; and then I'm being pulled out of the house. The cuffs go on, and the metal bites cold around my wrists; the police car door is thrown ajar, waiting for me to slip inside.

I see that Lisa is standing in her driveway, in men's pajamas, gaping at the spectacle unfolding before her. Her graying curls fly wild around her head. She looks stunned, or stoned, or maybe both. She inches toward us, carefully picking her way across the dirt with her bare feet.

"Nina? Is everything OK? What's going on?"

"Ask them," I say, and jerk my head toward the nearest cop. "I have no idea. I'm sure it's all just a terrible mistake."

She frowns and comes to a stop a safe distance away. "Let me know what I can do to help."

The policeman's hand is on my head, gently pressing me down, but before I duck into the back of the police car I manage to call out to Lisa. "Just . . . keep an eye on my mom for me," I say. "Make sure she starts her radiation treatments. I'll be back home soon, I promise."

Of all the lies I have conjured up in my life, this is the only one I never intended to tell.

■ ■ ■ ■

VANESSA

■ ■ ■ ■

24.

Week One
I wake up a wife!

I wake up a wife and I don't even realize it, not at first, because my brain is burning and my mouth is chalk and I can still taste the tequila in my throat. I forgot to draw the curtains last night so it's the morning sun that wakes me, too early, *awfully* bright because of the reflection off the fresh snow outside. It's been a good long while (was it Copenhagen? Miami?) since I woke up in this state and it takes a minute to orient myself: I'm in the velvet canopy bed in Stonehaven's master suite, where my parents once slept, and my grandparents and great-grandparents before them, and so on and so forth for the last hundred-plus years.

I wonder if any of *them* ever woke up like this: blind with pain, still drunk, mind wiped clean of memories from the night before.

But no — not *entirely* wiped.

My eyes fly open. Memories are surfacing, startling creatures swimming up from the dark. I roll to one side to check if I'm remembering correctly. And there he is, naked in bed beside me, wide-awake and smiling at me like I am a warm latte that he is about to drink up.

My husband. *Mr. Michael O'Brien.*

I wake up a wife, and I wonder what on earth have I *done*?

"Good morning, my love," he says in a voice still crackled with sleep. *"Wifey."*

A callback to a moment the night before, after we said *I do;* I remember that much, and I also remember what I said back. *"Hubby,"* I whisper. The word is strange in my mouth, but also comforting, a feather duvet settling over my limbs. Then I giggle, because of all the impulsive things I have done in my life this has to beat them all, and laughter seems the appropriate response.

Oh. Smiling hurts.

When I wince he brushes a thumb over my brow. "You doing OK?" he asks. "That was a new side of you last night, one I didn't expect. Not that I'm complaining."

So it's true. Last night we got drunk on tequila and champagne, and he asked me to marry him, and we called a town car to take us across the border to Reno, where we got married at a shabby little place called Chapel o' the Pines just before midnight. There was an officiant in purple nylon vestments and a professional witness who knitted baby socks while we took our vows. I seem to recall that we laughed, a lot.

He asked me to marry him!

Or maybe we asked each other?

I can't quite remember.

Do we even have photos from last night? Blindly, I feel around for my phone — under the pillow? next to the bed? — thinking that my social media feeds will help fill in the gaps. (How many names and faces and *unforgettable moments* would I have lost, were it not for the convenience of hashtags?) But then I remember that Michael made me leave my phone behind at Stonehaven before we climbed in the car, whispering "I want this to be just for us, just about us" as he gently pried it from my hands. A little burp of panic: If we didn't document our marriage, if it isn't in my public photo stream, did it really happen?

I peer over the edge of the bed and see a heap of clothes on the floor. Apparently I got married in a pair of jeans and a stained Yeezy sweatshirt. (So maybe I *am* glad there are no photos.) This, despite the fact that somewhere in the packing boxes that still line the edges of this bedroom there is a wedding gown, a custom Ralph & Russo, that has never been worn. Also, I do believe that I walked down the aisle to "Love Me Tender." This is not how I once dreamed that my wedding would go. ("Halo," that was always the plan.)

Do I care?

"You're awfully quiet, yeah?" He pulls back to study my face. "Look, I know what we did is kind of crazy, but I don't regret it. Do you?"

I shake my head, suddenly shy. "Of course not. But shouldn't we maybe talk? About what it all means."

"It means what we want it to mean. We figure it out as we go." His eyes are such a clear blue, so translucent, there is nothing to hide behind as he gazes down at me with an expression that strips me bare. He puts his mouth to my ear and whispers lines of his poetry, with that Irish burr that vibrates something deep in my bones: "We shall always be alone, we shall always be you and I alone on earth, to start our life."

And I think to myself: *Does it matter, really, who asked who?* The outcome is the same: That I *won't* ever be alone again. I am thirty-two years old and I have a husband. I am about to build a whole new family again; and it didn't happen at *all* in the way I imagined, but here I am, regardless. Loved, for better or worse. Something wild flutters inside me, like doves set suddenly free, until I think I might burst.

And I think of my friends back in New York

City and wonder what they'll say when they discover that I married a scholar and a writer, a *poet,* and from an old aristocratic Irish family to boot. A man I've known only eighteen — no, nineteen! — days. How *surprised* they'll be! (Oh, Saskia: Take *that* for an unexpected narrative line.) Most of all, I think of Victor, with a pleasant throb of vindictiveness. *You thought I was shallow and predictable; well, look at me now.*

Outside, the snow is falling again, veiling the pines that I can see through the bedroom windows. Stonehaven is cold and silent, except for us in our velvet-lined room on the second floor. Just a few weeks ago, this place was a tomb. Now, with Michael in bed beside me, it feels like the beginning of a new life. I think that maybe I can be happy here, after all. *I'm happy already!*

Michael's arms slide around me and he pulls me into his furred chest and I settle there, waiting until the throbbing in my brain matches the slow, calm beat of his heart. His lips on my forehead, his hands in my hair, as if all of me now belongs to him. Which — I do, I do, I do.

"I love you," I say, and I mean it.

I wake up a wife, and I practically *overflow* with joy.

There's something foreign and heavy weighing down my left ring finger. When I lift my hand to look, I see an antique engagement ring, diamond baguettes surrounding a plush emerald. Five carats, maybe; a Deco design; overly ornate in the way of antiques. The ring droops on my finger and I use the tip of my pinkie to push it back and forth so that the stones catch the light. It's pretty, even if it's fussier than something I would have picked out myself. Another memory that rises up from the murk of the previous evening: The two of us stumbling into my father's study with a bottle of Don Julio in hand, Michael weaving slightly behind me as I open the safe and pull out a ring that I'd stashed there in the dark. Michael kneeling in front of me and slipping it on my finger. Or maybe he didn't kneel at all; maybe he just slipped it on while gazing deeply into my eyes.

Or maybe I put it on myself, without even asking his permission. It's possible.

Michael closes his hand over mine. "When I have a chance, I'll get you a new ring, one without any baggage. We'll go down to San Francisco and find a jeweler and get one made. As big as you like. Ten carats, twenty."

And I remember first seeing this ring in *her* hand, the way she clutched at it as if it were a rope that was going to tow her up and out of her seedy little life. It clearly meant so *much* to her, and now it's mine. So even though, by Liebling family standards, it's a fairly modest

428

ring, I know that *this* is the ring that I want. Maman would've approved of what it symbolizes.

"It's your family heirloom and I love it. It doesn't matter to me if she had it first." Then I catch on the word that he just used — *baggage* — and reconsider. "As long as it doesn't remind you too much of . . . her?" I can't make myself say her name. I'm not even sure which name I would use.

I study Michael's face for grief or regret, but what's there is inscrutable. Maybe it's anger. Maybe it's resignation. Maybe it's just love. He leans in and kisses me, so hard it's almost painful.

"Not a bit," he murmurs.

I wake up a wife, and I think: *I won.*

25.

Ashley felt so real to me, for a moment there. That morning when we sat in the library, I *believed* in the empathy in her eyes, the way she held my hand while I cried, how she teared up about her own father's death. When I clutched at her on the couch — *Tell me what it's like to be a healer!* — she looked me straight in the eyes and said she slept well at night. She *hugged* me! She assured me that we were friends.

What a fake. What a liar.

And oh! The irony that I felt so *intimidated* by her. Her cool detachment; her serene poise; the way she seemed to float around Stonehaven, above it all, occasionally gracing me with that knowing smile. That morning, after I wept on her shoulder about Daddy and Maman, I actually *felt embarrassed*! I stood at the window and watched her meander back down to the caretaker's cottage, her yoga mat tucked under her arm, and convinced myself that I'd somehow screwed it all up. Because I'd noticed the way she hesitated to embrace me in the hall. And so, as she walked away, I convinced myself that she was repulsed by my messiness, my neediness, by the way I'd bragged about my *Instagram fame.*

I let myself believe she was better than me. What a fool.

For a few days after our conversation in the library, I slunk around Stonehaven, acutely conscious of Michael and Ashley down the hill in the cottage, too self-conscious to go knock on their door. Certain that I'd screwed everything up. Barely climbing out of bed, the black funk having once again descended with its curtain of self-loathing. Occasionally, I'd spy Ashley doing her yoga out on the lawn, or the pair of them walking the grounds — bundled up in their parkas, bumping up against each other as they walked — and I'd long to go out to them.

I forced myself to stay inside, my skin breaking out in anxious hives that I scratched at until they were bloody and raw.

You'll know they genuinely like you if they come to you, I told myself.

But they didn't.

On their fourth day in the cottage — two days since Ashley and I had talked — I lay in bed for most of the morning, watching the shadows move across the room as the sun

431

crossed overhead. I could see myself reflected in the mirror on the front of the giant armoire that hulked on the other side of the room and the sight of myself (a greasy-haired wraith, so pale and weak that I might as well just disappear) made me want to break something; so eventually I got up and threw open the armoire doors just to make the damn mirrors go away.

And oh! *My mother's sweaters.* I'd forgotten they were still there, beautiful pastel stacks of cashmere folded into neat rectangles. (Lourdes had a way with laundry; we did love her so.) My father had never cleaned out the closets in Stonehaven and I hadn't ever bothered to unpack myself and so there they still were, the last vestiges of Maman, filling the ancient armoire. I touched one: thin and soft, the very essence of her.

I pulled a pale pink angora cardigan down from a shelf and pressed it hopefully to my nose; but it didn't smell like her perfume anymore. It smelled of must. And when I unfolded it there were moth holes on the front and a stain around the neck, which Maman would never have tolerated. A pang of frustration: It was just a shabby bit of cashmere after all. I tossed the first sweater to the floor and grabbed another — this one a faded blue, and in no better shape — and then another, and then when I reached for the next one something hard and square came flying out with it.

I leaned down and picked it up: It was a journal, bound in red leather, edged in gold.

A diary. How did I never know that my mother kept a diary? I opened it to the first page, my heart kicking to life at the sight of my mother's finishing-school cursive, so neat and symmetrical. ("You can tell an educated woman by the beauty of her hand," she used to tell me. But of course, that was before computers made handwriting irrelevant.) The first diary entry was dated August 12, just after they'd moved into Stonehaven for Benny's junior year.

This estate is my albatross. William wants me to see it as an opportunity but dear God, all I see is work. But we're here for Benny and honestly I couldn't bear how everyone in San Francisco was starting to look at us anyway — everyone speculating about his problems behind our back, practically gleeful to see us suffering. So I will smile and behave like a good little wife even though inside I'm screaming that this place is going to be the death of me.

I flipped quickly through the pages. Some entries were short and dutiful, and others were rambling and long, and yet more seemed to end mid-thought, as if she was still unsure about committing them to paper. *Benny's grades are improving at the Academy but he is still so uninterested in anything but those ghoulish comic books and I keep wondering if —.* Or: *I left three messages with William's new secretary and he hasn't called me back so either he's screwing the secretary and she's trying to pull a power move on me or else he's avoiding me for other reasons which means —.*

I sank, wobbly, to the floor, coming to rest in a nest of abandoned sweaters, my dead mother's presence all around me. I knew I shouldn't be reading her diary. Wasn't this a violation of her trust, her privacy? But of course, I couldn't stop myself. I flipped through the pages, my eyes occasionally seizing on my own name. *Vanessa seems to be doing well at Princeton, but of course we knew she would* (I liked this!) and *Vanessa is home for the holidays, which is wonderful, but I can't help noticing that she's so insecure and desperate for validation — from me and her father and also the world at large* (this I liked less) and *I wish Vanessa would visit us more often but I guess that's what happens when they go off to college; they eventually forget you.* (Oh, the spasm of guilt at *this*!)

Mostly, though, the diary was about Benny and my father and herself.

Benny has started sneaking around with this girl, her name is Nina Ross and she's polite enough but strange and not <u>quality.</u> Single mother (a cocktail waitress in the casinos, for God's sake) and no father in sight. (I think he might be Mexican?) She dresses like one of those kids who shot up that school in Colorado and honestly I am worried. We didn't uproot our lives and move up here so that Benny could fall in with a bad influence. I do not understand why he is drawn to her of all people, but I can't help feeling like it's a rebuke of me, like he wants to thumb his nose at my concern for him. So he sits out in that cottage with her for hours every afternoon and I'm honestly afraid to go knock on the door and see what they're doing because I don't think I could bear to have to tell William if it's something bad, because he'll blame me for everything. Benny's failures are my failures, never his. It's terribly unfair but of course I'm used to it because my whole marriage is that way.

A few pages later:

The doctor prescribed me Depakote for my mood swings but I took it and I gained three pounds in two weeks so I'm throwing the rest in the trash. Anyways most days I am fine except for the ones when I just want to erase myself from the world. So maybe I should be taking the pills on those days, or as an example to Benny — to be a good mother to him! — but I'm afraid getting fat

435

might also make me feel depressed; so what's the point? Anyway William thinks I'm taking them and I just keep telling him that I'm fine because that's what he wants to believe and God knows we are used to pretending.

And later:

I thought I smelled pot on Benny's clothes the other day and so I looked in his room when he was at school and there was a baggie of marijuana under his bed and I don't know what to do because the drugs are so bad for his condition, that's what the doctors say, and I want to absolutely kill that Nina girl for feeding drugs to him (because God knows that must be where he got it). This is not what he needs, not right now when he seemed to finally be doing so much better. I told Benny he is not allowed to see Nina anymore and he told me he hates me and now he's not talking to me, which hurts so much but I can bear it because it's for his own health even if he doesn't see that now.

After that, a gap of three months — when she was at the spa in Malibu, presumably — and then just two more entries. First, a short, terrible one:

Benny is back from Italy and he is not well and I think it might be too late to fix it.

And finally (oh, I knew I shouldn't read it, not *this* entry, but I couldn't stop myself) an even more terrible long one:

As if life couldn't get any more unbearable it turns out that William has been having an affair. An envelope arrived at Stonehaven addressed to him and when I saw that it was a woman's handwriting I knew. It's not the first time, of course. So I opened it and it's a blackmail letter from some woman saying if we don't pay her a half-million dollars she will expose him (us!) to the tabloids. And she's included some ghastly photos of the two of them, naked, doing things — I ran to the sink and vomited as soon as I saw them. The worst of it is I figured out who the woman is — it's the horrible mother of that horrible girl who Benny was palling around with last spring. Lily Ross, a cocktail waitress at one of the casinos where William has been frittering away our fortune. How could William be so stupid to get involved with a scam artist like that?? Meanwhile Benny is still in a downward spiral because of the druggie daughter and I want to kill them both, mother and daughter. The two of them are single-handedly RUINING US and I don't understand why they have it in for the Lieblings. William isn't even here to clean up the mess so it's all on me, and anyway there's nothing I can do because we don't have that kind of cash sitting around to pay the blackmail because William's been so reckless. I am so humiliated. What has been the point of all this? Coming up here and pretending things can be fixed when in fact it's all so broken, more broken now than ever. If those photos end up in the papers — it will kill me, I'll be the laughingstock of the West Coast, of the whole country. I might as well end it all before Lily Ross does it for me because God knows I am not doing any good here and even Vanessa and Benny are better off without me.

And then — nothing.

I couldn't breathe. I closed the diary and threw it away from me, hands shaking. *Lily Ross.* Not some San Francisco trophy wife after all, but a local cocktail waitress — a con woman? The mother of Benny's *amour fou?* And — my God, *blackmail.* No wonder my mother had been so distraught. Public exposure was one thing my mother could not handle: the whole world knowing how messy her marriage really was, how cheap the tart was who took her husband away. Yes, she'd been unstable — but this, *this,* would of course have sent her over the edge. Lily Ross might as well have pushed her right off the *Judybird.*

I thought of my father's words: *We're Lieblings. No one gets to see what's in our basement and no one ever should; there are wolves out there, waiting to drag us down at the first sign of weakness.* Apparently he'd already met the wolves by then, and they were named Lily and Nina Ross.

I tried to remember the faces of the mother and daughter that I'd met in the café that day but they'd already blurred out of focus; I remembered only the dark dour smear of the daughter, the cheap blond tart that was her mom. *Them?* How could my father and brother have been so taken in by *them*? How could those two nobodies so quickly and effectively destroy my entire family?

I rose and retrieved the diary from where it had landed, near the bed, and then turned back to the last page of the diary. I read and reread the entry. Twelve years of questions and *finally* I had answers. I had a scapegoat (a pair of them!) on whom to heap blame for all my family's problems. *They* were the force that had knocked my world off its axis. (*My mother's suicide, my brother's schizophrenia — not my fault at all! Their fault!*)

Lily and Nina Ross. Something violent rose inside me at the sight of their names in my mother's elegant handwriting. It was too much to bear. I grabbed a pen and scrawled over the names with furious black scratches, but their presence in my mother's diary still felt like a violation. So I tore out the last entry and crumpled the paper up into a ball, then retrieved a shoe from the closet and hammered the ball of paper as hard as I could until the paper shredded and the heel of my shoe began to splinter. Then I gathered the scraps and marched them down to the library and threw them in the fireplace.

Rage had gripped me and I did not want to let it go. I moved through Stonehaven for the rest of the day in a hot, destructive fury, throwing books to the floor, smashing wineglasses in the sink, each unsatisfying *crack* a surrogate for the two women whose faces I *really* wanted to break. I stalked through the house in a circle, around and around, as if by doing enough circuits through the rooms I might somehow rewind all of our lives back twelve years.

And then I collapsed. Because, of course, there are good emotions and bad emotions and anger falls in the latter category. I *knew* that. Wasn't there a quote about just that on Ashley's home page? I pulled up her website and — oh yes, there it was. *Buddha says: You will not be punished for your anger, you will be punished by your anger.* I felt abashed, ashamed, then — as if Ashley could see me from down there in the cottage, and she knew

I'd fallen short.

I climbed back in bed under the velvet coverlet and for penance I read motivational quotes, which didn't help much, until finally I took three Ambien and slept for the rest of the night.

By the time I woke up the next morning, I almost felt calm again, as long as I didn't think too hard about the *Judybird* still parked in the boathouse down at the lakeshore.

And still, Michael and Ashley didn't come.

On their fifth afternoon in the cottage, I watched through my bedroom window as the BMW crawled down the driveway toward the gate. Ashley sat behind the wheel, window down, the breeze moving her hair. I wondered where she could be going. And then a little while later — a knock on the back door. *Michael?* I slapped my cheeks until they stung with life, threw my unwashed hair back into a ponytail, and raced to answer it.

He stood there on the rear portico, rocking back on his heels, his hands shoved into his pockets. An afternoon wind was blowing off the lake; it picked up his curls and flew them around his head like a halo.

"I've been wondering if you were still alive in there," he said. His hypnotic blue eyes ran across my face, his brow wrinkled with concern. "You all right, then?"

I was! *Now* I was. It did not escape me that this meant Michael had been thinking about

441

me. It also did not escape me that he'd waited until Ashley left to knock on my door. "Just had a bit of a cold. I'm better now."

"Well, we thought maybe you were avoiding us. Ashley in particular was worried she'd done something to put you off?"

"Oh, no, not *at all.*" Relief bloomed through my chest. *So much time wasted in unnecessary self-flagellation!* Why did I always do this to myself? "Is she upset? Ashley?"

"Nah. She just thought you were going to do some yoga with her. Was a little surprised when you didn't come out and join."

"Tell her I'll be there tomorrow."

His eyes flickered over my shoulder; a nervous smile as he surveyed my kitchen. "You going to invite me in, then? Ashley's gone to town for groceries and I'm desperate for a break from my work."

"Oh! Yes! Want to sit down for a few minutes? I could make tea." I ushered him in toward the kitchen table.

He hesitated, looking down at a plate of congealed eggs that had been sitting there since yesterday. "Show me another room. It's a big house, this is. Curious to see it all." He studied the half-dozen doors leading from the kitchen to various parts of the house, and then headed toward the farthest one, seemingly at random. I chased him down as he flung it open and then, with a look of surprise on his face, coughed out a laugh. "What's *this*?"

"The games room."

I followed him in and flicked on the light. This was one of the rooms I never used, because what's the point of a games room if you don't have anyone to play with? There is nothing in the world more desperate and lonely than a game of solitaire. I looked around the room, taking in the billiards table and the sterling silver chess set just gathering dust in the corner, and wondered if I should suggest a game of pool. But Michael was already making a beeline to the opposite wall, where a pair of gold-and-mother-of-pearl pistols hung over the fireplace.

He leaned close to examine them. "These things loaded?"

"No! The ammunition is locked away in one of the closets. I think they once belonged to Teddy Roosevelt? Or maybe it was FDR."

"But they work, yeah?"

"Oh yes. I remember once my uncle shot a squirrel out of a tree with one of them." The same uncle that later attempted a boardroom coup against my father; perhaps we should have seen *that* coming. "My brother went mental about it. He was a vegan." I corrected myself: "*Is* a vegan."

Michael tore his eyes away from the pistols and looked at me. "I didn't know you had a brother. Are you close?"

"Yes, though I don't see him a lot. He's living in an institution. Schizophrenia."

"Ah." He nodded, as if filing this away for later reference. "That must be tough."

"Very."

A blast of wind slammed at the windows, rattling them in their casements. *"Blow, blow, thou winter wind,/Thou art not so unkind as man's ingratitude."* He smiled at me. "You know, it reminds me of back home in Ireland. My family's castle was near the sea, and the wind would blow up the cliffs so hard that if you were standing up on the battlements you could literally get blown right off and dashed on the stones below."

"Where's your family living now?"

"All over. My parents died in a car accident when I was young. And my siblings and I all went our separate ways. There was some ugliness over the inheritance." He walked over to the chess set and picked up a pawn, weighed it in his hand. "That's why I left Ireland, yeah? I hated all the squabbling over money. Decided I'd rather find a way to live on my own devices, in a place where my name didn't come with so much baggage. I wanted to do some real good, teaching kids who came from nothing. You know what I mean?"

I leaned up against the billiards table, a little faint. "I do."

"Yeah? I bet you do." He gave me a sideways look. "We're awfully alike, you and I, aren't we?"

444

Were we? I let the notion roll around my mind, and found it pleasant. (To not have to explain myself! To be understood! Isn't that what everyone wants?) "Where was your family's castle? I did a tour of Ireland with my family when I was a child, we must have visited a *hundred* castles. Maybe I saw it?"

"Doubtful." Michael abruptly put down the pawn and walked over to the sword display, mounted on either side of the hearth. There had to be at least thirty, the leavings of some ancestor with a military fetish. He lifted one sword off its stand — a heavy silver thing, with an engraved handle — and hefted it in one hand. Then he pointed it toward me, and lunged. "En garde!"

The sword tip flew through the air, stopping perilously close to my chest. I shrieked and scrambled backward, my heart ready to fly right out of my chest. Michael's eyes went wide; in his hand the sword quivered, then drooped toward the floor. "Oh, shite, I didn't mean to scare you. I used to do fencing. Sorry, I didn't think." He placed the sword back on its stand, then reached for my wrist, gripping it tight. I could feel his thumb gently probing, feeling for my racing pulse. "You're just a delicate thing, aren't you? All nervy and sensitive. Emotions written right on your face."

"I'm sorry." It came out as a hoarse whisper. Why was I apologizing? I was acutely conscious of the ball of his thumb, rubbing against the soft flesh of my wrist.

"Nothing to be sorry for." His voice was low. His eyes seized mine and held them fast. "I like it. *So much* going on in there. Ashley, well, she's not . . ."

He didn't finish the thought; his eyes fell to the carpet and stayed there. The space between us felt dangerously electric with static. I could feel the heat of his body through the flannel of his shirt, smell the spiced tang of his sweat. And I wondered, suddenly, about Michael and Ashley's unlikely pairing: A yoga teacher and an academic? A middle-class American and an Irish aristocrat? How *did* that work in reality?

Maybe their connection is sexual. I recalled the intensity of their kiss in the car that first day, felt myself flush hot at the thought. But now there was Michael's thumb on my wrist, and the memory of crying in Ashley's arms, and the disorienting rattle of the wind against the windowpanes. It was suddenly all very close and confusing. My mouth was dry and sour; it tasted of betrayal.

Metal glinted through the trees outside the windows: A car was coming up the drive. The BMW. I jumped away, my wrist slipping from his grasp. "Ashley's back! She'll want your help with the groceries, right?" I darted toward the door.

Michael hesitated, then followed, but

446

slowly. He was working his way around the perimeter of the games room, stopping to examine the golf cups and sailing trophies, picking up photos and peering at them before setting them down. My pulse was still on fire, but if he felt as guilty as I did — if he agreed that we'd just had a *moment* — he wasn't showing it.

At the door to the back porch, he stopped to gaze down the lawn to the lake, churning gray and cold. "So now. You won't be a stranger anymore, yeah?" His smile dangled precipitously from his lips, casual as could be; but then, right before he turned down the steps, he touched two fingers to his eyes, and then pointed them at mine.

"I see you," he said softly.

Did he? It felt dangerous, but God, it also felt *good.*

I barely slept that night, tossed by exhilaration and dismay. When I finally drifted off I had dreams in which I was a goose feather being snatched in the wind off the lake, never quite managing to land. I woke and lay there in the dark, hating myself. I didn't want to be *that* sort of woman; he had a girlfriend, a girlfriend whom I *admired.* And yet, the undeniable tug I felt when I was around him — Was I expected just to *ignore* that?

Maybe our greatest strength as human beings is also our greatest weakness, I thought.

447

The need to love and be loved.

By the time the sun rose, I was determined to reach out to Ashley, to return some balance to this strange equation. By seven, I was in my yoga clothes and at the window, waiting. But the temperature had dropped overnight, and the lawn was covered with a lacy crust of frost. Ashley never came outside.

I paced the house all morning, manufacturing excuses to go knock on their door.

I presented myself at the cottage door just after lunch, backpack in hand, a gristly lump of nerves. But when Ashley threw the door open, her face lit up, as if she'd been waiting for me all week. (I suppose she *had* been, though not in the way I was imagining it at that moment.) She flung out her arms, and pulled me into a hug.

"There you are, I missed you," she purred. The warmth of her cheek against mine numbed the memory of Michael's thumb on my pulse, even as I was acutely conscious of Michael gazing at me from the couch across the room. I closed my eyes, and let myself sink into the safety of her embrace.

Today I'll make it up to Ashley, I told myself. *Today I'll prove to myself that I'm her friend, not her enemy.* I would like myself more that way; *that* was the person I wanted to be.

If only I'd known, I wouldn't have bothered.

But I didn't, so I hoisted the pack high: "What do you think of a hike?" I asked.

448

■ ■ ■ ■

It was Ashley who I focused my energy on as we drove south down the lakeshore; Ashley who seemed so absorbed with the local lore that I giddily rattled off; Ashley who sang along to Britney Spears with me. (I was so *pleased* that she liked pop music!) In the back seat, where he grumbled about Ashley's taste in music, Michael felt like an afterthought. I was surprised that he'd decided to join us at all. (Or was I? *I see you.* I thought of his words from time to time, with a shiver.)

But by the time we parked, I was beginning to feel like equilibrium had been restored. We started up the path to Vista Point, Michael walking behind, Ashley alongside me. She hummed quietly to herself as she hiked, a faraway look on her face. *She seems at home here,* I thought to myself. *Even more so than me.* I stupidly chalked this up to her athleticism, to her comfort in her own body, her peace in the world. (God, the *irony*!)

I hadn't been back to Vista Point since I returned to Tahoe. Maybe I was avoiding it because it was *our* spot, Benny's and mine, our favored hiking destination whenever my family came to visit our grandparents during the summer holiday. It's not that Benny and I were really so keen on the hiking itself: Going to Vista Point was mostly a way to escape the claustrophobic house, where my mother and grandmother paced around each other like wary lionesses. There was a flat rock at the very top, which overlooked the lake, and I would lie there in my bikini and listen to my Walkman while Benny sat and drew in his notebooks. We'd stay up there until the sun got dangerously low in the sky before slowly making our way back to the house for the formal dinner that awaited us: waitstaff in stiff uniforms, vichyssoise in china bowls, my father drinking too many G&Ts while my grandparents frowned at the water marks on their silver.

I loved those hikes with my brother. Up there, as we silently gazed out at the mountaintops, it would feel like Benny and I had temporarily tuned in to the same channel, and were for once experiencing the same thing at the same time. Those moments were rare, especially after Benny started to slip.

The path up to the top hadn't changed since I had last been there, years before. The way was still marked with splintered wooden signs, mile markers in fading yellow paint. But the pines had crept in closer, and the boulders seemed smaller, as if in the intervening years I'd come to take up more space in the world. With Michael and Ashley there, I felt larger than life; I felt *alive.*

But next to me, Ashley's breath was growing ragged, her steps less sure. (Maybe I should have noticed and suspected at that point, but I was still so *determined* to be her friend.) When we got to a clearing near the summit, she stopped, and braced a hand against a tree.

I turned to wait. Michael had vanished far behind us. "Everything OK?"

She ran the hand up and down the bark of the tree, gazed up into the branches. Her placid smile suddenly looked an awful lot like a grimace. "Just taking it all in. I think I might stop for a minute and meditate."

She closed her eyes, shutting me out. I waited, looking out at the view. Storm clouds were gathering. A particularly ominous cloud had impaled itself on the peak of the mountain directly across the lake. The wind had whipped up whitecaps across the surface of the water, blowing south toward the casinos on the Nevada shore.

How long was she going to stand there? Did she expect *me* to be meditating, too? The stillness made me twitchy; I instinctively reached for my phone and lifted the camera to frame Ashley where she stood silhouetted against the lake. Her cheeks were flushed pink with exertion, her lashes trembled against her skin. *So pretty.* I snapped a photo, applied a few filters. I was typing the caption: *My new friend Ashley* when the phone suddenly flew out of my hand.

"No!"

451

Ashley stood before me, her face purple as she jabbed at the buttons on my phone. (*My* phone!) "Sorry to be such a stickler but . . . I'm a very private person. I know social media is your thing, but I'd really rather not have you post photos of me online." She handed the phone back to me. She'd deleted the photo entirely.

I blinked away the tears that had sprung to my eyes. It had been ages since I'd spent time with anyone who didn't *want* their photo taken: An appearance in someone else's feed was the best sort of validation, a flag staking your place in a world that you *hadn't* curated yourself. But not for Ashley, apparently. "I'm sorry," I murmured.

"No, it's really my fault, I should have said something earlier. Don't worry about it, OK?" She smiled, but her lower lip was pulled tight against her teeth. I'd clearly made a terrible faux pas.

She turned away from me and looked down the hill. "Let's head back down and find Michael. I'm starting to think we may have lost him forever."

I nodded, but I was thinking of the photo that I had already uploaded, days before, of Ashley doing yoga on the lawn. *I need to delete it before she sees it and gets upset.* "You go ahead," I said. "I'm going to take one more minute. I'll catch up."

As soon as she was out of sight I turned my

phone back on, and opened up Instagram, where the photo of Ashley was still at the top of my stream: 18,032 likes, 72 comments. It really *was* a good portrait — one of the best, artistically, that I'd taken since getting to Tahoe — and I hesitated, a little torn. How identifiable was she, really? I scrolled quickly through the comments, just to see what my followers had to say about it. *So idyllic / Whose the yoga hottie?! / Looks fun but R U ever going to start posting fashion again??? / Tired of nature shots, unfollow.*

And that's how, right at the bottom of the page, I came across a comment from my longtime follower *BennyBananas.* BennyBananas, *haha,* a joke that I had never found funny at all. The Orson Institute had clearly given Benny cellphone access again, a privilege they only conferred when he was a safe distance out from one of his paranoid phases (otherwise, he'd just end up in a Reddit conspiracy theory spiral), so this was a positive sign about my brother's current mental state. Distracted by this — and by the lingering sensation that I had made a critical error — it took me a minute to fully absorb what Benny had written under the photograph. When I did, I felt as if the entire mountain was about to collapse under my feet. Boulders shaking and rumbling, tearing themselves from the earth in order to tumble in unison down the hill and smash everything that lay below.

VANESSA WTF ARE YOU DOING HANGING OUT WITH NINA ROSS WITHOUT ME?

I stood too long on the top of the mountain, trying to wrap my head around my brother's message. *Nina Ross?* That name again. At first I thought that I might have conjured it up, a vestige from my mother's diary earlier in the week. But I read Benny's comment again, and the name *NINA ROSS* was still there; and it still made no sense. Benny had to be hallucinating again. Because there was absolutely *no way* that Ashley Smith was Nina Ross.

But Benny had phone privileges. Benny only got phone privileges when he was lucid.

What did Nina Ross even look like? I still had only the haziest recollection from that day we'd crossed paths at the café. Didn't she have . . . pink hair? Wasn't she chubby? A pimply Goth, with self-esteem issues. That hardly sounded like the toned, self-assured woman who was waiting for me down the hill. And yet . . . it had been twelve years. All that could have easily changed with a diet and a makeover. (Just ask Saskia.)

Was it possible?

I dialed my brother's phone number with

numb hands, half-frozen with the cold, my heart thumping so hard I worried that it might jump out of my chest.

My brother answered on the first ring, his voice breathless and squeaky. "Seriously, Vanessa, what the hell? Nina Ross! Oh my God. What's she doing there? Did she ask about me? How long has she been back in town?"

"That's *not* Nina Ross," I said. "It's my rental guest. She's a yoga teacher named Ashley and she's here with her boyfriend, Michael, who's a writer. She's from Portland. Her dad was a dentist." I willed this into truth with the conviction of my voice.

"Well, maybe she changed her name. It happens. Seriously — ask her!"

"Look, it's *not* her," I said, my words a little too sharp. "Sorry, Benny. Probably you're just remembering her wrong. It's been a long time. Do you really remember what Nina Ross looked like?"

"Of course I do. I still have photos of her from back then. And I already looked at them to double-check because I knew you were going to say I was crazy. Here, I'll send you one." I could hear him fumbling with his phone, the scrape of his sleeve across the microphone, and then a moment later my phone chimed with a text.

It was a low-res selfie, taken with an early-model camera phone. The shot was grainy, but I immediately felt an uneasy *ping* of recognition: It had been taken inside the caretaker's cottage. Benny and a teenage girl lay side by side on the gold brocade couch, their faces pressed up against each other as they made silly faces at the camera. They looked young and unfiltered and pleased with themselves, tangled up in each other like puppies tumbled in a pile.

The girl had dark brown hair with fading pink tips; her eyes were rimmed with heavy black liner. Her skin was lightly pimpled and there was a softness to her chin although she was certainly not as overweight as I remembered. There was something else underneath all that though: the raw, unformed material from which a harder, more savvy woman would someday be carved.

Benny was right. The girl lying there was Ashley. (Or: Ashley was Nina?) The years had passed, and she had changed a lot (she *was* much improved, aesthetically speaking); but it was there in the curve of her smile, in the wide dark eyes against the olive skin, in the self-assured conviction with which she gazed at the camera: *Nina Ross.*

And then there was Benny, still a boy as he lay next to her, his eyes unclouded and the purple shadows of madness not yet bruising his skin. I couldn't remember the last time I saw him so happy, so free of anxiety, so *clear.*

Oh Jesus, had he been fixated on that horrible girl for all these years? I thought about his comment on my Instagram photo. It wasn't *Why are you hanging out with Nina Ross?* but *Why are you hanging out with Nina Ross without me?*

My mind was firing so fast that I felt faint. *Why is this woman here? Why is she lying to me about who she is? What does she want from me? What do I say to her?* And also: *Oh God, if Benny knows Nina Ross is here, what will it do to him? Will he have another episode?*

"OK, I get what you're seeing, there's definitely a resemblance," I said slowly. "But it's not her, I swear. She said she'd never been here before. Why would she lie about that?"

"Because she didn't think you'd be nice to her? Because our family was *awful* to hers?"

What I wanted to say: *It was the other way around. They blackmailed us, Benny. Nina's mother drove Maman to suicide and Nina got you hooked on drugs and together they destroyed our family.* But how would that help him if he didn't know this already? If anything, it might set him off. I never knew exactly what would trigger his episodes; but dredging up the horror of that time seemed like a pretty sure bet. "Look," I said soothingly. "I am ninety-nine percent sure it's not her. It makes no sense at all. But if it makes you feel better, I'll ask her."

"Will you?" His voice was pleadingly childlike. My heart was breaking for him; I wanted to wrap my baby brother in a bubble and protect him forever against the evils of an unpredictable world.

The sun was falling behind the mountains to the west, shadows creeping across the patchwork of water below. The wind blasted over the peak so hard that I felt like it might blow me backward over the edge. "Look I've got to run, Benny. I'll call you later, OK?"

"I'll be waiting." I hung up to the echo of his hoarse, excited breath, and I knew he was not going to let this go.

I hiked back down the trail in a cloud of confusion, still trying to convince myself that it was all a mistake. Maybe Ashley was just a doppelgänger, her presence here some sort of strange coincidence. Or she was Nina's long-lost twin! (Ridiculous, I knew, but possible?) Or, if it *was* Nina, maybe there was a legitimate reason why she was pretending to be a stranger to Stonehaven.

But I *knew*. I moved blindly, seeing nothing but the smug face of the girl in the photo, ready to tear our world apart. *What gall could possibly bring Nina fucking Ross back here?* I stumbled over the rocks and tree roots that I had leapt over so neatly just an hour ago, my equilibrium lost. And then: I came around a stand of pines and saw Michael and Ashley in the clearing just ahead.

They hadn't heard my approach, not at all. Instead, they were wrapped in a tight embrace, kissing each other *hard,* as if on the verge of tearing each other's clothes off right there on the trail.

I stopped short, hidden behind the trees.

I watched as Michael ran his lips down the side of Ashley's neck, bending to bite the exposed flesh of her clavicle. She gripped his neck and pulled him closer, her other hand clawing at his sweat-drenched shirt, and something churned inside me. Was it — envy? The ghost of Michael's body, his finger testing my pulse, that left me feeling naked and needy? (Of course it was; but it was also so much more.)

Unexpectedly, Ashley opened her eyes and looked straight at me over Michael's shoulder. And *that* was when I knew for sure. Because she didn't blush with embarrassment, didn't demurely pull away like the Ashley I knew would have. Instead, she coolly maintained eye contact with me even as her boyfriend slid a hand under her shirt. *She wants me to see how desired she is,* I realized. *She wants to make me uncomfortable, make me jealous.* I saw it then, the cruel darkness flashing across her eyes as she locked her gaze on mine, a sharp flicker of the real person hiding underneath that copacetic yogic poise.

Michael was cupping her breasts now, and

she was *still* looking at me; I could barely breathe. Her lips moved, almost imperceptibly, into a tiny smirk: *I see you.* Now that I was looking for it, it was unmistakable. This woman was no stranger to Tahoe, haplessly landing at my front door. She was Nina Ross and she knew *exactly* who I was.

She knew exactly who I was, and she *hated* me — quite possibly as much as I hated her. *Why was she here?*

Liquid anger lit me up. I thought of my mother's diary entry: *I want to kill them both, mother and daughter. The two of them are single-handedly RUINING US.* The woman across the way from me was responsible for our family's demise. I had to *do something* about that, for Maman's sake, for Benny's, for the sake of all the Lieblings they'd connived to destroy.

I found myself running through all the ways I might confront her, the *righteousness* with which I could expose her. Wasn't she going to be shocked — *Mortified! Frightened, even!* — to realize that I knew who she *really* was? I took a breath, ready to call her by her real name: *Nina Ross you BITCH!*

But then she closed her eyes again, and the moment passed. On and on they kept kissing. She *knew* I was watching, it was so *brazen.* I moved closer, impatient. There was a stick on the ground; I put my boot on it, and snapped it, *hard.* Michael's eyes flew open and met mine. He jumped back, pressing Ashley (*Nina!*) away with a palm.

She blinked. She gave her wet mouth a quick swipe with the back of her hand and then she smiled at me, that familiar mask settling back across her features. "Oh, *there* you are!" she chirped, all sweetness and light. *Ashley* had returned, but now I could detect the mockery in her voice. That smile, so wide I could see her crooked incisors — how could I ever have been convinced it was genuine?

She was babbling an apology now — her leg had cramped up! Different muscle groups than yoga! So *sorry.* And I thought to myself, *You liar. You're probably not even a yoga teacher at all. Who the hell are you? What do you want from me?*

I couldn't figure it out. Had she come back here looking for Benny? But then, why the disguise? Was there something here that she'd left behind? The more likely scenario, I thought, was that she'd come here to finish the job that her mother had started: She wanted money. Maybe she thought I could somehow be blackmailed, too?

I realized that I had an advantage now: I knew who *she* was, but she didn't know that I knew. I had time to figure out what I was going to do about it.

Meanwhile, Michael was looking from her to me and back again, his brow furrowing with concern. Surely he could sense that something had just shifted between us all?

"Sorry to cut this short, but I'm knackered," he said. "Let's get off the mountain before we freeze."

"Too late," Ashley said, and pasted herself to Michael's side. "Brrr." She tucked herself underneath his arm, preening for my benefit. He looked over her head at me, and I could see in his eyes how uncomfortable he was with her little possessive display. *Sorry,* he mouthed at me. But I was the one who felt bad for him: *He didn't know.*

I wondered, with a little flip of my stomach, what past she had manufactured for Michael's sake. If she was lying to me, she was surely lying to him, too. And what was she trying to get from *him*? But then, it was obvious, wasn't it? He was rich. *She was after his money.*

Like mother, like daughter. I might be her short con, but *he* was her long con, and she'd dragged him along for the ride.

My heart flew out to Michael. Maybe I should have been frightened for myself, but I felt strangely calm instead. Stonehaven was *mine;* I could send her away anytime. I had so little left to lose, so little that I really loved. But what about *him*? Sensitive, thoughtful, intellectual Michael: He had no *clue* how dangerous she was. I needed to warn him.

But — how? A confrontation might backfire.

I had no proof to shove in her face, other than an out-of-focus picture from twelve years back. She would deny everything, and then she'd leave Stonehaven in a huff with Michael by her side, having lost nothing at all. And I'd be alone again, licking my wounds.

What I wanted instead was to take from this woman everything that *she* and her mother had taken from me: family, security, happiness, sanity.

Love.

And suddenly, I knew what I was going to do. I was going to save Michael from her. And in the process, I was going to make him *mine.*

Anger is a magnificently blinding force. Once you step inside its scalding beam, it's impossible to see past that light. Reason vanishes into the darkness beyond. Anything you do in fury's service feels justifiable; no matter how petty, how small, how nasty or cruel.

The thing is, the anger made me feel so giddily *alive.*

That night, back at Stonehaven, I went around the house locking every door. I drew every curtain on the ground floor (shaking out a pound of dust, an army of dead spiders.). And then I retrieved one of the pistols from its mount on the wall in the games room, loaded it with ammunition that I found locked in a drawer, and tucked it under my pillow.

Yes, I was angry, not frightened; but I also wasn't about to be *stupid.*

26.

And so: a dinner party. Time to play the part of *elegant hostess.*

With each whack of my butcher knife against the chicken, I imagined that *her* neck was on the cutting board and my knife was a guillotine. I pared potatoes, imagining the peels as her flayed skin. When I fired up the burners on the behemoth of a stove, I thought of what it would feel like to shove her hand into the flames. I cooked all day, my anger simmering and bubbling along with the stew on the stove.

By five, darkness had settled on Stonehaven. The wind had died away and everything was still out on the lake outside. I could hear the migrating geese down at the water's edge, honking in protest as they prepared to flee the coming storm.

From my father's bar, I prepared three martinis, ice-cold gin with a generous splash of vermouth and an even bigger slosh of olive brine: not a perfect martini, but sloppy by design. The brine and booze would serve to disguise the presence of an additional ingredient I'd put in one of the coupes: the contents of a bottle of Visine.

The coq au vin was almost done, a simple salad was cooling in the fridge. I polished off my martini as I waited for the potatoes to boil, and then mixed myself another. The rain announced itself with an artillery spray of drops hitting the windows. I looked up, startled, and spied Ashley and Michael running up the path from the cottage, their jackets held over their heads.

I went to greet them at the back door with a cocktail in each hand and a smile on my face, and they flew through the door in a sodden flurry. Already, I was thankful for that second martini. The gin had loosened me, it pleasantly blurred the whole surreal endeavor so that I didn't have to look past this moment — the martinis, the chattering guests, and the surprised pucker of Ashley's brow as she took the first sip of her cocktail: "Wow, you pour a stiff drink."

"Should I have made something else for you? Matcha tea? Green juice?" I could pretend, too. My lips stretched unnaturally over my teeth: *You fake.*

She looked a little alarmed at this. "Oh, no. It's delicious."

I wanted to slap her.

Michael wandered to the stove, lifted a lid,

and sniffed at the contents. "Smells amazing, Vanessa. And here we are, empty-handed."

He followed me around the kitchen as I finished the meal, asking questions about my cooking technique, casually flipping through the stained cookbooks on the counter. He was more interested in me than the girlfriend who sat impatiently at the table. She raked her damp hair back into a ponytail and gazed around the kitchen, tipping back her martini quickly. I had set the kitchen table with the everyday plates (none of the monogrammed Liebling china for *her*), and she surveyed the settings, straightened a fork.

"We're not eating in the dining room tonight?" she asked.

"Too formal," I offered.

"Of course. It's cozier in here, right? But is there any chance we could get the grand tour of Stonehaven?" Her eyes darted to the kitchen door and the dark hall beyond. "I'd really love to see the rest of the house."

I bet you do, I thought. I imagined her hands greedily fingering the surfaces of my family heirlooms, and I wanted to shudder. Was she planning to slip the silver into her pockets when I wasn't looking? I would *never* let that happen. "Maybe after dinner? I'm almost done cooking."

I took my time about it, though, watching her from the corner of my eye as I mashed the potatoes, stirred salt into the coq au vin.

By the time I put the food on the table, she was tipping back the last of her martini.

We sat, and I poured the wine — a dusty bottle of Domaine Leroy that I'd found in the cellar. A challenging wine, all smoke and leather, the kind of thing only someone with a refined palette (and presumably not the daughter of a *casino cocktail waitress*) might appreciate. Michael lifted his glass and tipped it toward mine: "To new friendships." He caught my gaze over the rim and held it for so long that it felt inevitable that Ashley would notice.

But Ashley seemed oblivious. She leaned across the table and clinked her glass against mine so hard that I thought it might shatter. "Sometimes the universe brings you together with someone that you just feel like you were *meant* to know," she said, faux sincerity dripping off her tongue. I wanted to spit in her face; instead, I smiled sweetly. She took a tiny sip of her wine and grimaced. *Plebeian.*

The table went quiet as we dug into the food. Ashley managed only a few bites before her face went white; she grabbed a napkin and pressed it to her lips. I watched coolly as she lurched out of her chair.

"Where's the bathroom?" she asked.

I pointed to the door. "There's a powder room down the hall, third door on your right."

She rushed out of the room, stumbling as

she doubled over, her hand pressed against her stomach.

I plastered the appropriate look of concern on my face and turned back to Michael: "I hope she's OK. I hope it wasn't the food." I examined my own forkful of stew with scientific opprobrium.

Michael was gazing after her with a look of mild confusion. "I can't imagine that's the case. I feel fine. I'll be right back." He stood and disappeared into the hallway.

I drank another glass of wine; and then I reached over and picked up Ashley's glass, tipping its contents into my own. Why waste a fine wine? She wasn't going to drink it now. A few minutes later, the two of them reappeared in the doorway; Ashley was pale and trembling, sweat glistening on her brow. "I think I have to go back to the cottage and lie down," she gasped.

"What's the matter?" My voice was as smooth and sweet as the dulce de leche ice cream I had stashed in the freezer for dessert with Michael. I studied her, wondering: There were seven side effects she could be experiencing, according to the Internet. Clearly, she already had vomited. What about the drowsiness, diarrhea, lowered heart rate, difficulty breathing? I had given her just enough Visine to make her ill, to get her out of my house, but not enough to send her into a coma. I made sure of that. (Although, *yes,* I did consider the alternative.)

Michael was at her side, his arm draped over her back as she doubled over with another round of cramps. He whispered something in her ear and she shook her head. He turned back to me. "I'm so sorry but I think we have to cut this short."

Oh. That was *not* the plan: She was supposed to leave *without* him. "But there's all this *food*. . . . Michael, maybe you could come back for it later?"

But Ashley was shaking him off. She managed to stand upright and gather her coat from the hook by the door. "No, Michael, you stay and eat. It would be a shame for all of Vanessa's cooking to go to waste. I'm just going to lie down and sleep anyway."

Michael looked at her and then at me. "Well. If you insist. I won't stay long."

Ashley's skin had taken on a greenish cast. She didn't even bother to acknowledge Michael's response, she just flung the door open and raced out into the night. We watched her through the window, careening down the path toward the cottage in the rain. Just before she vanished out of sight, I saw her double over and vomit into a stand of dormant azaleas. I flinched, wondering whether Michael would go to her then; but maybe he didn't see her, because he didn't move.

Or: Maybe he *did* see, and he just didn't care.

And then we were alone, Michael and me. I turned to smile at him, suddenly feeling almost shy. I reached for another bottle of wine and grabbed the corkscrew.

"So," I said. "You wanted the grand tour?"

Michael followed me through the rooms of the mansion, wine in hand, as I maintained a giddy patter about the history of Stonehaven, all the family legends passed down to the Liebling heirs. "So, the house was built in 1901, story was that my great-great-grandfather had a crew of two hundred working on it so that it could be finished within a year. This was the biggest house on the lake back then, the family came up only in the summers but kept a full-time staff of eleven to maintain it year-round." I flipped on the lights in each room that we passed through, hoping to make the house seem cheery and inviting, but the dim old sconces couldn't illuminate the shadowy corners. I hadn't even been in many of these rooms since I arrived, and it looked like the housekeeper hadn't, either. Dust lay thick on the sideboards, a musty smell lingered in the old nursery, dark stains bloomed in the draperies in one of the guest bedrooms.

But Michael didn't seem bothered by Stonehaven's state of neglect. Instead, he seemed fascinated by — even knowledgeable about — everything he saw; because of his

471

family's heritage, presumably. He sipped at his wine as we wandered through the halls, asking me about specific pieces and their provenances — my grandmother's hand-painted Louis XVI chairs, the old master still life in the stairway, the gold-and-alabaster clock in the study. He lingered in each room, going up close to paintings, touching the panels on the walls, peering behind doors and inside closets. Sometimes, I'd turn around mid-sentence and discover that he was still in the room that I'd already left, studying the antiques.

I didn't want to be talking about antiques.

I saved my bedroom for last. I led Michael to the big wooden doors: "See that? The coat of arms with the boar's head and the scythe? It was passed down from my family's ancestors back in Germany." Or so Grandmother Katherine had told me. I'd always suspected that this wasn't quite true, but myths are so *easily* burnished into truths through the power of self-regard.

Michael reached out to trace the carvings with a finger. "A lot of history in this house."

We stood side by side, admiring the door. Lingering there, the moment so magnificently fraught with tension (*Entering the boudoir! The bed lies beyond!*), as I wondered, a little dizzily: *Do I tell him now, or later? How do I reveal my history with his girlfriend without driv-*

ing him away? "So," I heard myself ask. "Have you and Ashley been together a long time?"

He looked sideways at me, surprise on his face. And I was sure I could read his thoughts: *Why are you bringing her up now, of all times?* "A long time? No. About, oh, six months? Eight?"

"How well do you know her?"

"That's an odd question. How well do I know my girlfriend?" He frowned, and kept tracing his finger across the grain of the door. "Where is this coming from?"

"Just curious." And I was! I was curious despite myself. I ran through all the things I wanted to know about Ashley/Nina. Where *had* she been all these years? When did she adopt the Ashley Smith persona, and why? Was she a scam artist like her mother? And what *about* her mother? Was Lily Ross still around? Did the law ever catch up with her? Oh, I wanted Lily Ross to have *suffered.* But maybe she had? There was that sob story Ashley had told me in the library, about her "ailing" mom. Was that another lie? Somehow, I didn't think it was. Something about the way she said it — those tears, they'd felt authentic. (But then, I'd been so gullible!)

"Do you know her family? Because Ashley said her mom is sick, and I wondered: What's wrong with her?"

"She told you that?" Michael frowned. "Hmmm. Honestly, I'm not exactly sure, something chronic."

So it was true; that, or she was lying to him, too. "You've never met her?"

He was still staring at the door as he shook his head. "No. She lives far away and we haven't made the trip together in the time that Ashley and I have been together. We were planning to go at Christmas." He put his hand on the doorknob and raised an eyebrow. "Can we go in now?"

He pushed open the door then, and stopped short. The bedroom was cavernous, the pulsing red velvet heart of the house. The walls were covered with mahogany paneling, decorated with the same coat of arms; the fireplace sat in a stone hearth that stretched taller than my head; and the pièce de résistance was a massive carved bed with a velvet canopy fit for royalty. A wall of windows overlooked the lake. It usually offered a spectacular view, but at that moment all that was visible was the pouring rain and the darkness beyond.

Michael laughed. "This is your room?"

"What did you imagine?"

He shook his head. "Something more modern and feminine. More like . . . you. Silly, I suppose."

He's been imagining me in my bedroom! A delicious realization. "Not in this house. There's nothing modern here, anywhere."

I watched as Michael wandered around the room, examining the trinkets on the bookshelves and the painting of Venus and Hephaistos over the mantel, opening the doors of the walnut-inlaid armoire that hulked against one wall. He walked over to the moving boxes stacked against the wall, and tilted his head to read the labels. "You haven't unpacked?"

"Why? I don't need any of that here, anyway. There never seemed to be much of a point in taking it out."

"You're still looking for a reason to leave." He tossed back the last of his glass of wine. "Or to stay."

"Maybe you're right." And then, feeling bold (or maybe I was just a little bit drunk?): "Can you give me one?"

"To what? Leave, or stay? It would depend." He turned and took in the bed, in all its monstrous glory. I wondered if he was imagining *us* in it, naked, swaddled in velvet. (*I* was!) Outside, the rain had turned to hail. It battered the roof overhead; a wind-tossed tree branch raked against the window as if trying to make its way to the warmth inside. Michael closed his eyes, and recited a few lines of poetry, so softly that I had to crane my head to hear his words.

"Western wind, when will you blow,
So that the small rain down can rain?
Christ, that my love were in my arms,
And in my bed again."

475

He opened his eyes and met mine, on the other side of the velvet expanse, and it was *that* look again, the one that made me feel as if he were looking straight inside my head. The martinis and wine had me spinning, but surely I wasn't imagining this, the static buzz heavy in the room between us. "Did you write that?" I asked.

He didn't answer. He just walked around the bed and directly toward me, his pale eyes still fixed on mine. The border between my body and the room around me felt blurred, I was vibrating with anticipation: This was it, he was going to kiss me. But then, when he was just a few feet away, his gaze shifted and suddenly he was not looking at me but over me, to the door. Two more steps and he was passing right by me. The first flush of excitement dissipated, leaving behind a tight knot of disappointment. All *that,* just in my head?

And yet. He passed by me so close that I could feel the heat coming off of him and — was that? *Yes,* it was his hand brushing against mine, just the tip of a finger catching on my pinkie. His hand pressed there for a meaningful second. Then he let out a sigh — *the sigh of a broken heart; the sigh of life conspiring against you* — and slid away.

I hadn't imagined it at all. Of course I hadn't. He had told me as much, two days earlier, in the games room: *I see you.*

(But if he sees me then that means he also

476

sees all the awful things about me, the things that no one could possibly like.)

(Or maybe he sees them, and likes me despite them?)

The moment was now; I needed to confess. "Look — I have to tell you something," I began. But he was glancing at his watch now, and my voice was too small, too timid, too fuzzed with gin. He didn't hear me as he reached for the door and swung it open. Instead, he smiled sadly, and gave me a courtly bow. "Ladies first."

I hesitated, and then walked past him and out into the hall, fogged with confusion and desire and alcohol. I was halfway down the stairs before I realized that he wasn't right behind me. What was he doing up there? A little clot of hope: *Maybe he's leaving me a message.*

But just moments later, he appeared on the landing. "Sorry, Vanessa, but it's been *hours.* I really should go check that Ashley is OK or she might eat me alive."

He tumbled down the stairs past me and toward the back of the house. I chased after him, rebuking myself for having missed another opportunity: *Fool! Coward!* And then, just like that, he was gone, jacket over his head, disappearing off into the liquid darkness of the garden. All that was left in his wake was a scattering of hail from where I held the door open too long, watching him go.

After he left, the house returned to being a deserted island on which I was once again marooned. I scraped the remains of the coq au vin into the trash, and wiped up the puddle of melted hail on the floor. I left the dishes for the housekeeper to address when she arrived in the morning. Only when all that was done did I allow myself to go up to my room to check if Michael had left something for me.

There was no quickly scrawled missive detailing his forbidden desire: nothing dropped on the velvet coverlet, nothing propped on the mantel, nothing scribbled in eye pencil on the mirror in the bathroom. And yet: a little hiccup in my heartbeat as I looked at my bed. There was a dent on the pillow that I was *sure* hadn't been there before.

Did he get in my bed and imagine lying here with me?

I climbed in bed and rested my head in the divot; I inhaled and — yes! — I could *smell* him, smoke and lemons. His shampoo, lingering in my linens.

I closed my eyes, and I laughed.

When I woke up the next morning, the quality of the light had changed. Overnight, the hail had turned into snow. Silence had settled in around Stonehaven, as if someone had dropped a blanket over the house. I rose from my bed, shivering in my flimsy nightgown, and unlatched the window sash. Snow was falling, softly, a delicate lace balancing on the pine needles outside my window. Below, the lawn was a featureless wedding quilt, punctuated by frozen ferns. The lake was gray and still. When I breathed, the cold air burned in my lungs.

The stairs felt treacherous under my feet. I was horribly hungover. Downstairs, the kitchen was still a disaster zone, and a text from my housekeeper informed me that she couldn't get in because of the snow on the roads. I made myself a cup of coffee and went to lie on the couch in the library, pondering my next move.

My phone *ping*ed with a text from Benny: *So?? Is it her? Nina?*

Didn't have a chance to ask.

A sharp knock on the back porch made me jump: *Michael.* I walked to the kitchen and peered out the French doors and was surprised to see Ashley standing there, apparently fully recovered.

I cracked open the door. "You're feeling better already?"

"Like new," she said. "Whatever it was, it's gone." Her face was back to its normal color and her hair was freshly washed; she looked radiant and healthy and young. She looked

479

better than I felt, which was manifestly unjust. How could she have bounced back so quickly? I should have put more in her drink.

"Food poisoning, you think?"

She shrugged, peering at me from under those long lashes, and I wondered if she suspected something. "Who knows. The body is a mystery sometimes, isn't it?"

"Well, I'm glad you're on the mend. We missed you at dinner." *We didn't, not a bit.*

"Michael told me what a nice time you had," she said. "I'm so sad to have missed it. I hope you'll offer a do-over."

I looked over her shoulder, in the direction of the cottage. Would Michael come to me on his own accord? I needed to give him an excuse to return, so I could get him alone. "Tomorrow."

She smiled. "Look, can I come inside?"

I hesitated. I wasn't so sure I wanted to be alone with her; I thought of the pistol I'd stuffed under my pillow upstairs. "I'll just go get dressed."

"Oh, please don't bother for my sake! It's just — there's something I need to talk to you about."

A spike of adrenaline: *Wait, is she going to confess her real identity to me?* I pulled the door open wider and invited her in. Ashley kicked off her boots and stood there by the back door, snow dripping off her jacket. She gazed at the mess of dishes and empty wine bottles. "Wow. You really did have fun last night. How many bottles of wine did you drink after I left? Michael was smashed when he got in. Now I can see why."

Jealous, then. *Well, you should be.* "The housekeeper was supposed to come in today but she got snowed in, poor thing. I just haven't gotten to the dishes yet." I picked up the wineglass closest to me and moved it over to the sink.

She watched me with a little smile hovering over her lips, as if she knew perfectly well that I was not planning to clean this mess myself. "I'll send Michael over to help. He made the mess, he should help you clean."

I shook my head in protest, although secretly I was thinking, *Oh yes, please do that, please give us more time alone.* My head throbbed, as if someone had taken pliers to my skull and was pulling out pieces of my brain. She didn't *look* particularly anxious. Was she going to confess or not? If she did confess, could I still hate her? I plopped down in a chair, pressed a finger on the pulsing vein in my temple, and waited.

Ashley sat down next to me, so close that our knees almost touched. She leaned in conspiratorially and I waited for the words to come: *I need to be honest with you. My name isn't Ashley Smith.* "So, I'm not sure if Michael told you this last night — he can be so

481

private, sometimes. . . ." There was a curious little smile on her face, and with that smile I suddenly knew that this was not going to be the confession that I was expecting. "But he asked me to marry him. We're engaged."

I was blind, red spots floating in my vision. Engaged? Why would he do that? When did it happen? Why *her*? Her smile grew stiff as she waited for my reaction, and I realized that I'd waited a beat too long to respond. I opened my mouth and the sound that came out was a horrible squeal. *"Tremendous! Fantastic!"*

I did not find the news tremendous in the least.

But my shrieks of delight must have been convincing because she started talking and talking and *talking.* She told me about how he got on his knee on the steps of the caretaker's cottage, as they stood looking at the lake on the first night they arrived; how he had an heirloom ring that belonged to his grandmother and she cried when he gave it to her. She was tugging off a mitten and thrusting a hand at me and there it was, a big cushion-cut emerald surrounded by diamonds, not a pristine stone judging by the color, but a pretty enough ring nonetheless.

Merde. It was too late. She'd conned him already.

She went on and on, about how *demure* she was, how uncomfortable she was with ostentation and money (*Oh, bullshit*). I was barely

482

listening to her as I stared at the ring drooping off her finger, thinking, *But he doesn't
even like her that much. I'm sure of it. They
have nothing in common. He likes me. How
could this happen?* She was still talking, about
her fear of the ring falling off, the need to get
it sized, and how until then she couldn't wear
it, because oh, she was so worried about losing it. So could I put it in my safe? For —
pardon the pun — safekeeping?

"My . . . safe?"

She nodded.

But of course I had a safe. The safe in the
study, where my father used to keep his *go-
cash.* That's what he'd called it, the day years
ago when he called me into his study and
opened the vault to show me stacks of neatly
bundled hundreds. "Cupcake, if you ever
need go-cash, this is where you look. There's
a million dollars in there. For emergencies.
Another million in the safe in the house in
Pacific Heights."

Why would I ever need that much cash? I'd
wondered then. *What kind of trouble does he
think I might get into?* Benny used to steal
hundreds from it, as if it were his own
personal piggy bank.

Of course, the safe was empty now. Like all
of the Liebling money, it was long gone.

Oh, I haven't mentioned that yet, have I?

That I am *broke, penniless, destitute.* Don't let appearances deceive you: After my father's death, when the trustees sat down to go through the accounts with me, I was shocked to discover that my father was teetering on the edge of bankruptcy. Since even before my mother's death, it seemed, he had been making bad investments with his fortune, throwing good money after bad, including a massive casino on the coastline of Texas that was obliterated by the hurricanes. There were gambling debts, too: poker games with million-dollar stakes that my father lost, week after week, according to a black ledger I found in his desk.

I remembered then, with sickening understanding, the fight between my parents that I overheard through the heating ducts: *Your addictions are going to destroy us all. Women and cards and who knows what else you're hiding from me.*

The trust that Benny and I had been drawing off of was nearly empty — drained dry by the cost of Benny's private institute and my high-flying Insta-lifestyle, and never replenished. Even our family's holdings in the Liebling Group weren't worth much anymore. The company never did quite bounce back from the recession, its debt load was staggering, and the Liebling family shares had been so sliced and diced throughout the generations that each branch now possessed just a sliver. Benny and I couldn't sell them even if we wanted to.

What we did have left after Daddy died: our house in Pacific Heights, the Stonehaven estate, and everything inside their walls. Benny inherited the former — which we immediately put on the market; the proceeds to cover Benny's living expenses — and I (as you know) inherited the latter. This was no small thing; it was still a fortune on paper, albeit a far more modest one than I once imagined.

That, however, didn't take into account the staggering *cost* of maintaining Stonehaven — the reality of which I discovered upon my arrival in Lake Tahoe last spring. The cleaning alone was really a full-time job; and then there was the general maintenance, the landscaping, snow removal in winter. The old stone boathouse needed to be repaired. The roof required replacing. The exterior wood paneling was rotting. The gas and electric and water bills were astronomical. And then property taxes! Altogether, upkeep of Stonehaven threatened to cost me in the high six figures annually.

And, with my *V-Life* sponsors fleeing in droves, I had no consistent income, either.

I could have sold off Stonehaven's art and antiques — I knew it was what I *should* do! — but every time I started to put together an inventory list to send to Sotheby's, I faltered. Those things, that house — they were my legacy, and Benny's, too (as well as all of those Liebling uncles and aunts and cousins to whom I rarely spoke but still felt some sense of duty). If I auctioned them off, or even sold off the house, was I eradicating my own history?

And if I eradicated *that,* what did I have left?

So instead, I rented out the caretaker's cottage, solving two problems in one blow — isolation *and* income — and thereby setting in motion the string of events that had landed me there, in Stonehaven's kitchen, looking at Nina Ross's engagement ring and *seething.*

In any case — the safe, of course I'd checked it, first thing after moving into Stonehaven, and the stacks of cash that I remembered were no longer there. Why would they be? In reality the go-cash was probably just my father's gambling stash; he likely blew it all on high-stakes poker at the casinos across the border, where Lily Ross served him cocktails with a side of blackmail. All that he'd left us in the safe was a stack of old files and the deeds to the house; plus a few last pieces of my mother's jewelry, which I promptly shipped off to the auction house where I'd already sold the rest.

Did this woman somehow think there were

treasures to be found in our safe? Was *that* what she was after here? If so, she was going to be sorely disappointed. I would have laughed out loud, if I wasn't already fighting tears.

Something heavy was in my hand: I looked down to see that Ashley had taken the ring off and dropped it in my palm. Surprised, my fingers closed around it. "Please?" she said. "I trust you to take care of it for me."

I looked down at my fist and then back at her, feeling exhausted and overwhelmed and confused. And then — *Oh God, no, not again!* — I *was* crying. Crying about my father, who did his best for us but still fucked it all up; and crying about everything that had been lost; but most of all, crying at the unfairness that *she* of all people was getting married to *him,* and I was not.

When I looked up, Ashley was staring at me. Was that stricken expression one of genuine concern? Or was she just marinating in my unhappiness, getting some sick vicarious thrill from it? I saw her hesitate, considering something, and then she reached out and put a hand over mine. "You were engaged earlier this year, right?" Her voice was low and soft. "What happened?"

She thought I was crying about *Victor.* I almost laughed. "How did you know about my fiancé?"

"Your Instagram. It was pretty easy to

figure out."

"Oh. *Right.*" I tugged my hand free of hers and wiped my face dry. She'd made a mistake: She already told me she didn't "do" social media. Obviously, she'd been tracking me from afar: For how long? And to what purpose? I imagined her carefully clicking through my photo stream, entertaining herself with the details of my life, and felt ill. It's too easy to forget about the invisible people out there on social media, the ones who observe in silence, the ones who never alert you to their presence. Not the followers, the *watchers.* You can never really know who is in your audience, or what their motives are for looking at you.

"So, is that why you moved here? Because of your broken engagement?"

"That's why I moved here," I began. *Don't tell her anything,* I thought to myself. *Don't let yourself be vulnerable.* But I was feeling so . . . off-balance. The words tumbled out regardless. "I needed a change of scenery and up popped Stonehaven, at what seemed like the right moment. Daddy left it to me, and I thought . . . maybe it would be comforting, to be back here, in our old family home. I thought it was serendipity. Turns out, I forgot that I hate this house. *Terrible* things happened to my family in this house, things we didn't deserve." I was getting overly emotional now; I was getting too *honest,* but I couldn't seem to stop myself. I couldn't control it, this exhausting *compulsion* to be seen and understood, even by (especially by!) my enemy.

But more than that: I wanted her to know what she and her mother did. I wanted her to know *exactly* how they'd destroyed my family. I wanted her to feel sorry for me; and in doing so, to hate herself.

"Stonehaven is just a shrine to the tragedy that is my family: Everything bad that happened to my mother and father and brother started here. Did I mention that my brother is schizophrenic now? It all began here. And my mother committed suicide right out there." I pointed out the window toward the lake.

Ashley's face went pale. "My God. I had no idea."

Oh yes you did, I thought. (But was it possible she didn't?)

And still I went on, and on, I couldn't stop myself. Years of pain and insecurity and self-doubt pouring out; why was I telling *her* of all people? But it felt good, so good, to tear off the facade and expose the truth of being *me.* "I'm Vanessa Fucking Liebling," I heard myself say. "Maybe I *am* fatally flawed; maybe I *am* somehow less worthy of empathy."

When I looked over, *Ashley* had fallen from

489

the face of the woman sitting in front of me. Nina was there instead, coiled up tight, her eyes dark and watching. I expected her lips to curl up in disgust, or cold calculation. Instead, she leaned in, and spoke in a voice I hadn't heard before. *"Pull it together.* And stop asking other people to tell you that you're worthy. Why do you care what they think, anyway? *Fuck them all."*

Her words were like a bucket of ice water, shocking me silent. *No one* talked to me that way, not even Benny. Did she really mean it? (And was she right?) "Fuck them all?" I repeated, dully.

She shifted in her seat, looked down at the ring in my palm, and seemed to do some mental calculation. When she looked back up at me, Nina was gone again, and Ashley was back; with her little smile and her faux empathy and her goop-like prescriptions for serenity. She started nattering on about the need for mindfulness and self-care and suddenly I couldn't stand it anymore. How dare *she* tell *me* how to be centered and peaceful?

I stood up abruptly. "Here. I'll go put the ring in the safe," I said, if only to remind myself that I shouldn't throw it in her face.

The safe was behind a painting in my father's study, a murky English hunting scene with grim aristocrats in wigs and plumed hats, their dogs lunging at a terrified fox. I pried the painting back, punched my brother's birth date into the keypad, and opened the lock.

The engagement ring was warm from my palm. I held it up and turned it, but the light from the sconces was too dim to draw a sparkle from the stones. I placed the ring in the safe and then swung the door shut with some small satisfaction.

I had her ring. And now I was going to get her fiancé.

Another night, another meal with the enemy.

But this one would be different. I was so *done* with this whole charade: It was time to blow it all open. (Or: *Pull it together.*) To put the imposter in her place, I decided to pull out all the stops and host a feast that would make the Lieblings proud. I summoned a caterer from South Lake Tahoe to produce a six-course meal; I hired a staff to serve and to clean, because I certainly would not be serving Nina Ross myself or scrubbing her lip prints off my crystal.

I was mistress of Stonehaven; it was time for me to act it. (*No more talk of fatal flaws! No more thoughts of unworthiness!*) Let Nina see everything that she was not; let her burn with envy that she would never be a Liebling, no matter how she might connive to be. And when dessert rolled around, I would finally expose her for who she was, and claim Michael for myself.

Before they arrived for dinner, I dragged the packing boxes from the corner of my bedroom and tore them open. I rifled through the dresses that had been hidden away in the dark for the better part of a year now: party dresses and prairie dresses, resort wear and club wear, clothes intended for day and for night and for every single moment in between. I dragged them out one by one and spread them around the room. Heaps of silk and chiffon and linen, in pink and gold and lime, a sartorial rainbow that piled up on the bed and the settee and, eventually, the carpet. The clothes breathed life into this musty old room, as if I'd thrown open the windows and let in fresh air. Why hadn't I unpacked these sooner? Each dress was an old friend; each one came attached to a specific visual memory, stamped with a date and time and memorialized on my Instagram feed: the crocheted dress I wore in that shoot on the beach in Bora Bora; the gown I wore eating breakfast on the balcony of my suite at Plaza Athénée; the sparkly shift from that shoot on the Hudson Pier.

I unearthed a floor-length green chiffon dress that I once wore to a Gucci dinner party in Positano — we took pictures on the boat on the way in. (22,000 likes! A near record!) Could that have been only eighteen months earlier? It felt like a lifetime had passed.

I tugged the Gucci dress on over my head and studied myself in the mirror. I was thinner than I used to be and my spray tan was long gone; but still, there *she* was again, and I was happy to see her looking back at me. *V-Life Vanessa,* fashionista and bon vivant, liver of the good life, *#blessed,* was back. No, I wasn't going to ask anyone else to tell me I was worthy: I knew I was.

Dinner was awkward and strained. I drank too much and talked too loudly. Ashley was too quiet, nudging the food around on her plate with the tines of a fork. Only Michael seemed relaxed, sprawled comfortably in his chair, regaling us with stories from his childhood in Ireland as he tore through every course placed in front of him.

I noticed that Ashley and Michael were avoiding looking at each other. Every once in a while, their eyes would snag and they'd give each other a long, indecipherable look. I wondered if they'd fought. (I was thrilled by this possibility.)

The caterer uncorked a bottle of French champagne, unearthed from Stonehaven's cellar. Michael and I each took a flute, though Ashley put a hand over her own to prevent the waiter from pouring. ("Still recovering from food poisoning," she said.) The food kept coming: *amuse-bouche,* then a *plateau de fruits de mer,* followed by a salad course and a tomato bisque. Our meal was an hour in and we had yet to even get to our entrées; I still had to figure out how to get Michael alone. Ashley kept glancing at the clock on the sideboard, as if this was an ordeal she couldn't wait to end. It was all a bit too much, I knew, but I was enjoying the uncomfortable expression on Ashley's face as she struggled over the place settings. Michael seemed unfazed by the formality of it all; but of course, he had been raised with money, too.

I would count the silver after she left, just to be safe.

Finally the main course was served, a wild-caught salmon roasted with blood orange. A momentary silence fell over the table as we lifted our forks and prepared our stomachs for battle with yet another dish.

The silence was broken by the faint trill of a cellphone. Ashley blanched and dropped her fork. "Oh God, I forgot to turn off the ringer." She reached into the back pocket of her jeans and tugged out her phone, muttering apologies; but when she saw the name on the display, her eyes went wide. She stood up abruptly: "So sorry, but I have to take this." As she backed out of the room, phone pressed to her ear, she gave Michael a significant look and mouthed a single word: *Mom.*

Lily, I thought, and my heart gave a little jump.

And then she was gone. And Michael and I were alone. We could hear Ashley's footsteps as she wandered farther and farther into the depths of Stonehaven, the murmur of her voice fading away, and then all was silent.

"What's that all about?" I asked. "Her mom?"

"I'm not entirely sure."

The chiffon of my dress was fluttering against my skin and I realized that I was trembling: How much time would we have before Ashley came back?

He cleared his throat and smiled awkwardly at me. "So. I still haven't told you about the college I've been teaching at, have I? It's the greatest group of students, disadvantaged but so intellectually curious. . . ." He launched into a speech about the joys of bringing knowledge to open young minds, a soliloquy so long and loud that it was clear that he was talking just to fill the silence.

"Michael, stop."

He stopped. He picked up his cutlery and looked down at his plate with resolve. I could hear his knife hitting the china as he cut the asparagus into neat segments. *Click, click, click.*

"Michael," I said again.

He remained intently focused on the salmon, as though if he broke his gaze the fish might swim off his plate and disappear. "What a treat this has been," he said stiffly, forking up a neat square of salmon. "I haven't eaten like this in years. It's so rare to find people in Portland who appreciate formal dining."

I leaned in closer, so close that I barely had to speak aloud for him to hear me. "Don't leave me hanging like this. There's something going on between us, right? I'm not crazy."

His forkful of salmon stopped halfway to his mouth and hovered there, quivering and pink. He looked to the door, as if Ashley might be lurking right outside, and then he turned and finally gazed straight at me. He leaned in close. "You're not crazy. But, Vanessa . . . it's complicated."

"I don't think it's as complicated as you think it is."

"I'm engaged." He looked forlorn. "I didn't tell you that before. And I'm a man of my word. I couldn't do that to her."

Finally, here it was, the opportunity I'd been waiting for. *"But she's not who you think she is."*

His hand tilted, and the salmon slipped off his fork. The fish hit the table and scattered pink flakes across his lap. He dabbed distractedly at the mess with a napkin and I watched as a parade of emotions marched across his face: confusion, alarm, denial. "I don't think I understand what you mean," he said finally.

I was about to launch into the whole sordid story, to run through a dozen years of history for him, but there was no time for that because we could hear Ashley's footsteps coming back down the hallway. "Look, we need to talk, in private," I whispered quickly. He was still gazing at me with a dazed expression when Ashley materialized in the doorway. She was flushed, gripping her phone with bone-white knuckles.

Michael stood up quickly. "Ash? What's the matter?"

She looked wildly around the room, as if she'd just woken up and was perplexed to find herself *here* of all places.

"My mother is in the hospital," she said. "I have to go home. Now."

Ashley left at dawn. I watched the BMW pick its way along the front drive, slipping in the fresh snow. Was that it? Was it all over, just like that? I felt almost . . . disappointed. Part of me wanted to know what she'd had planned, and if I'd managed to foil it.

And what about Michael? In the flurry of action that had followed Ashley's announcement — dessert and coffee bypassed altogether, the crème anglais forgotten in my fridge as the two of them hurried back to the caretaker's cottage to confer — I hadn't had a chance to ask whether *both* of them would be leaving.

If he goes with her, it means he chose her,

I'd told myself. *If he stays, he's staying for me.*

Now, as I stood in the parlor, watching the car vanish down the drive, I could see that there was only one person in the front seat of the old BMW. She was leaving alone.

I had won.

The pines closed in around the car, she turned the corner, and she was gone.

I went upstairs, got the gun from under my pillow, and went down to the games room. The lights danced merrily off the swords hanging on the walls as I placed the pistol back in its position of honor over the hearth. I wouldn't need *that* thing anymore. (*She was gone! I had won!*)

My phone chimed with a text: my brother again.

Stop treating me like a child. Is it Nina or not?

I was still giddy with victory; it seemed safe enough to tell him, now that she had vacated the premises.

You were right. It was her. But she's not here anymore. That woman was bad news, Benny. It's better for everyone that she's gone.

Wait, I don't understand, she left? What did

she say? Why was she at Stonehaven? Was she looking for me?

IDK. She never admitted who she really was. But it doesn't matter now because she's gone. And she's not coming back.

She left?? With her boyfriend?

Her boyfriend stayed behind. He's still here.

So there's still a chance.

A chance for what, Benny??

For ME. She's in Portland?

FFS, Benny. I have no clue where she went. But all that was in the past and it was no good for any of us, we're both better off letting it go and moving on. DO NOT MAKE YOURSELF CRAZY OVER THIS. Please don't fixate on some untrustworthy girl from your childhood, OK? She was bad for you. Then and now. I love you.

My phone immediately started to ring, with Benny's name on the display. I ignored it. Instead, I drew on my snow boots and parka, dabbed a little gloss on my lips. Then I opened the back door and stepped out into the yard. It was snowing again. The cold air

499

stung as it hit my face, and I welcomed it, because my cheeks would be flushed and pink and alive.

I left a neat track of footsteps across the snow, down the path to the caretaker's cottage. The lake stretched out before me, dormant and gray. The geese were gone. The pines quivered under the weight of the snow, showering me with soft flakes as I passed underneath.

Michael opened the cottage door so fast that I wondered if he'd been waiting for me.

"You stayed," I said.

He blinked at me. "I stayed."

I blew on my hands, rubbed them together. "Her name is Nina Ross," I said. "It's not Ashley Smith. I know her, from years ago, from *here.* She's a liar and a fake, and she's after your money. The same way she came after mine. Her family destroyed my family. You can't trust her."

He looked over my shoulder at the lake, his eyes darting left and right, as if he was looking for something out there on the surface of the water. Then he sighed. He reached out and put his hands on my shoulders, gripping them so tight it hurt.

"Fuck me," he said to the pines that danced above my head.

And then he kissed me.

The storm raged, the wind screamed, the

trees groaned and swayed, and inside the walls of Stonehaven everything was about to be overturned. Soon, Michael would know everything that I knew about his fiancée. Soon, he would call her, and inform her that the engagement was off, and that he didn't want her coming back to Tahoe. (I would hear him screaming into his phone from six rooms away.) Soon, he would move his possessions out of the caretaker's cottage and into Stonehaven.

Soon — so soon — we would be married.

27.

Week Two

My husband! I like to watch him when he's not aware: Shoveling snow on the path down to the dock, his muscles flexing with each bite of the blade. Sitting by the window working on his book, the winter light illuminating him as he hovers over his laptop. Tangles of black hair tucked absently behind his ear, his pale eyes fixed on the screen. He has a face from a Jane Austen novel, all weathered and worldly. (Or would that be Brontë? I should have paid better attention in English lit.)

I *just can't stop* looking at him.

Already he's taken over Stonehaven as if it's been his home forever. He lies on the silk couches with his shoes on, not caring a bit that the soles are leaving black marks on the fabric. He puts his beers right on the inlaid mahogany side table, leaving ghostly white rings that won't scrub out. He smokes cigarettes out on the veranda and, since I have no ashtray, crushes the butt into a bone china plate monogrammed with a gold letter *L.*

My grandmother Katherine would be horrified by this behavior, but I'm *thrilled.* He's brought this house down to earth, dominated it, made it his own in a way I never could.

We've been married eleven days now, and after months of feeling trapped by Stonehaven, suddenly I have no interest in leaving it. We've talked a bit of taking a honeymoon, someplace warm and tropical. (Bora Bora! Or maybe Eleuthera? Where *is* everyone going now? I've been out of the loop too long.) But then the snow is falling outside and we're drinking martinis by the fire in the library, and it's so cozy that I can't see the point. I spent so many *years* constantly in motion; I suppose I was looking for something I couldn't name, and now that I've finally found it, it's a relief to just be *still.*

The constant, distracting chatter in my brain — all those exhausting highs and lows — has vanished entirely. I feel like I'm truly *in the moment.* (Oh, fake Ashley would be so proud!)

I've stopped Instagramming altogether, not a single photo since the day that we got married. Michael discourages it. He hides my phone from me. But that's fine! I'm finding that I don't need the approval of a half-million strangers anymore, either. The only person whose opinion matters is sitting right next to me. Honestly, it's a relief to let all

503

that go: the reflexive *yank* of that empty square tugging me inside it, the exhausting artifice that comes when you put yourself on-stage, and ask to be judged.

You see? You can't wound me anymore, because I no longer care what you think.

"Maybe we should go to Ireland," Michael says to me. "I can introduce you to my aunties. We could even go and visit the castle." I make him tell me stories about this castle, the ancient O'Brien seat, a fortress even more forbidding than Stonehaven. He demurs that it's a "modest" castle — "there are thousands of castles in Ireland, practically everyone's got one in their family history." Still, I can't help thinking that great houses have been bred into his bones. It explains why Stonehaven doesn't intimidate him a bit.

Add this to the long list of things we share. His parents, like mine, are long dead — *an Aston Martin,* he wept in my ear one night, *a flock of sheep that materialized unexpectedly on a dark country lane* — and his siblings have been lost to alcoholism or estrangement. He knows what it feels like to wake up in the morning in a panic, feeling like someone has untethered you during the night. Like you could disappear one day and no one would

504

even notice, because the people who love you the most are already gone.

I don't have to feel that way anymore.

Also like me: His family lost its *real* money a while back, the steady chipping away of a dwindling family estate with too many heirs and too many expenses.

He doesn't know we have this in common yet.

This is our new routine: I sleep in late in the morning, until Michael brings me coffee in bed around ten. We make love, sometimes twice. By noon, Michael is at work on his book, and I am at my sketches. We sit in happy silence like this for hours. Dusk comes early in December, so we take a break in the midafternoon and pull on our snow boots to go for a walk along the lakefront. We'll wander down past the boathouse, onto the snow-covered pier, and then sit on the bench at the end, taking in the stillness of the lake. Sometimes we'll bring a flask of tea and stay there, happily *not talking* (but not because we don't have anything to say!), until the sun dips behind the mountains.

Then back to Stonehaven, perhaps some more writing and sketching. I'll cook dinner for us, digging through the stacks of old French cookbooks I've found in the kitchen until I find something that sounds appealing:

sole meunière, boeuf Bourguignon, salade Lyonnaise. My jeans are starting to get tight. In New York, in my old life, I would have immediately done penance with back-to-back spin classes, but here, I don't care. It doesn't matter if I can't fit into my Saint Laurent leather pants; I have nowhere to wear them anyway.

Then: cocktails by the fire, more sex, more cocktails, maybe an old movie on my laptop as we lie in bed.

The days slip past, fuzzy with lust and alcohol, everything pleasantly sticky and new.

My sketchbook is slowly filling with drawings of outfits: tops with pleats that undulate like the wind on the surface of the lake; delicate toile dresses that fly off the shoulders like raven wings; jackets embroidered with feathery spines, reminiscent of pine needles. At first, the sketches were hesitant and shaky, but increasingly they are growing bolder: a single silhouette rendered in a few, thick lines, the details shaded in with pastels. I'd almost forgotten how good it felt to draw; until this month I hadn't held a pencil since the art classes that I took in high school. I was good at it back then, good enough to be invited into the gifted program at my school, but my parents didn't encourage me to take it any further: Lieblings were supposed to *collect* art, not make it ourselves. Also, I was aware enough to know that I had *some* talent, but nowhere near enough. Benny was the Liebling who had something urgent he needed to put on the page, whereas I lacked the singular vision that it takes to be a real artist. If I'd kept it up, I would have ended up a dilettante, producing adequate landscapes that would be politely bought by friends, but never hung in museums.

So I let it go.

And then, Michael happened. *I can tell that you have the soul of an artist even if you don't know what to do with it.* He said this to me in bed one morning, not long after Ashley left. I laughed, but his words stayed with me. And so later that day (yet another idle mountain day; a life of leisure *does* get dull, especially when you don't have your phone to distract you) I thought, *Why not?* I had already spent most of the year sitting around Stonehaven with nothing to do, filling the time imagining a remodel that would never happen because I couldn't afford it, fiddling with my dwindling financial portfolio. Dutifully, dully *liking* things on social media.

That afternoon, I retrieved a dusty pen-and-ink set from the recesses of the study and sat in the sunroom, looking out at the snow-covered lawn and the lake beyond. But when I lifted the pen, the image that emerged on the paper was not another landscape but a picture of a dress. A soft white ballgown, with an asymmetrical bustline and a dishabille skirt that floated and draped like a fresh snowdrift.

As I sat there considering what I'd drawn, I felt Michael's breath on the back of my neck. "That's beautiful," he said as he leaned in closer to examine it. "Have you ever designed clothes before?"

"I wear clothes. I don't design them."

He pressed a declarative finger on the page, right in the center of the dress's bust. "You do now," he said.

I laughed. "Come on. I'm hardly a fashion designer."

"Why not? You have the platform. You have the taste. You have the resources and *clearly* you have the talent. Did no one tell you that before?"

I stared at the page, trying to see it through his eyes. Was it possible I had greatness in me after all? Something that had been unacknowledged all these years, a flicker of light that no one had ever bothered to fan into flame?

Pull it together, a familiar voice whispered in my head. *Stop asking other people to tell you that you're worthy.*

People don't take the time to really look at each other anymore. We live in a world of surface imagery, skimming past each other, registering just enough to assign a category and label before moving on to the next shiny thing. It's the rare person — *Michael!* — who pauses to *really see,* to think about what else might be outside the frame.

Maybe I'm emerging from a chrysalis! Maybe I'm on the verge of becoming a *whole other person.* Maybe I'll change my name to O'Brien, and shed Liebling forever.

I'm already halfway there; why not just go the distance?

28.

Week Three

Michael wakes me up with a grave expression on his face. "I have to go back to Portland for a few days," he says. He thrusts a cup of coffee at me.

I scoot up the bed until I'm pressed against the carved mahogany headboard. The bed smells of sex but also dust: The red velvet swags of the overhead canopy are surely housing a collection of dead spiders and flies. Another thing on the list of issues I need to point out to the housekeeper, who I am pretty sure is quietly abandoning one cleaning duty every week. Sometimes I think Stonehaven is trying to return to its natural state: a haunted mansion in some Halloween theme park.

I take a coy sip of the coffee, frown as if I don't understand. But I've known this would come eventually, the moment when the spell would be broken and real life would intrude. Michael came to Tahoe on vacation. He never intended to fall in love and get married and

510

stay forever. Of course he would have to go back home at some point.

"You want to retrieve your belongings?" I ask.

He nods. He climbs in bed beside me and lies next to me, on top of the coverlet. It tightens over my legs, like a straightjacket. "That, yes. And also to tell the administrators that I won't be back to teach in the fall."

I smile. The coffee tastes of citrus and chocolate, it burns pleasantly at the back of my tongue. "Oh *really*. Presumptuous of you."

"I mean, you'd prefer to stay here than to move back to Portland with me, yeah? Your house is much more spacious, and private. . . ." He nuzzles his nose into my neck, kisses me on the edge of my lips even though my breath must be abysmal. When I laugh, he stops and draws back. "But there's something else, my love. And I'm a *wee* bit embarrassed to tell you this."

"What?"

"*She* . . . and I — well, looking back this is the stupidest thing I've ever done. Call me naïve, but I tend to trust people, yeah? I never could have thought . . . and it's still hard to get my head around . . ." He looks lost, his hand fiddling with the creases in the coverlet. "OK, look: I let her talk me into combining bank accounts. Back in the summer, before we left to go traveling. So we had a shared

511

credit card, yeah? And a household bank account linked to our individual ones. And she's cleaned it all out. Maxed the credit card, took all the cash. And now I need to go back there and deal with the situation."

That bitch. I thought we'd gotten rid of her when she drove off in the snow last month. I thought I'd warded off disaster; but apparently I was too late. "Oh. Oh, honey. How much?"

"A lot." He shakes his head. "You were right about her. I still can't believe it. How could I have been such an *idiot*?"

"I was an idiot, too." I take his hand. "I believed in her, too, for a while. I *still* don't know what she was trying to get from me, but I figure I got off easy."

He shrugs and squeezes my hand. "It'll be fine, I'm sure, I just need to go back and meet with some people at the bank, maybe talk to a lawyer. It was stupid of me not to deal with it weeks ago, when you first told me who she . . . what she really . . ." He can't finish, his voice strangling. "But in the meantime, and I hate asking this of you . . ."

I suddenly understand what he's trying to say. "You need money."

"Just enough to get me to Portland and back." He ducks his head like a little boy, clearly ashamed to even be asking. "I'll pay you back."

I set my coffee down on the side of the

table, next to the engagement ring that glints in its tiny silver dish. It charms me, how embarrassed he is. "Don't be ridiculous," I say. "You're my husband. We share things."

He closes his eyes, as if overcome. "This is not how I wanted to start off our marriage. Unequal footing, right? And to be clear, I know we haven't talked about this yet, but: There's money in the family trust in Ireland. It's not what it *used* to be, but there's still some millions in my name. Thing is, I've had issues withdrawing it directly while living in the States. I need to meet with the trust solicitor first, sign some documents. Maybe when we go visit — maybe next summer, when Ireland's not so bloody cold. I'll settle it all then, get it set up in accounts over here." He tugs the coverlet tighter, smoothing the creases over my belly. "Probably I should have done that years ago, but money has never really been that important. I've never cared that much, you know? As long as I've got my books, and pens, and coffee . . ."

"And me."

He laughs. "Of course. You, too. But now" — he leans in and kisses me, hard — "now I want to spend it all on you."

"Look," I say. "I'll call this morning and get you added to my credit card. It might take longer to get you attached to my accounts; I'll have to call my lawyers and get some paperwork drawn up."

"Ach, Vanessa, there's no urgency," he says quickly.

"*Of course* there is."

"Let's deal with it when I get back, yeah?" he says. "Let me get the past off my plate first, before we start talking about the future."

I pick up the engagement ring and slip it on my finger, spinning it slowly back and forth. Michael and I look at it together in silence, until he finally closes his hand around mine and hides it inside his fist.

"You're not saying something," he says. "You can ask me anything, you know."

"Are you going to try to see her while you're in town?"

"Her?"

"Ashley. *Nina.*"

I've never seen him so indignant. "Are you kidding? Why would I put myself through that?" He squeezes my hand once, a little too tight, then lets go. "As far as I see it, there never was anyone named Ashley. Our whole relationship was a sham. She's a liar and a con artist, and I want nothing to do with her. I don't even want to speak her name. Either of them." There's a tiny purple vein in his temple that's popped out, and it pulses angrily. "Besides, I hear from our mutual friends that she left Portland a few weeks back. Took my money and ran. She's long gone."

I nod. Outside, the pine trees rustle and

sway. It has been warm for the better part of the week and much of the first snow has melted, leaving only icy crusts on the needles and slush along the drive. Another storm is due before the holidays, only a week away.

"And there's one more little thing." He closes his eyes, embarrassed to meet my gaze. "When she left here, Ash took the car, right? So . . ."

Michael drives out the following afternoon, in a new silver BMW SUV that we buy him at the dealership in Reno. Once I would have thought nothing of a purchase like this — a trinket, a toy! — but now the expense feels like a splurge. I have to learn to live within my new means, I remind myself, as I drive back over the summit alone. Michael won't care, will he? *All he needs is books, and coffee, and me.*

When I get home the house feels oppressively silent without him. I walk through the empty rooms, pick up things that Michael has left behind: a sweater that I press to my face that smells of spice and cigarettes; the charger for his cellphone, which he left plugged into the wall by the bed; a water cup with the imprint of his lips along the rim. I press my lips against the outline, like a besotted schoolgirl.

I flop down in the library, the coziest room in the house. With Michael gone (To Nina?

Despite his assurances, I worry), my internal chatter is starting up again; the whispers of self-doubt are back. I pull out my sketchbook and flip through the pictures of dresses, but they look flat on the page now, derivative and dull. Are these *really* any good? What if Michael's just flattering me because he doesn't want to hurt me?

I put the sketchbook down and go hunt for my phone; finding it hidden in the drawer of a sideboard in the parlor. I can't help myself: I click on the Instagram app for the first time since we were married. There, I see that the world has continued apace even as my life has taken a radical left turn. Maya and Trini and Saskia and Evangeline are off in Dubai, wearing Zuhair Murad sundresses as they pose on the backs of camels. Saskia has uploaded a photo of herself in a leopard-print bikini with the phallic thrust of the Burj Khalifa tower rising up behind her; it has 122,875 likes and a long stream of comments. *Beeaaautty — Maravilhosa — That bod is on fire — Girrrl, ur so hot can u follow me back?*

When I click over to my own Instagram feed I see that my following has dropped again, dipping below 300,000 for the first time in three years. The natives are getting restless — *Yo V, where u at these days? You on a social media fast? We want clotttttthhhhhhes*

516

— and I realize that I'm in danger of obsolescence.

Do I care? I wait to feel jealous of my old friends, or like I've lost something meaningful, but I feel nothing. No — I feel *superior.* I've finally learned to *turn off the cameras and live in peace.* (Again, her voice! I wish it would go away, even when it's right.)

I force myself to put the phone back in the drawer. And then a moment later, I pick it up again and dial Benny's number.

It rings for a long time before Benny answers. I wonder if they've taken his cellphone away again, but eventually he answers. His voice is thick and slurred. Have they increased his meds again? "Benny, I've got news."

He's been ignoring me for weeks now, my texts all going unanswered. He's still mad at me. He still thinks I drove his *one true love* (good grief) away from him.

"News about Nina?"

"*No.* Jesus, Benny. Let that go."

I can feel him pouting. "OK then, what? You've finally come to your senses and are getting out of that hellhole? Burning Stonehaven to the ground?"

"Not exactly," I say. "I got married."

"Married." There's a long pause. "To whatshisface? Victor? I didn't know you two were back together. That's great."

"Not him, Jesus God, *no.* To Michael."

An even longer pause. Finally, he speaks: "You got me. Who's Michael?"

"The writer? Who was staying in the care-taker's cottage?" Nothing. "He's Irish? Old family? I told you about him." Still nothing. "For chrissake, Benny. He's the guy who came with Ashley — with Nina. When she left, he stayed. And we . . . well, we fell in love. I know it sounds strange, but I'm really happy, Benny. I really am. The happiest I've been in a really long time. And I just wanted you to know."

The pause this time goes on so long that I start to wonder whether he's fallen asleep on the other end of the line.

"Benny." There's a sinkhole opening inside me, and with every moment of silence it widens.

"I heard you."

And I *know* what he's thinking, because he's my brother. And his soundless whisper of doubt exposes the fear I've been avoiding myself. "Benny . . . ?"

There's a strange sound on the other end of the line, a strangling cough, or maybe it's a laugh. "You married a guy you know nothing about?"

"I know enough," I say. "I know how I feel."

"Vanessa," he says slowly. "You're an idiot."

I remind myself that this is Benny's disease speaking: a version of the same pessimism and paranoia and nostalgia that has torn his life apart. And yet, his words are a kind of poison, which seeps into my happiness and threatens to destroy it. *You married a guy you know nothing about?*

Do I? Do I know anything about Michael other than what he's told me himself? Of course I don't. I haven't met his family, or spoken to his friends (other than *her*!). And yet I also can't disregard this sense of *knowing and being known* that he's given me: that he is the only person who has seen *Vanessa Liebling* as I really am, outside of the elaborate trappings of my name and public image. The truth of that emotion trumps his uncorroborated autobiography.

And yet. A day after hanging up on Benny in a huff, I find myself sitting in front of my computer, surreptitiously doing research on my new husband. I type *Michael O'Brien* into a search engine and get . . . nothing. Or rather: way too much. There are thousands of Michael O'Briens, maybe tens of thousands: dentists, musicians, spiritual healers, financial advisers, party clowns. By adding some parameters (*teacher, writer, Portland, Irish*) I find his LinkedIn profile, with a list of the schools he's taught at, as well as a basic personal website with some of his poetry, a black-and-white portrait, and a *Contact* button. The same things I found on my original cursory Google search before we'd even met, but nothing more.

I try searching *O'Brien* and *Ireland* and *castle* and am relieved to discover that yes, there is a castle that belonged to the noble clan of O'Briens. In fact, there appear to be eleven, so it's not clear which O'Brien castle belonged to his particular branch of the family.

And that's it. If there's anything else about him online, it's been drowned in a sea of other Mikes and Michaels and O'Briens. He has no Facebook profile, no Instagram feed, no Twitter handle. But I already knew that about him. He warned me that he has no interest in putting his life out there for the world to see. And I get it, I do! (*Now* I do, at least a little.) A desire for privacy shouldn't be cause for suspicion; privacy used to be something people even *valued,* once upon a time.

I stare at the blinking search field, feeling sticky and soiled. I sense something tenuous and vulnerable on the line, something that could be so easily broken if I'm not careful. So it's almost a relief when there's a clatter from the front of the house and then I hear Michael calling out my name. He's home, a day early. I shut the whole thing down and dash away from the computer, saved from the precipice.

And there he is, *my husband.* His new car

outside is crammed full of cardboard boxes, and the smell of exhaust and roadside food lingers on his clothes as he throws his arms around me and squeezes me tight to his chest.

"How was Oregon?"

"Torture," he says. He sounds despondent. "It's going to take longer than I thought to sort the whole mess out. My credit has been utterly destroyed. She cleaned me out. I don't know what I'm going to do."

"You'll start over," I murmur. "With me. It's OK. I have enough money to cover the both of us." *For a while,* I think, but don't say out loud.

I can hear his slow, measured breaths, the steady drum of his heart. "I'm so embarrassed, Van. I'm so sorry to have to put you through this."

"It's not your fault," I say into the soft flannel of his shirt. "It's hers. She's a *monster.*"

"You saved my life, really. I can only imagine how much worse things might have gotten if you hadn't exposed her as a fraud. What if I'd actually gone ahead and *married* her?" He shudders. Then he tips my head up and studies my face. "You're my savior. This place is like heaven. I couldn't wait to get back to you."

See? I have no good reason to doubt him.

29.

Week Four

Michael is spending more and more time on his laptop, writing. He has moved from his favorite position on the couch in the library, next to me, and instead now works at the desk in my father's old study. "Better for my back to sit on an actual chair," he tells me. (I understand! Really I do!) He's moved a space heater in there, and closes the door to keep the room warm. When I pass by I can hear the clatter of keys, the murmur of his voice as he sounds out words. At dinner, he's distracted, as if he's left most of himself back in the overheated study. When I call him on this he looks startled.

"Sorry, honey. I should have warned you that I get like this when I'm on a roll with my writing." But he reaches across the table and squeezes my hand. "This is a good thing, though. I'm inspired. You're inspiring me. My *muse.*"

I've always wanted to be a muse!

I wander into the study one evening and catch him working in the dark. His face is buried in the screen, so immersed in what he's typing that he fails to notice me entering the room in my stocking feet. I'm almost around the desk when he finally registers my presence just a few feet away. He looks up with alarm, the blue glow from the screen illuminating the shock on his face; and then he quickly snaps the lid of his laptop shut.

He puts a flat hand on the computer, anchoring it to the desk, then looks up at me with a frown. "No peeking," he says. "I'm serious."

I slide into his lap and tug playfully at the lid of the computer. "Come on," I say. "Just one chapter? One page? A paragraph?"

He shifts his weight so that I slide off his lap and end up back on my feet next to him. His features are shadowed in the gloom, but I can tell that he is annoyed. "I'm serious, Vanessa. When people read my work-in-progress it makes me self-conscious and then I can't write at all. I need to work in a vacuum, without anyone's judgments or opinions."

"Even mine?" I *hate* that I'm pouting, but I can't help it.

"*Especially* yours."

"But you know I'm going to love what you write. I love your poetry."

"See? This is what I mean. You'll love it no

matter what, which means I'll end up wondering whether or not I can trust your opinion, and then I'll start second-guessing myself. That makes it even worse."

"OK, OK, I get it. I'll leave you to it." I turn to stalk off but he grabs my wrist before I get far.

"Vanessa." His voice is cajoling. "This isn't about you."

"But *she* read your work. She said so." I am surprised by the spite in my voice.

His hand tightens painfully on my wrist. Am I being too petulant? Do I sound whiny and jealous? I wish I could take it back, but it's too late. "Why are you *still* worrying about her? Vanessa, you have to let that *go*. And besides, *no,* she didn't get to read what I'm working on now. She saw some old material, against my better judgment, but I've got something new in the works."

I tug my hand away. "Forget I said anything."

His voice softens. "You shouldn't be jealous of someone who didn't actually exist, you know. Especially *her*. It's really not worth getting worked up about."

"I'm not." I'm lying. I'm upset. *He shut me out.* That's not supposed to happen, is it? Not when you're in love; when you're supposedly *seen*?

He's not a fool, so he knows I'm lying, too. *Of course* he registers the anger in the way I

524

stomp up the stairs and climb straight into bed, even though it's barely eight o'clock. I wait for him to come to me, but he doesn't. It's the first time we've gone to bed separately since we've been together.

I lie in the icy sheets, shivering. Our first argument: Was it my fault? Am I too shrill, too controlling? Have I fucked everything up for good? I know I should go apologize and beg for forgiveness, but an old, familiar inertia descends. The dark curtain, falling around my bed, and I find I can't muster the will to get up; so instead I curl up under the velvet coverlet and cry myself to sleep.

When I wake up, it's pitch-black, and the faint radioactive gleam of the old alarm clock tells me that it's close to midnight. Outside, a winter wind has picked up. I lie in the bed, my eyes raw and puffy from crying, listening to the groaning of the pines and the rattle of ice on the windowpanes. I can hear the wind whipping around the corners of the house, a faint high whistle like a distant train rushing through the dark.

And underneath *that* — the slow, steady thrum of human breath. I roll to my side and reach out for Michael, but the bed is empty. And only then am I aware of the shadow falling over me, a spectral presence here in the dark, silently watching me from across the room. I sit up, gripping the sheet to my chest and think — *Ghost!*

But of course, it's just Michael. He walks slowly over to the bed, his laptop gripped in both hands.

"You scared me," I say.

He sits down on the edge of the bed next to me, then unfolds the laptop. It flicks to life, illuminating the room with a pale blue glow. "Peace offering?" he says. He holds the computer out toward me.

I take it gingerly. "You changed your mind."

"I was being unreasonable," he says. "But you have to understand that I was burned pretty hard by Ashley."

"Nina," I correct him.

"See? I don't even know what to call her." He wrinkles his nose. "You get why I'm having a hard time learning to trust again? But I also don't want you to think that I'm keeping secrets from you. That's not our relationship. You aren't *her,* I need to keep reminding myself of that. So . . ." He pulls open a document on his home screen. "Read. It's just a little snippet, but . . . you'll get the gist."

The laptop is warm in my hands, as if it's alive under my palm. "Thank you." I'm a little weepy: This is more like it. All is forgiven.

He stands over me while I read, studying my face as I scroll through his words.

My love — ohmylovemylove. When I look at

her, her green eyes stirring in that feline face, the words (worlds) whirl within me. My beauty my love my savior. All my life I've been a wanderer but she makes me still. Life pivots around us. A shared center, two people one point, it is within and it is without but always it is us us us and we need nothing beyond that.

It goes on like this for paragraphs. My first reaction is one of dismay. It's not very . . . good, is it? Nothing like the lovely poetry that he'd quoted to me in the bedroom. Nothing like the Maileresque masterpiece I'd been envisioning. But I take a beat, second-guess myself the way I always do: Just because it's *un petit étrange,* not to my taste at all really, who am I to judge? (Postmodern literature: Just one of the many classes I failed at Princeton.) I sense Michael studying my reaction, the tiny twitches of my face illuminated by the glowing screen; and it's then that I am able to summon the only important realization, the one that makes my judgment of his writing skills irrelevant.

"It's about *me*?" I whisper.

I can't really see his face, but I feel his cold hand on my cheek. "Of course, it's about you. My *muse,* remember?"

"I'm touched. Really." But when I try to keep reading the next page he gently tugs the laptop from my hands and chides me. "You can see the rest when I'm done."

His words inhabit me as I dream that night, and are still in my head when I wake the next morning. *My love — ohmylovemylove.* I fly out of bed — *alive again!* — and go to find him.

But he's gone. In the kitchen I find a note by the coffeepot: *Drove to the store to get the paper.* His laptop is sitting there on the kitchen island, emitting a faint whine. I run my hands over the lid, feeling the hard drive vibrate under my palm. *I shouldn't. He trusts me!*

I just can't resist — I flip the lid open. Just to see! If it's still open to the document, I'll let myself read *one page only,* I tell myself. Just to see what else he's written about me. That's hardly a betrayal.

But the screen is locked. I toy with the password field for a moment, fingers hovering over the keys, and then realize that I have no clue what his password might be. All those significant names and dates and numbers that comprise a person's personal history — I've yet to familiarize myself with any of them. I don't know Michael's mother's maiden name, or his childhood pets, or his favorite sister's birthday. I'm frozen, standing there, realizing that my husband is still a mystery.

(Is it possible I've been *too* impulsive, for

once? Did I get myself into something I wasn't prepared for? I stand there spinning with self-doubt.)

But numbers and names mean nothing, I remind myself. They lend us a false sense of security, the belief that verifiable facts are a girder against the loss of love. As if a person will never leave you once they know the name of your favorite teacher, your mother's star sign, the age at which you lost your virginity. All the ephemera that forms the ladder of our identity — where does it ultimately lead? We act as if it's meaningful, but it says nothing about the state of our hearts.

All Michael and I really possess of each other, for now, is trust. And I trust him! I do! I *have* to.

I close the computer. *I wouldn't peek even if I could,* I tell myself.

(Or is it the other way around?)

30.

The holidays creep up, and suddenly Christmas is just a week away. One morning I wake up to discover that Michael has installed a tree in the parlor, a sweetly tilting pine that he's decorated with the same silver and gold ornaments that Grandmother Katherine once put on her trees. Somehow, he's even managed to place it in the same spot where she put hers: in the window that looks out toward the portico, an invitation to guests coming up the drive. Looking at it, I am suddenly six years old again, and afraid of a spanking.

As I stand staring at it, this hallucination from my past, Michael comes up behind me and wraps his arms around my neck. "I saw that tree when I was walking around the property last week and thought, *Christmas tree,*" he says. "Betcha didn't know that I'm handy with an axe."

"I have an axe?"

"Of course you have an axe. What, you've

never used one?" He kisses me on the cheek as if he finds me adorable, his pampered little princess, and then steps back to admire his handiwork. As he squints at it, his smile falls away. "Shite. It's lopsided."

"No, it's *perfect*. Where did you find the ornaments?"

"In a closet in one of those rooms upstairs that we never go in." He senses my hesitation. "Was that OK? I wanted it to be a surprise. Our first Christmas together, I thought it should be special."

I can't quite pin down what about this bothers me. Is it that he's been poking around the house without me knowing about it? That he suddenly knows more of Stonehaven's secrets than I do? But why would this be a problem? I *wanted* him to feel at home here.

"It's beautiful," I say. "But I should have warned you sooner, we need to spend Christmas down in Ukiah, with Benny."

Michael tilts his head slightly, as if trying to straighten the tree in his mind. "It's a little creepy to spend the holiday in a psychiatric ward, yeah?" He reaches out to adjust an ornament but it falls to the floor and shatters, scattering tiny shards of gold glass across the floor. We both freeze.

I bend over and start to pick up the broken pieces of ornament. "It's not what you're thinking, it's nice there. Look, you haven't even met Benny yet. He's wonderful, you'll see. Eccentric, but wonderful." My face is hot, something twisting and squeezing in my chest.

Michael grabs my shoulder, stopping me. He plucks a piece of glass out of my hand and cups it in his own. "Don't cut yourself," he says. "I'll do it."

I watch him as he crouches over the polished floors, gently sweeping up bits of glass with the side of his palm in a way that reminds me — with an ache — of Maman, and the little glass bird. "Why don't we just have Benny here?" he asks.

"Benny won't come here. He hates it here, remember? Besides, I'd still need to go down to sign him out. He can't just leave there on his own."

"Right." He looks up at me from where he's crouched on the floor. "Is he in line to inherit Stonehaven if something happens to you?"

What a strange question! "Of course he is. Unless I redo my estate and designate a different trustee."

"Right. It's just —" He frowns. "You told me that he said he wanted to burn this place down, is all. And he's not so rational, is he?"

"God, that's morbid. Can we not talk about that kind of thing?"

Michael nods. He crawls across the floor to retrieve a piece of glass that's landed up against the wall. He picks it up and then sits

532

there for a moment, his back to me. I see his breath rise and fall faster than it should and it looks like he's upset. Have I said something wrong?

"Benny's the only family I have," I say softly. "I can't spend the holidays without him."

"*I'm* your family now, too," he says. He sounds wounded; I've hurt him. I didn't even think of that. It never crossed my mind that marriage requires a reshuffling of your priorities, with spouse on top and parents and siblings in the middle and your own needs somewhere far down below. (*Where do children fit in all that?* I wonder. We haven't even discussed the fact that I want a baby, sooner rather than later. Was it wrong of me to assume he wants one, too?)

I stand there, my jaw working up and down, not sure how to respond. Eventually he rights himself, his hands glittering with brutal flecks of gold, and looks at me. I can see him measuring the distress in my face, and I also see the shift in his own when he makes a decision. He's done some shuffling of his own. He softens, and reaches for me. "I want to make you happy, and if it makes you happy to go to Benny, we'll go. End of story."

And that *would* be the end of the story, except that the morning we're supposed to leave for Ukiah, my car already loaded with gifts, Michael wakes up sick. He lies there in bed with his teeth chattering, complaining of aches and fever. "Crikey. How the hell did I get the flu?" he murmurs, as I pile the bed with extra blankets. "I've barely left the house in weeks."

When I finally locate a thermometer in the nursery (an ancient mercury thing, probably dating back to the 1970s) and bring it back to our bedroom, Michael's temperature is 102 and his forehead is beaded with sweat. I know it's unfair of me to be bitter (or worse: *suspicious*) about the timing of this illness, but when I think of Benny waiting for me in Ukiah I want to cry.

I stand over Michael as he huddles under the covers, his eyelashes fluttering with fever. "We can't go now," I murmur.

He opens one blue eye and fixes it on me. "You can go," he says. "You *should* go."

"But you need me to take care of you."

He tucks the blanket tighter under his chin. "I'll be fine," he says. "Your brother is the one who needs you most right now. It's your first Christmas without your dad, yeah? You two should be together. We'll have other holidays together, you and I."

A tide of gratitude rises in me: that he can see the rightness in this decision, and is willing to sacrifice our first holiday together so that I can be with my brother. *He understands!* I forgive the untimely flu.

"I'll only be gone a few days," I promise.

"Take all the time you need," he says. "I'm not going anywhere."

The Orson Institute does their best with the holidays — the staff in Christmas sweaters, "Silent Night" piped soothingly into the reception area, the doorways festooned with pine garlands (but not, of course, poisonous poinsettias or toxic holly berries). There's a tree in every room, and a giant menorah on the lawn, and a holiday meal for visitors featuring ham, duck, and sixteen different pies.

But when I arrive at the facility, the day before Christmas, Benny isn't festive at all. At some point since we last spoke, he slipped into mania again, and so his dosage has been upped and his phone taken away.

When I find him in one of the common rooms, he's sedated and blank. He sits on the couch with a Santa hat tugged over his unruly red curls, watching a SpongeBob SquarePants holiday special.

His main psychiatrist — a trim woman with a no-nonsense cap of silver hair — pulls me aside.

"Something triggered him, maybe the holidays," she tells me. "We caught him trying to break out of the facility. He stole a nurse's car keys and was driving out the lower gate when we stopped him. He was raving

535

about going all the way to Oregon." She frowns. "And he'd been doing so well, too. We were going to talk to you about putting him on a reintegration plan."

Oregon: *fucking Nina Ross.* Why won't she go away for good? Why does she keep *haunting* us? I go over to Benny, who is slumped into the cushions of the couch as if trying to sink all the way inside them. He's attempting to eat a carton of strawberry Yoplait while in this position, and dribbling yogurt down the front of his sweater. He glances down at the mess, runs a finger through one particularly large blob, licks it clean, and then looks back at the TV screen.

I sit next to him, dropping a pile of gifts at his feet.

"Oregon? Benny, you have to let it go."

He ignores this, and gestures at the TV with his spoon. "This show is really funny," he says, but his words are slow and mirthless.

"Seriously, Benny. That girl is poison."

This seems to jerk him out of his stupor. He sits up, shakes his head as if to clear it, and I glimpse the glimmer of mania lurking there behind the drugs. "She's the only girl I ever loved. She's the only person who ever loved me."

"*I* love you." So much. Doesn't he see that?

He looks at me balefully. "You know what I mean."

"For God's sake, Benny. You were sixteen

years old, just a kid. You have no idea who she really is, now. Her mother —"

"Her mother had an affair with Dad and then tried to blackmail him."

I stare at him. "You knew about that?"

"Of course I knew. I was there when the letter came. Never saw the point in telling you because Dad asked me not to. Besides, I figured you'd lose your shit about it and spend the rest of your life fuming instead of being a *productive member of society* and all." He blinks a few times, takes another bite of yogurt. "But Nina's not her mother. Think about it: What did she ever really do to *you*? Because all she ever did to *me* was be my friend when no one else was interested. And Mom and Dad fucked *that* up."

"*Think* about it, Benny. She got you hooked on drugs, which set you on a downward spiral and triggered . . . well. All this."

He yawns. "Bullshit. She'd never even smoked pot before I gave her some."

This stops the words in my throat. She hadn't? My mother had it wrong? "Wait. *You* gave pot to *her*? But Maman said —"

He groans. "Mom was too fucked-up to see straight. Really, Van, there's no reason to be pissed at Nina. Her mom was a piece of work, it's true. But Nina didn't do anything to me. I'm *here* for the same reason that Mom's dead: We both had some faulty genes that screwed with the chemical balance in our heads. It's no one else's fault."

It isn't? My jaw works up and down, as I try to come up with another reason to hate Nina Ross. I feel lost, like I've let go of a thread and the path I've been following has disappeared. What *did* she do back then, really? Besides failing to be one of us. (*Strange and not quality,* I remember Maman writing. Oh.)

The characters onscreen screech and wail. "But still: You can't deny that she faked her identity as Ashley Smith. Why would she *do* that if she wasn't up to something shifty? And don't forget that she stole money from Michael!"

He raises an eyebrow. "You sure about that?"

"What do you mean?" Something lurches inside me. *He's paranoid,* I tell myself. *He's manic.* But he doesn't seem manic at all; if anything, he seems pretty lucid.

"All I'm gonna say is, I'm not convinced that you're the best judge of character, sis."

"This isn't about me," I say. "This is about your health. And fixating on her isn't healthy for you."

He proffers the half-empty container of yogurt toward me, with the spoon sticking out of it. "Speaking of my health, apparently I'm not allowed a fork anymore, unless I have supervision. Twenty-nine years old and I can't cut my own goddamn food."

I put my arm around him. Even like this, he's still *Benny* to me; that sticky, warm toddler whom it was always my job to protect. "Do you want to come live with me?" I hear myself say. "It would make me so happy if you did." *Could* I bring him to Stonehaven to live with me? Maybe it's not so unfathomable after all. I always thought that Benny would be too much for me to handle alone. But I have Michael now! We could take care of him *together.* A family again, finally!

"I dunno." He shrugs and slumps back, succumbing to the drugs in his system. "It's not so bad here at Orson, actually. It's safe. No voices."

"Oh, Benny." I don't know what else to say.

He leans his head on my shoulder. "Merry fucking Christmas, sis."

When I return to Stonehaven two days later, I discover Michael has recovered from his flu, but is in an inexplicably sour mood. The kitchen is a mess — I gave the housekeeper the week off for the holidays, and Michael has apparently used every pot in the place in the meantime. We forgot to water the Christmas tree and it's shedding dead needles everywhere. They crunch underfoot when I walk through the house in search of my husband.

I find him in front of the fire in the library, hunched in the big leather chair with his laptop on his knees. He's wearing a scarf and hat indoors.

I wait for him to stand up and take me in his arms, to make some noise about missing me, but he barely turns his head from the screen to acknowledge my presence. "How was the drive?" he asks, as if I'd just gone on a grocery run.

"Fine."

Is he punishing me for leaving him alone for Christmas? I can't quite understand what's going on. I point at the woolly hat. "Don't you think that's a little overkill?"

He reaches up and touches it, as if he's forgotten he is wearing it. "It's freezing in here. Are you sure this place has central heat? Because I cranked the thermostat up to eighty and I still can't feel anything."

I think of the heating bill we're going to get next month, and cringe. "The furnace is sixty years old," I say. "And this house is almost twenty thousand square feet."

He makes a face at his screen. "Well, we should replace the furnace, then."

I laugh at this. "Do you have any idea how much that will cost?"

Now he's looking at me, straight on, with an expression of disbelief. "Seriously? You're worried about the cost of *central heating*?"

The tone in his voice is one I've not heard from him before: mocking and petty. And I realize that this may be the moment to honestly disabuse him of the notion that I'm limitlessly rich, but my hackles are raised. "Well, it's not like you're the one paying the bill," I say flatly. "Go ahead. Wear your scarf and hat. Can I get you a blanket while I'm at it? A cup of tea? Hot-water bottle?"

He seems to realize that he's upset me, because something in his face shifts and softens. He reaches up and grabs my hand and tugs me onto his lap. "I'm sorry. I just think the weather is getting to me. So cold and dreary." He pulls me in closer. "I hated being alone for the holiday. I missed you. It made me grumpy to be away from you. Don't go away ever again, OK?"

The smell of him, spice and soap; the heat of his skin under my hand. *There is friction in every relationship,* I remind myself. *We're only just discovering ours, and that's OK.* I could continue to be indignant, but it's easier to succumb to his demand for forgiveness.

"I won't," I say into his sleeve.

And yet. I am unloading bags from my car that night when I stop and look at the silver BMW parked next to mine. Still off-gassing with newness, this indulgent, impulsive gift I gave my husband. Why am I so hesitant to tell him that I am not as rich as he thinks I am? Is it because I'm afraid that he won't love me as much? That he won't believe we

541

are alike anymore? Because I still worry that, if I'm not *Vanessa Liebling, heiress,* I'm no one at all?

I sit down in the front seat and inhale the smell of him, still lingering in the leather from his road trip earlier in the month. He's left the key sitting right there in the console, an act of ease or perhaps just laziness. I turn on the radio, and to my surprise a hip-hop music station blasts through the speakers. My husband, the pop culture snob — How did he put it? An *aesthete* — likes Kendrick Lamar? I could have sworn he said he only listened to jazz and classical.

Maybe this little *ping* of surprise, like a sonar pulse mapping out the gaps in my understanding of him, is what triggers me to reach over to the car's GPS control panel. I pull up the list of prior destinations and, with one eye on the door to the house, scroll quickly through them. There aren't many addresses in the list, the car hasn't been many places. The supermarket, the hardware store, a few other Tahoe City destinations. I realize that I'm looking for Michael's Portland address. This would be the very first place he headed after the dealership, so I run my finger down to the bottom of the list.

And then I stop, my hand skittering across the screen, my fingers thrumming with electric shock. Because the first address that my husband went to in his new car wasn't in

542

Oregon at all.
It was in Los Angeles.

31.

Week Six

"What were you doing in Los Angeles?"

Michael stops in his tracks in the doorway of the kitchen, the morning papers in his hand, snow in his hair. This has become his new daily routine, the drive down the road to the general store, where he buys a stack of newspapers that eventually end up scattered across the chairs and the tables, half-read. One of the papers under his arm, I can't help but notice, is the *Los Angeles Times.*

He places the newspapers carefully on the kitchen island, next to yesterday's papers and our dishes from last night's meal of frozen pizza. Neither of us has much of an inclination to clean up, and the housekeeper has been off for the better part of the week.

"Los Angeles?" He enunciates the syllables as if sounding out the name of an exotic destination. "What makes you think I've been to *Los Angeles?*"

"I saw it programmed in the destination

history in your car. It was the first address in the list."

A mottled purple shadow darkens his face. He stares at me, his jaw tucking tight into his chin. "For fuck's sake, Vanessa. You're checking up on me? You're *spying*?" He paces around the island until he's on the same side as me, standing too close, his chest thrust out in a pugilistic stance. "We've barely been married a month and you're already turning into a jealous wife? What next, you're going to start looking at my text messages and my emails? Jaysus *fuck.*" His hands are clenched into fists that tremble at his side, as if waiting to be unleashed.

"Michael, you're scaring me," I whisper.

He looks down at his fists, and releases them. I can see the white crescents where his fingers were digging into his palms. "And you're scaring *me.* I thought we had something special, Vanessa. Jaysus, what happened to *trust*?"

"We *do* have something special." What have I done? I stumble over myself with apologies. "No, I swear. I wasn't spying. I came across it by mistake. It just . . . I didn't understand, because you said you went to *Portland . . .* and the history said *Los Angeles.*" I want to cry.

He's breathing heavily. "I *did* go to Portland."

"But Portland wasn't in the list of addresses . . ."

"Because I didn't need directions! I know how to drive to my own goddamn house!"

He's still towering over me; I feel tiny in the face of his fury. And I think, *If I upset him he might leave and then I'll be alone again.* "OK," I say, hating how pathetic my voice sounds. "But I still don't understand why there's a Los Angeles address in the destination history."

"Christ, Vanessa. I. Don't. Know." He throws himself down on a stool and buries his head in his arms. I stand there, helpless. Have I ruined everything? The kitchen is silent, except for our labored breathing. And then, suddenly, he lifts his head, and he's smiling. He grabs my hand and pulls me onto his lap. "You know what? I figured it out. The car probably originated in Los Angeles, right? That's where it came from, before they shipped it up to Reno. The address you saw was probably from the Los Angeles BMW dealership, or something along those lines."

"Oh." I am flooded with relief. "OK, that makes sense."

He laughs. "Silly goose. What did you think? That I have a lover hidden in Los Angeles? That I'm living some kind of double life?" He cups his hand along my cheek, shakes his head with bemusement. What *did* I think? That Nina was in Los Angeles, and he'd gone looking for her. That he came back

546

with a car full of his belongings that weren't in Portland at all. And that would mean . . . what? That at least something of his history was a lie?

But I prefer his version of events, even if it all feels just a hair too convenient.

I put my hand over his, pressing it tighter against my cheek. "I don't know very much about you, you know. We're still strangers."

"My Vanessa, we're not strangers in the ways it counts." He tips my chin up, so that he's looking directly into my eyes. "I'm not hiding anything from you, my love. I'm an open book, I swear. If you are worried about something, just *ask* me. Don't snoop around behind my back, OK?"

"I won't," I promise. I bury my face in his neck, because that seems like the safest place to be. He pulls my face up again and kisses me, and then picks me up in his arms and carries me up the stairs to the bedroom. And that's it, the subject is closed. We're both relieved to move on.

Everything is fine. Everything is fine. Everything is fine.

We make martinis, we cook dinner, we chat about tomorrow's plans for New Year's Eve. It's decided that we will leave the house, for a change, and go to a nice restaurant to celebrate. Things are shifting; we are settling into a new routine, ready to leave the cocoon and face the greater world. We smile, we laugh, we make love, and everything is fine.

I think.

New Year's Eve. I have dragged another dress out of retirement, a wool Alexander Wang with leather detail. Tights, knee-high boots. Nothing too ostentatious: This is Tahoe after all. Most of the people at the restaurant will probably be in jeans.

Michael has unearthed a suit from one of the duffel bags that he brought back from Oregon — a very modern Tom Ford, I'm surprised to note. It drapes easily across his shoulders and chest, perfectly tailored; he shoots his cuffs with a practiced flick of his wrists, as if he was born to wear formal clothes and not the lumberjack duds he's been living in. I feel like I'm seeing a whole new side of him, a glimpse of the aristocratic life he was born into. Who knew that my academic husband followed men's fashion trends? (I confess, I'm just a little pleased!)

It's like we're playing at dress up, donning the roles of husband and wife for our first public appearance. He zips up my dress. I fiddle with the knot in his tie. We laugh at how *conventional* we are being, how *domestic*. I'm high on champagne, and happy: This is the fullest that Stonehaven has felt since my mother died and my brother landed in a mental institution. This is what I've longed for, for years. It feels like *home.*

We have reservations at a lakefront restaurant in Tahoe City, where there will be live music and dancing. I settle into the passenger seat of his BMW. When I go to type the address into the navigation system I notice that the destination history has been completely erased. I sit back, say nothing. Michael turns on the radio and soft jazz swells from the surround-sound speakers. He reaches over and takes my hand, and I smile blankly out the windshield as we back out of the garage.

The destination history has been erased. The Los Angeles address is gone.

But it's not gone, because I already memorized it. I already memorized it; and yesterday afternoon, while Michael was having his postcoital nap, I plugged the address into Google Maps. So I already know that it doesn't belong to a BMW dealership at all. It belongs to a tiny, vine-covered bungalow in the hills of East Los Angeles.

Why am I so relieved to discover that the New Year's party is at a family-style restaurant? We are seated at long communal tables, surrounded by friendly strangers on all sides; strangers whose wine-soaked curiosity about Michael and me prevents us from having any one-on-one conversation. It's been so long since I talked to anyone but Michael and

Benny, and I feel positively high from all this human contact.

Michael keeps his arm clenched possessively around my shoulders during the meal, proudly announcing to anyone who will listen that we are newlyweds, it was *love at first sight,* he *swept me off my feet* in a *whirlwind romance.* (Nina's role in our history is quietly abandoned to the ash bin.) For a literary writer, he certainly enjoys a cliché. He makes me splay my hand out over the table, showing off the ring that rattles loosely on my finger. "An heirloom, from my family's estate in Ireland," he announces proudly.

It feels so *good* to be the blushing bride, everyone admiring us; it squelches the murmur of doubt at the back of my mind. Maybe everything *is* fine! Maybe it's just my own twisted brain that's been interpreting the signs in the wrong way.

The woman sitting next to me, the elderly wife of a venture capitalist from Palo Alto — herself dripping in diamonds — pulls my hand close to examine the ring and then gives me a funny little smile. "The first few months of marriage are the best, when you're just screwing yourselves into oblivion," she says to me, and gives my hand a squeeze. "Enjoy this time while you can. Because the blinders will eventually come off and what you see after that is never quite as pretty." I look at her, startled — *What does she know?* — but of course, her gaze is blank, generically kind, and it's just my own fear whispering in my ear again.

I drink some more to mute it.

The food is good, the cocktails strong, the company pleasant. Michael is almost manic, ordering the waiter to bring a round of Jameson Rarest Vintage Reserve to everyone at the table, and then leading a collective toast to our marriage. Then he orders another. We dance to a swing band (Michael is a quite capable dancer — another surprise!) and just before the clock strikes midnight the waiters circulate with complimentary prosecco. I'm breathless and giddy with drink, abandoning myself to the horn section, letting my husband swing me in increasingly out-of-control circles while I shriek with laughter. *Everything is fine!* Then it's midnight, and everyone on the dance floor is cheering. Michael holds me tight to his chest and kisses me. "Farewell to the past, hello to the future. *You* are my future. Now and forever."

Maybe it's the cheap prosecco mixing with the expensive whiskey, maybe it's all the dancing, but when he spins me again, I feel like I'm going to throw up. "I think I need to go home," I murmur.

Michael pulls me off the dance floor. "Of course. I'll settle up."

The waiter materializes with the check and

551

Michael reaches for his wallet. "Two thousand forty-two. Jaysus, maybe I shouldn't have bought that second round for everyone." He laughs, seemingly unconcerned, but then freezes with his hand halfway to his pocket. "Oh God, I forgot. My credit card, I had to cancel it. Because of . . . you know. *Her.*"

I reach for my evening bag. "I've got it." I sign the bill, feeling my stomach clench at the ludicrous number, once again wondering how I'm going to tell Michael about our finances. Because as much as he protests that he doesn't care at all about money, I'm starting to suspect that this isn't quite true. We need to get to Ireland sooner rather than later, so he can tap into his inheritance.

As I hand over my credit card to the waiter, I see that the venture capitalist's wife has been watching us from across the room. She smiles thinly, and turns away.

It's snowing outside. Michael goes to retrieve the car, so that I won't have to trudge through the slush in my designer shoes. I wait inside the restaurant's vestibule, peering out the window at the icy street and the cars slowly slipping past. I feel someone come up behind me and turn to see the venture capitalist's wife. She takes my hand and lifts it, so that we are both looking at the ring on my finger.

"It's not real," she says quietly. "It's not real, and it's not an antique. A very good fake, but *definitely* not an heirloom."

I stare at the ring for a long time. *Maybe he doesn't know?* "Are you sure?"

She presses my palm between hers. "Honey. I hate to be the bearer of bad news. But yes." Outside, the BMW slides silently into view, and I wait for Michael to climb out and come get me, but he stays behind the wheel. I stand frozen in the vestibule, waiting for my stomach to stop tying and untying itself in knots. Michael honks the horn, three short blasts that shatter the starless night.

The venture capitalist's wife winces. "I hope you got a prenup," she says.

And then, just like that, she's gone. I wrap my scarf across my face, concealing my expression, and gird myself for the long drive back to Stonehaven.

I feel like I'm driving back to jail.

32.

Week Seven

Michael's been on the phone in the study for days now, the door closed so that all I can hear as I walk past is the faint swing of his cadence as he speaks to someone in a low voice. He's trying to locate Nina and recover his money, a project that seems to involve endless hours talking to lawyers and private investigators and the authorities in Oregon.

I spend my waking hours lying in front of the fire in the library, my sketchbook open to an empty page on which I'm failing to draw. Here I am *again;* wasn't finding love supposed to make all this go away? But this time, the dark chatter in the back of my mind isn't about my worthlessness; instead, it's about my *fear.* The faint whisper: *What have you done?*

I'm listless, fatigued, nauseous; I haven't drawn a thing since New Year's. I feel acutely aware of my body, the uneasy shifting of my intestines and the dryness of my eyeballs against the backs of my lids. When I pick up the pencil I can feel the bones inside my hand, pressing against the lead. It's unbearable.

Instead, I lie here on the couch, huddled under blankets. The hives on my arms are back, and I scratch at them until they bleed, blooming red stains through the fabric of my robe. I barely even register the pain.

This is where Michael finds me on the fourth day of the New Year. He materializes at the library door with a cup of tea for me, in my grandmother's best rose china. "My love. You look awful." He puts the tea on the coffee table and draws the blanket over my legs. "I'll drive to Obexer's and get you some chicken noodle soup, yeah?"

I shudder. "Maybe later. I don't have much of an appetite."

"Drink your tea, then. *Tea with milk and honey will fix any ill.* That's what my grandmother Alice back in Ireland used to say. Of course she also laced hers with whiskey, so maybe that's why she felt so good." He laughs, hands me the teacup, but I've grown *tired* of hearing about Grandma back in Ireland. (Another whisper of doubt: *Does she even exist?*) The liquid is so hot that I have to put it back down immediately. He draws a finger through a droplet of tea on the table, rubs it on his jeans. "Are you feeling well enough to talk?"

"About what?"

He settles on the couch next to me, his hand on my leg. "So, I've been talking to this private investigator, yeah? And he has a lead. He thinks Nina is in Paris, living large on the money she stole from me. But I can't do anything about it as long as she's there. We need to find a way to bring her back to the States — *drag* her back if need be — so that we can press charges against her. The lawyer suggested I hire this fixer he knows, someone who specializes in this kind of thing."

I frown. "In *what* kind of thing? Kidnapping? Couldn't you just extradite her?"

"Do you have any idea how long that will take? How many legal hoops we'll have to jump through? You think she's gonna stay in one place for long?" Michael sighs. "Look: She's a thief, and an imposter. Apparently she's been working her grift for years, faking identities so she could get close to wealthy people and rip them off. She stole from me, and I'm *sure* she was planning to steal from you, too. That must be why she brought me here in the first place. This place — it's full of valuables, yeah? *I* think she was planning to slip some things in her pockets before leaving town." It makes sense; I nod. "So then. She deserves whatever she gets, and if that means, say, knocking her out and then putting her on a private plane, so be it."

"Knocking her out — how? You mean, getting her drunk? Or are we talking about roofies here?"

Michael's fingers on my leg tighten and release, tighten and release. His hair has grown longer in the two months he's been in Tahoe, and nearly touches his collar. He's tucked it back behind his ears in a way that I don't find particularly attractive. "Honestly, I would have thought you'd be *happy* to see her go down. I'm not sure why you're ambivalent. Didn't you try to poison her, for chrissake?"

He's right, of course. I remember the Visine that I squeezed into Nina's drink, ages ago now. I *was* thirsting for revenge then, it's true. But that was a harmless prank: a night spent over the toilet, nothing permanent. (Not poison! Not technically.) And yes, I stole her fiancé (and her ring) but that was *love,* and forgivable. Kidnapping sounds so . . . violating. And illegal. I imagine her waking up on a plane, her wrists bound, with no idea where she's headed. The image isn't satisfying; it's *disturbing.*

"It sounds like a complicated endeavor," I murmur. "Legally dubious. And expensive."

He runs his hand up and down my leg. "Mmm. Actually, that's what I need to talk to you about. The fixer and the private investigator and the lawyer . . . they all work on retainer."

I suddenly see where this is going. "You need money."

"Temporarily. Until I disentangle my finances."

"How much?"

"A hundred-twenty."

I'm relieved. "A hundred and twenty dollars? Sure, I'll get my checkbook."

He chuckles: *So charming*. "No, darling. A hundred twenty *thousand* dollars."

I pick up the tea again, and take a sip that scalds my tongue. It's too strong and too sweet. The dark knot inside my belly is twisting and twisting and twisting. "Michael. Maybe you should just let it go. That's an awful lot to spend on what sounds like a wild-goose chase. How much money of yours did she even take? I can't imagine it's worth the expenditure."

He stares at me. "It's the principle of the thing. She should pay for what she did."

"But she brought us together, too. So maybe we call it even and move on."

"If we don't stop her, she'll just go on to target other people. And it will be our fault."

"But isn't that the job of the police?"

He jumps up and starts pacing the room. "I *called* the police. They said their hands were tied because we had set up joint accounts, so it was my fault. It's up to me to bring her to justice. It's up to *us*." He picks up the poker and prods at the dying fire, sending sparks flying. "Vanessa. I can't believe you're fighting me about this. With all the money you have at your disposal."

This is the moment. "Actually, I don't have any money at my disposal."

He laughs. "Very funny."

"I'm dead serious, Michael. I don't have much money. Not that I can give you."

He stands turning the poker in his hand, the light from the fireplace reflecting shadows across his face. "You mean it's not liquid."

"I mean it's *not there.*" I put the tea down and it splashes across my wrist, leaving a red welt. I press my lips against it, suck the pain away. "I'm house rich and cash poor. My father was near bankruptcy when he died. My trust is down to nothing. My Liebling Group stock is underwater. Everything I have is going into the upkeep of Stonehaven right now. Do you even know how much it costs to maintain an estate this size? Hundreds of thousands of dollars *annually.* Didn't you ever think about why your family sold their castle?"

He is staring at me. "You're kidding. Haha, right? Funny joke, getting a rise out of me, right?"

"Not kidding. I should have told you before, but the moment was never quite right. I'm *sorry.*"

"Well *that* explains . . ." His voice dwindles off, leaving me wondering what it explains.

He dances the end of the poker on the floor as he thinks, little jabs that leave divots in the wood. Every time it lands, I flinch. "OK. But the house. And all the stuff in this house. It's got to be worth, what, millions? Tens of millions?"

"Probably."

"Then *sell* it."

Is he really suggesting that I sell the house to pay for a vendetta against Nina Ross? "Maybe someday. But not yet. Not for *this.*" I hesitate, thinking, and then — *oh, it feels devious, but I can't help myself* — I hold out my hand. "I could sell the ring," I say carefully. "How much do you think it's worth? Six figures, surely?"

I watch his face, but if he knows, he's hiding it well. Instead, he scowls. "We're *not* selling my grandmother's ring. It's an heirloom."

"Well, we're not selling my great-great-grandfather's house, either. Also an heirloom."

"You don't even like this place!"

"It's more complicated than that."

He weighs the heavy poker in his hand and I feel a familiar little *ping* of fear. I wonder what's running through his mind. "Well, we're going to need to get cash *somewhere,* Vanessa. Now or later."

"I thought you had all that money in a trust in Ireland," I say pointedly. "Now would be the time to retrieve it, it seems."

He drops the poker on the hearth and walks to the doorway. "I need to get out of this fucking house. I'm going for a drive," he says darkly. He stalks out of the room and, in a minute, I hear the front door slam. I wonder if he'll bother to bring me back chicken noodle soup from the market. I have a feeling he won't.

I pick up the tea and take another sip. My stomach twists when the liquid hits it, and I feel the bile rising. I have just enough time to lurch to the garbage can on the other side of the room before my body starts ejecting the tea. The trash can is made from embossed leather, and the thin brown liquid that I regurgitate immediately sinks into the calfskin and ruins it. I'll have to throw the can away, I think feverishly, before I vomit again.

I lie there on the floor, my face pressed against the cold boards. *Pull it together,* that familiar voice whispers to me. I find myself thinking again of the Visine that I squeezed into Nina's martini, of how helpless and confused she must have felt when she was throwing up in the bushes; and it's no longer satisfying. Instead I wonder if what goes around comes around; if Nina and I have somehow been caught in an endless cycle, chasing each other in circles, snapping at each other's tails.

I can't help but wonder if we've both been chasing the wrong person.

■ ■ ■

A day passes, and then two, and the subject of money doesn't come up again. I hope that Michael's just given up the vendetta against Nina and moved on. But I find myself watching him more, noticing the way he walks around the house, touching objects with a casual possessiveness. He studies the furnishings with an attentiveness that I once ascribed to curiosity; now I wonder if he's doing inventory.

Once, I come across him standing in front of a Louis XIV commode in the parlor with his cellphone in his hand and I could swear that he had just snapped a photo of it. And when I open the armoire one day to look in the box where I keep the last of my mother's jewels (nothing particularly valuable, just the baubles with sentimental value, like her favorite diamond eardrops and a tennis bracelet that's missing a stone): Am I paranoid, or did it move three inches to the left?

And yet, after our fight, he's been all *sweetness.* He brings me tea in bed (which, after my vomiting the other day, I can't help but regard with suspicion, letting the first sip linger on my tongue while I check for the bitter taste of Visine; but of course, there's none). He cleans the kitchen unasked. He massages my back when I complain of stiffness. And I have to recognize that he's right: We *do* need money, whether for kidnapping schemes or just to pay the bills, so why am I so defensive about selling off a few antiques? Maybe I'm looking for reasons to be angry with him, because we had our first real argument and I'm scared that I'm the one in the wrong.

As I listen to him snore next to me in bed — unable to sleep because of the voices in my head — another horrible thought occurs to me. Did I only ever want Michael because *Nina* had him, and now that he's mine I'm losing interest? Or maybe love sparkles the most when it's elusive, a diamond hanging just out of reach. Once you have it firmly in your grip, the glimmer fades and it's just a cold rock tucked in the palm of your hand.

No, I love him, I *do*! I have to, because what is all *this* for if I don't?

Still. A wall has fallen between us, and we are going about our lives together but separately. I go to bed before he does now, and when I wake up in the mornings, it's a relief when I open my eyes and discover that he's not there. He locks himself in the study most of the day, coming out only for meals and the occasional walk. *What's he doing in there?*

Because I'm fairly certain it's not writing.

This morning, following a hunch, I typed a

few lines from his book into Google.

> When I look at her, her green eyes stirring
> in that feline face, the words (worlds) whirl
> within me.

I closed my eyes while the search engine churned, praying to myself. *Please please please let me be wrong.* But I wasn't. There it was, on the second page of results: a lesbian love story by an MFA student named Chetna Chisolm, published in an anthology called *Experimental Fiction for Lovers.* He'd changed a few details — a name here, a verb there — to make it sound more masculine and muscular. But it is unquestionably the same story.

Stupid me, I know, but I still feel compelled to give him the benefit of the doubt. *He didn't want to show you his writing; he said he was private about it. Maybe you badgered him so much that he felt obliged to show you something — anything — just to get you off his back. Perhaps* (optimistically) *maybe what he's really written is better?* And then I remember another fragment that he'd claimed to have written — lines from a poem, the ones he recited to me in bed the first day we were married, the writing I'd actually liked:

> We shall always be alone, we shall always
> be you and I alone on earth, to start our life.

That one is even easier to find: "Always," by Pablo Neruda. Quite a famous poem, actually. I probably read it in high school or college, and the fact that I didn't recognize it makes me feel like a fool.

At dinner, over steak and roast potatoes, I ask him how his writing has been going.

"Oh great," he says, vigorously salting his meat. "I'm really on a roll."

"When do you think you'll be done with the book?"

"Could be years. Creativity isn't something you can rush. It took Salinger ten years to write *Catcher in the Rye.* Not that I'm saying I'm Salinger. Except that maybe I am, who knows, right?" He laughs as he lifts a piece of steak to his mouth. He's pulled his hair back into a tiny ponytail, which reveals the receding hairline at his temples.

I push my own meat around my plate, watching the fat congeal into glassy little bubbles. "You know, I was remembering that poem you recited to me, the day after we got married. *We shall always be alone, we shall always be you and I alone on earth, to start our life.*"

He smiles, pleased. "Nice line, that. Guy who wrote it must be a genius."

"Neruda, right? It was Neruda who wrote it, right? Not you?"

Something flickers across his face, like he's rifling through mental file cards, trying to pull the correct one. "Neruda? No," he says. "Like I said, I wrote that. I never much cared for Neruda."

"Because I think I read it in college."

He bites into the steak and the juices run down his chin. He lifts a napkin to his face and speaks from behind it. "I think you're remembering wrong."

"It's OK if you didn't write the poem. Just . . . tell me the truth."

He puts down the napkin and looks at me with those piercing, pale eyes. How did I ever think that they were clear and open? Because right now they might as well be a wall, concealing everything going on in his head. "Baby, what's wrong?" He says it softly. "I hate to say this, but . . . you're kind of starting to worry me, with all this weird paranoia. First Nina, and then the car thing, and now *this.* Do you think you need, maybe, some help? Should we call a psychiatrist?"

"A *psychiatrist*?"

"Well." He sounds like a cowboy, gentling a horse. "You do have that family history. Your brother's schizophrenia. And your mom was mentally ill, too, yeah? I mean, think about it. It's worth considering."

I stare at him, and can't decide whether I should laugh or cry. Because how *do* I know? What if I *am* being paranoid, a symptom of the same disease of the mind that took down

566

half my family? How do I know if I'm going insane?

"No," I insist. "I'm fine."

I hide in the bathroom of my bedroom and make a phone call to the police station in Tahoe City. The front desk connects me with a weary-sounding detective, who asks me what my trouble is.

"I think my husband might be a fraud," I say.

He laughs. "I know a lot of women who say that about their husbands. Can you be more specific?"

"I don't think he is who he said he is. He said he's a writer but it turns out he's just a plagiarist. And he gave me a ring that he said is an heirloom but is actually a fake." I think I hear footsteps on the stairs, and lower my voice to a whisper. "He lies. About everything. I think."

"Does he have government identification?"

I think about this. I haven't looked at his driver's license; but he must have had it when we got married, right? And our marriage license, the one we got from the late-night county clerk in Reno — it definitely says *Michael O'Brien*. I think back to that night, wade through the memories left behind after the haze of tequila faded, and yes, I remember him handing over a driver's license, along with mine. "Yes," I say. "But a driver's license, it could be fake, right?"

I know how I must sound. And so when the detective speaks again and his voice is louder and brighter, as if he's speaking to someone in the room with him, my heart sinks. "Look. Have you considered divorce?"

"But can't you investigate him? And tell me if I'm right or not? Isn't that what the police are here for?"

He clears his throat. "I'm sorry, but it doesn't sound like he's broken any laws. If he's a problem, kick him out." I can hear him writing on paper. "Look, give me your name? I'll make a record of our conversation, in case anything escalates and you want to file a restraining order."

I almost say *Vanessa Liebling* but then I imagine the awkward silence on the other end — or worse, the suppressed laughter. *Another Liebling bites the dust, that family sure is a mess.* Instead, I hang up.

I call Benny at the Orson Institute. He sounds a little better than he did when I saw him two weeks back, as if he's surfaced above the scrim of the drugs that dull him. It's possible he's been boycotting his meds again.

"How's married life?" he asks. "Actually, I don't want to know. Talk to me about something nice."

"OK," I say. "I have a serious question for you, and it's not actually that nice."

"Shoot."

"How did you know that you were, well, *mentally ill*?"

"I *didn't* know," he says. "You were the one who knew. They had to drag me off to an insane asylum and even then I was convinced that they were the crazy ones and not me."

"So I could be schizophrenic, too, and have no idea."

He's quiet for a long time, and when he speaks again, he sounds more emphatic and clear than I've heard him in years. "You're *not* crazy, sis. Maybe you're a moron sometimes, but you're not crazy."

"But I have these wild swings, Benny. And it's been getting worse, the older I get. Like, I'm careening around a racetrack at high speed, just barely in control, my mind a tangle of thoughts, for days or weeks or months; and then out of the blue, I crash and burn, and then I can barely stand to look at myself in the mirror."

He's quiet. "Like Mom."

"Like Mom."

There's another long moment. "Mom was manic-depressive, you know, bipolar. Not schizophrenic. I know schizophrenia, and you're anything but. You're not hearing voices, are you?"

"No."

"Good. Look, go see a psychiatrist and get yourself some decent drugs and you'll be fine.

Just for God's sake, don't go out on any boats, OK? For my sake?"

"I love you, Benny. I don't know what I'd do without you."

"OK, forget it, maybe you *are* crazy."

The nausea is back, a tightness at the back of my throat that threatens to choke me, from morning to night.

It's growing clear to me that I don't know this man, my husband, at all. I feel like a hostage in my own house: Do I continue tiptoeing around him, in fear of provoking him and watching my life tumble back into lonely uncertainty? Or do I confront him, and risk angering him and making everything worse, when I don't have any *real* proof of anything?

Because he has an answer for everything, I'm learning. He will gaslight me until I question my sanity, rather than his.

All I want to do is climb into bed and stay there forever. But it feels too dangerous; it feels like giving up; and *that* voice (*her* voice) keeps telling me to *pull myself together.* So instead I get up each morning, and I smile, and I laugh at his stories about Ireland. I cook him elaborate French dinners (ones that I have no appetite to eat myself), and I rub his shoulders when he sits at the kitchen table. I walk with him down to the pier at dusk and sit with him on our bench near the boathouse, holding hands and not talking. And when he reaches for me in bed I close my eyes and let myself give in to the physical sensations and try to suppress the doubt that numbs my nerves. If I pretend everything is still OK, maybe it will magically be OK.

Except that I already know that this won't work. Magical thinking didn't save my mother, or my brother, or even my father. Why would I think that it might save me?

And there is something else, something on the periphery of my consciousness that's been nagging at me, something I can't quite put my finger on. The day after I talk to Benny, I find myself looking at the calendar, and a cold understanding spreads through me. Why I've been so nauseous, the mysterious exhaustion and the unexplainable tenderness in my breasts.

I am pregnant.

I could have an abortion, of course. This would be the rational move of someone in my current position: Make an excuse, slip out of town, have it finished within a day. But then I imagine the butter-soft gaze of a baby, looking up at me adoringly, and something fiercely protective rises in me. I know I won't be able to do it.

I can't sleep. I lie awake as Michael snores soundly beside me, thinking I can hear the spiders weaving their webs in the bed's velvet swags, the limbs of the trees *tap-tap-tap* ping at the windows. I am having a child with this man; he will be the father of my child, in my life forever. I know less about him every day; as if the person I thought I loved has been vanishing, and soon all that will remain will be the outline of a man with a void at the center.

I lie there thinking: I should kick him out, right? This is *my* home, not his. But why am I so afraid to confront him? Why do I find myself curling my hand protectively over my belly, as if anticipating a blow?

Who is he?

I didn't get a prenup. We have a child coming. He could take me for all I have. He could take *Stonehaven*!

I am so alone in this.

And then I realize: There is one person who could answer my question.

I want to laugh out loud in the dark room, because I can't believe what I'm thinking. Desperation drives you to do unlikely things; what was once unthinkable becomes the one hope that sustains you.

This might be a wild-goose chase. She might really be in Paris, or *anywhere,* it's true. But deep inside, I *know.* There's a reason I memorized that address in Los Angeles, even if I didn't realize it at the time. Something about the house, with the scarlet vines out front — I knew who lived there, from the very start. I know where I need to go now.

I'm going to go find Nina Ross.

■ ■ ■ ■

NINA

■ ■ ■ ■

33.

I have always been a sound sleeper, at rest in my convictions, but jail turns me into an insomniac. The need for constant vigilance, plus an unsettling awareness of my own culpability, conspire to keep me in an endless twilight state: never asleep, but also never quite awake, either. I float here, in limbo.

The cacophony of county jail is deafening: That's what happens when you jam thousands of women into concrete rooms that were intended to house a population half our size. We sleep in bunk beds in the common areas, feet away from the tables where we play cards and read all day. We urinate in overwhelmed toilets that clog and overflow. We stand in lines for showers, meals, haircuts, telephones, meds. At all hours of the day and night, the concrete echoes with screams and prayers and tears and laughter and curses.

There is nothing to do here but wait.

I mill around the common room in my canary-yellow prison suit, watching the hands of the clock in the cage on the wall slowly ticking away the minutes of the days. I wait for mealtime, though I have no interest in eating the gray slurry that slides around my tray. I wait for the library cart to come around, so I can pick out the least offensive romance novel on offer. I wait for lights-out, so that I can lie in my upper bunk in the semi-dark, listening to the snores and whispers of my fellow inmates while I wait for sleep to come.

It hardly ever does.

But mostly, I wait for someone to come help me.

My lawyer is a harried public defender with gray corkscrew hair and orthopedic shoes, who I meet only once, before my bail hearing. She sits across the table from me and pulls a folder off the top of a stack and examines it with purple drugstore bifocals. "They've got you for grand theft," she explains. "Your name was on the lease of a storage unit that was filled with stolen antiques. They traced a pair of chairs back to a robbery that had been reported by someone named Alexi Petrov, who then made a positive ID of you in a photo lineup."

So much for my theory that billionaires are too rich to be bothered with police reports. "How soon is my trial?"

"That. Right. Well, I hope you're patient,"

she says with a sigh. "Because you're probably going to be in here for a while. The backlog on cases right now is outrageous."

At the arraignment, the judge sets my bail at $80,000. It might as well be a million dollars, because I have no way to pay it. When I look around the courtroom, I see no one I recognize: Lachlan hasn't come, nor has my mother. I realize that they probably don't even know that the bail hearing is taking place — I have no funds in my prison account to make phone calls, so I haven't been able to get in touch. Secretly, I'm glad that they aren't seeing me like this, uncombed, exhausted, sticky with guilt and drowning in my yellow jumpsuit.

My public defender pats me sympathetically on the back and then races off to her next client, a pregnant teenager who shot and killed her rapist.

I go back to county jail and prepare to wait some more.

The days crawl past and still no one comes for me. *Where is Lachlan?* I wonder. He's the only person I know who might have the money to bail me out. Surely my mother has tracked him down by now, told him what happened, sent him to find me. But after one week passes, and then another, and he still doesn't show up, it dawns on me that he's not coming, ever. Why would he show his face anywhere near a police station, and risk being identified? Quite possibly he thinks that I'm planning to implicate him in order to save my own skin.

Or worse. I think about his muted fury when I left Lake Tahoe; his suggestion that I'd somehow screwed up everything for us both. And I wonder: *How* did *the police know that I was in Los Angeles, anyway*? It seems an unlikely coincidence that they showed up at my house, less than an hour after I'd arrived in town. Someone must have tipped them off.

Only two people knew that I was home: My mother and Lachlan. (Three, if Lisa noticed my car in the driveway.) Of the three, I know exactly which one was most likely to have made the call.

Of course it was Lachlan. Our time together ended as soon as I stopped being useful to him, and started being dangerous. The minute that safe was empty, my fate was sealed. *He never had any loyalty to you,* I think as I walk the dusty square of the prison yard, razor wire glinting in the pale December light. *You knew that. He was always going to toss you aside eventually. You're just lucky it took this long.*

So then: Who else might come for me? My mother? Lisa? The landlord of my neglected antiques shop in Echo Park, who has surely tossed my stuff on the street by now? I feel untethered, entirely cut off from the world outside. As I lie on my lumpy plastic mattress, trying to make myself invisible to anyone who might be spoiling for a fight, I see for the first time how isolated I've become, how small the circumference of my existence really is.

Finally, after three weeks in county, I get summoned to visiting hours. I make my way to a room jammed with folding chairs and chipped linoleum tables, a garish beach-scene mural painted on one wall alongside a chest of broken toys. The room is packed with life: children and grandparents and boyfriends, some wearing little but their tattoo sleeves and others in their beribboned Sunday best. It takes me a minute to pick out my visitor: It's my mother. She sits alone at a table in the back, wearing a bright green dress that gapes around her neck and hips, with a silk scarf wrapped around her head. Her eyes are red-rimmed and fixed on a point on the wall across from her, as if she's trying to center herself amid the madness.

When she sees me, she lets out a little cry and lurches up from the table, her pale hands fluttering in the air like little birds that have fallen from their nest. "Oh, baby. Oh, my baby girl."

The security guard is watching us with cold

eyes. We're not allowed to embrace. I sit down across from my mother and slide my hands across the table to take hers.

"What took you so long to come visit?"

She blinks rapidly. "I didn't know where you were! I didn't know how to find you and every time I called the inmate information hotline I just got an automated menu instead of an actual human being. There's an online database but you didn't show up in the visitation system until just last week and then I had to register and it was just . . . I'm so sorry."

"It's OK, Mom." Her hands are slight and bony in my grip, and I'm afraid to squeeze them too hard. I eye her head wrap, wondering if the radiation made her lose her hair after all. Underneath it, her face is drawn and narrow, making her blue eyes even more prominent.

"How are you feeling? Have they started the radiation therapy yet?"

She unfurls a palm in front of her face: *Stop.* "Oh, honey, let's not talk about that, please. I've got it all under control. Dr. Hawthorne is very optimistic."

"But how are you going to pay for the treatment?"

"I mean it, Nina. You have enough to worry about without thinking about *that.* That's what got you here in the first place, right?" She places her palm against my chin, pressing it hard against my jawbone. "You look terrible."

"Mom."

Her liquid eyes threaten to spill over. She sniffles and tugs a crumpled tissue from her sleeve. "I can't bear to see you like this. It's all my fault. If I hadn't gotten sick. If I had better insurance. I should *never* have let you come back to L.A. to take care of me."

"It's not your fault."

"It *is.* You should have just let me die three years ago."

"Mom, *stop.*" I lean in. "Look, have you heard from Lachlan?"

She shakes her head. "I tried calling him but his phone's been disconnected. God, that was such a mistake, introducing you two. This was all his idea, wasn't it? And now he's gone and you're stuck holding the bag."

She peers at me as if waiting for me to pile on Lachlan with her, but I'm not in the mood to place blame; I know why I'm here. It's only a small miracle I didn't get caught doing worse. I think of Vanessa: What if I had been caught taking a million dollars from her safe? It's a strange relief that I found it empty.

"I wish I had the money to bail you out of here," she hiccups. "Look, there's still about eighteen thousand left in our checking account, I know that's not enough, but maybe if I made some calls. Maybe I could go to Vegas for the weekend and try my hand at the tables, or . . ." Her eyes go big and far away and I try to imagine her at a casino bar, working her hustle in her weakened state, keeling over in a marble-tiled hotel bathroom and being left for dead.

"For God's sake, don't do *that*. I can handle it in here. It's not so bad," I lie. "Use the money you have left to cover your medical bills. That's more important. When I get out of here, I'll find legitimate work, I promise. There's got to be a local interior decorator who will hire me. I'll work at Starbucks. Anything. We'll make it work."

She presses a fingertip to the corners of her eyes. I can barely hear her whisper, "I don't deserve such a good daughter."

"Mom," I say gently. "When the treatments are over and you're healthy again, go find a real job. For my sake, please? One where you sit at a desk and get a regular paycheck. With healthcare and benefits." She stares blankly at me. "Talk to Lisa, I'm sure she'll help you out."

A bell jangles overhead, signaling that visiting hours are over. Before it even stops, the security guards are already yelling at us to stand and line up against the wall. My mother looks at me with panic in her eyes. "I'll come back soon," she calls, as I back away from the table. She blows kisses that leave pink streaks on her palms.

"Don't," I say. "It's too hard to see you in

here. Just — focus on getting healthy. That's the best thing you could do for me. Don't die while I'm in here, OK?"

I turn away so that I can't see her crying as I get in line. I can smell sweat and hair oil and astringent soap emanating from the other women standing in line with me, and I know that this must be what I smell like, too. I close my eyes and follow this scent of humanity back to the room where we will all sit and wonder what comes next, hoping we won't be forgotten.

And so I go back to waiting, but I'm no longer sure what I'm waiting for.

If there's one thing you *do* have in jail, it's time to think, and so I've found myself thinking a lot about blame. I've spent my whole life looking out, trying to locate the architects who constructed the walls of this world that I found myself in. I used to blame the Lieblings: It was easy to hate them for everything they had that I did not, and for the way they shut me out of their world. As if one door that closed in my face was the reason that everything else went sideways. But I'm finding it harder and harder to believe that now.

I could blame my mother, for dragging me along in her bad decisions; for failing to give me the leg up in life that I longed for. I could blame her, too, for failing to take care of herself, so that I had to do it for her.

I could blame Lachlan, for seducing me into joining his schemes and for turning on me when I became inconvenient to him.

I could blame society, I could blame the government, I could blame capitalism gone awry — I could tug on the threads of social inequality and watch them unravel all the way back to the beginning and pin my blame on whatever I find there.

And surely all these elements were pieces of the reason why I am where I am. But wherever I look to lay my blame, I always discover the same person: myself. I am the common denominator. There is no one path in life that is set before you, I'm starting to realize; no one is making your decisions for you. Instead of looking out at the world to find a cause, it's time for me to start looking inward.

Especially here, in county jail, where I am surrounded by the truly downtrodden — women born into circumstances that drove them inevitably into drugs, prostitution, abuse, and desperation; women who never had a chance at all — I see for the first time how fortunate I have been. I have a college degree, I am healthy. I was raised without stability or good role models but I at least knew I'd always have food to eat and a place to sleep. I always had a mother's love. That is more than so many of the women I see around me can claim.

So I suddenly find that it is hard to blame. Instead, what I mostly feel is shame. Shame that I did not do more with what I *did* have, and shame that I pretended that the road I'd taken was the only option I had.

Because it wasn't. I chose that road. I made it mine. And if this is where it took me, it's my own fault.

If I ever get out of here, I swear, I'll find a better path.

A month passes before I'm summoned to visiting hours again. I assume that it's my public defender, with news about my upcoming trial. But when I get to the visiting room, I stop short. Because the person sitting there waiting for me is Vanessa Liebling. She looks pale and exhausted, with black circles under her eyes; she is somehow simultaneously bone-thin and bloated. Her jeans strain at the waist, her sweatshirt droops at the chest. But it's definitely her. Her eyes are bulging with the effort it takes not to stare at her surroundings; her hands are jammed in her lap as if she's trying to make herself as invisible as possible.

I'm surprised by the little kick of my heart, the flutter of happiness I feel at her presence. Am I *that* desperate for a familiar face? I slide into the chair in front of her and she looks almost startled to see me.

587

"Hi, Vanessa." I grin. "It's good to see you. Really."

"Nina," she says rather primly.

It takes me a second to realize that she's used my real name. But of course, if she's here, it means she knows who I am. How did she find out? Did Lachlan tell her? "So, you know who I am," I say. "Who told you?"

She wraps her hand in the hem of her sweatshirt. "Benny figured it out," she says. "He recognized you in a photo on my Instagram feed."

"Smart Benny." How much of the truth does she know, then? How much of the rest do I want to tell her? I sit there silently, overwhelmed by the web of lies I spun, wondering where I should start unwinding them.

As I puzzle through this, I feel her eyes on me. "You've gotten thin."

"The food here leaves much to be desired."

She looks me up and down, taking in my unwashed hair and the stiff prison jumpsuit I'm wearing. "Yellow's not your color, either."

I can't help it: I laugh. "How did you find me in here?"

"Long story. I went to your address, and no one was there. But I talked to your neighbor, and she told me where you were." She looks down at her hands. "She told me about your mother, too. How sick she's been. I'm . . . sorry."

588

I sit back in my chair. "Are you really? Sorry?"

She shrugs. "I don't know how I feel about anything anymore, to be honest. The woman who murdered my mother has cancer, shouldn't I feel some kind of karmic retribution? But I don't feel good about it."

My feeling of goodwill vanishes as quickly as it came. Is this what we're going to do now? But of course it is. Our first chance to uncork and air all those years of bottled-up resentment; I dig in deep, let my voice go cold. "Your mother killed *herself,* I seem to recall."

"Your mother gave her a nice little push, though. She would never have killed herself if my father hadn't gotten blackmailed by your mother. It *destroyed* her."

Oh. I hadn't anticipated *that* turn. It makes sense that if my mother mailed her letter to Stonehaven, Judith Liebling would have come across it. But I'm not about to take on this burden, too. "Are you really sure about that? Your mother was completely fine until my mother showed up?" She blinks at this and doesn't answer. "If you're going to blame anyone, blame your father. He's the one who was having an affair."

"He was a *mark.* She targeted him."

"Your father was an asshole. He treated me like dirt and broke up my relationship with your brother."

589

"He was *protecting* Benny. And you, really. Think about it: How would you have handled being in a relationship with a schizophrenic?"

"He wasn't schizophrenic yet."

We stare at each other across the table, chairs tipped, both of us ready to jump up and leave. It is at once oddly exhilarating to finally be getting all this out in the open, and yet the words make me feel dirty and small. Why are we fighting our parents' battles as if they are our own? What will this accomplish now that they are all dead or dying, anyway?

"So." I stare daggers at her. "Exactly why are you here? To gloat at my situation?"

Her eyes flick around the room. At the next table over, a prostitute missing a front tooth is trying not to cry as her daughter, in pigtails and a *Moana* T-shirt, weeps in her grand-mother's lap. Vanessa watches them with anthropological curiosity.

"You know, I thought it would feel good to see you like this: that you'd finally gotten what you deserved. But it doesn't." She turns back to me. "Your neighbor Lisa, she told me you were arrested for grand theft."

"Antiques," I say. "I stole antiques from a Russian billionaire."

She furrows her brow. "Is that what you were going to do to me? Steal my antiques?"

I shrug. "Tell me why you're here and I'll tell you what we had planned."

"*We.*" Her face turns the color of nonfat

590

milk. "You and Michael. You were in it . . . together?"

I hesitate for only a second: Do I throw him under the bus? Then again, he already sold *me* out. "His name's not really Michael. Does that answer your question?"

She nods. She slowly draws her hands out of her lap and sets them flat on the table in between us. And that's when I see it: the emerald engagement ring, on her left hand.

"Oh no," I say, realizing.

"Oh yes," she says, stiff as cardboard. "And here's another fun fact: I'm pregnant."

I'm shocked into silence. We both stare at her hand on the table, the pale skin of her fingers, my mother's fake ring looking garish and out of place against the worn lino. *What have I done?*

"What's his real name?" she finally asks. "If he used a false identity when I married him, the marriage isn't real, right? It's illegitimate?"

I think about this for a long time. Do I even know his real name? With all the slippery lies I saw him tell, I never thought to wonder whether he was lying to me, too.

"Bail me out of here," I say, "and I'll help you find out."

Lachlan's apartment is a blank beige box: a generic stucco condo in a big complex in West Hollywood, the kind of place where the walls are thick and no one speaks to their neighbors. I've only been here a handful of times over the years: Lachlan usually came to me, which I always assumed was out of respect for my need to be near my mother. Now I wonder if this had more to do with his own desire for secrecy.

I am back in the clothes that I was arrested in: the clothes I was wearing when I drove away from Stonehaven that November morning. The shirt is still powdery-smelling from the deodorant I was wearing that day, the pants still stained from the coffee I spilled in the car. My clothes are baggy on me now; they feel like the costume of a stranger. After nearly two months in county jail, the sun is blindingly bright, the air so sweet that it's almost painful to breathe.

I direct Vanessa to park her SUV down the street from Lachlan's apartment, just to be safe, and then we walk the rest of the way to the complex. Vanessa trails a half step behind me as we walk between the buildings, her eyes darting left and right as if expecting Lachlan to leap out from behind a stand of oleander. Palm trees keen softly in the wind, lost fronds curling at their feet like plucked feathers.

"Where does Lachlan think you are, anyway?" I ask.

"I told him I was going to visit my brother."

"Benny. How is he doing, anyway?"

She keeps her eyes fixed on the sidewalk, gingerly avoiding the blackened nubs of long-abandoned gum that pepper the asphalt. "Up and down. He was doing better, but lately he's been having trouble again." A slight hesitation. "Since he heard you were back, actually. He's been rather fixated on seeing you again. He tried to break out of his institution to go look for you. In *Portland.*"

I hear a jab in the emphasis she puts on this last word, but I choose to ignore it. My heart twists at the thought of Benny, fruitlessly trying to hunt me down. Poor Benny. "Maybe I can go visit him, after."

She gives me a sideways look, full of distrust. "You'd do that?"

"Of course." The thought fills me with lightness, in fact: to be wanted. It is something to look forward to, something to hang in my future and move toward. When was the last time someone actually wanted to see me, even if it is a mentally unstable childhood ex?

I lead Vanessa around the back of one of the buildings, to where the condos face onto a narrow strip of gravel and a high wooden fence. Above the fence line, I can see the Hollywood Hills, and the eight-figure homes that perch up there among the palm trees, aloof in their isolation. Alexi's house is up there somewhere, the Richard Prince nurse still on the wall, bloodied and watchful. Already, it feels like another lifetime.

Each condo in this complex has a tiny little deck, most of which sport a bike or a plastic chair or a cluster of browning plants. Vanessa follows me to a deck at the far end of the building, fronting a unit with windows that are empty and dark. I leap lightly over the railing as Vanessa gapes at me.

"Come on," I say.

"Aren't we going to get in trouble?"

I look out at the wall of windows with their blinds closed tight for privacy. People are always so worried about strangers looking in that they forget to look out. "No one is watching."

Vanessa clambers over the rail and stands next to me, panting from the effort. "Do you have a key?" she whispers.

"I don't need one," I say. I lift the handle of the sliding door and press my shoulder against the glass, jiggling the door in its frame until the catch releases. The door slides silently open.

Vanessa has a hand pressed over her mouth. "How did you know how to do that?"

I shrug. "It's the one thing my father bothered to teach me before my mother kicked him out. He was always too drunk to keep track of his keys."

She frowns. "Who *was* your dad? Not a dentist, I take it?"

"No. He was drunk, a gambler, and a wife-beater. I haven't seen him since I was seven.

He's probably dead or in jail. At least, I hope he is."

She can't seem to stop staring at me, as if she's never seen me before. "You know, you're a very different person when you're honest. I think I like you more this way."

"Funny. I think I prefer Ashley myself. She's not nearly as cynical. And a lot nicer."

"Ashley was a fake. Really, I should have known it from the start." Vanessa sniffs. "No one is that self-possessed in real life. On social media, sure, but not in person. Ashley was always too good to be true."

We step into the cool darkness of Lachlan's living room, and draw the curtains closed behind us.

The condo is a bachelor pad, stark and severe. Leather sofa and chairs, giant TV, a bar cart stocked with expensive alcohol, vintage movie posters on the walls. The condo could belong to anyone: There are no framed photos, no trinkets on the sideboards, no bookshelf reflecting quirks of taste or education. It is barren, as if Lachlan had made a conscious decision to sweep himself off the surfaces and render himself invisible.

We stand in the gloom, waiting for our eyes to adjust. In the distance I hear a horn honking, the tinny vibrations of distant hip-hop coming through an open window. I turn in a slow circle, taking in the familiar surroundings.

"What are you looking for?" Vanessa asks.

"Shhh," I whisper. I close my eyes and listen to the room, waiting for it to speak to me. But the wall-to-wall carpeting sucks all the sound from the room and so what remains is a void. I imagine Lachlan moving through these rooms, his footsteps silent because of the rug underfoot. He must have left an imprint of his real self somewhere in between these walls, something underneath the careful mirage that he is so good at building.

There's a sideboard pushed against the wall. I throw the doors open and begin rifling through its contents: old electronics, a stack of books on human psychology, and a Hugo Boss shoebox filled to the brim with cellphones. I pick up a few phones at random and try to turn them on. Most are dead, but one still has battery life. When it flickers to life, I scroll through it. There are no photos, and the texts have been erased, but in the call history I find a long string of phone calls to a number in Colorado.

I call and listen to it ring. Eventually a woman answers, breathless and angry.

"Brian," she barks. "You have some *gall* calling here . . ."

"Sorry, who is this?"

"Brian's ex-girlfriend. Who is *this*?"

"Ditto," I say. "What did he do to you?"

The woman starts to yell into the phone so loudly that I have to hold the receiver away from my ear. "He racked up forty-three thousand dollars in charges on my credit card, took out a loan in my name *without* my permission, and then skipped town! That's what he did. You tell him that Kathy is going to *cut* his *fucking head off* if he comes back to Denver. . . . No, wait, tell me where *you* are and I am going to call the police."

I hang up.

Vanessa is watching me closely, her face wide and fearful. "Who was it?"

"A mark," I say. I look at the pile of phones in the box, repulsed. So this is what Lachlan was doing on the side, when he would disappear for weeks at a time. How many women are in there? Two dozen? Three?

She tips over the box of phones, her hair falling across her face, and I think she might cry. "Did you know he was doing that?"

"No." I put the lid back on the box and push it away with my toe. "OK, let's keep looking. You take the kitchen, I'll take the bedroom."

The bedroom is dark, blinds drawn, dust thick in the air. The drawers of the dresser are stacked neatly with shirts and chinos; the closet filled with designer suits and polished leather shoes. I dig around in the drawers and shelves, peer inside the shoes, but the only thing of interest that I find is a wooden box with a collection of a dozen expensive watches that I didn't help him steal and have never seen him wear. I am starting to realize how busy he has been without my assistance. I almost wonder why he bothered with me at all.

I can hear Vanessa in the kitchen, rifling through the cabinets, then a hollow clatter as something wood — a board? — is dropped to the floor. She comes back in with a box of McCann's oatmeal in her hands, and an odd expression on her face. "Look," she says. The box is packed tight with hundred-dollar bills, rubber-banded in thick stacks. "I found this behind the toe kick, under the cabinets. It came right off when I pulled at it."

I stare at it. "How'd you think to look there?"

"I watch a lot of TV shows, like *Criminal Minds,*" she says. "It's got to be tens of thousands of dollars. And there's six more boxes just like it."

Looking at the money in her hands I feel a quick kick of adrenaline: *money for my mother's treatment.* I reach into the box and retrieve one of the bundles of cash — gritty with cereal dust — and instinctively start to tuck it in my pocket. And then I stop. I can't do this anymore.

I hand the money back to her. "You keep it," I say. "I'm done taking other people's things."

Vanessa drops the box on the bed, as if it's radioactive. "You want *me* to steal Michael's money?"

"Jesus, Vanessa — it was never his in the first place. God knows where it came from. Just, take it. For the bail you covered. And to pay you back for whatever he's inevitably already taken from you. Did you buy him anything?"

"A car."

"Did you add him to your credit card?" She nods. "Uh-oh. Then he's probably already figured out how to draw off your bank account."

She looks like she might cry. "I can't believe I fell for his shtick. *Both* of you — you just . . . suckered me. Like a fool."

"*No.* You saw exactly what we wanted you to see. We put on a good show, tailored just for you. So you believed it: That makes you an optimist, not a fool." I pick up the box and hand it to her. "Here. You earned this."

"Well, I don't want it."

"Fine. Donate it to charity, then. But for God's sake, don't leave it for *him.*"

She picks up the box again, peers inside. Shakes it around, then sticks two fingers deep into it, and pincers out something else: a small manila envelope. She looks at me, then

599

opens it and removes a piece of paper. Unfolded, it reveals itself to be a birth certificate, soft with age. The name is almost obscured by the fold lines, and for a few seconds the strange truth fails to register. Michael O'Brien, born in Tacoma, Washington, October 1980 to Elizabeth and Myron O'Brien. There's a yellowed Social Security card in the envelope as well, and an expired U.S. passport, all belonging to *Michael O'Brien.*

He used his real name.

Vanessa's face pales. "Oh God."

I look at the birth certificate for a long time, remembering the moment in that hotel room in Santa Barbara when Lachlan rolled over in bed and suggested his new pseudonym. *Michael O'Brien.* No wonder it rolled off his tongue so easily, far more easily than *Ashley* ever fit onto mine. Did he already see Vanessa as the big fish he had been waiting all these years to hook? I wonder what he has planned for her. A cushy marriage? An even cushier divorce? Or something far worse than that?

"He's not even from Ireland," I mutter.

Vanessa leans over to study the birth certificate, touching the edges lightly as if fearful of leaving her fingerprints on it. "He's waiting for me back at Stonehaven. If I file for divorce, he's going to take me for half of everything I have." Her voice grows softer.

"I'm having his baby. I thought about not going through with it, but I *want* this baby. I just . . . don't want Michael in our lives. I need him gone before he finds out I'm pregnant. Otherwise I'll never be rid of him."

"You need to kick him out."

She peers at me from behind a tangled strand of hair. "He's not going to leave that easily, is he?"

Guilt gnaws at me, sinking its sharp teeth into my conscience: *I* dragged Michael to her front door, and then I left him there for her to deal with. "Probably not."

She stands up, a little wobbly. "I'm not going to let him drive me out of my own home."

"Are you going back there? To Stonehaven?"

She shrugs. "Where else can I go? It's my *home.*"

"Don't go alone, at least. Maybe you could take Benny with you? You could confront him together?"

"You don't know how Benny is now. He's not reliable that way."

"For God's sake, just — give it a minute. Stay at a hotel for a night or two. Come up with a better plan than *I'm asking you to leave.*" I know what I should tell her to do — *call the police* — but if she does, it'll just be a matter of time before they find the Jet-Set profile Michael and I put up and figure out that I was a part of his plans, too. I'm already in enough trouble. So I keep my mouth shut.

Vanessa picks up the oatmeal box full of money and holds it stiffly out from her body, as if it might accidentally detonate and take off a limb or two. She turns, and goes back to the kitchen.

The minute she walks away with the money, I regret giving it to her. What was I thinking? I probably just signed my mother's death warrant. And I'm going to need money for a decent trial lawyer, unless I want to spend the rest of my life rotting in jail. What is my piousness going to gain me in the end? Is a clear conscience really worth all *that*?

Too late now. But presumably he has other stashes of cash in other hiding places. I drop to the floor and peer under the bed — nothing but dust — and then lie on my back on the carpet, thinking. The last time I was here must have been six months back. After finishing a job (a B-list rap star, whom we liberated of six figures' worth of diamond-crusted finger bling), Lachlan took me out to dinner in Beverly Hills and then, too drunk to drive back to Echo Park, back to this condo. I remember waking up hungover in his bed and hearing him rustling around in the bathroom, the soft click of a door being pressed back into place. When Lachlan came back in the bedroom and saw that I was awake, he smiled and dropped onto the bed next to me; but not before I saw his face rearrange itself, as if he was taking a mental eraser to his own expression.

So: the bathroom.

I open the bathroom door and flip on the vanity lights, blinking in the sudden glare. A woman is standing there, looking back at me, her face sallow and hair wild. I almost don't recognize myself. Sometime while I was in jail, the poised and polished Nina Ross shriveled up and vanished. I'm not quite sure who the person that remains inside my skin might be. I think of Vanessa's words — *I like you more this way* — and wonder how this could possibly be true.

The medicine cabinet has nothing but toothpaste and Tylenol, a single bottle of dextroamphetamine, and a very expensive shaving kit. Under the sink, a stack of toilet paper and Kleenex, plus a supersized bottle of Drano. I pull it all out and spread it on the tile floor, just in case something might be tucked in back. There's nothing there, just some dead silverfish and a square of Con-Tact liner paper emblazoned with yellowing daisies. But I notice that the edge of the paper is curling and bent, as if it's been pushed at too many times, and when I tap on the base of the cabinet, it sounds hollow. I wedge a fingernail under the corner of the pressboard, and the bottom pops out easily.

There's a flat shirt box underneath. I tug

off the cover and study its contents, heart racing.

Eureka.

Vanessa gives me a ride back to Echo Park. Night has descended on Los Angeles, and rush hour traffic clutches at our car as we join the river of taillights heading east. Her SUV smells like leather and citrus air freshener; the seats are so deep and cushioned after my eight weeks of plastic and metal that I feel like I might suffocate in them. The silence in the car is a thick soup. I can't bring myself to ask Vanessa what she's thinking; I can't afford to care.

She slows to a stop in front of the bungalow, her eyes flicking nervously at the front door, as if wondering whether my mother is going to materialize to confront her. But the lights are out in the house, windows staring black and empty-eyed at the street.

I pause before I open the car door. "Are you going back to Stonehaven now?"

"I've got a room at the Chateau Marmont," she says. "It's too late to drive back tonight. I'll leave in the morning."

I blink. *I could go with her. I could go back to Stonehaven and clean up the mess that I made.* "Don't go," I try instead. The path of least resistance.

She turns toward me, her whitened teeth glinting sharply in the dark, and I see from

604

her impatient expression that our tenuous truce has ended. "Stop saying that, as if this mess you made can be cleaned up just by ignoring it. I mean, *honestly.* Who are *you* to give me advice on what to do?" Her breath is quick and hot. "No, really: Who *are* you, anyway?"

I don't see as much as hear her father then, in the condescending tone of her voice, her words echoing his: *Who are you?* I bristle, despite myself.

I'm no one, I think. *I'm nobody. But so are you.*

"Fine. Figure it out yourself, I don't care," I say as I fumble for the door handle.

"I *know* you don't care, you never did, only about yourself," she says flatly, and maybe she has more barbs to cast at me but I don't hear them because I'm already scrambling out of the car, away from Vanessa Liebling and Stonehaven and back toward my mother, and home.

Vanessa's headlights offer just enough illumination to locate the key under a succulent, and then she's pulling away and the darkness settles in around me as I let myself into my house.

Inside, nothing has changed; but there's a close quality to the air, still and stale, as if the house has been unoccupied for some time. I quickly walk through the empty rooms, looking for recent signs of my mother, but I find no dishes in the sink, no residual coffee in the pot, no dirty clothes on the floor. On a hunch, I look in the front closet: My mother's overnight bag is missing. I run back out to the porch and peer in the mailbox: There's at least a week's worth of mail spilling out.

Oh God: She's in the hospital.

The prison guards gave me back my cellphone when I was discharged, but the signal is disconnected — my mother didn't pay the bill while I was in jail. So I use the landline to call Dr. Hawthorne; and when I reach his answering service I leave a frantic message begging him to call me.

Three minutes later, the home phone rings, with Dr. Hawthorne on the other end of the line. I hear the clatter of dishes in the background: I've caught him during dinnertime. "Nina, it's been a while," he says, and I'm sure I can hear accusation in the carefully neutral tone of his voice. *How could you abandon your mother when she's so sick?*

"Is my mother OK?"

I hear the faint whine of a small child, which he dismisses with a hush, then footsteps moving through rooms: He takes a long moment before answering. "Your mother? Well, I wouldn't feel comfortable answering that without examining her first."

"Why was she admitted?"

Silence on the other end of the phone.

"Admitted?"

"To the hospital. I'm sorry, I've been out of town for the last few months, so I'm out of the loop. My mother didn't tell me what was going on. Has she started radiation therapy? And the, the" — I rack my brain for the word — "the Advextrix?" *How is she even paying for it?* I wonder.

A soft cough, the whispery rustling of papers. "Your mother isn't in the hospital, Nina. At least not as far as I'm aware. And she isn't taking Advextrix. She's been in remission for over a year. Her last few scans were all clear."

"Remission?" The word echoes from somewhere far away, three syllables whose meaning I suddenly can't reconcile.

"We've got our regular follow-up scan scheduled in March, but my prognosis remains optimistic. As I said before, stem cell transplants have a success rate exceeding eighty percent. I can't make any guarantees, but I would assume that your mother is doing just fine. Have you spoken with her recently?"

The phone receiver is slippery in my hand; something cold slides down my throat and lodges, like an ice cube, in my esophagus. *Mom is healthy.* A little boy shrieks in the background — *"Daddy"* — and I hear Dr. Hawthorne covering the mouthpiece as he says something soft and placating to his son.

Shaking, I replace the receiver.

Mom is healthy.

Mom has been lying to me.

I spin in a circle, looking blindly around the dark bungalow as if my mother might somehow materialize out of a closet. My hands flail, reaching out to the walls to steady myself. I seize on the sight of the file cabinet, hunkering in the corner of the dining room: her medical records. I lurch toward it and yank at the handles. The drawer resists, jammed, until it finally gives way with a metallic shudder.

I rip through folder after folder of paperwork and bills, tossing them to the floor in a blizzard of pink and yellow and blue. Tissue-thin printouts, lab results, hospital invoices: All the evidence points to how terribly sick she really was. But I know she was sick: I was *there* during those weeks in the hospital after the stem cell transplant. I was *there* during the long hours of her chemotherapy. I pulled the blond hairs from her brush and held her hand as the poisonous chemicals dripped, dripped, dripped into her veins. She was sick, she was *dying*.

But she's not dying anymore.

I don't know what I'm looking for until I come across it jammed toward the back of the drawer: a letter from Dr. Hawthorne dated last October, the word *REMISSION* jumping out at me from the middle of a string

608

of otherwise incomprehensible numbers and medical jargon. Right behind this is a folder with the dire CT scan results that she waved in front of me that day that I picked her up from the hospital. There they are, the familiar shadows lurking in the soft tissues of her body, clinging to her spine, her neck, her brain. But now that I look at the scans more closely I can see how the dates were gently rubbed out, the year smudged and doctored with pencil until a *7* was reimagined as an *8.*

She used old scans to convince me that she was still sick.

But why?

I'm still staring at the scans when I hear the sound of a key rattling in the lock, and then I'm blinking at the bright wash of light as the lamp in the front room flicks on. My mother is standing there in white pants and a batik top, a sun hat folded in one hand, frozen at the sight of me.

"Nina!" She drops the hat to the floor, and steps toward me with arms wide in order to gather me into an embrace. "Oh, my baby! But how did you manage to post bail?" I note, bitterly, the strength of her stride, the faint blush of tan on her skin, the cheeks that are once again growing plump. Now that it's no longer concealed by a scarf, I can see her hair, and it's blond and shiny. I take a step backward.

"Where have you been?"

She stops. She reaches up and tentatively touches her hair, as if remembering its unseemly health. I watch calculation creep across her face; and I think I might be ill. "The desert," she says. Her voice has gone soft and fluttery again; there's a purposeful hitch in the movement of her arm. "The doctor said it'd be good for me. The dry air."

I feel it like a needle in my heart, then, the horrible realization: *I* am my mother's mark.

"Mom. Stop it." I hold out the CT scans. "You're not sick."

The soft curve of her lip sucks in and out with her quickening breath. "Oh, honey, that's ridiculous. You *know* I have cancer." But her eyes fix on the paperwork in my hand and then slowly rise to meet mine, with a timorous wobble.

"You haven't had cancer for a year." My voice is a cracked vase, broken and hollow. "You faked the test results and pretended you were sick again. What I don't get is why you lied to me."

She droops against the edge of the couch, her hand feeling around for something solid to keep her upright. She looks down at her toenails — pale pink seashells against the white of her sandals. "You were going to go back to New York. You were going to leave me alone again." She blinks, black curls of mascara sweeping across her swimming-pool eyes. "I don't know. . . ."

"You don't know what?"

"I don't know how to take care of myself. What I'm supposed to do now." Her voice is tiny, like a little girl's, and I am suddenly exhausted by my mother, by all her years of excuses and apologies.

"Just tell me the truth," I say.

And so she does.

We sit side by side on the porch, in the shadows, where we don't have to look at each other directly. And she tells me the truth, going all the way back to the very beginning. How she first met Lachlan four years ago when she tried to steal his watch off his arm during a poker game at the Hotel Bel-Air, and he immediately recognized what she was. He grabbed her wrist and looked her in the eyes and said, "You can do better than that, can't you?"

But she couldn't, not without him. She was spinning rapidly toward her fifties and men's eyes slid over her at the bars now; they wanted the younger prettier ones and increasingly she knew she gave off a whiff of desperation. Lachlan seemed amused by the determination in her hustle, though. He enlisted her to help him in his cons, using her as a wingwoman to lubricate the path toward his female marks: lovelorn types gullible enough to hand over credit cards and account num-

611

bers. (The women on those cellphones, I realize.) After all, women trust men who have female friends to vouch for them.

For the first time in years, she had enough to cover her rent and more.

And then she got sick. She ignored it as long as she could, hoping it would go away on its own; but then she fell and got the fatal diagnosis. Cancer. Who was going to take care of her when she couldn't take care of herself? Lachlan would certainly move on without her once she wasn't useful to him anymore. She knew I would come when she summoned me, but how was *I* going to pay the bills? She wasn't stupid; she knew what kind of salary the second assistant to an interior decorator was making. She sensed, in my hedging phone calls, my own financial desperation.

Her solution was to offer me up to Lachlan. Her smart, pretty, sly daughter, conversant in *billionaire* and learned in *fine art:* Surely Lachlan could find a use for me, surely he would seduce me with just the right kind of con, train me up. He was intrigued, amused; and when he met me in person that day in the hospital, a little smitten, too. She told him the words to whisper in my ear: *Only people who deserve to lose what they have. Only take what we need. Don't get greedy.*

And it worked. I was a natural. There was grift in my blood.

"There's no grift in my blood," I tell her, my face tight against the creeping nighttime damp, my eyes fixed on the dark gravel of the driveway. It hurts to keep my eyes open. "You made me this way because you wanted me to be like *you*. If I was like you, then you'd feel better about yourself."

Her words are so small, they are nearly drowned beneath the groan of the freeway traffic at the bottom of the hill. "I wanted you to go make a grand life for yourself, far away. But you didn't, so what was I to do? I had bills. I was *sick*. I needed your help, and you couldn't help me out with the way you were living."

She hadn't quite anticipated that the hospital bills would be so huge, or that she would come so very close to death, or that I would get so wrapped up in the escalating costs of her illness that I would end up taking as many risks as I did. She also didn't anticipate that I would start sleeping with Lachlan —

"Although, of course, I could see the appeal," she says with a sly glance in my direction. I wonder if this is true; or if my seduction by Lachlan was an unacknowledged part of her plan. After all, it kept me closer to her and it kept outsiders away.

"Of course it was alarming," she continues, to see me slipping so easily into the lifestyle that she had spent so long trying to help me escape. When she didn't need my help anymore, she promised herself, she would make me leave. She would send me back to the East Coast a little savvier, a little wiser in the ways of the world, and free to make a clean life for myself. Except that last October when the test results came back negative, and the bills were almost paid off, she found that she couldn't let me go. She would lie in bed at night, feeling the poison finally ebbing from her blood, and ask herself: *What now?* Once I left she would be back where she started, with no savings, no skills, her better grifting days behind her.

So, she came up with a plan: one last big con, to pad her nest egg, and she'd let me go.

Tahoe was her idea. She'd been watching the Liebling family from a distance for years, just as I had. Stewing up a bitter little pot of vengeance, waiting for just the right moment to bring it to boil. She had read the news headlines when William Liebling died; she followed online when Vanessa moved back to Stonehaven. For twelve years, she'd been thinking of that safe full of money, the house full of precious antiques and paintings, wondering exactly how she could get inside. And now I was primed and ready, with a decade of my own festering resentment of the Lieblings just waiting to be ignited. Plus, I was far more familiar with the secrets of Stonehaven than she'd ever been.

"You knew about the money in the safe?"

And then I remember — she was there in the coffee shop with me, the day that Benny and his sister were talking about it; studiously pretending not to listen while she absorbed every word he said. But: "How did you know I had the code?"

The golden cap of her hair swings along her jaw as she shakes her head. "I didn't. But you're my smart girl." She offers a proud little smile. "I knew you'd find a way in somehow. Besides, Lachlan knows how to crack a safe if you couldn't figure it out yourself."

All she had to do was plant a seed — the recurring cancer, the massive bills about to come our way again — and then get Lachlan to give me the tiniest of pushes in the right direction. (I remembered that now, the way he so casually plucked that destination from the air as we sat in that Hollywood sports bar: *What about Lake Tahoe?*) And voilà, off we went.

"But the police were looking for me," I say. "*That's* why we left. They caught Efram and he gave me up."

She nudges a sandal off one of her feet and rubs her toes, slowly, between her palms. "There were no police. Not then. Efram moved back to Jerusalem, last I heard. It was a story we ginned up, Lachlan and I, just to convince you to leave town, and then keep you away for a time while I was" — she hesitates, the next word half-swallowed —

615

"cured."

"But they arrested me," I object. "For God's sake, Mom. I'm facing criminal charges. That's not pretend."

And this is when my mother finally cracks. I hear it first, the break in her throat; and when I turn I catch the glint of tears filling the tiny wrinkles around her eyes. "That wasn't the plan," she whispers. "I swear, it wasn't. Lachlan double-crossed me. He screwed us both."

Maybe everything would have been OK if the money had still been in the safe when I opened it. Maybe then we could have split a million dollars and walked away into the sunset, no hard feelings, bon voyage. Or — maybe Lachlan had another plan of his own all along. Michael O'Brien's plan. But my mother knew when I arrived back in Los Angeles, both empty-handed and without him in tow, that something terrible was about happen. It just happened so much faster than she'd anticipated: the knock on the door, the handcuffs on my wrists, and suddenly I was in jail.

The police hadn't found that storage unit all on their own. They'd received an anonymous tip, someone had dropped the name Alexi Petrov, and they'd put it all together from there.

Who else could have done that but Lachlan?

I'm too furious to speak. I tip my chair back

and lean against the shingled wall of the bungalow. Splinters slip through my T-shirt and tug at my skin but I don't move; I let myself feel the sting of this betrayal fully.

"You should have known. You should have seen this coming. You knew who he was — he's a *con*. How could you just *give* me to him like that?" I am trying not to cry. "You spend my whole life telling me to trust you, that all we have in this world is each other. And then you do *this* to me."

My mother is silent. I feel her body vibrating beside me, as if something inside her is spinning out of control. "I'd kill him if he gave me the chance," she says. "But I don't know where he went. He hasn't returned my calls."

"He's still at Stonehaven. He got Vanessa Liebling to marry him. Presumably he's going to make her life hell and then divorce her and take her for all she's got."

"Oh." Then, in an odd voice: "Poor girl." A car turns up our road, and we both go quiet as headlights sweep across us. I look at my mother then, and when I do I see the lie on her lips. Her smile is a twist. She is not sorry for Vanessa, not at all.

I stand up with a lurch, stumbling on the old boards of the porch.

"Where's my car?"

She gives me a blank look. "I sold it. I didn't think you were going to be getting out any time soon and . . ."

"What about Lachlan's car, the one I drove home from Tahoe?"

"That one, too." She ducks her head, and her voice pitches to a whine. "I had *bills.*"

"For fuck's sake, Mom." I fling open the door to the bungalow. The keys to my mother's Honda are sitting just inside the door, and I grab them from the dish, along with my purse.

When I turn, my mother is standing behind me. She grabs my wrist, blocking my path, and I'm shocked by how strong her grip has once again become. Or maybe she was just feigning weakness all along. "Where are you going?" she asks.

"I don't know," I say. "Anywhere but here."

"Don't leave me." In the light from the living room lamps, I can see her ravaged face, mottled with panic, mascara tears worming darkly down her cheeks. "What will I do?"

I look down at her hand on my arm, at the shell-pink fingernails and the telltale tan lines that whisper of secrets. Where *was* she last week anyway, and who was she with? But the answer is obvious, really: Once I was in jail and she saw that the Liebling money was not going to feather her nest after all, she realized she was going to have to start grifting again and found herself a mark. Exactly what scheme was she cooking up, out there in the desert? The question itself exhausts me, and I realize I have no interest in finding out the answers anymore.

"You'll do what you always do," I say. "But this time, when you screw it all up, I won't be there to help you."

VANESSA

34.

When I walk in the door of Stonehaven, he is waiting for me. A smile on his face, blue cashmere turtleneck that brings out the color of his eyes (my Christmas gift to him!), a wineglass in his hand. He stands there in the foyer, next to my grandfather's Delft vases, as if he is welcoming a guest into his home. (*His!* Oh God, what have I done? Maman, Daddy, Grandmother Katherine, I am *so sorry.*)

My husband: Michael O'Brien.

I struggle in the door with my suitcase, shaking snow from my hair, and he leaps forward to grab the bag, trading it for the glass in his hand. I find myself looking down into a dark pool of claret, my fist clenched around the crystal stem, unsettled.

"Château Pape Clément — found it in the cellar," he offers, noting the confusion on my face. "Here, I didn't kiss you."

And then his lips are on mine, the heat of him melting the snowflakes that cling to my skin so that cold droplets trickle down my face like tears. His arms sweep around my back, pressing me against the soft nap of his sweater, underneath which I can feel the placid beat of his heart. There's an unwelcome throb coming from my groin. And I *swear* the life growing in my womb recognizes his presence; something fluttering and trembling inside me. Against my will, I feel myself relax into him, the ease of just letting it all be, letting him take care of me. Of *us.*

I spent the whole long drive back from Los Angeles preparing to confront a criminal — grinding my way through the storm, thinking, *I can do this! I am capable, I am strong! I am Vanessa Fucking Liebling!* — only to find this, an attentive husband, harmless as a teddy bear. I remind myself that this — *he!* — is just an illusion. But it's such a convincing one.

Who is *Vanessa Fucking Liebling,* anyway? A basket case; a weakling, hiding behind a name that's lost all of its weight.

I pull back. "You got a haircut," I notice.

"You like it, yeah? I remembered you preferred it shorter." He runs a hand through his hair, tousling it so that a black curl falls over one eye. He smiles at me from underneath it, and I feel desire rising inside me despite myself. I follow him into the kitchen, where a fire leaps in the hearth and something roasts in the oven — a chicken? potatoes? —

that smells of home. I'm so overwhelmed I want to weep; the conviction drains from me along with the snow from my boots.

He pours himself a fresh glass of wine and then turns to look at me. I stand just inside the door, motionless, still in my coat, the wine in my hand untouched. The smile falls off his face in tiny pieces, then all at once.

"Is something wrong?" he asks.

Outside, the snow is coming down thick and fast, burying Stonehaven in a silent shroud. Three feet is expected tonight. The weather report is calling it the biggest storm of the season: a *dump.* (Oh, the irony!) I'm lucky I'm here at all: I had barely driven over the summit before the highway patrol closed the roads entirely.

Despite the warmth from the fire, the steam clouding the windows, I'm freezing cold.

I don't realize that I'm about to speak until the words are suddenly out there, like a grenade slipping thoughtlessly from a hand. (*Too soon! I'm not ready!*)

"Who *are* you?"

He places the glass of wine down, his brows puckering with mild puzzlement. "Michael O'Brien?"

"That's your name. But who are you *really*?"

He's smiling again, bemusement twitching his upper lip. "Asks the queen of duplicity."

This stops me. *Me?* "What do you mean?"

"Your career has been all about spinning lies. Putting up a pretty facade for public consumption when you're a mess underneath. Selling a life that doesn't really exist. You don't see that as a lie?"

"That doesn't *hurt* anyone!" (Does it?)

He shrugs and sits down on a stool. He settles the glass on the marble counter with a soft clink, spins it until it is perfectly aligned with the edge. "You can see it that way if you like. I'd disagree. You've been profiting off a mythical version of yourself, promoting un-achievable aspiration, giving your half-million followers insecurity complexes and dooming them to a lifetime of FOMO therapy. You're a huckster, darling. Like the rest of your kind."

My head feels thick, muddied. It's mad-dening, how calm he is. He's trying to confuse me; he's succeeding, too.

What do I say? I'm afraid of upsetting him. I still remember the horrible heft of that poker in his hand, the fury on his face when I told him I wasn't as rich as he thought I was. There are knives in this kitchen; there are heavy cast-iron skillets and burning logs and all sorts of dangerous things. I don't want a big confrontation. I just want him to *leave.*

I try again.

"Look, I've just been thinking." (*Gentle!* I make my voice sound so *gentle* and unsure; which, really, isn't much of a stretch.) "Is this really working, you and me? Together?"

He spins the glass of wine on the counter. It wobbles drunkenly, threatening to tip over and shatter; and I'm about to lunge to grab it when he stabs the stem with a finger, anchoring it in place. "What? You're unhappy, is it?"

"I was just *thinking.*" I glance at the clock over the door. It's only five P.M., but outside the kitchen windows I can't see anything, only darkness; not even the lake, not even the falling snow. The stones of the mansion absorb all the sound from the storm; it's so quiet in the kitchen that I can hear the hiss of the stove's pilot light. "I was just thinking that maybe we could use a little space from each other. Our whole relationship happened awfully fast, and in such *pressured* circumstances, and maybe we didn't know what —"

He interrupts. "You were just *thinking.* Well *I* think maybe you're *always* unhappy, yeah? I think your issues aren't with me, they're with what's going on in your head." He taps a finger to his temple. "You don't *really* want me to leave. You just can't quite believe that you don't deserve to be alone. So I'm not going to go, because I know you'd regret it. I have no intention of letting your self-doubt dictate the parameters of our relationship." He slides his hand across the counter, palm up, ready for me to slip my hand into his. "It's for your sake, Vanessa. You'd be so lonely if I left. You'd hate yourself for throwing away what we had. I'm the only person alive who really *sees* you."

I stand there, frozen in place, chewing on this. Because, oh, he's *right*. He does see me; he always did. I believed that he loved me despite my failings as a human being (or *because* of them!), but now I know that what he *really* saw were vulnerabilities that he could exploit. And that makes me hate myself even more. *He doesn't love you, because you're unlovable. He was only ever trying to con you.*

And yet he still stands there, pinning me in place with those blue eyes of his, so tight with concern.

He comes around the island to stand in front of me. "I can make you happy, Vanessa. You just have to *let* me. You just have to stop doubting me." He reaches out and plucks at the zipper of my parka, as if trying to pull me into him. And for a brief moment, this does *seem* like the path of least resistance: To just lean into him, and *let it all be*! To relinquish my agency, accept my weakness, and let him wrest control. He *is* the father of the baby that is growing inside me; wouldn't it be easier to raise a child with him than to try to do it all by myself? To try to reform him, so we can be a family? To continue to bathe myself in warm lies of convenience?

I could just give him everything he wants, instead of waiting for him to take it from me.

Why do I need any of this, anyway? Why not just hand it over to him and be rid of it?

Instead, I put my hands on his chest, and push him — *hard* — away from me.

As I do, there's an unmistakable sound from the far end of the kitchen: squeaky hinges protesting, the groan of wood scraping against the floor. One of the kitchen doors has just been flung open. And Michael and I both turn around to stare at the farthest door, the one that leads to the games room, the door that almost *never* gets used.

Nina is standing there. Her jeans are soaked from the knees down, her cheeks are slapped pink by the cold, and her bedraggled parka is dark with snow. In one hand, she holds one of the dueling pistols from the games room wall. The gun is pointed in our direction, though I can't quite tell from where I stand if she's trained it on Michael or on *me.*

The floor gives way underneath my feet, my knees buckle, and I think to myself, *This is the end, finally.*

"Don't waste your time," she says to Michael. "She knows. She knows all about you."

■ ■ ■ ■

NINA

■ ■ ■ ■

35.

We aren't born monsters, are we? At birth, don't we all have potential baked into us, the possibility to be good people or bad or just some nebulous area in between? But life and circumstance do their work on the biases that are already written into our genes. Our bad behavior is rewarded; our weaknesses go unpunished; we aspire to ideals that can never be achieved and then grow bitter when we can't reach those goals. We look out at the world, we measure ourselves within it, and become more and more entrenched in one position.

We turn into monsters without even realizing it.

That's how you wake up, twenty-eight years into life, and find yourself looking down at a gun in your hands. And you wonder where the *Rewind* button might be, the button that might take you back to the very beginning so that you can try it all over again and see if you land somewhere new.

On the other side of the kitchen, Vanessa and Lachlan are frozen in place, just a few feet from each other, their mouths shaped into identical, wordless Os. "She knows," I say to Lachlan. "She knows all about you."

Lachlan looks from me to Vanessa to me again. It may be the very first time I've ever seen visible surprise on his face. "Where'd *you* come from?"

"Jail," I say.

His brows squeeze together in a parody of confusion. "Oh, yeah?"

"Please, show me the courtesy of not pretending to be surprised."

He hesitates for a moment, then laughs. "Fair play. OK, so how'd you get out, then?"

"Posted bail, of course."

He's calculating this, still not quite understanding. "Your mum did?"

"No." I waggle the gun in Vanessa's direction, which is more difficult than I'd expected. It must weigh at least five pounds, with all that gold and engraving, and my sweaty hands keep slipping on the grip. "*She* found me and sprang me out."

"Eh?" He swivels to look at her. "Well, *shite*. I really didn't think you had it in you!"

I'm not sure whether he's referring to *her* or me. Probably the both of us, the more I consider it. His Irish accent, now that I know it's just an affectation, grates on my nerves.

Lachlan — no, *Michael,* I remind myself —

634

takes an exaggerated step backward from Vanessa. I have to make a choice then — at whom should I point the gun? — and I note the relief on his face as he realizes that I've left it trained on *her.* Our original mark. The privileged princess that we came here, together, to con. I watch his eyes flicker between us, and then settle on me, with a tiny smirk. He's shifted his alliances back to me, and I am reassured to be back in his graces again. At this point, that's my only hope.

I look down the barrel at Vanessa and she is trembling as she stares nervously back at me, question marks in her eyes. I summon all those years of Liebling hatred, bring them back up to the surface — *Who are you?* — and glare steadily at her. She shrinks under my gaze, until she is just two moist, green pools of panic, ready to spread across the floor.

When I turn to look at Michael he is smiling at me, a watching smile, tight and false. He's waiting for me to show my hand.

"She knows," I say again. "She knows what we were up to. She knows you're not who you are pretending to be."

He doesn't even look at Vanessa; it's as if she isn't even there. "All right. Let's talk. What's your game, Nina? Why did you bother coming back here, then? Why didn't you just fuck off to Mexico while you could?"

"With a felony theft conviction hanging

635

over my head? How far would I get? And about that — I need money, a lot, to pay for a good trial lawyer. Because of *you,* darling. Thanks for that."

"No hard feelings, yeah?" He is showing far too many teeth; I can see the strain on his face. "I hope you didn't take it personally. I just saw a better opportunity. You always thought too small. Always so worried about not taking *too much.* It wasn't working for me anymore. You and I — We'd run our course, don't you think?"

Vanessa has started slowly inching her way backward, one tiny step at a time; her hand groping behind her as if feeling for the handle of the kitchen door. "Go sit down over there," I bark at her. I wave the gun at the table on the other side of the room.

She goes and sits, like an obedient pet.

"Here's the deal. Whatever it is you've got going on with *her*" — I gesture at Vanessa — "I want in on it. Or I'll go to the police. I'm sure they'd be happy to give me a plea deal if I turned you in, too. You're a much bigger fish than I am."

"For fuck's sake, Nina." He looks down at his cashmere sweater, plucks an invisible thread from the front. "Sure, right. I'll cut you in. Except you've just gone and cocked it all up with this little trick, haven't you? What am I supposed to do now? Like you said, she *knows.* Besides, it turns out she doesn't actually *have any money."*

"I do have money," Vanessa objects softly. Her hair has fallen out of her ponytail and it covers her face so I can't see her expression. She's got her hands placed flat on the table, pressing hard, as if trying to anchor herself in place.

Michael turns to look at her, with a snarl of disdain. "You have this heap of a house. You have *antiques*. Not the same thing at all."

"We'll take the antiques, then," I say to Michael. "We'll find a way."

But Vanessa swings her head and peers up through the curtain of hair. "But I *do*. I do have cash, *lots* of it. At least a million. And jewels, my mother's jewels, worth *way* more than that. I'll give it all to you if you'll just *leave,* the both of you."

Michael hesitates. "Where is it?"

"The safe."

Michael throws his hands up. "My love, you're a terrible liar."

"The safe was empty," I offer. "I already looked inside."

Vanessa's hands are pressing down so hard on the tabletop that they are turning white. Her eyes are pink and wet. *"Not* the safe in the study. The safe on the *yacht."*

"Where the hell's the *yacht?"* Michael asks.

"My mother's yacht. It's dry-docked. In the boathouse."

"Why the hell would anyone put a safe on

a *yacht*?"

"Of course yachts have safes. Have you ever even *been* on one?" She straightens a bit in her seat; shoulders pulling back, almost indignant. "Where *else* are you supposed to keep your valuables when you're cruising around Saint-Tropez?"

Michael glances at me, looking for backup. "Tahoe isn't exactly Saint-Tropez."

"Well, there's still a safe on our boat. And that's where Daddy stashed a lot of the valuables because he figured people like *you* would never be smart enough to look *there.*"

She sounds like her father again; the cool contempt in her voice makes my stomach curl reflexively. I study her face, looking for signs of prevarication — shifting eyes, a hitch in her breath — but there's nothing to suggest that what she's saying is a lie. She stares steadily back at me, her whole demeanor suddenly calm and collected.

"Wouldn't it have been easier to get a safety-deposit box?" I ask.

She shakes her head. "He didn't trust banks."

I turn to Michael. "Look — it can't hurt to go check it out. If it's true, it would be easier than the antiques."

Michael's eyes drift to the window, as if expecting to see a boat parked down on the pier, but of course there's nothing to see but snow swirling in the pitch-black night. "You

638

want to go out in *that*?"

"It's just snow," Vanessa says. "If we go down and get it now, will you get the hell out? Tonight?"

Michael turns to me. I shrug: *Why not?*

"Sure," he says. "We'll go."

We trudge across the great lawn and down the hill in the dark. The snow is so deep already that it sucks at our boots, fills our socks; we lurch and stumble and sink, leaving a path of destruction behind us. Vanessa leads, a few feet ahead of me, instinctively feeling her way down the path.

It feels good to be so cold; it dulls the feverish voices that vibrate inside my skull. When I breathe, it hurts, but at least it means I'm still breathing.

Michael falls into step beside me. The snow is falling fast and thick, but the storm is windless and still. It's so deadly silent out here that I can hear the crunch of each footstep, as the fresh snow gives way to the harder crust beneath.

Michael grabs my arm for balance, reeling toward me to mutter in my ear. "Hate to tell you this, but that thing's not loaded."

It's too hard to walk with the gun in my hand; I've tucked it into the waistband of my soggy jeans so that I have both hands for balance. "Actually, it is," I say. "I checked."

He scrunches his face. "Huh. Wonder when

she did *that.*" He steps into a snowdrift up to his knee, and swears. "Do you think there's actually a boat? Or you think she's trying to pull something over on us?"

"Like *what*? She's about as threatening as a kitten. Besides, there's two of us and one of her. What could she possibly do to us?"

"It's weird, is all." He sighs. "She's a fucking liar, that one. Said she had no money."

I sink so deep in a drift that my boot comes off my foot. I reach into the snowbank and retrieve it, jam it back over my soggy sock. "So what *were* you planning? You might as well tell me."

He scowls. "It was gonna be divorce, right? Get hitched, no prenup, simplest con there is. Legal, even! California is a community property state, right? I figured, probably couldn't get *half* of everything she had, but I'd at least get her to give me a couple million just to go away. But then she finally informs me that she has no *real* money, it's all tied up in the fucking house. Which makes everything a lot harder, divorce-wise, yeah? Not like her lawyers are going to let me walk off with the keys to Stonehaven. So *then* I figured, I'd play nice husband instead, get her to rewrite her will and leave everything to me. Wait it out for a bit, and then . . ." He shrugs.

"Kill her." I fail to keep the disgust out of

my voice.

He gives me a sideways look. "Don't get like that. For chrissake, isn't that what *you're* getting at, here? Waving that gun around? Because, darling, we're not going to be able to just *let her go.* She'll go straight to the police."

"I'm aware of that." But he shrugs, skeptical, as if he can't quite envision me as a murderer. And I wonder, with a jolt of panic, if this is the gaping hole in the plan, after all: the plausibility of me killing in cold blood, if I needed to.

Snowflakes are catching in his eyebrows; he wipes his face violently with the arm of his coat. "Jaysus, this *fucking* snow." He stumbles and rights himself. "Just so you know, you can't just *shoot* her, either. It's going to have to look like suicide, yeah? Good news is that her family is barmy — her mum offed herself, and there's that schizo *brother* of hers. No one's gonna question it."

"You already had it figured out, then. How you were going to do her in."

"Sedative in the martini, knock her out, string her up from the staircase. Boom: *She hung herself.* Hell, I thought maybe I'd even talk her into doing *herself* in. She's halfway there already, the loony git." He kicks petulantly through another hillock of snow. "That plan won't work now. We'll have to come up with another way. An accident, maybe. She

641

fell in the lake and drowned?"

The lake appears out of nowhere, a black void suddenly opening up at our feet. Vanessa is waiting for us on the edge of the shore, her hands jammed in her pockets, pale face moonlike in the dark. Her hair is so full of melted snow that it's starting to freeze into icicles around her face.

"There." She points to a stone boathouse, just a few steps farther down the shore. The building huddles there in the trees, buried in snow, waiting.

Michael kicks the snowdrifts from the threshold of the boathouse so that we can pry the door open (the wood splintering under his grip) and then we're standing inside, out of the storm. The interior is cavernous, a damp stone cathedral. The lake softly laps at the dock under our feet; there's a rustling coming from up in the eaves. Something huge looms above us in the dark: a yacht, battened down for the winter. The silvery script along its side reads *Judybird.*

Michael and I stand staring dumbly up at this strange apparition. Then there's a terrible grinding sound that echoes off the stones and sends me reaching for the gun. But when the spotlights click on overhead I see that it's just the rusty boat-lift hydraulics, slowly lowering the yacht to the lake's surface.

Vanessa stands at the edge of the boathouse,

her hand on a switch, watching the *Judybird* sink down, down, down, until finally it's back in the water and rocking gently in its own wake.

"How about that," Michael mutters.

I've got the gun out again. I keep it loosely trained on Vanessa as she walks around the yacht, unsnapping the protective canvas cover sheathing the back of the boat with surprisingly steady hands. She heaves the cover to the side of the deck, wipes dirt from her cheek, and then turns to us.

"You coming?"

We climb aboard.

The *Judybird* isn't an enormous yacht, as far as yachts go, but it's obvious that it was once a fairly impressive boat, all polished wood and chrome. Neglect has done a number on it. On the *Judybird*'s upper deck stuffing oozes from cracks in the leather upholstery, and yellow stains mar the paint along the bridge. The aluminum safety bars that line the prow are rusty. An orange lifeboat lies deflated on the lower deck, its wooden oars scattered across the stern.

What kind of people just leave their yacht to rot in the dark? I wonder. *Such wasteful decadence.* A familiar coil of resentment unspools in my chest and I seize it: *Use your anger.* I hoist the gun even higher. My hand isn't sweaty anymore.

A few feet from where we stand in the stern, there's a door; and when Vanessa opens it, we can see a staircase vanishing down into the darkness. The boat's cabin. A rank smell — mold, rot, forgotten things — rises up through the open door.

"There are two bedrooms down there, plus a living room and a galley," Vanessa says. "The bedroom on the right — that's where the safe is. Just above the vanity, you press the wooden panel and it swings open."

Michael turns to Vanessa. "What's the code to the safe?"

"My mother's birthday: 092757," she says.

He peers down the stairwell. "It's dark. Is there power down there?"

"There's a light switch, at the bottom of the stairs."

He swivels his head and looks at me. "I'll go check it out. You keep an eye on her."

He takes a step down the stairs, ducks his head to avoid the low doorjamb, and lifts his phone over his head. The flashlight sheds a thin blue light into the hallway below. He hesitates, takes one more step — *my pulse is going wild* — and another and he's clear of the door and that's when I kick Michael square in the rear.

He pitches forward, falling down the remaining steps — I catch just one flash of his expression of shock, illuminated by the tumbling light of his phone — and then

Vanessa is beside me, heaving the door closed and shoving an oar through the handle to jam it shut.

Vanessa and I stand on the deck staring at each other, motionless, just listening.

There's a groan, and then a howl of anger. *"Bitches!"* His voice is muffled. I hear him running up the steps, a lopsided gait — he probably twisted his ankle — and then I can hear him banging on the other side of the door. *"Fucking let me out!"*

His Irish lilt is finally gone.

I turn to Vanessa. She's breathing heavily, her fingers clawing at the skin on the back of her hands, leaving bloody welts. "Will the door hold?"

"I think so?" She doesn't look convinced.

It's a relief to finally put the gun down, to shake out my shoulder and flex my palm until the circulation comes back to my hand. "OK," I say to her, "let's go."

Vanessa finds another switch in the boathouse wall and the rolling door at the far end of the building starts to rise, creaking and groaning in its track. Halfway up, the door gets stuck — maybe from ice, or maybe it's just rusted shut from lack of use. Vanessa's eyes go wide with alarm, and I think, *Oh God what now,* but then the door shudders and lifts free. In a minute, we are peering straight out at the lake, where the snow is coming down so thick you can barely see five feet in front of you.

Another little lurch of panic, as Vanessa fishes a key from a drawer in the cockpit and turns it in the ignition and nothing happens; but when she tries it a second time, the engine kicks to life and roars. The *Judybird* vibrates in its berth, like a dog straining at the leash.

She turns off the lights on the boat, and we motor slowly out into the storm.

I can hear Michael slamming around the locked chambers belowdecks, screaming curses. The oar in the handle shudders, but holds. He starts banging on the ceiling, making the fiberglass vibrate under our feet.

"You OK?" I ask Vanessa. She sits in the cockpit, steering straight out into the veil of snow like she's done this every night of her life. She's eerily calm now.

"Oh, I'm fine! I'm *great!*" But I can see how tightly she's gripping the wheel, the welts on her hands purple and raw from the cold. "You? You were so *convincing,* but it also looked like you might lose your lunch back there in the kitchen."

"I almost did," I say. She laughs, a giddy little trill, although I wasn't trying to be funny. I wonder whether she is completely disconnected from reality, or if she's just in denial about what's happening. Michael thumps once — hard — directly underneath her chair and her eyebrows shoot up, then settle back in place.

Vanessa drives straight out into the dark, and I pray that she knows where she's going, because I can't see a thing ahead of us. When we're clear of the dock and a little ways out into the lake I turn around to look back at the lights of Stonehaven, but the shoreline has vanished entirely behind a curtain of snow. We might as well be on the moon.

After a few minutes, Vanessa stops the boat. How far out into the lake are we? Maybe a half mile? I can't tell, but it's certainly far enough. In the short time that we've been out in the storm, a layer of snow has accumulated on the boat's exposed surfaces. Down belowdecks, Michael has finally gone quiet, so when Vanessa cuts the motor an eerie stillness falls over the *Judybird.* The boat slaps up and down in the waves and Vanessa turns to meet my eyes and everything is *so quiet.* It feels like the calm before the storm; except that the storm is already raging all around us, snow coating our hair and catching in our eyelashes and melting on our freezing hands.

I think about what is supposed to come next.

"You need to go to the police," I had said to her. "They'll arrest him. Maybe there's already a warrant out for his arrest, somewhere."

I sat on the bed in Vanessa's room at the Chateau Marmont. My heart was bruised and hollow. The long day had left me with nothing but this one conviction: I *did* care about the mess I'd made. I cared enough to help Vanessa even if she didn't realize that she needed me to do it. I cared enough to help her, even if it hurt me.

Vanessa clutched the neck of her hotel bathrobe tight around her neck, covering the vulnerable hollow of her throat. "I already called the police," she said. "They laughed at me."

"Right, but now you have *me*. I'll testify against him."

She blinked at me. "But wouldn't that mean you'd be implicated, too? As an accessory?"

"In all likelihood." I nodded and I swallowed, because *that* — another decade to add to my upcoming prison sentence — was what I had come to terms with during the drive from Echo Park to the Chateau Marmont. I was prepared to be noble, to take my lashes, to finally do *the right thing.* But she was already shaking her head, dismissing the idea out of hand.

"No. No police. No big trial. No publicity. Think about it — Vanessa Liebling, taken in by a hustler? It'll be *everywhere, Vanity Fair, New York* magazine, all the blogs. My whole family history dragged out into the light for everyone to gawk at. I'll be absolutely destroyed. Benny, too. And then my baby, she'll grow up and find out everything about who her father was. I can't do that to her. She can't ever know she's an O'Brien; she has to be a Liebling." She must have noticed the baffled expression on my face — *that* was what she was worried about? — because she shrugged, straightened up a little. "All I have left is my name."

"OK, then. We go up there and confront him together. Two against one, maybe he'll leave on his own accord."

She shook her head again. "You said it yourself, he's not going to just leave because we've asked him politely, is he? I think he's fully capable of violence, don't you? You should have seen what he did with my great-uncle's sword." The tendons of her neck worked up and down. "Besides, even if he does leave, I'll still have to spend the rest of my life hiding from him — no way could I ever be online, because what if he somehow figures out that we have a kid together? He'll come back, he'll use her to get at me." One of her hands crept to her stomach, cupped it protectively. "You know it's true. Nothing is ever going to stop him as long as he thinks he has power over me."

She leaned in closer to me. She blinked at me, her breath sweet in my face. "We have to do something drastic. We have to show him that he can't mess with us. We need leverage, something that will really scare him."

Silence fell on the room. Below, in the courtyard, a group of teenagers giggled in the hotel pool; a wineglass shattered on stone. I looked over to the console by the door, where I'd left the bag I'd brought with me: a paper lunch sack, stuffed with papers.

"I think I might have something," I said.

I pick up the gun again and point it at the door while Vanessa creeps forward and removes the oar, then flings the door open. We both flinch, waiting for Michael to explode out the door. There isn't anything dangerous down there — at least Vanessa didn't think there was — but who knows what could be repurposed into a weapon? A lamp, a fork, a coffee table.

Instead, we see him sitting there at the top of the stairs, blinking out at us from the dark.

He stands, his eyes moving from the gun in my hand to the lake beyond my shoulder, likely trying to pinpoint exactly where we are. Then he steps out onto the deck, his shoes squeaking in the snow.

"So, what now?" he snarls. "You gonna make me walk the plank?"

Vanessa and I look at each other. I recall Vanessa's shivery whisper as she sat beside me in the hotel room last night, the fragility of her voice undercutting the darkness of her plan. (Vanessa, the privileged heiress, a natural con underneath it all.) *First he has to think you're on his side, so that he drops his guard,* she said. *I'll figure out a way to get him out of the house and down to the boat. Out on the lake, he'll be vulnerable. Out there, we'll be in control. But here's the thing: He has to think we are capable of killing him.*

"It would probably be easier just to shoot you," I say now.

"This is madness." He shivers, blows on his hands, looks imploringly at Vanessa. "You could've just let me go, for chrissake. I'm no threat to you."

Vanessa moves a little, so that I'm standing in between him and her. "I'm not so sure that's true."

"*You,* then." He turns to me. "Shit, Nina. You've given me a good scare. So, OK, you win. Take me back to Stonehaven and I'll go away. Let's just the both of us *forget* that we ever met this loony bird and her tomb of a home."

"Shut *up!*" Vanessa screams at him. I can hear her breath accelerating, hot little puffs just behind my ear, she must be near hyperventilation; and I think, *Please pull yourself together.*

He ignores her, flaps his hand at her as if she's an annoying little gnat that can be dismissed with a wave.

651

Meanwhile, I say nothing, and he must sense that as an opportunity — after all, I am still the one with the gun — because he keeps talking, his voice hoarse and dry. "You don't need her. I have money hidden away, we could share that." And then: "Why are you siding with her anyway? She *hates* you. You hate her!" Finally, creeping closer, his voice soft and cajoling (the same voice that has seduced more women than I can count, coaxed them away from rationality, spun them into self-doubt — now finally turned against *me*): "You *love* me. I love you."

I am hypnotized, half-frozen, but *this* finally jolts me back to life. "Love? Hardly. You called the *cops* on me. You conspired with my *mother.* I was just another mark you could use to your advantage."

He laughs. "OK. Touché. But murder is a whole different playing field, my love. Do you really have it in you to *kill* me, for God's sake?"

"Do *you*?" I reply.

He doesn't answer. The wind has picked up. His breath billows in ghostly plumes around him as he squints at me through the swirling snow.

I feel Vanessa's hand pressing gently against the base of my spine. *Go on.*

"Look: We *could* kill you, if we wanted to," I say. "But here's what we're offering you instead. We're going to drop you off at the

Chambers Landing pier, and you can make your way into town by yourself from there. You will leave Tahoe entirely, as soon as the roads clear. You will not return to Stonehaven, or make any kind of contact with Vanessa *or* me, ever again. If you do, we will send copies of these to the police."

At this, Vanessa reaches into her parka, and retrieves a paper sack from the inside pocket. She holds it out in the air between us all, and then — as if unclear what else to do — she simply lets go. The bag falls to the deck; and out slide the documents that I found hidden in the bathroom of Michael's condominium.

In the pile are fake identity papers that date back a dozen years: passports, driver's licenses, bank paperwork, government IDs. There's a passport for Lachlan O'Malley in there; but also one for Lachlan Walsh, and another one for Brian Walsh, and one for Michael Kelly with stamps from several South American countries. Driver's licenses for Ian Burke, Ian Kelly, Brian White, all with the same familiar face but different states of origin. There are even two marriage certificates in the pile — Arizona and Washington, neither with names I recognize — and a University of Texas college ID for Brian O'Malley dated 2002. In the photo, his hair is in a buzz cut and he's wearing a muscle tee.

"Fuck *me*." He leans over to study the pile,

his chest rising and falling.

"And there's this, too." I fish a small tape recorder out of my jacket pocket. "I recorded everything you said on the walk down to the boathouse just now. About your exact intentions for Vanessa. Behave yourself, or the police will get that, too."

"Blackmail, eh?" His eyes slide up to meet mine. "That's a new one. Your mom teach you that trick?" He smiles, as if amused, but I can see the tightness in his lips, the churning behind his eyes.

On the very top of the pile of IDs, now dusted with snow, is the passport for Michael O'Brien that we found in the oatmeal box. He leans down to pick this up, wipes the snow from it, and gazes thoughtfully at the photo. I wonder what he's seeing as he looks at his one true self.

And then he turns, and flicks the passport over the side of the boat.

Instinctively, I lurch to catch it. My focus shifts just long enough for Michael to leap forward, quick as a snake, and knock me sideways. My boots lose their grip on the slippery deck and I'm falling, the gun flying out of my hand; and by the time I right myself it's in Michael's hand and he has it pointed straight at *me.*

He doesn't even hesitate before pulling the trigger.

The snow falls in wild spirals, tossed by the

654

currents of the storm. The lake laps greedily at the hull of the boat. The gun goes *click.*

Nothing happens. But of course it doesn't — it isn't loaded. Why take chances when it didn't need to be? We were never actually going to *kill* him.

Michael looks down at the gun in his hand, a stupid expression on his face. He pulls the trigger again — *click* — and then once more, panic creasing his face.

On the third click, Vanessa slams him in the side of the head with the lifeboat oar.

"Go fuck yourself!" she screams. When he falls, stunned, to the deck, she hits him again, and there's a sickening crunch that can only be the sound of a cracking skull. She's still screaming and hitting him — *"fuck yourself go fuck yourself"* — when I wrestle the oar from her hand and wrap my arms around her chest to stop her from screaming. She shakes in my arms, fighting to break free. She's soaking wet, and for a moment I think that this is from the melting snow until I realize that no, she's *sweating.*

Blood is pooling along the fiberglass under Michael's head, staining the snow underneath him pink. We stand there for what feels like forever, as Vanessa's breath slows; she stops quivering, and stills, and I finally release her. She walks over to Michael and looks down at him. His pale blue eyes stare sightlessly back up at her.

"Well," she says softly. "That's it, then."

I run to the side of the boat, and vomit.

Vanessa is the one who takes care of the rest, with a crisp efficiency that shocks me. How does she know how to do all this? The bathrobe that she retrieves from the bedroom closet and ties around Michael's stiffening body; the heavy boat manuals that she tucks in the robe's voluminous pockets; the way she knows to push his body off the side, rather than the back, of the deck. "We don't want him getting stuck in the motor," she explains flatly.

At first, Michael's body floats, the white silk bathrobe wrapped around him like a mummy's shroud. Snow gathers on his back, which still bobs above the surface of the lake. But then it's not even a minute before his clothes grow sodden with lake water; and then — just like that — he slips under and is gone.

I sit shivering on the side of the boat, numb to the snow that is melting on my face, and watch him sink.

Vanessa mops up the blood with a rag and Windex from the utility closet — it wipes so easily off the fiberglass, no worse than a spilled cocktail — and then tosses it in the water after him, along with the bloody oar and all Michael's forged documents. Then she wordlessly starts the engine and slowly turns the boat around, and we start motoring back through the storm.

As we drive away, I look back out at the water once more and think I see something slick and dark floating out there in the infinite blue. A log, maybe. A mysterious creature, risen up from the depths of the lake. A drowned man.

And then it's gone.

I look away, and back toward the shore, and wait to see the lights of Stonehaven.

EPILOGUE

Spring arrives early at Stonehaven. We throw the windows open on the first day that the temperature tops sixty, let fresh air into Stonehaven's rooms, chase out the must of another winter. The last crusts of ice are still melting in the shade under the trees, but in the flower beds near the house the first crocuses thrust spikes up toward the sun. One day we wake up and the great lawn, previously brown and matted, has erupted in a carpet of bright green.

We move cautiously around the house, the four of us, blinking in the clear spring light, still as skittish as fawns around each other. Only one of us is fearless enough to fill the house with shrieks and giggles and wails of disappointment, but she's only seven months old. Her name's Judith, but we all call her Daisy; and we dote on her, mother, grifter, and broken brother alike. Daisy looks like a doll with her flaxen hair and her fat pink

658

cheeks and those pellucid blue eyes, the last of which none of us ever comments on, although we all occasionally experience a shiver of discomfort when they fix directly on us.

I've been spending my days going through the rooms of Stonehaven, one by one, documenting the contents of each — this time, with the owner's permission. Each painting, each chair, each silver spoon and porcelain clock is to be noted, described, photographed, cataloged, and archived. I'm already on my fourth binder. Sometimes I'll look up and realize that I've just spent five hours researching the provenance and history of a Bourbon-era armorial vase, so consumed with cartouche and fleur-de-lis that I forgot to eat lunch.

So far, after six months of work, I'm on room sixteen out of forty-two. Vanessa and I haven't discussed what will happen once I've finished them all; but I have at least a year to figure it out.

The job was Vanessa's suggestion. She came to see me during prison visiting hours, two months before I was released and only a few weeks out from her due date. Her swollen body barely fit in the molded plastic seat of the visiting room chair. She was one of those women whose bodies cling to pregnancy, and every part of her — hair, skin, chest, belly — seemed to be bursting with life. I wondered if she was making up for all those years of fashion-induced starvation.

"I'm offering you a job as an archivist," she said, not quite meeting my eyes. "I can't pay a lot, but I'll give you room and board and cover your expenses." She picked at her fingernails, glossy from prenatal vitamins, and smiled nervously at me. "I'm looking into long-term options for Stonehaven. I might donate it to this organization my mom used to support, Mental Health Association in California. They're interested in starting a school for kids with special needs. Like, you know, Benny?" She flashed a nervous smile at me, and I thought, *Oh, so that's going to be her penance.* "Anyway, it's going to take a while, and in the meantime I'm going to get rid of a lot of the antiques. I need someone to help me figure out what to sell, what to keep, and what to donate." Another pause. "I figured you've probably paid more attention to the contents of that house than anyone has in decades."

At first, I wasn't so sure about this. I'd assumed I'd head back to the East Coast after my release, and see what kind of art world jobs my damaged record might allow. I wanted to get far away from the West Coast and my sordid history here, start over fresh. And it was possible she was just trying to buy my silence. But about what? We both had a lot to lose with exposure.

The more I thought about it, the more Vanessa's idea made sense. We were tied together now, she and I; even if I moved four thousand miles away I would never be able to escape that bond. Vanessa was probably my best shot at reclaiming some legitimacy in life. Plus, if I was going to be honest with myself, wasn't there also a little surge of excitement at the idea of really getting to study Stonehaven up close? To truly learn its secrets after all these years?

"You trust me not to steal the silver?" I said. "Remember, I'm a convicted felon."

She gave me a shocked look, then laughed, a slightly hysterical sound that broke through the cacophony of the visiting room. "I think you've already paid your debt to society."

I arrived back at Stonehaven eight months after my trial and conviction. I'd been sentenced to only fourteen months, thanks to the work of the expensive attorney that Vanessa hired on my behalf (paid for, I'd later learn, with the money we found in Michael's kitchen). Instead of a felony, my grand larceny charge was reduced to a misdemeanor. With good behavior and time served, I was back at Stonehaven by November, six weeks after Daisy was born, almost exactly a year since I'd shown up on the same doorstep as *Ashley.*

Benny was living here by then, too, helping

his sister with the baby. Vanessa had finally talked him into moving out of the Orson Institute and in with her. It was to be a "trial run" at independent living, which so far seemed to be fairly successful, even if the ghost of failure always lingered in the stones: *What happens if?* But nothing had happened yet, and in the meantime, they were both so careful with each other. Vanessa hovered over Benny constantly, watching as he took his meds, buying him notebooks and fancy pen sets for his drawings. (Mostly, now, he drew Daisy.) He, in turn, was a consummate uncle, content to spend endless hours reading *Pat the Bunny* and *Mr. Silly,* drawing on the infinite patience of someone who has spent the last decade of their life just watching bugs crawl.

They both seemed happy, and honestly, I was happy for them.

He and I went on a long walk on my first day back, down to the shore — both of us going a little stiff and awkward as we passed the caretaker's cottage — where we sat watching the boats out on the lake. He seemed a little slower, dulled, not quite the Benny I remembered; and yet something of the teenager I'd known was still there, too, in the way he smiled sideways at me, his neck flushing with embarrassment.

"I'm surprised to see you here," I said. "I thought you said you'd never come back."

"I didn't think I would, but someone needs to keep my sister sane so I figured who better to do it than someone who is even less sane than she is?" He picked up a flat stone from the shore and threw it out toward the water, with a schoolboy flick of the wrist that sent it skipping four times before it sank. He turned and smiled awkwardly at me. "Also she promised me that *you* were going to be here."

His smile spoke of heartbreak and loss but also a bit of hope; and just like that I understood the *other* reason that Vanessa had invited me back here. It wasn't for my incomparable curatorial knowledge of antiques, or even to buy my silence. I was a lure for her brother. I was there to help glue her family back together.

Maybe that was to be *my* penance. If so, I thought maybe I was OK with that.

"I'm not going to moon over you or anything, if that's what you're worried about," he continued. "I'm not delusional. I mean, I *am,* but not that way. I don't expect you to save me, or anything. It'd just be nice to be friends again, you know?"

"I do." I thought of the superhero Nina that he had once drawn of me, the one who could slay dragons with her fiery sword. I wondered if maybe I'd finally lived up to the promise of his drawing, and my dragon was currently floating at the bottom of the lake. Or maybe *I* was the dragon, and I'd slain my worst self;

and now that there was nothing left to slay I could finally put the sword down and *just be.*

"I'm sorry," he said, fingering another rock that he'd plucked up from the shore. "I'm sorry that I didn't stand up to my father when he humiliated you that day. I'm sorry that I let my parents make you feel bad about yourself, and I'm also sorry that I didn't tell you that I was sorry sooner."

"God, Benny, it's OK. You were a kid," I said. "I'm sorry that my mom was an opportunistic thief who did terrible things to your parents."

"That part wasn't your fault."

"Maybe. But I still need to apologize for a lot more than you ever will." He gave me a funny look, and I wondered — not for the first time — how much of the rest he suspected. *He knows nothing about what you and Michael were up to,* Vanessa had told me before I arrived. *As far as he's concerned, Michael just up and vanished on me, and I tracked you down in order to apologize for doubting you. That's what he wants to believe, so let him.*

I reached out and squeezed his hand, his fingers as long and soft as a child's. He smiled at me, and squeezed back.

We sat there quietly for a long time, watching the speedboats, and I thought maybe I could finally be happy, too.

■ ■ ■ ■

And I still do, although there are nights when I wake up in a sweat, something visceral and cold having risen from my dreams. The feeling of the snow blowing across the bow of a yacht, of boots slipping in a wet slick of blood and ice, of the cold heft of Michael's body as it slipped into the lake. Of the syrupy blackness of the night; and the adrenaline lift of the storm suddenly clearing long enough to see the distant lights of Stonehaven, a beacon in the dark.

No one seems to have noticed Michael's disappearance. Then again, who would? And who would they even know to miss? Lachlan O'Malley? Brian Walsh? Michael Kelly or Ian Kelly or someone else whose name I never learned? His true footprint in the world was kept small by design; this has helped us get away with his death.

The only person who I know that might be wondering about him is my mother; but I haven't spoken to her since the day I left her sitting on the porch in the dark. We exchanged just one text, when I informed her that the lease on the bungalow had been terminated and she had thirty days to find herself a new home. *You're going to have to forgive me someday,* she replied, almost immediately. *Remember that all we have in the end is each other.*

But I'm not so sure about that anymore. Perhaps my mother's greatest con of all was convincing me that this had ever been true.

There are days when I am torn with guilt, imagining her living in a cardboard box on skid row, the cancer having returned despite it all; but I know my mother better than that. She is resourceful; she will always find a way. I just don't want to know what it might be.

Did I mention that Vanessa is a mommy blogger now? She's gained a quarter million new Instagram followers in the last year, and has started sketching out a branded line of organic-cotton children's clothes called *Daisydoo.* The porch is constantly piled with boxes arriving from her new social media sponsors: eco-friendly diaper companies, makers of artisanal Norwegian handcrafted cribs, and purveyors of pureed superfood pouches. Benny has found his calling as her photographer: He follows her around Stonehaven, shooting mother and child in beatific tableaus that get uploaded to Instagram and cooed over by Vanessa's voracious flock. Every dirty diaper, every midnight tantrum, is an opportunity for Vanessa to upload motivational platitudes about *being in the moment* and *knowing how to appreciate the lows along with the highs* and *striving to be the person that your child already believes you are.*

Last week, I noticed that she'd told her fans that Daisy was the progeny of a sperm donor.

Guys, I realized that I needed to take agency and reach for what was most important to me, instead of waiting for someone to give it to me! I wasn't going to wait for other people to tell me that I was worthy anymore: I knew I wanted to be a mother and so now I am a mother. I didn't need a man to define myself.

The post had 82,098 likes and 698 comments. *Go Grrl / You're an inspiration to all of us mommies / #sostrong / OMG I feel the same / LUV UUUUU.*

Looking at her social media feed, you'd never know that we murdered Daisy's father and then dumped the body in the lake. But I suppose that's the point of it all, for Vanessa: to throw herself into the world she *wants* to inhabit in the hopes of forgetting the one in which she really lives. Who am I to say she's wrong to try? We all build our own delusions and then live inside them, constructing walls to conveniently hide the things we don't want to see. Maybe it means that we're crazy, or maybe it means that we're monsters, or maybe it's just that the world we live in now makes it so hard to separate truth from image from dream.

Or maybe, as Vanessa more bluntly puts it, "It's just a way to pay the bills."

We've spoken about Michael only once, one night when we'd had a little too much to drink. She and I were sitting in the library — now missing a half-dozen pieces that had been sold to cover expenses (that horrible painting of the prize horse was actually a John Charlton, and brought $18,000 at auction) — and watching Daisy sleep on the baby monitor. Out of the blue, Vanessa reached over and gripped my leg.

"He was evil," she said flatly. "He would have killed us both if we hadn't killed him first. You know that, right? Because we had to do what we did. We *had* to!"

I looked down at her hand, the fingernails clipped maternally short now, but still buffed and polished to a shine. *But the gun wasn't loaded,* I wanted to say. *Maybe we could still have found another way.* "Don't you feel . . . bad?" I asked, instead.

"Well, *yes*! Of course." Her eyes looked yellow in the flickering firelight. "But I feel *good*, too, if that makes sense? I feel more . . . self-assured, I think. Like, I know I can trust my own instincts, finally? Though maybe that's just the meds that my psychiatrist's making except for the one nightmare that we both share. That one is big enough to tie us together for now; it's the bridge that helps us cross that ravine, as precarious as it may sometimes feel.

Vanessa sat down in a rocking chair, and clutched her baby to her chest, her skirt sort of flung around them both like a cloud. Daisy lifted the goldfinch with two greasy fists, inserted its beak in her toothless mouth, and began to suck. "See?" Vanessa laughed, delighted. "He's a teething toy now."

I could hear tiny teeth clicking against the porcelain, the rhythmic rasp of baby breath. Daisy's pale blue eyes, so eerily like her father's, gazed calmly at me over the bird's head, and I swear I could see the thought in her head: Mine.

Vanessa looked up to see me watching, and smiled.

"Where's Benny?" she asked. "This would make a good photo."